Crying From One Eye

By Pete Waterhouse

Unintended Consequences
(short stories)

Crying From One Eye

Pete Waterhouse

ISBN: 978-1-8065-4023-5

Perfect Bound

First published in 2025 by Bookvault Publishing, Peterborough, United Kingdom   .

An environmentally friendly book printed and bound in England by Bookvault, powered by printondemand-worldwide

Cover design by Creative Covers: www.ccovers.co.uk

For
AJJW
&
LJW

CHAPTER 1

With the rucksack pulling on her shoulders and the handles of her shopping bag sculpting grooves into her hand, Beth trudged home, wondering about one of life's great mysteries. How, did the bag always end up in her right hand? Once again, and with an audible exhalation, she swung the bag over to her left hand. As if flicking water onto the pavement, she shook out her right arm. If her shopping was going to stretch her arms, she should at least try to make any increase equal. Her lips tightened into a grim smile. Most people already thought she was monster – to them, any deformity would be confirmation, yet also inadequate punishment.

Flexing her fingers, she raised her eyes from the dusty pavement. Ahead was what she thought of as the mysterious roundabout, its centre containing an eye-catching display of well-tended shrubs, all delicately positioned and trimmed. She'd seen formal gardens that hadn't received as much love and investment. But there were no sponsorship signs. Did the council really play favourites with traffic junctions? Beyond, sat The Midland Oak Park – an open space so small she could stroll around it in ten minutes. In the nearest corner, in the shade of an oak tree, lay a plaque on a plinth.

I'll take a breather once I get there, she promised herself, shifting the rucksack on her shoulders, trying to make the weight less uncomfortable.

By the time she had crossed the road, the supermarket Bag for Life had somehow reappeared in her right hand again. Shaking her head in wonderment, she approached the brick plinth which supported a granite slab. *You,* she thought, *it was you that brought me here to Leamington Spa.* Her sigh turned into a puffed-cheek exhalation. She understood, agreed it was for the best, but it still didn't seem fair: she was twenty-two and this structure was the nearest she had to a friend.

Has to be this way though. Safer for everyone.

Her back complained as she lowered her shopping bag to the pavement. She should have packed the bottles better. It would be her own fault if she returned home with a bag sodden and full of broken glass. She didn't dare remove her rucksack though – she didn't think she'd have the strength, or the courage, to heave it back onto her shoulders.

This, she vowed, taking a deep breath, would be her last pause before home. The air tasted as though someone else had already breathed it.

She rolled her shoulders. The rucksack hung slightly lopsided and annoying, dragging her bra strap off. Irritation buzzed inside her, threatening to escalate into something worse. The back of her T-shirt felt saturated. In the town-centre supermarket she had been confident that, despite the sweltering August day, it would be easy to carry everything she needed home in a rucksack – and then she'd found herself among the wine and spirits. Her lack of willpower could be infuriating.

Trying to relax, and counting to ten as she curled and uncurled her fingers, she stared at the plaque. She still thought it looked lost and lonely, as if banished from the town centre. She'd been disappointed when she'd first seen it. A year ago, on the day she'd moved into her flat, she'd ventured out to find what had pulled her to the Midlands. Her initial impression of the granite slab was that it looked like a mushroom cloud. It wasn't, of course, it was just shaped as a stylised tree, with a thick trunk rising up to a scalloped misshapen mass. It looked nothing like the oak tree growing behind it, whose branches overshadowed both plaque and plinth.

She'd paused here so many times over the past twelve months she knew the wording and capitalisation by heart. The slab, according to the inscription, 'commemorates the MIDLAND OAK, which for centuries grew close to this plaque and was reputed to be at the CENTRE OF ENGLAND'. This claim was what had caught her eye on Google Maps, and what had attracted her to Leamington Spa – being about as far as possible from any coast.

According to the inscription, the oak tree that shaded the plinth was a descendant of the original Midland Oak. The locals called it 'Son of Oak'.

Typical, she thought. Not 'Child of Oak' or 'Offspring of Oak'. Not even 'Chip Off the Old Oak'. But 'Son of Oak'. It was never going to be 'Daughter of Oak'.

That day, when she had first seen the plaque, Beth had been horrified at the other official signs, positioned around the Midland Oak Park like sentries. On each were printed the words 'Important Hazard Notice' above a large yellow triangle, inside which was an illustration of what looked like someone standing on a cliff edge, peering into water lapping below. Under the triangles were the words 'Danger' and 'Deep Water'. On some of the signs, the 'W' was capitalised, on others not. Thanks to her work, she noticed things like that. Trembling, she had stared at the signs, fearing someone had already recognised her and put them up for her benefit. Ridiculous of course. Besides, despite the implication, she knew from experience that water didn't need to be deep to drown someone. A half-filled paddling pool would do.

Especially if that someone had a knife embedded in their chest.

When she had managed to release her breath she had been relieved to see no water at all, just a grassy hollow fringed with rushes and reeds. This part of the park, it appeared, was used for flood defences; run-off rainwater was collected here, and could pool so deep that warning notices were required. There appeared to be no sturdy fence though. It was as if the council thought well-intentioned signs would suffice.

Today, there was no danger of drowning: the long, dry summer had left everything a sickly yellow-brown, the colour of a fading bruise.

Beth sucked in another deep breath and grimaced; it tasted like used cooking oil. Even though she remembered cool sea breezes with nostalgia, she knew she was safer here. Better for everyone. She wiped a hand over her forehead. It came away wet and glistening, and her grim smile returned. For someone in hiding, a fine sheen of perspiration was not much of a disguise.

She gave her arm one final shake, flicking off her sweat, and once again pulled her bra strap into place. A groan escaped her as she stretched her back and shoulders before once again shrugging her rucksack into a less uncomfortable position. There was a muffled clink. Fearing what she might find, she pressed her hand to the bottom of the rucksack. It was okay, unlike her back it was dry.

Inhaling, but failing to find much oxygen, she bent at the knees and grabbed the handle of her shopping bag. She exhaled as she straightened her legs, and then began the final slog home, feeling the heat bouncing off the pavement. Any hotter and the tarmac would become sticky. An oncoming cyclist caught her eye and raised his eyebrows as if in recognition of their mutual madness at being outside in this heat. She looked away, to her right, as if something had caught her attention in the park.

She waited until the cyclist was behind her before looking ahead. Another roundabout sat about a hundred metres ahead. This one she could relate to. Compared with the Midland Oak roundabout this smaller one was unloved: it was covered with straggly, unmown, yellowing grass. Beth intended to follow the pavement to the right here so that, in about twenty or so minutes, she would be opening the door to her flat. The first thing she would do, she told herself, was christen the tumbler she'd just bought. She licked her desert-dry lips at the thought of cool, clear water. Maybe, if she could finish her work, she'd have a gin and a slice. She licked her lips again.

From behind her, the distinctive sound of a bus grew louder. The bus – a number 664 – passed her, then pulled in at a bus stop on the opposite side of the road. It could, she knew, take her almost all the way home. In fact, she could even have caught a 664 in the town centre, outside the supermarket. She sighed, checking out the passengers. It wasn't full but there were enough people aboard to confirm walking home had been the sensible decision: on board they were safe from her, and she was protected from them. She wondered what they would do if they knew who was watching them. Nothing good, that's for sure.

The bus pulled away, leaving a middle-aged woman at the stop, adjusting her own shopping bags. She began walking parallel to Beth, a few metres ahead, then turned to check for traffic. Beth looked away and accelerated. If the woman crossed, Beth wanted to be in front, where the woman couldn't see her face.

A cluster of cars came from behind, forcing the woman to wait. Beth recognised the lead car, and the driver who turned towards her.

No. Please.

The vehicle passed, signalled right at the roundabout and Beth prayed it would take the right-hand exit. It didn't. It circled the scrubby-grassed roundabout and returned towards her. Her heart thumped hard as it plummeted. The car began slowing, drawing in to the kerb, stopping ahead of her, facing her. It was huge and tall and painted a shade of red that screamed 'look at me'. Bull bars, polished to a shine that made Beth squint, protruded from the bonnet. Yeah, like they were a necessity in a royal spa town. It was the sort of car that would have Ryan, her brother, salivating. And if he was a fan, then Mum and Dad would have loved it. Ryan had five years over Beth, with the consequence that when they were kids, his knowledge of the world appeared encyclopaedic. Also, thanks to his childhood passion for toy cars, she recognised the triangular Mitsubishi logo; it reminded her of a radiation warning sign.

As she approached, the passenger window slid down. Beth accelerated. She'd stride past without looking. A male voice hailed her. 'Hi there.'

She continued walking, increasing her speed. Her heart hammered harder, and not only at the extra exertion. Once, when she'd been recognised, a housemate had ended up in hospital. Poor Jackie. Life-threatening burns the doctor had said. The car reversed a few metres and once again stopped ahead of her. It was, she thought, a dangerous manoeuvre.

The woman from the bus was now crossing and watching this encounter with undisguised interest, as if it were a scene from a soap opera.

The driver leant over the passenger seat, smiling. 'Hi. Look, I've seen you about. We haven't been introduced. I'm Jacob. Well, Jake. I've just moved into the flat below yours. You look as if you might need a hand. Can I give you a lift? I'm going back home. Jump in.'

Beth halted. She wasn't going to get away, and she couldn't afford to bring any more attention to herself. Once again, her bag was in her right hand, and she lowered it to the pavement. She didn't have to bend much to peer into this bright red beast, just enough to make her back ache from the weight of her rucksack. She looked in at the driver, as if expecting something to jump out. Jake had an open, round face, the sort that made it obvious how he had looked as a boy. It was also several shades too pink, as if someone had tweaked the colour settings. She'd seen him unloading his things from this car over the last few days and, while it would have been neighbourly to take him a cool drink, and maybe a hat and sun cream, she hadn't.

His fair hair was so fine it just had to be thinning already; she thought she could see his pinkish scalp through the wispy strands. She put him in his late twenties or early thirties, a few of years older than her brother.

She glanced up and down the road, not so much looking for traffic as an excuse. Neither could be found. The woman from the bus was getting closer, clearly intrigued by this encounter. Beth touched her cheek, pulling away a strand of damp hair that had come loose from her ponytail.

Oh God, would he see that as flirtatious?

Flustered, she calculated what would attract least attention or curiosity: accepting a lift from a neighbour, albeit a relative stranger, or insisting on struggling home? And the woman from the bus was closing in, curiosity growing with each step.

'It's up to you,' Jake said with a shrug. 'I just thought, your bags… you know, like, they look heavy.'

At their mention, Beth felt the full weight on her shoulders. It was still almost a mile to walk and it was blisteringly hot. And yet…

'Sorry,' she said, shaking her head as if she'd just awoken, trying to sound normal. 'I'm Liz.'

She was trying the name for size. She'd already used Ellie,

Lizzie and once even Betty, along with some even more ill-fitting names, all now discarded, like worn-out clothes, in other places in her past.

'Pleased to meet you, Liz.' He leaned across and opened the passenger door; it was as if by giving a name, allowing him to use it, she had given her acceptance.

Beth stared into the car as Jake picked a couple of things from the passenger seat and threw them into the back – an extension lead with a four-way adapter, and a hammer.

'You know what it's like,' Jake's laugh sounded genuine. 'A new place and never enough sockets. Never picture hooks where you want them.'

She knew all right.

Beth was silent for a second. But a second, she knew, was a long time. He was waiting and she couldn't get out of this now. Not without causing a scene. And she couldn't face yet another relocation.

She took a decisive step forward and opened the rear door. With great care, she heaved her shopping bag onto the back seat, and then, with difficulty, shrugged off the rucksack. The hot sweat running down her back cooled in an instant. She shivered. The rucksack joined her other bag, with almost no tell-tale clinking, and she wanted to cheer at this. Instead, she climbed in next to Jake. The passenger seat was higher than she expected and she stiffened, feeling vulnerable, as if on display. A shudder rocked her as the air con chilled her perspiration, but she couldn't lean back for fear of her sodden T-shirt staining the upholstery.

'Day off today?' Jake asked while she reached for her seatbelt. She couldn't tell whether his perkiness was an act.

'Sorry?'

'It's a Wednesday. I thought you'd be at work. I've got the week off while I move in.'

'I work from home.' She hoped her tone made it clear: so I don't have to deal with people.

'No commuting, then. Nice. Is that why you don't drive?' he glanced across, checking she was buckled in.

Another shiver ran through her. 'Sort of.'

I wouldn't trust me with a car.

'So,' he asked when she offered nothing more, 'what do you do when you're working from home?'

She stopped herself from saying: I mind my own business, as should you. 'I'm self-employed,' she said. 'What about you?' She wanted to move the conversation away from herself.

He shot her another glance before putting the car into gear and checking the mirror. She could see his mind considering possibilities – how does a single woman working from home make money? 'A freelance copyeditor,' she added before he reached any wrong conclusions. 'And you?'

'On anything I might know?'

'Probably not. Academic books and journals. What about you?'

He nodded, considering. 'I tried working from home in the pandemic. Couldn't get on with it.' He smiled. 'So difficult to get up in the morning.' A soft clicking came from the car's indicator and he pulled into the right-hand lane.

'It's something you get used to,' she said. 'Besides, if you don't work you, like, starve.'

'Isn't it lonely? I missed the people. I'm a software developer,' he said it as if it was something he'd won. 'Leamspa Games. You know, one of the games companies around here. Leamington isn't known as Silicon Spa for nothing.'

'Computer games?' She shook her head. 'Too techy for me.'

They approached the well-loved roundabout with its secret benefactor.

'You mean nerdy.' His smile broadened, showing there was no offence.

'I never said that. Besides, I work on stuff like the *Journal of Chinese Economics and Business*, and *Urban Family Studies*. Niche stuff. So, I think I can out-nerd someone in the games industry. Games are popular.'

They circled the roundabout and headed towards home. He glanced at her. 'You a gamer?'

She shook her head. 'Working from home, if it's a choice between making money and wasting time then...' Immediately she regretted her words. 'I've got a few games,' she said, trying to be placatory. 'For my laptop. But I guess they're pretty old now. I don't play much these days.'

'Yeah? What did you play?'

'I don't like shoot 'em ups.' She folded her arms. 'Or anything that involves too much killing.' She saw his expression and knew he'd misunderstood.

'Yeah?' He contemplated her answer. 'Okay.' He nodded, then spoke as if offering a secret. 'Sometimes though, sometimes a shoot-em up is just what I need. A safe way to deal with life's frustrations, if you know what I mean. They're – the good ones, that is – cathartic. I can save the world without actually having to, you know, compromise. I can be brave. So... what? You prefer puzzles, role-playing? Strategy? Exploring open worlds rather than killing their inhabitants?'

If only you knew, she thought, and a memory slipped free: Owen's blood slicking her hand. She felt the urge to wipe her palm even though there was nothing there. No blood.

'Something like that.' A small part of her ached to tell him. Just to see if telling someone, anyone, would reduce the burden. *I'm a killer – no, I'm a murderer. Everyone, but everyone – from the Youth Offending Team to the appointed psychiatrist and even*

Mum and Dad – said I must be honest with myself. I'm a murderer. I'm dangerous. I can't be responsible for hurting anyone else. I just can't.

She looked back, trying to see her only friend, the Midland Oak plaque, before it passed from sight.

CHAPTER 2

Beth kept her arms folded, her right hand clutching the seatbelt. She still wasn't sure why Jake had offered her a lift home. Did normal people actually want to help others? Half her attention she kept on the road ahead, the other half was on Jake, ready for any unexpected movements.

Had he recognised her? Did he know who she really was? It was possible, she supposed. It may have been over a decade ago, but she'd made the national news. Depending on your favourite tabloid, she was either the *Island's Killer Kid* or the *Maid of Murder*. One redtop had even tried the *Baby-faced Killer*, but that was never going to catch on, especially when juxtaposed with the leaked photograph. Somehow, it managed to make her look evil rather than the child she had been. She was thirteen years older now, had grown her hair and changed its colour, but knew from dreadful experience she could still be recognised, particularly by anyone actually looking for her. The tabloids occasionally reminded everyone of Jon Venables and Robert Thompson and their horrific murder of two-year-old James Bulger in 1993, and – while Beth had been younger than her victim – she knew she was one of the next on the reporters' wish list.

Sitting in the car, the five-minute drive home seemed to last half a day.

Regency Court was an L-shaped block of flats that loitered on a corner of a crossroads, opposite the local library. Tucked behind it, in the right angle, was the residents' parking spaces. Beth always pictured the route to the open-air car park as a spiral: left at the crossroads, then next left, then an immediate left into the car park, passing between two brick pillars. Beth was convinced she had seen residents accelerate to take the final sharp corner, as if they liked the thrill or the challenge. Today, she had no doubt the man driving would do the same to tease or impress her.

'Here we go,' he muttered as if preparing to go on stage.

Beth gripped the seatbelt tighter in readiness. Instead, the car slowed. Remembering how her brother used to taunt her, Beth tensed, waiting for Jake to stamp on the accelerator, spin the wheel and laugh. He didn't. She blinked in confusion and surprise. It was as if Jake were delaying arrival or wanted to remind himself of the sign by the entrance: 'Private Property. Residents Parking Only'.

He fed the steering wheel through both hands, as if worried the gap between the rough brick pillars had shrunk. The block of flats dated from the seventies, and even though the car park entrance was not designed for a vehicle of this size there was still room between the wing-mirrors and brickwork. However, Beth was certain that, even carrying her shopping, she could walk faster than they were now moving.

The parking places, marked out with faded and broken white lines and numbers, came into view and Jake spoke a single word, 'Yessss'. It turned into long exhale. His relief couldn't have been clearer. He glanced at Beth, as if only now remembering she was there, and his colour deepened. There was no way she could not have heard him. 'This,' he said, clearly embarrassed and feeling the need to explain, 'is so much better than my last place. You have no idea.'

His expression was a mixture of disbelief and pleasure, the look

13

of a child who'd finally received a present they'd been promised months ago. Beth looked ahead, her right arm now across her body and her hand gripping the door rest. 'What's so much better?' To her, the parking area, surrounded as it was by a brick wall that was taller than she was and topped by sharp arrow-headed black railings, had the appearance of a prison exercise yard.

'Well, look.' Jake halted the car and nodded. 'Spaces. Even my parking space is free.'

Of the parking spaces for the twelve flats, only two were in use. Both spaces marked for visitors were also empty.

To Beth, it looked as it usually does this time of day. 'Yes,' she said, sure she was missing something. 'And...?'

'Oh, you have no idea.' Jake repeated, his voice catching, and for a terrible moment Beth thought he was about to cry. She gripped the door rest harder. 'Really, no idea,' he muttered, 'what it's like to come home from work and find someone's stolen your parking space. Your space that's clearly signposted and numbered, that's for your use only. My heart used to sink when I saw I had nowhere to park. It was a horrible feeling.' He shook his head, whether to dislodge the memory or at the strength of his own emotion Beth couldn't tell. 'It was getting to the point,' he said, getting the car moving again, 'when I dreaded coming home. You have no idea how bad that feels.'

Oh, I have.

Slowly, and with – Beth thought – unnecessary care, Jake steered into his allocated spot. The car slid into shadow; the sun had not quite hauled itself above the roof of the three-storey block.

'And what can you do?' He spoke as if trying to justify his actions to himself more than Beth. 'Leave a note on the windscreen of the intruder? The spaces were numbered, with the flat number, like here.' They both stared at the other parking spaces, odd on this side, even the other. Beth's, marked with the number '3', was beside the one they were in, the once white paint broken in places but the number still legible. 'All that meant, of course,' Jake said, 'was that they then knew where you lived. Once, I did bump into some guy returning to the car he'd left in *my* space. Stupidly, trying to be brave: I asked him – politely, I thought – not to park there in future. That went well. At least the sight of my black eye amused my dad. I hadn't heard Dad laugh so much since he and mum split.' He touched the cheekbone under his left eye. 'And as the guy then knew which flat was mine, I spent months, when some car was parked in my spot, expecting it to be him, waiting for him to come and humiliate me further. Every noise keeping me awake. Waiting…'

He gave out a little laugh, almost a cough. 'And, of course, if someone was in my space, then I had to go and find somewhere else to park, somewhere where I wouldn't get a ticket. Not so easy.' He looked at his hand as he switched off the engine.

Realising she was tense, Beth concentrated on relaxing. She stretched her fingers, brushing them against the door handle. 'You must have, like, good self-control,' she said. A memory of her mum came to mind, of broken plates, flying cutlery. 'I know people who'd have definitely caused a scene,' she thought of the hammer Jake had placed on the back seat, out of reach. 'Probably even lost it, their temper, and damaged whoever's car it was.'

For a moment, Jake's lips tightened. Beth could see him considering his response. 'Not me,' he said after a pause. 'I'm…' he began, then his whole body sagged, as if relaxing after lifting something heavy. 'Really,' he said, after another breath, 'I'm such a coward I used to drive to a car park half a mile away, and pay, just to avoid confrontation. It's not like computer games.' Another deep breath, this time followed by a half smile. 'Sorry. It must mean nothing to you, sounds ridiculous and, now, even to me, it doesn't seem so important. Back then, though…, well, back then it was horrible. It felt like a theft. It felt personal, like someone taking advantage. Laughing at me.'

'Is that why you moved here?' Beth tried what she hoped was a reassuring smile, one that didn't reveal how uncomfortable she felt. Was it normal to be this open with someone you've just met?

'Yeah. Anyway, what's your story? How long have you been here? Do you come from around here?'

Beth almost laughed. She recognised someone changing the subject. Not only had she done it often enough, she knew she had to do it again.

'Look,' she indicated her own parking spot. 'I, like, don't have a car, so you can always park in my space if, you know, someone takes yours.'

He turned to her, his surprise as obvious as if that word had been tattooed on his forehead. 'Oh, thanks,' he said, and for a fraction of a second they locked eyes.

Beth looked away, concentrating on finding and pressing the button to release her seatbelt.

'Shouldn't need it though.' Jake scratched his chin. 'It looks as if people here are more law abiding.'

If only you knew.

'So,' Beth held her seatbelt as it released. She wanted to get out, away from such confessions. 'Where was it you were living before?'

He wrinkled his nose as if remembering a bad smell. 'Doesn't matter. None of that matters any more. It's not important.' He shook his head. 'What matters is I'm here now. I don't believe in looking back, not if I can help it.'

Beth paused, unsure she had understood. 'How can you not look back?'

He spoke as if the answer was evident. 'Well, the past is the past. Back then I had trouble parking, and it was horrible. Now I don't. So, whatever may have happened back then, it's over. I'm here, where I am now. And happier.'

'But...'

'I'm not saying you can't learn from the past, but why spend time looking behind you?'

'Because we, like, need the past.' Beth found herself struggling both to understand and to express herself. 'How can we make decisions if we don't know who we are? And how can we know who we are if we don't know where we've come from?'

He looked at her, but there was the twinkle in his eyes of one who's enjoying the discussion. 'Because it's our decisions *now* that define who we are. Our actions now. Not those of the past, and especially not those of other people in the past. What is it? "The past is a foreign country"?'

'But surely our futures are prescribed by our pasts?'

'Only if you let them be.' Jake laughed, and it sounded relaxed and genuine, the sound of someone taking pleasure in a debate with a close friend. 'Is it a good idea to be going forward while looking backwards?' He shook his head to answer his own question. 'Most times, I reckon, it's best not to look back at all. In fact, if you have to look at the past, then it's only to confirm how much better things are now. Otherwise, what's the point?'

He unbuckled his seatbelt and, twisting around, he looked between the seats at the shopping he'd thrown into the back, now lying beside Beth's bags. The movement brought him closer to Beth and she couldn't stop herself from tugging at the hems of her shorts, stretching them taut. The tops of her legs were no one's business but her own. She was grateful he didn't seem to notice her leaning away.

'Yeah,' he nodded at her bags, 'I'll get them for you.'

17

'I can manage.'

She'd clambered out before Jake had opened his own door. The ground felt a long way down. She opened the rear door, leant in and heaved her bags out, Bag For Life first, taking care to avoid too many giveaway clinks. When she returned for the rucksack Jake was plucking his hammer and four-way adapter from the seat.

'You sure you don't want a hand? I can at least carry one bag.'

'No.'

He shrugged. 'Okay.' There was a thunk as the car's central locking engaged.

'Thanks for the lift.'

Beth swung her rucksack onto one shoulder, then fought to find the strap and force her other arm through it. Just that movement was enough for new perspiration to begin trickling down her neck. She and Jake were standing towards the rear of the car and, due to the shadow of the flats, both their heads were exposed to the sharp, bright sun while their legs remained in the shade. Jake's features were definitely too pink and, Beth thought, heading for a full-on – and painful – burning. She took a step towards the building, hoping Jake would follow so they could both find relief in the shadows. Jake didn't move. Instead, he cleared his throat. The hammer and adapter swung at his side.

'Actually,' he said, 'it's been lucky meeting you. Otherwise I would have had to, you know, come up and knock on your door.' His tone had changed, and Beth was unsure whether he was preparing to give bad news or ask a favour – or whether there was a difference. 'I'm having a party on Saturday. A sort of, well, housewarming.' His gaze flicked from Beth to the roof of the car between them, as if there was something more important there.

She was amused by his embarrassment, but also amazed that part of her felt sorry for him.

'You'd better warn Mr Grumpy,' she said. 'He complains at anything. Like, walking downstairs too heavily.'

He looked up at her. 'Mr Grumpy?'

'The landlord, Mr Lottan. Don't know how many flats he owns, but certainly yours and mine.'

'I've already asked him. Told him to come along if he wants. Persuaded him it'll all be okay. Quiet. Refined. Not sure he was convinced, but a bottle of wine seemed to help.' A shy smile touched his lips, and he looked back at the bright red roof of the Mitsubishi. His fingers brushed some dust from it. He glanced at her, then returned his gaze to his fingertips, as if willing them to remain stationary. 'Would you like to come along?' Before she could reply he added, 'It'll be nothing big or formal, just a few work colleagues and friends. They're okay. Well, most of them.' He smiled, and this time his eyes remained on hers. 'You can't always choose who you work with… well, actually I guess you have. But if you'd like to come, that'd be great. And,' he blinked as if just remembering something important, 'please bring anyone you want, of course. Of course you can. Please do. But, you know, just in case there is any noise, I thought I ought to let you know. Being neighbourly. And, if you're not doing anything, I thought, well, please come down and join us.'

'Well…' She considered her usual evenings: reading a book or watching a movie accompanied only by wine or G&Ts to help the time pass quicker and to get her though another night. Or maybe sitting at her laptop, working, a mug of tea beside her. If she'd been given some freelance work, then that's what she'd prefer to be doing. It kept her mind fully occupied, stopped her from thinking.

Her pause was too long for Jake.

'Okay.' Jake nodded, too fast. 'You have other plans. That's all right.'

'No.' Mentally she kicked herself. She should have agreed. That's all it would have taken, a simple yes, she was busy. Instead she said, 'No, I don't have anything else to do.'

'Oh, okay.' He looked at her, blinking again. 'So you might as well come along then? At least pop down and give it a go.' His smile turned into one of recognition. 'Yeah,' he said. 'At parties, I always end up in the kitchen as well.' Beth was annoyed at how easily he had read her expression. 'Look.' He held out a hand, fingers splayed, as if showing there was nothing hidden. 'The offer's there. Eight o'clock. Just come down if you want. Bring anyone. If not... I'll try to keep the noise down, but you know what it's like.'

Before she could stop herself, and feeling the weight of the rucksack on her shoulders, the rivulets of sweat racing down her back, Beth said, 'Okay, yes,' and proceeded to give herself another good mental kicking. She'd be bruised at this rate.

There would be people there. Strangers. And, of course, there would be drink.

That mixture, Beth knew, could be combustible. Dangerous in so many ways for her and — especially — for others. Was it a risk worth taking?

'Please do, Liz. It's good to be neighbourly. Sure you can manage with those bags?'

'Yeah.'

They walked to the rear entrance to the flats, into the shadow of the building. He unlocked the door and held it open for her.

'Oh,' Beth said, 'and in this weather you should really wear a hat.'

CHAPTER 3

The screaming seemed to start the moment Beth unlocked the door to her flat. Her whole body went rigid, as if everything inside her knotted and locked. Was it possible, she wondered, that the baby upstairs had been awaiting her return? The inconsolable howls sliced into her, peeled back her recriminations and exposed her latest mistakes. She shouldn't have even got into Jake's car, let alone considered his invitation. Perspiration stung her eyes. She squeezed them shut, trying to make her muscles hurt. Still Dashee wailed. She squeezed tighter. Beth knew what was coming. Shreeya would soon lose patience with her unhappy son and then her impotent yelling would join the racket.

Incandescent anger exploded within Beth at the injustice. She didn't disrupt Shreeya and Dashee's lives, yet they were always stopping her from concentrating. And if she couldn't work, she couldn't earn money, couldn't pay rent to Mr Grumpy, couldn't live. It wasn't fair she had to suffer like this. It just wasn't. What supplied real fuel to her fury, though, was the knowledge that her ire shouldn't just be directed at the flat above. By far the greatest part of it should be aimed at herself. She was an idiot for not dismissing Jake's invitation the moment he made it. She had been stupid to get in his car, and – most damning – she had only been walking home because she was lazy. Work had become difficult that morning so, rather than persevering, she had gone gallivanting into town instead. Another howl and her hands clenched into tight fists, her nails digging in as if desperate to draw blood. Her jaw clamped shut to stop her shouting the words her brain screamed.

Unable to make her stiff legs move, she remained in her hallway, her breaths rapid and shallow. Danger signs flashed in her head like a migraine; sirens blared, desperate to be heard over Dashee's wailing. Today, she threatened herself, she would take note of the warnings. Today she would control her temper. She could do it. Yes, she could. Using all her willpower, she forced herself to take a deep breath, filling her lungs. If she could just quieten everything in her head then she could recall some of the techniques she'd been taught. Count, slowly.

One.

Thin the anger through movement – stretch, roll shoulders.

Two.

Use all senses to be aware of the situation.

Three.

Concentrate on counting.

F…

Dashee, or Dash as Shreeya called him, paused – a single sobbing breath – and screamed again.

Wincing, Beth tried to focus on her surroundings, anything to distract her from the wailing; it had an almost physical, powerful presence. She looked along her low-ceilinged hallway, concentrating on anything other than the cacophony. To her left was the door to her bedroom, opposite that was the closed bathroom door. At the end of the hall, to the left, was the kitchen, to the right her living room. At the very end, the airing cupboard.

Finally, she managed to move, and her hands shook while she locked the door and slipped the chain on. She tried to imagine herself sitting on the sofa, calm and counting.

Four.

Five.

Six.

She used to picture her anger as something flammable, nitro-glycerine maybe, swirling in her blood, coursing through her body. Every now and then – often for no obvious reason – volatile fumes would be compressed into the tight space between brain and skull, waiting for the inevitable spark. She had never been diagnosed as being neurodiverse or on any spectrum, but often wondered if she was. External sensory stimuli could easily overwhelm her, and when forced into social situations she sometimes just needed to flee. Whether she was neurodiverse as a result of her experiences, or the other way round, was something she had begun to wonder, but been too scared to investigate. Now, taking two tentative paces along her hallway as if it were a minefield, she tried to imagine the fuel feeding her anger being re-absorbed into her body, thinning. Slowly, fraction by fraction, the tension in her shoulders began to dissipate.

One final deep breath as she reached eight. Nine. Ten. And…

Relax.

Another howl came from the flat above, followed by Shreeya's own cries. 'Please. Please shut up. What is it you want?'

She tensed again, and remembered the work she had left unfinished. It wasn't fair!

She kicked off her trainers; so hard they bounced off the wall and she was forced to bend to gather them. A sudden urge flooded through her to fling them away but, with effort, she controlled herself. As if she were drunk, she placed the trainers – with exaggerated care – beside two other pairs, all the time ensuring there was clear access to what she had named her 'Fleebag'. Peeling off her ankle socks, she flung those towards the bathroom door. They could go in the washing basket later. Her cooling bare feet felt the rough threads of the thinning carpet; it was beginning to fray in places. Something would have to be done about it soon. She sighed. It meant dealing with Mr Lottan again. Considering the fuss he'd made when she'd pointed out his stained and peeling wallpaper, it was a confrontation she could do without. He'd complained even though she'd volunteered to do the wallpapering herself (after watching many YouTube tutorials). All he had to do was pay. Of course, he'd continued complaining and making sexist remarks about how a girl couldn't possibly do it – right up until he saw the result. Even then, his approval was begrudging. Mr Grumpy, indeed.

At first she'd been pleased with her choice and her work. Now, she wasn't convinced. She thought she'd chosen wallpaper that would lighten the place, was bright and cheerful. Jolly. It reminded her of a time when she was happy. Now though, the repeating vertical lines of coloured blobs and splotches, on a light jasmine background, just looked childish. And once she'd put it up, taking care to get the first roll perfectly vertical, her mistake had become obvious. The pattern highlighted the lack of perpendicularity of the walls and ceiling. Thanks to her eye for page design and layout, a lack of symmetry rankled. Looking into the corners gave a strange sense that nothing was quite straight, nothing was true, everything was a fraction out of kilter. Also, the vertical pattern reminded her of bars.

Sweat trickled down her back and a bead ran from her temple to her cheek. It felt as though something alive was crawling down her face. Jake's air-conditioned car had just been a respite. She was glad her only mirror was in the bathroom. The thought of seeing how she looked now was too much.

To the continuous torture of Dash's cries, she carried her bags to the kitchen, went to heave them onto the worksurface, groaned and gave up. Leaving them on the floor she began pulling her shopping out. The two lemons she left on top of the fridge freezer. She took out the new tumbler and stared at it, pleased. It went beside the sink.

One of the two bottles of cheap Rioja she put aside. For Saturday, she thought, staring into the bottle, trying to lose herself in its contents, wondering again why she hadn't refused Jake's invitation outright.

Upstairs, the bawling slowed, faded (Beth held her breath and glanced at the ceiling), until a coughing fit exploded, and then little Dash began howling again. Beth was sure it was louder; she could barely hear the sound of her own teeth grinding. There was a *thump*, as though someone had thrown something on the floor, a pause, and then more wailing. It was all so unfair. Everything. Jake's invitation, Jake's offer of a lift, the walk home, the difficult editing job. Her head felt chaotic, thoughts bouncing all over the place, accelerating then rebounding, and her brain felt distended, unbalanced. Then came thoughts of Jake's party, of encountering new people, their well-meaning curiosity, the same old questions, and the answers she couldn't give.

One.

Two.

Three.

She reached seven before she could focus on pulling the other two bottles from the rucksack. Supermarket own-brand gin. Maybe, one day when she had some spare money, she could afford some of the branded stuff. Both gins went in the fridge, next to an opened bottle, but she found her fingers did not want to release the smooth glass. No. No, she must finish her work first. She felt herself stiffen and so rolled her shoulders in an attempt, before it became too late, to release some of the accumulating tension.

Her skin prickled, and she knew she ought to shower, to clean herself of the gunk and sweat accumulated from the journey home. But no. This was her own fault. If she'd persevered with her work, not taken the easy way out, she might have had it finished by now. Remaining sticky and uncomfortable was what she deserved. She licked dry, rough lips. Okay, maybe she could permit herself a glass of water. Yes, in the tumbler she'd just bought. Hydration would help.

Above, Dash interrupted his cries with sobbing.

Still angry with Dash, with work, with life's injustices, but most of all with herself, Beth picked up the tumbler. She weighed it in her hand. It had been a choice between this single embellishment-free glass and a cardboard-wrapped pair on special offer. They had had hearts engraved on them. But while they had been cheaper, Beth just couldn't bring herself to buy them. Not with all that intimation of romance. Dash howled again, somehow even louder, and she almost dropped the glass.

'Dashee!' she hissed through rigid lips. It would be just her luck to break the tumbler before using it.

She rinsed it, dried it and held it up to the light, partly to distract herself from the sound of the temper tantrum upstairs and partly to admire the clarity of the glass.

She filled it with lukewarm water from the tap, thinking as she did so of the gin cooling in the fridge, contemplating the taste, the brain-numbing effect, then shook away such thoughts with a violence they didn't deserve. Licking her lips, she walked to the living room, where Dash's cries seemed louder, as if he were inhabiting a black cloud above her head. She felt herself wincing with every wail, her breathing becoming shallower.

Yanking out the high-backed office chair, she sat, rigid. She may be working from home, with a dining table for a desk, but with the hours she put in she was glad she'd bought an expensive, comfortable chair. She wasn't bothered by how out of place it looked: it was practical. When she saw the Word document still open on her laptop she grimaced and recalled what had driven her to walk two miles into town.

The sentence, in the paper's abstract, read:

The penetration of corvée under state's egg crucible and defends nearby élite who can look at potential in the meadow.

Her self-imposed deadline was to have the whole paper edited by the end of today. It was going to require all her concentration to—

Howls and screams fell from above and she flinched as if they had physical weight. It was as if the room were contracting and her head swelling. She tried to focus on the screen, squinting. Words juddered in time with the cries. If she couldn't get this done… Dash wailed again, louder, and she put her face closer to the screen, as if that would help, and stared at the words. Corvée, she knew was effectively unpaid labour, but the rest… The letters leapt. Her head was bursting. She gulped a mouthful of water so hard it hurt her throat. If only she could concentrate, if only she could have silence, if only she could remove all thoughts of her stupid mistakes, of Jake, of his party. Dash screamed again, cutting through her thoughts and Shreeya yelled once more, 'Stop, please stop. I don't know what it is you want.'

She put the tumbler down before her grip shattered it. She pressed her fingers against her eyes, hard, and in an unexpected moment of quiet heard an email arrive. When she looked, it was from the Production Editor of one of her Asian cultural studies journals, addressed to the nice genderless name she used.

Sam
We are implementing a new process for copyediting,

whereby papers will first be assessed for language quality by our Indian typesetting partners, and only passed on for a full copyedit if deemed necessary. This will result in a significant drop in work we will be sending you. It is not, of course, a reflection on the quality of your work.

What? No. You can't do that. That's my income.

She stared at the message, reading the words over and over.

That journal's written by overseas authors. Their English needs...

The letters on the screen began to fade as everything else became brighter.

Of course that journal needs editing. Every paper. For quality. For sense. How are readers going to trust it if they can't understand it?

She clutched the edge of the table.

And I need the work. I need *to* work. Yet I can't even do this piece. How will I survive? You can't just...

Her combustible rage was no longer being diluted. Her breaths were scarcely pulling in any air, yet becoming ever shallower.

Dash gave out an almighty howl, deafening. Shreeya screamed, 'No!' Everything too loud.

And, in Beth, an explosion.

'*Fuck!*'

She hurled the tumbler. The glass exploded near the skirting board. Shards, sharp bright slivers, spun in the air. Water spattered the wall.

Upstairs there was momentary quiet, as if Dash were shocked at the competition.

Beth slumped; as usual an eruption consumed all her fury in a single blast. Not a solitary angry ember remained. All she felt was the familiar shame and self-loathing.

Her mind was now as cool and clear as a mountain lake. *Now* she was aware of her breathing. *Now* she could control it. *Now* she could count to ten. She wanted to laugh like a maniac – a common reaction, she knew from experience. Hysteria after release. She looked back at the screen and, with a hand that felt heavy, minimised the email window. Behind it, like a dark threat, lurked the badly translated sentence. In a moment of clarity, she began to see in it a shape, an intention, a meaning.

One again she leant forward. Yes… yes… if…

Knocking.

Oh, for heaven's sake.

On her front door.

'Are you all right?' A man's voice. Muffled. Concerned.

Jake?

Taking a deep breath, as if readying for a plunge underwater, Beth stood and – thinking of the shattered glass and checking where she placed her bare feet – walked carefully out of the living room. She doubted any splinters had reached as far as her desk, yet – if she were honest – she wasn't sure what she'd do if she saw something sharp and enticing embedded in the carpet.

'It's okay,' she called once in the hall.

'Are you all right?'

'Just dropped something.' She shouted, slipping the chain free and unlocking the door. She opened the door as if distrustful of what she might find.

'It sounded like a bomb going off. Are you sure you're okay?' Jake stepped back when he saw her, as if expecting violence, his chest heaving. He'd clearly sprinted up the stairs. Beneath his pink complexion, there was a pallor, as if he'd had a shock. She kept one hand clutching the door, the other pressed into the pocket of her shorts. He wasn't to see her hands shaking.

She pinned a smile to her face. 'An accident. It's all okay now.'

Jake moved his head from side to side, his gaze trying to slip past her.

'You're sure you're okay?' he said. 'Nothing I can do?'

She wanted to tell him there was no one else here. 'Everything's fine,' she said instead, speaking with care, both her hands balling into fists. 'But, as you're here, I've just checked my diary. I can't make it on Saturday.'

'Oh. But…' He looked at the floor. Behind him, the stairwell window looked out over the car park. In a fit of optimistic exuberance, Beth had placed a peace lily on the windowsill. Each time she passed it she resolved to return with more water. Its yellowing leaves drooped, becoming more brittle by the day.

Jake looked up, his mouth making strange shapes as he tried to find a smile. He failed and offered a perfunctory nod instead. 'Okay. I understand.' His voice cracked until it was just a whisper, 'It was just an idea.' His shrug was that of someone accepting defeat. 'Maybe another time.'

'Maybe.'

Upstairs, Dash filled his lungs and began again.

Jake looked at the ceiling, as if he could see through it. 'Poor little mite. That must get annoying for you.'

Beth followed his glance. 'The terrible twos. Think he started early.' The sound of Dash reminded Beth of the sentence, the gibberish, and – in a burst of intuition – she suddenly saw a way in. She needed to get back to it while the idea was clear.

'Look,' she said, 'I've gotta go; clean up the mess.'

'Oh, right. Yeah. Of course. If you want a hand…?'

'I can manage.' She begun closing the door.

'I understand,' he said again, but his expression said the opposite. He took a step back as if to leave, then stopped. 'If your plans change on Saturday or, you know, if you can make it, just come down.'

'Yeah.' She stopped as a new, and confusing, realisation sideswiped her. 'And, er…' she wasn't quite sure how to say what she wanted, '…I mean, like, thanks for coming up to, you know, check on me.'

He shrugged again, but this time his mouth found a genuine smile. 'It's what neighbours do. I—'

'Bye.' In her rush to return to work Beth closed the door harder than she intended. Its slam set Dash off yet again. She looked up at the sound and then ran the few steps along her hall; she had to get to her computer before inspiration evaporated. The shattered glass and the drying wallpaper could wait. They always did.

She sat so fast that, even on the carpet, the casters rolled backwards and she had to pull the chair closer to the table.

She could barely hear Dash now; his cries obscured by her excitement, by the sound of synapses firing. Everything was just background noise. Her focus was fully on the unintelligible sentence.

The penetration of corvée under state's egg crucible and defends nearby élite who can look at potential in the meadow.

Yes, of course. The author didn't mean egg. They'd tried to be clever, had used an online translator or a bad thesaurus. The author had looked up a synonym, thinking the word was *yolk*. It wasn't. What the author meant was *yoke*. The yoke of the state. So, *crucible* should clearly be *crucial*, and *defends* was just a typo. Which gave:

The penetration of industry under the yoke of the state is crucial and depends on the local elite who can see potential in the...

Meadow. Meadow? Pasture? Grass? *Field.* In the field.

The penetration of industry under the yoke of the state is crucial and depends on the local elite who can see potential in the field.

It was still far from correct, but she was certain she was now heading in the right direction. She breathed easier, relieved she was finally getting a grip on the author's intentions. A little more time and she was positive she could intuit the full meaning.

'Yes,' she said aloud, grinning.

She wasn't, however, the sort of person who could let herself enjoy any achievement for long. Her expression faded, she shut her eyes, as she recalled her outburst. 'Thanks, Mum,' she muttered. There was a tacit agreement amongst her family that she'd inherited her mother's temper. She could remember, before the murder, back when she was young and happy, her dad using racial stereotypes and joking that if Mum was having a bad day, she'd get through more plates than a Greek wedding. As a family, they'd never had sausages again after that time when Mum had...

No.

Beth shook the memory from her head. Blaming her mother for her own short fuse was like blaming rain for wetting her hair – it was a choice to venture outside, a choice not to carry an umbrella, a choice not to wear a hat. Sometimes, in bed and unable to sleep, she also wondered if this was another symptom of being neurodiverse, and whether she should see a doctor. She fetched the dustpan and brush she always kept ready, and some newspaper in which to wrap the broken glass. She knew how to do this. One way or another, it felt as if she'd spent her whole life cleaning up after a temper tantrum.

The wallpaper would dry – it was only water this time, not wine – and, besides, any marks were close to the floor. She doubted the landlord was observant enough to notice, and no one else was ever going to visit.

The larger pieces of glass she wrapped in the free local newspaper, breaking off any blade-like points to ensure nothing would poke through, resisting the urge to see just how sharp they were. She brushed up what she could, and ran the vacuum cleaner over the carpet to pick up any remaining shards, amusing herself by thinking about adding the ground glass to the food of whoever in the publishing company had decided it was speed of publication that mattered, not quality, not accuracy, not legibility or even professionalism.

At the thought of the email, of losing her income, she felt her muscles tense, her breathing again becoming shallower. Colours became brighter, Dash's cries less muffled, everything coming into sharper focus. This time, however, after the explosion she had the calm clarity to detach herself, to watch herself from a distance rather than be overwhelmed by her own fury-saturated blood. Too often, the warning signs were obvious but obscured by a claustrophobic red fog.

I need to cut back.

She smiled at the thought, which in itself made her feel a little better.

No more than one outburst a day.

She put the newspaper-wrapped broken glass by the kitchen bin, ready to be taken out to the recycling wheelie bin, and the dustpan and brush in the cupboard beneath the sink, ready for its next use. It wasn't just a matter of being tidy, of it being safer not to live amidst too much clutter. It was a matter of being ready if she had to relocate again in a hurry. Her 'Fleebag' – an essentials-filled rucksack that she could just grab and run – was always kept by the door. She was putting the vacuum cleaner away in the airing cupboard – the only suitable spot for it – when she heard, between Dash's increasingly breathless cries, a *bleep*. A new email.

For a second she hoped it was some new work, or the Production Editor telling her to disregard the previous message; of course they wouldn't be removing her livelihood, in fact they were going to offer her more work and increase their rate of pay. Yeah, right.

Losing her work meant losing more than just her income. It was dangerous. And not just to her.

After years of therapy and introspection – and working and living on her own with only her own thoughts – she was well aware that work wasn't just a means of paying bills. She used it to fill her empty time, to occupy her mind. Usually she could focus all her concentration on whatever text she was editing, deciphering its meaning, use her intuition to understand the intentions of the authors. It was all–consuming, preventing her from considering existence, thoughts of life and death, and, of course, remembering the past.

Above, Dash seemed to be exhausting himself. The gaps between his gasping wails were becoming longer. His sobbing and wailing now sounded pitiful. Beth thought the worst might be over. For today.

She returned to her living room, looked at her laptop, saw who the email was from and found her legs could no longer support her. She landed on the office chair with a thump. The hydraulic base hissed under the sudden pressure.

The email was nothing to do with work. It had been delivered to an account she kept separate. Only Mum, Dad and her brother,

Ryan, knew the email address.

She clicked on the account, stared at the screen and the room started spinning, the air being sucked from it. Two names leapt out: the sender's name – her mother – and the name in the subject box – Mary Calbourne. Beth gripped the edge of table so heard her fingers whitened. She knew the name, of course. After all, she had murdered Aunt Mary's eldest son.

Beth managed to release the edge of the table, and her trembling stiff fingers reached towards the mouse, intending to open the email.

No.

She'd open it when she was ready. She wasn't at her mother's beck and call. She needed to reassert control.

She released a shuddering breath, surprised she had been holding so much in, stood and made her way to the kitchen.

To hell with work. Now is most definitely the time for that gin and a slice.

She took the opened gin from the fridge, grabbed a bottle of cheap tonic, put them both on a tray. Picking up a lemon, she rolled the citrus fruit around in her hand, feeling its dimpled skin as she located what she wanted from her knife-block. A finely serrated edge, she knew, was best for the initial cut.

She added the lemon and knife to the tray and pulled an old wine glass from the cupboard: she was now out of suitable tumblers. Grabbing a towel, she took everything into the living room. The towel she placed on the office chair – it was a nice chair, and she wanted to keep it that way – then lowered herself onto it. Everything else she put on the table. She squeezed her eyes shut, knowing she shouldn't be doing this.

Fuck it.

Licking her lips, she poured gin into the glass, topped it up with a splash of tonic. Two quick cuts with the knife gave her a decent thin slice of lemon. She watched the juice drip from the blade.

Holding the knife with one hand, she pulled up the left leg of her shorts with the other. It looked as if a badly made wicker basket had been pressed into her skin. A multitude of short pale lines pointed in all directions. A scatter of en-rules and em-rules: she thought of them as her hyphens. She chose a spot, as clear of recent scars as possible and drew the juice-coated blade across her flesh, slicing with care through one layer of skin, then another. She sucked air through her teeth and shut her eyes. *She* was doing this. No one else. Even though she could never get the sharp sting as exquisite as she anticipated, with each cut she felt she was regaining a valuable fragment of control.

Once blood appeared, she found another spot on her upper thigh and again pulled the blade across, adding the slightest of pressures. Then she picked up the slice of lemon, held it over the wounds, and squeezed.

Okay. Ready for you now, Mum.

She leant forward and opened the email.

Bethany

I've spoken with Ryan on the phone. In case you're interested, he says he's well. He suggested I contact you. However, you still haven't given us your home address or telephone number, only this email address. Ryan says he hasn't got any other address for you either. I must say it seems a bit ungrateful after all we've done. Still, I'm sure you know best. Anyway, Mary Calbourne died a few days ago. Callum, her other boy, has returned to make arrangements for the funeral. I don't know whether he's been let out on compassionate grounds or he's done his time, but I heard he's been asking after us. We agreed we'd better warn you. I'm sure you remember last time you met. You should be thankful Ryan saved you.

Ryan thinks we should meet up to discuss what to do about Callum. You've seen fit not to tell us where you're currently living, but Ryan suggests meeting in Guildford. It's convenient for everyone, and Ryan won't have to give up too much of his time. He's very busy these days. He can only make this Saturday lunchtime. I'm sure that'll be okay with you.

We're all fine. We haven't heard otherwise so I assume you are okay.
Love
Mum & Dad

Beth made another cut.

CHAPTER 4

By next morning, the latest scabs on her leg had hardened; each enticing crust just asking for a sharp fingernail to be inserted under it. Through habit, and through her pyjamas, Beth's fingertips caressed the fresh scabs and old scars as though they held a braille message. She was sure she had spent most of the night awake, her head awash with various replies to Mum's email. Now she was fully awake though, and sitting before her laptop, she just couldn't recall the wording she'd thought best or even why it had seemed so perfect.

Blowing over the first coffee of the day, rippling its surface, she re-read Mum's email once again. So, Ryan had suggested meeting in Guildford, had he? She let out a dry laugh. Well, he would. He lived in Guildford. And for Mum and Dad it was pretty much a straight drive up the A3 from Havant. For her, of course, it was a matter of a long walk to the station, an hour's train journey to Reading, followed a lengthy wait for the Guildford train. A half-day's journey.

Mum said it was, 'convenient for everyone else'. And that Ryan wouldn't have to give up too much of his valuable time. Well, good for him. She, however, normally worked on Saturdays to make up for shopping mid-week when there weren't so many other customers around.

Of course, she couldn't blame the family: they didn't know her situation or even where she was currently living. That didn't prevent her from being irritated at Mum's assumption she was available on command. Beth thought of refusing to attend but knew that would be self-defeating. Mum would tell her, and everyone, she was 'just being silly'. Looking at where she'd angrily thrown the glass yesterday, Beth knew that wasn't the case. Besides, she'd already turned down one invitation for something on Saturday, a refusal that still felt like an unscratched itch.

She pressed on her scabs, realised what she doing and stood up. She began pacing, attempting to dilute the irritation before it turned to anger. Not for the first time she wished she could call someone. She thought of Jackie, poor burned Jackie, but Beth hadn't spoken or seen her since petrol had been poured through the letterbox and set alight. Beth knew it was cowardly, but still couldn't bring herself to make contact. After all, what could she say? The police had never caught the culprit, but Beth was convinced it was Callum Calbourne. And now he was out of prison and, according to Mum, asking about her. If he ever found her again...

Three steps to the window and she stared out: innocent people on the street below, oblivious to her presence. The way it should be. But, for once, she felt having someone to talk to would be a comfort. Maybe the people at Jake's party would be all right. Maybe Leamington Spa would turn out to be the place she could safely make some friends. Perhaps even someone she could just call up for a chat, or to meet for a coffee? Was that too much to ask?

Yeah. It seemed it was.

She shook her head and returned to pacing. It was more likely Leamington would be yet another place she had to flee. Yes, Jake seemed nice, but then she probably seemed a normal person to him – and look at her history. She sighed. It must be yesterday's gin, she thought, making her feel sad and desirous of company. Looking around her living room, at the not-quite-true walls, and the wallpaper with its pattern like vertical bars, she sighed again. Yes, it was definitely the after-effects of the gin.

She fought against it but couldn't stop herself picturing Jake's round, open face, his soft, fair skin beginning to burn in the strong sun, his thinning hair. And he had been so honest about himself. She found herself in the hall, heading to the front door. She should go and thank him for the invitation; it always pays to be on good terms with your neighbours. The thought of knocking on his door, speaking to him, sent her back to the living room. Maybe she should watch out for him today? To catch him, to say thanks. Maybe she should move her laptop to the bedroom, closer to the window that overlooks the car park? Just in case?

'Oh, come on,' she muttered and laughed drily. She was thinking like a teenager. She picked up her mug again and took a mouthful of coffee. It was still too hot. She swallowed it anyway, feeling it burn her throat, knowing she deserved the discomfort.

Sitting back down, and putting the coffee mug on a closed notebook – despite her good intentions, she had never treated herself to coasters – she re-read mum's email.

Taking a deep breath, she typed a brief reply, cc'ing it to Ryan, simply asking for details of where they proposed meeting and what time, not even saying she'd be there. She left the email on the screen while she showered. Nothing further came to mind so – clean, dressed and before making breakfast – she clicked on 'send'.

Standing in the kitchen, waiting for the kettle and toaster to do their jobs, she tried not to imagine Mum's response. Instead, she readied herself for a renewed attack on her overseas author's work, to try to get into his thoughts and intentions. It was getting close to her deadline now, and yesterday had been a waste.

Actually though, not a complete waste. There was Jake...

The kettle clicked off and the toaster ejected its two slices of brown bread. She heard neither: her thoughts had tripped again at the memory of Jake's kind invitation and her refusal. She thought now she'd been too hasty. She'd been having a bad day. She hadn't been invited to anyone's party in a decade or so. Surely she ought to be able to go to a party to which she'd been invited, like a normal person.

Except, of course, she wasn't normal.

Supposing she lost her temper? After a few drinks, surrounded by noise, maybe flashing lights, in the company of strangers, people who might say anything, might – however innocently – probe her background, might upset her, might rile her... It had happened before. And worse, supposing someone did recognise her? What then?

The risks were too great.

Last time she'd been recognised, one tabloid had given just enough information that – while they could deny it – her address was discoverable. Obscenities had been scrawled on the wall outside and petrol had been poured through her letterbox, followed by a match. (It was you, Callum, wasn't it.) She'd been lucky, and had been out shopping. Jackie, one of her housemates, had not been so fortunate. Beth had not dared live in shared house since.

Staring into space, she eventually became aware of the silence. Blinking away thoughts of violence – on her, and by her – she made herself another strong instant coffee, knifed butter and chocolate spread onto the cooling toast, and carried it all into the living room.

Today, her commute – the journey from kitchen to work – felt long. The plate of breakfast she put between the laptop and her reference books – the most recent edition of the *Oxford*

English Dictionary, a thesaurus, *Harts Rules for Compositors and Readers*, and the *Oxford Dictionary for Writers and Editors*. Not for the first time, she noticed her desk, like the room, held nothing personal. No pictures, no keepsakes, no mementos. She wondered again whether she should put something somewhere. Other people did. She shook her head. Even though no one ever visited, she'd be uncomfortable with anything that could be used to identify her, and that may have to be left behind.

Grabbing a piece of toast, and taking a bite, she used her other hand to open the document she was trying to edit. At least there was no noise from the flat above this morning. Beth had heard Shreeya taking Dashee out, bumping his pushchair down the stairs. Knowing she ought to get as much done as possible before they returned, Beth settled down to concentrate.

Like a cautious kitten at an open door, a stray thought poked its head into view: the invitation had been kind of Jake.

He probably only did it out of sympathy, or so you wouldn't complain about the noise.

The voice in her head was her mum's, and Beth found herself nodding. It really was unlikely that a stranger would think her attendance would improve an event. Besides, being trapped in a small flat with loud music and a bunch of strangers, possibly all men from the computer games industry, and probably drunk, was amongst – other things – just too risky. She shivered and inhaled, as if spectral fingers had run down her spine.

And yet...

Jake seemed all right. Kind. He...

A bleep announced the arrival of an email. From Ryan.

She double clicked to open.

Hi Pudge
So good to hear from you again. I do hope life's treating

you well. You deserve it.

We need to discuss what to do about Callum. You've got to keep away from him. If he's looking for you, for your own safety we can't let him find you.

We can discuss plans on Saturday in Guildford. Considering Mum and Dad's attitude to fine dining, I figure a pub meal would be best. There's a pub on Bridge Street, The Rodboro Buildings, not far from the station. I told Mum to tell Dad it's a Grade II listed building, one of the first purpose-built factories for car production or something. I figure that might interest him and give Mum some leverage to make him come along. It'll give him something to talk about if nothing else. :)

See you there a 1 o'clock.

It'll be great to see you again and catch up.

Love Ryan

She smiled and felt a comforting warmth deep inside that had nothing to do with coffee. Already she was looking forward to seeing Ryan again; he could always make her laugh. And he would protect her, that she knew. After all, it had been Ryan who'd dragged Callum – screaming and threatening murder – off her in their last encounter. Yes, she'd ended up in hospital, bruised, with cracked ribs, a fractured wrist and a broken tooth, but if Ryan hadn't been there, it would have been so much worse. At the time, she was convinced it was the right decision not to press charges. The publicity would have been unendurable, much more so than her injuries. Now though, she wondered if she hadn't been selfish, if she could have saved more lives from being ruined if she'd been braver.

She thought of Jake and what he'd said about avoiding

confrontation – the opposite of Ryan. Unconsciously, she shook her head, scowled and rubbed her hand hard over her scabs: she knew better than to make unfair comparisons. Thinking of Jake, though, she wondered what he was doing downstairs, at this very moment. No. Stop it, work needs to be done.

She stared at the screen but the words meant nothing. Time had become unimportant.

Callum.

Callum Calbourne. She could, with ease, bring his innocent, enthusiastic young face to mind. And just as easily, she could remember his screwed-up hate-filled features. One way or another, it seemed he'd always been part of her life, just not always the same part.

Standing, she paced to the window again and looked out. Nothing new to see. She found herself walking to the bedroom, from where she could see into the car park. Maybe she'd see Jake, moving more of his stuff in? No, there was no movement. His car was still there though, still the biggest and brightest vehicle in sight. Turning away and glancing at her crumpled duvet, her eyes fell on the two soft toys – Pickle and Rascal – that sat at the end of the bed. They had been given to her, she'd been told, when she was about two. They had lost their looks, their fluffiness, their colours and one of them was far from his original shape. A seam had split and stuffing had spilled before she'd noticed and repaired it. Looking at them, she realised, shocked, Callum had been part of her life for longer than they had.

Beth had no idea how long Mum had known Mary Calbourne; she assumed they had been childhood friends. Aunt Mary had been closer that any real aunt. According to Mum, when Mary's husband left, a week before Callum was born, it had seemed natural the two families should stick together. The fact that the Calbournes lived on the Isle of Wight, at Yaverland, not

44

far from a beach, meant Beth and Ryan had always looked forward to visiting – right up until Beth had murdered Owen. As Dad said, something like that was bound to put a crimp into a relationship.

She pulled the duvet back to air the mattress, and picked up the teddy bears, smiled at their familiar worn faces. Callum would now be, what, twenty-five? Twenty-six? He'd been in the school year below Ryan. For kids though, one year was a significant difference. Ryan and Owen, being older, just didn't want him hanging around with them. She could remember feeling pity for Callum as his attempts to join in with the older boys' games were – often none-too-politely – rebuffed. Even now though, she couldn't decide whether Owen wanted his space away from his younger brother or, for some reason, felt threatened by him. Probably a bit of each. Then again, maybe the fact that their father had deserted the family just before Callum's birth had some bearing on his actions.

She returned to the computer and stared at the screen. Right, she really must concentrate on work. The words on the screen had no meaning, they could have been an artistic design, and her mind – ignoring all instructions – recalled Callum's rejections by the two older boys and how she found herself comforting him. When she pictured it now, it must have appeared odd, an eight-year-old girl leading a sniffling twelve-year-old boy along the beach near Yaverland to play.

She focused on the screen before her again, but knew it was useless. She was trapped in here with her thoughts. What she needed was fresh air. Shaking her head, the way she would if a fly were buzzing too close, she slapped one hand on the table and almost leapt to her feet. Time for a walk, return a library book, and do what she had to do.

She locked the door after leaving her flat and made her way

downstairs, looking away from Jake's front door as she passed it, even though it meant looking at Mr Grumpy's. Blinking, she exited the flats into yet another bright, hot morning. It felt as though rain was something she had once imagined. She halted and looked right and left, investigating the passing traffic, parked cars, checking the pedestrians.

When she was positive no one was paying her any attention, she turned right, eventually crossing a main road, and went for a two-mile brisk walk. She only slowed to smile and nod at a lady in a blue T-shirt who was training a guide dog, a happy looking labrador with both a lead and a harness for a blind person to hold. The Regional Centre was in Leamington Spa, so such a sight was familiar to Beth and she always made a point acknowledging the good work being done. It was a reminder she should donate to the charity again. About thirty minutes after she left, she was back at Regency Court and passing Jake's windows. She resisted the temptation to look in, and headed for the library. It stood near the crossroads, no more than a few minutes away.

Over the years Beth had known a number of branch libraries; she thought Lillington one of the cheeriest. It was T-shaped, but with unequal arms, so to the right of the entrance was the children's section while on the left was the longer area for adults. The leg of the T had two stories, the upper one being for the staff. It also allowed square pastel-green panels to be set above the entrance. Large windows ran along the frontage, allowing Beth, as she walked up the sloped path to the entrance, to see how many people were inside. She was pleased to see that, apart from the librarian, the place was empty. No children being read a story and no one doing the current jigsaw that had been left out. The building had the feel, Beth always thought, of being designed in the fifties or sixties and trying to look futuristic.

Behind the counter, the librarian – a middle-aged woman

who reminded Beth of an enthusiastic but ineffectual teacher she'd once had – looked up and smiled, expectant. 'Morning,' she said, cheerfully.

'Hi,' Beth kept her head down and pointed towards the computer monitors. 'Okay?'

'Can you manage, love?'

'Yeah.'

'Help yourself.' The librarian returned to sorting books, still smiling to herself. Someone who enjoyed their work.

Using the self-service machine, Beth returned her book, a reference work on home plumbing, then made her way to the computer area. Well, as she was here…

Three tables sat pushed against a wall, on which were placed three monitors and associated keyboards. Beth chose the furthest; she could hide herself behind the monitor, peering around it to keep an eye on the librarian – just in case the woman started showing an interest in the only customer. She never had before, though.

Beth opened up the browser and began searching.

First, she typed in Jackie Noonen's name. Beth's fingers trembled, and she felt a familiar hollow sickness that she knew was guilt. There were old reports of the arson attack on Beth's old place in Caterham, descriptions of Jackie's injuries, the months of painful recovery, the permanent facial scarring. Beth had never been able to bring herself to visit, or to apologise, to explain the level of guilt that lived in her body like a cancer. But every now and then Beth checked to see if there were any updates or news on Jackie. Beth prayed that one day she'd find a marriage announcement. Not today though.

She gulped air, trying to fill the void in her with something other than guilt and shame.

Peering around the monitor she checked the librarian was still busy behind the counter and, with trembling fingers, for the first time in her life, typed the name 'Callum Calbourne' into a search engine. She half expected alarm bells to go off. When they didn't, she shifted herself closer to the screen, feeling sick and vulnerable, as if she were searching for something she shouldn't. Somehow it felt safer to do this on a public computer than on her home one. She didn't really believe such a search could be traced, but better to be safe...

'Oh no,' she muttered.

She knew from Mum and Dad that the death of his brother had sent Callum off the rails, but she hadn't realised how badly.

'Oh, Callum.'

The librarian looked over. 'Are you all right?'

'Yeah. Sorry.' Beth ducked, putting her face closer to the screen. She hadn't been expecting the answers to be so easy to find. Callum's name appeared in the *Isle of Wight County Press*, the *Island Echo* and the *Isle of Wight Observer*.

'Oh, Callum,' she whispered again. It felt as if she were being slowly immersed in freezing water.

As well as the newspaper reports there were pictures, most provided by the Hampshire Constabulary. Her breath caught at the mugshots, at the memory of his attack on her a week after Owen's funeral. She found she had to stare deep into the digital photographs to locate, inside that scowling, hardened face, the sensitive boy she had once known. The same guy but two different people. Mostly though, it was his eyes that fascinated her, and to which she kept returning. She wished there was someone she could call who could come and reassure her that she was being too fanciful, too imaginative, reading too much into the photographs. His eyes. Every time she looked at them – whether a quick glance or a long investigative stare – she'd swear they were brimming with a single dark accusation: *you made me this way.*

Her stomach churned and a sourness squirted into her mouth.

A noise. Beth looked up to see a woman enter the library, book in one hand, shopping bag in the other, and exchange greetings with the librarian. Beth held her breath while the visitor used the self-service terminal to return the book. The bleep of the terminal was just audible to Beth over the sound of her pounding heart. Fingers on the mouse, Beth waited, ready to minimise the browser in case the visitor walked further into the library. She knew she was doing nothing wrong, but that's not what it felt like. She tried to swallow the bad taste in her mouth, while praying the woman wouldn't decide she wanted a replacement book and, if she did, that she wouldn't investigate the shelves nearest to Beth and look over her shoulder.

Instead, the woman looked at her watch, smiled at the librarian and left.

Beth released the breath she had been holding and returned to her search. She clicked on another page and this time her own name leapt out. An icy band clamped around her chest, squeezing the air out of her lungs. She couldn't catch her breath. All she could manage were rapid and tiny exhalations, followed by equally shallow forced inhalations. She looked away from the screen but didn't have the strength to turn her back on the words and their implications. The text was always there in the corner of her eye. She wasn't looking at the library, she was looking at the dead, unchangeable, past.

After a few minutes her breaths became deeper, blood returned to her cold fingers and her light-headedness receded.

As if preparing herself for another plunge into chilled water, she pulled her shoulders back to open up her lungs, then forced her eyes to return to the screen.

She clicked faster through pages, always keeping old ones open, and amidst the reports of attempted classroom arson, school expulsions and fights, her own name and Owen's kept cropping up as one journalist after another tried to make the connection between Owen's murder and Callum's increasingly anti-social behaviour.

And then there were police cautions for violence. It seemed Callum didn't care where he picked a fight – inside and outside pubs, or clubs, or in shops – or with whom. Men and women were equally likely to suffer.

Then came the sentencing for ABH – actual bodily harm of some poor woman, reported to be an ex-girlfriend.

All these poor people, she thought, her body briming with familiar self-loathing.

So many lives affected – ruined – by me.

Sour bile flooded into her throat, and she stood, wondering whether she could make it outside before vomiting.

'Are you all right, love?'

Beth nodded to the librarian, swallowing hard, unable to speak.

'You've gone quite pale.' The librarian put her books down and stepped out from behind the counter.

Way to go, Beth thought, in not bringing attention to yourself. Should have stayed at home. Remained ignorant. She looked at the door, and swallowed again until she felt she had control.

Holding her hand up, she halted the librarian's progress. 'I'm all right,' Beth managed to say, although she thought her voice sounded too croaky to be believable. She didn't want the librarian to see what pages she'd been looking at. Too many questions.

Beth aimed for a reassuring smile. 'Came out, without having breakfast,' she said. 'I'd better go and have something now.'

She shut everything down, deleted the browsing history, and left, waving goodbye to the curious librarian. Outside, to her surprise, she didn't throw up. Somehow, though, keeping everything down felt worse than releasing it.

She turned away from Regency Court, needing another to walk, to see if she could reconcile the vicious and violent man Callum had become with the boy he'd been.

The last time she'd seen Callum he'd put her in hospital. Now he was looking for her again.

Of course he was, she thought, I killed – no, murdered – his brother. His older brother.

If someone had taken Ryan from her, would she find some way to extract vengeance on the world? On the person who had derailed her life?

Too right she would.

CHAPTER 5

Habit prevailed when, on Saturday, Beth boarded the train at Leamington Spa station: find a seat in the front-most carriage, as far forward as possible, as far from anyone else as possible. At Reading station, she spent the time between connections in the toilet with her book, only leaving to board the train to Guildford. Again, she found a seat as far forward as possible and kept her face turned from other passengers. When the train arrived at Guildford, she realised she hadn't even thought about her actions. Everything was now second nature.

She stepped down from the train, crossed the yellow safety line – painted but fading on the platform – and stood to one side. She was well away from the others disembarking and those standing, pushing forward, ready to board. Placing her handbag on the grey concrete, speckled with blobs of ages-old chewing gum, she squatted on her heels and pretended to rummage inside her bag, glancing up every few seconds before once again pretending to check its contents. To anyone who noticed her, she hoped it would appear as if she were searching for something. Her ticket, maybe. Her phone. Anything.

An announcement – a recorded female voice – echoed across the station, explaining that the train the train she'd just stepped from, the 11.47, now standing at platform 8, was about to depart, and continue its journey to Redhill via Gatwick Airport. The digital clock said it was 11.58.

She looked up once more, watching the guard at the far end of the now deserted platform. All the carriage doors were now shut. All the other passengers who had left the train were either climbing the staircase to the bridge over the platforms, or taking the ramp down to the subway that passed beneath them. No one appeared to be waiting for her, no one had a camera, no one, except maybe the guard, was paying her any attention. She stood, swung her handbag onto her shoulder and began moving down the platform. The guard blew his whistle and waved his arm. The driver acknowledged the signal and the train began to move. No one leapt off, no one had shown her any signs of recognition. Another journey survived, she thought. Mustn't get complacent though.

She let her breath out in a long sigh, unable to tell where the sound of her exhale ended and the noise of the departing train began.

She walked along the platform, between white posts that held up a roof of frosted glass panels. They would keep the rain off in the winter, but on a sunny day like today they just made everything too hot.

One of the consequences of working in publishing, she'd realised, was her attitude to deadlines. She had worked hard to get the reputation of never missing one, even those challenging deadlines where a Production Editor, under pressure, pleaded with her to work an evening, or over a weekend, sometimes even overnight. She'd never turned any jobs down. Now, never missing a deadline felt a matter of honour and integrity. While she'd come close sometimes – and on occasions deliberately so – she had never, ever been late. And so the never-be-late imperative had seeped into her private life.

She was due to meet Mum and Dad, and Ryan at The

Rodboro Buildings at one o'clock. Ryan would be late, as he lived the nearest and had never been on time in his life – Mum thought this was hilarious. And Mum and Dad would be late after arguing about parking. Despite knowing this, she'd still caught the train before the one she actually needed. It calmed and reassured her knowing there was contingency in case of delays or – much worse – if she felt someone had recognised her and she had to hide. It also enabled her to ensure the route to the pub had not changed. Being as prepared as possible, not liking surprises – were these other aspects of her character, she wondered, that put her somewhere on the spectrum? She had no one to compare with. As it was, being assiduously early, she now had time to kill in Surrey's county town. She didn't mind, she felt she'd practised the art of being anonymous in shops.

Ahead of her was a choice: the bridge over the platforms or the subway beneath. Up or down? From this angle, the slope down to the tunnel led to gloom. She broke into a humourless smile. She was meeting her family: down felt appropriate.

Her smile turned into a scowl as she thought about how much effort she'd put in to maintaining a reputation of never missing a deadline, of never refusing work. From Wednesday's email, it seemed her reliability didn't count for anything: the company was going to take her work away just to save money. Quality, it appeared, no longer mattered. The long-term consequences of publishing something that was ambiguous, or worse wrong, didn't matter. All those times she had saved the author and publisher from libel actions, all those professional reputations she had saved by catching things spell-checkers had missed, they didn't matter either. Normally she smiled when remembering how a professor had written 'uninformed police' when he meant 'uniformed police'. Today, though, when she thought about losing her work, her income, she couldn't stop her hands becoming fists and her fingernails digging deep into her palms.

Some years ago, and for a brief period before a neighbour started asking awkward questions, Beth had lived in Godalming, about five miles south-west of where she was now. Guildford, therefore, was not new to her. She'd visited Ryan before he'd dropped out of his studies at Surrey University. The station exit, she remembered, was on platform 1 at the far end of the subway. The tunnel felt dank and dismal despite its whitewashed concrete walls and the large flat-screen displays for bestseller books, blockbuster films, and productions at the Yvonne Arnaud – the local theatre. She was sure the walls would feel clammy if she touched them. Orange handrails bordered the slope up to the exit. The turnstile ate her outward ticket as if it were starving and released her into the station concourse.

An itchy sensation of vulnerability settled on Beth as she weaved through those arriving, leaving, queuing or just milling about. Bumping into someone could bring attention to herself.

All her life Beth had hated people making comparisons between things that just shouldn't be compared. Such as between her and her brother.

Thanks, Mum.

Even though she knew it was natural part of the human condition, she still hated herself when she caught herself doing it, like now... Compared with Leamington Spa station, this felt like walking into a pub having a half-price drinks promotion. She'd forgotten just how crowded Surrey could be.

She managed to leave the concourse and stepped out, squinting, into the bright sunlight. A few blinks and she got her bearings and remembered the way to the High Street.

Joining the back of an impatient crowd, she waited at a pedestrian crossing. The traffic lights turned amber, then red, and instead of stopping, several cars still accelerated through.

Eventually, some brave person stepped out, forcing the next vehicle to squeal to halt. In the seconds it took her to reach the far side of the narrow road she could see a long line of cars already queuing. The drivers either glowered and tapped their steering wheels or yawned, resigned to the heavy traffic.

Looking at the traffic and the crowd of bumping pedestrians, she remembered her surprise when she'd first moved to Leamington Spa, amazed at how wide the roads were, at how comparatively little traffic there was. It was as if everything had just breathed out, given itself a more room. Today, that felt the very opposite of Surrey.

Pedestrians jostling for space filled the pavements, battling to get to or from the station; Beth couldn't walk at a comfortable speed. To her right was a busy road, the obligatory one-way system; looking to her left, she saw the River Wey. She was thinking of Leamington's river, the Leam, also near its railway station, when, in the briefest lull in the traffic, she halted, shocked. Listening. Someone bumped into her from behind. She stepped to one side – and into her childhood. Shrieks filled the sky: seagulls. It was the raucous sounds of her childhood. And she hadn't realised how much she missed them. Living hours from the coast now, she barely heard the sea birds. For a moment she could almost taste salt, could smell wet sand and hear the crunch of sand and stones on the beach. Emotions, memories, flooded through her, filling her to overflowing, and she simultaneously wanted to celebrate, and bend over and vomit. She did neither, of course, just took a second or two to take deep breaths and gather herself. She looked behind her, picked her spot and joined the multitude making its way towards the high street.

On the right-hand side of the road at the next set of pedestrian lights stood the Wetherspoon's pub, the two-storey Rodboro Buildings, where she was due to meet her family in – she glanced at her watch – forty-five minutes.

It'll be at least an hour, she thought, until they're all there.

What to do?

If she hit the pub now, she knew she'd be drunk by the time her family arrived. Tempting…

No. The high street then. Anonymity in a crowd was easy.

Like Leamington's Parade, Guildford's High Street was on a hill, which she began walking up. Unlike Leamington's main street, though, it was cobbled. 'They're not cobbles, they're granite setts', Ryan had told her the one time she'd visited. Cobbles as far as she was concerned. Looking at the shop fronts, Beth thought the high street had more than its fair share of expensive jewellery and shoe shops, between the obligatory coffee franchises. It also had a gold and silver clock, dated 1683, that projected over the road at the end of a black metal beam painted. According to the clock, there was thirty-five minutes to go. Ryan, even if he were awake, wouldn't be out of bed yet, and Mum and Dad would still be arguing about the best route off the A3.

She turned around and gulped. Looking down the hill, she was surprised, scared even, at how many people she could see.

Steeling herself, she turned and made her way back down the hill weaving between sweaty bodies, feeling – not for the first time – grateful that she worked from home and could do her shopping mid-week. How long that would last if she lost her job, was something she dared not contemplate.

A glance at her watch told her she was still a fraction early, so it was either a visit to the M&S toilet or hide in Waterstones. The bookshop won. It wasn't difficult to be anonymous when people were looking at the shelves rather than other customers. Besides, surrounding herself with books, she knew, was like a magic trick – time just vanished.

Ten minutes later, which felt like two, she left the shop and made her way towards the pub. Arriving there a few minutes early would not only enable her to have a fortifying drink – *but only one!* – before Mum and Dad arrived, it would also enable her to pick the quietest table, the furthest from anyone else, and to choose the most suitable seat, one in the shadows. She needed to be able to watch for anyone showing undue interest in her, for anything resembling a flicker of recognition. Her picture – the famous one someone in the police had illegally leaked – occasionally appeared in the papers as a reminder of child murderers, and she knew she could never take it for granted that she'd changed enough to be unrecognisable. When she looked in a mirror, she thought she could still see, under the skin, the remnants of that scared nine-year-old girl.

It was unfair that men could grow facial hair to add to a disguise.

Finally, the obvious thought elbowed its way to the fore: it's not too late to keep on walking, to return to the station and get the first train back to Reading, then to return to the safety of home.

Yeah, but what about seeing Ryan?

More to the point, there was Callum Calbourne hunting her.

Prickles rippled over her skin, her fine hairs lifting, allowing the cool breath of fear to brush her flesh. Somebody bumped into her from behind again, and she realised she'd halted. She felt simultaneously hot and cold. Callum. She recalled the chill that had entered her bones when she'd gathered the courage to Google his past. Where was he now? Had prison rehabilitated him? Beth looked about her, at the passing faces. Overhead a seagull cawed. Suddenly sure Callum was waiting, watching, ready, she spun around – scaring a small gasp from the woman behind her.

She looked down the hill and focused on the traffic passing

the end of the High Street. Gripping her handbag tighter she started striding downhill. She was aware that those who saw her expression as she approached stepped out of her way.

The Wetherspoon's sat on the inside of a bend in the road, so the bar took the shape of an L, with the seating area curving around it. The walls had been taken back to bare red bricks – the original brickwork, Beth assumed – as if to show that there was nothing hidden and everything was revealed. She looked at her watch. Twelve forty.

Perfect. Time for a drink.

She ordered a gin and tonic at the bar and looked around while she waited. There were many empty tables, but she noticed there was an upstairs. That would be better. Out of the way.

She paid, watched the condensation appear on the cold glass, then she took a sip. Licking her lips and letting out a contented sigh, she carried her drink up the narrow stairway, taking care. It wouldn't do to trip and bring attention to herself.

She reached the top and scanned the area for a suitable table.

'Oh, shit,' she said. 'No.'

The glass fell from her fingers. She didn't feel its icy contents splash her shin.

CHAPTER 6

'Now, now, Bethany. There's no need to throw a tantrum.' Mum's voice was calm, irritating.

'No need?' Embers that had been glowing threatened to explode. Beth wanted to grab her mum's glass and fling it through the pub's window. Shattering both. At least the fresh air would cool her anger.

Ryan had been the first to notice her arrival, and he'd had the good grace to spring to his feet, weaving between tables to her, looking shamefaced. Dad had just sort of exhaled nosily through his nose and nodded. Beth had seen this many times before: it was what he did when he couldn't be bothered to say, 'I told you so'.

It was, however, Mum's actions that sprayed most fuel on Beth's fury. Seeing Ryan jump up, hearing Beth's initial shout of 'what's going on?' Mum had turned her head – slow and controlled – to look at her daughter. Triumph flickered on Mum's face, but so fleeting that Beth wondered whether she had imagined it – in fact, had she been expecting (wanting?) to see it?

Beth blinked at the thought, but what she saw now was sternness. Her mother's features were steel. It wasn't menacing as much as secure; Mum was, as always, utterly confident in her own righteousness. Beth had grown up under the weight of this expression; it still appeared in her dreams and she still loathed it. She was in her early twenties, for heaven's sake, she shouldn't still be made to feel like a naughty child. And yet she did.

Before Beth could unhook her eyes from her mum, Ryan had stepped around the table and was next to her at the top of the stairs. 'Sorry, Pudge,' he whispered as he bent to retrieve the glass she'd dropped. 'It was their idea.'

The glass had bounced, not broken. Iced G&T cooled Beth's shin. It would be sticky later.

Mum dipped her head and peered over the top of her gold-framed glasses. Serene. Annoyingly composed. 'Bethany,' she said, not feeling the need to raise her voice. 'I'm sure you don't want to make a scene.'

'A scene?' Her words were louder than she intended, despite her teeth being clenched together so tight it hurt. 'I'll make—'

Mum smiled and put a finger to her lips. Shhh.

Ryan spoke before Beth could respond, his voice soft and understanding. Always the peacemaker. 'It's okay,' he said. 'It is. It's okay.' He put her glass on the nearest empty table with exaggerated care, as if afraid of making a loud noise, and led her to the seats opposite Mum and Dad. The window beside her overlooked a major junction.

Beth looked at Ryan, at his disarming smile, and her anger subsided. He was the only one who could do that. Finally, her jaw unclenched. So did her legs and she managed to take a few steps. 'You tell me one o'clock,' she said, 'and I arrive, *early*, to find you've been here since, what?' She glanced at the almost empty glasses on the table. 'Half twelve? Twelve? What am I supposed to think?' She was now standing by their table, almost leaning over it.

'It's not like that.' Her dad offered a guilty smile, attempting reassurance. 'We wanted to talk to Ryan about his work. We didn't think you'd be interested.' Mum and Ryan ignored him; it was so clearly a lie. He shrugged, looked at his glass and finished off his lemonade, ice clinking as he returned the glass to the table.

Ryan returned to his chair and pulled out the one next to him, nearest to Beth. A photograph of a family of polar bears adorned his T-shirt. Beth was certain that if she'd worn it, it would have provoked a disparaging comment from her mother. 'Please, Pudge, sit down.' Ryan spoke, soft and understanding, and nodded at the empty chair. 'Take the weight off your resentment. You're right, of course.' He held his arms up in mock surrender. 'You caught us.' He lowered his hands and for a moment Beth thought he was going to stroke her forearm, attempting to be reassuring, the way he used to when they were young. She wanted to yank her arm away, unwilling to be touched or soothed by anyone. Yet he didn't touch her, which stoked her temper, the embers glowing bright again. 'Why'd you all lie to me? You…' she thrust an accusatory finger at her brother, glad she had nothing sharper than a fingernail, '…even *you* told me one o'clock. Why…'

Her mother hoicked an eyebrow – in that way she had perfected, the way that said, 'don't be silly, little girl'.

'Oh, come on,' Mum said. 'You know perfectly well why.'

'You wanted to talk about me. Without me being here.' As soon as Beth spoke the words, her anger dissipated like mist under a morning sun. It was so easy to get angry with family. They, after all, had installed all the switches and buttons and levers that triggered such a response. They wrote the manual. And they had years of learning when and how best to use such controls. Despite this, it was almost impossible for Beth to fully lose her temper with these three. Not like she could with other people. She sagged, and almost fell onto the chair Ryan had pulled out. She found herself facing her mum, and squeezed her eyes shut. The flickers of fire she saw on the insides of her eyelids faded. When she opened her eyes bright spots shot across her vision, and she turned her head to the window. The traffic outside came into focus and, for a second, it seemed strange that life elsewhere was continuing, oblivious to the deafening pounding of her heart and her clenching and unclenching fists. There was a low pulsing thrum as the traffic moved then slowed, then stopped at the traffic lights, then moved again once the lights changed. Life below, going on without her.

She took a deep breath and, composed, turned back to her waiting, expectant, family. 'Okay. So, what did you decide, then? Without me.'

'Do you want another drink?' Dad rose to his feet, as if getting ready to run. 'Let me get you a new drink. What can I get you?'

The largest gin they have. A bottle. Two.

Beth looked at the glasses on the table. Ryan had drunk almost a pint of lager; Mum a white wine; Dad – today's driver, it seemed – a lemonade. She knew if she had something strong now it would further expose the already raw nerve-endings of her temper. It would also disappoint Mum, and she didn't feel strong enough to face further disapproval. 'An orange and lemonade. Oh, and no ice.'

'Another Stella for me, please Dad.' Ryan finished his pint in a single gulp and placed it away from him, at the centre of the table. When she was younger, a lot of her friends had thought Ryan handsome, and had enjoyed telling her so. Yes, he had a thick mop of dark hair that, no matter what, always fell into perfect place. And yes, he hadn't suffered from teenage acne. But, no, Beth couldn't see it herself. He was just Ryan. Her brother, who'd never had any shortage of girlfriends.

Dad set off for the bar and Beth thought he looked older than when she had last seen him – at Christmas, she calculated. Lines, although soft ones, had appeared on his face. In his tight and faded black polo shirt and stretch jeans he looked exactly like what he was: late-fifties middle management who had reached as far as he was going to get, and was killing time cultivating middle-age spread. Compared with him, Beth always thought her mum looked exactly like what she wasn't: a strict headmistress, one who wouldn't tolerate insubordination. In fact, while she did work in a school, Mum was the staff secretary. Beth suspected each member of staff, each parent, each pupil, believed they were Mum's favourite.

Beth looked from Mum to Ryan and back. At that moment she thought the happy chatter of other customers and clink of glasses and cutlery sounded muffled, as if the three of them were in a bubble. She couldn't decide whether it protected them or separated them from the outside world.

Mum, of course, was the first to speak. She drew a deep breath that may have been a sigh. 'It was for your benefit, Bethany. With Callum asking after you, I thought it best that we discuss matters before you arrived. That way we'd be able to give you our advice. Which we'd all agreed on.'

'You said in your email he wants to find me.'

Mum nodded. 'He does.'

'How do you know?'

The slightest of smiles touched Mum's lips. She hoicked an eyebrow again. 'Oh, *I* know. *I'm* the one who keeps in contact with everyone.' She stared at Beth. 'I've kept in touch with all our old friends. So naturally I know many of those going to Mary's funeral. Of course I do. They told me about it. We're not invited, of course, thanks to you and… what happened. I've been thinking about it and I think I'll send flowers. Don't know what your father thinks, though. I'll send them from all of us. Even you, Bethany.' She glanced at her watch. 'I'd better do that today thinking about it, the funeral's two-thirty on Monday. I'll get your father to stop at the florists on the way home.' She turned to see her husband returning from the bar, a drink in each hand, menus bending under pressure from an elbow. 'I don't know how well that'll go down, but *I* think it's the right thing.' She looked at Beth again. 'Actually, I think it's a cremation. Your father says he wants a cremation.' She shook her head. 'I've got to put him right about that. I—'

'Here we are.' Dad grinned as if he'd achieved something important. 'I've brought back a couple more menus as well. I'm assuming we'll be eating here.' He placed Ryan's lager in front of him, dropped the menus on the table to join the one already there, propped between the condiments, and, with care, placed Beth's orange and lemonade in front of her. The ice in it rattled against the sides of the glass. She'd asked for no ice.

Beth took a deep breath and mentally began counting. She got to five before she was convinced she wasn't going to make a fuss. At least there was no slice.

'What did he say?'

'Who, dear?'

Beth sucked in a deep breath. 'Callum, who do you think?'

Mum sipped her wine. 'There's no need to get snippy.'

'Mum,…'

'You talking about the funeral?' Dad broke in, trying to be placatory. 'We won't go of course. But your mum heard from… from…'

'Rosemary Acton, and Julie Chenning, and Sharon Exton, and…' Mum rattled off women's names as if Beth should know them. A few Beth recognised as Mum's friends from a lifetime ago, others she had no idea about. She wondered whether her mother expected her to know these people or was trying to prove a point.

'To cut a long story short,' Ryan said, trying to hide his impatience, but Beth still saw him glance at Mum as if for permission to interject, 'Callum's been asking for our addresses.

He must want to track you down.' Beth was surprised Mum didn't look annoyed, but then it was her son, not her daughter, making the interruption.

'Did he say what he wanted me for?' Beth looked in turn at the three faces around the table.

Ryan shook his head, but his thoughts were clear. What do you think he wants you for? You killed his brother, ruined his life. Now his beloved mother's dead.

'Has he, or anyone, been in touch with any of you? Asking for my address?'

'We don't know your address,' Mum stared at her, making Beth feel as if she'd done something else naughty. 'You won't tell us.'

'Now you know why?'

'Don't you trust us, Bethany?'

'It's not that, I—'

'We can keep secrets, you know.'

'Yes, but—'

'Can you imagine what it's like to be a mother whose only daughter doesn't trust her enough to tell her where she's living? Who can't even go and visit her own daughter? Ryan keeps us informed about his job and everything.'

Beth glanced at her brother. He was looking down, deep into his drink, as if something interesting might be found there. 'Ryan,' Beth said, 'doesn't need to hide.'

'Bethany—'

'Are you still getting the phone calls, Mum?'

'No.'

'Sure?'

Mum pursed his lips. 'I told you, no.'

'Really?'

'Not for ages. Besides, it was all such a long time ago.'

'Dad?'

'I think there was one about six months ago.' He couldn't meet Mum's eye.

'You never told me,' she said, enunciating every syllable.

'It was at work.'

Beth could have sworn he shook a little.

'You should have told me,' Mum said.

'Might not have been a journalist. Might've been a prank.'

'Mum,... Mum.' Beth tapped the table, pulling her mother's stare back to her. 'Journalists don't care that it happened a long time ago, they care about selling papers. Child-murderers...' Mum winced at that, '...always make copy, especially if that can help track down those kids' new identities. It only takes a slow news day or someone planning a feature. Have you ever Googled my name?'

'Why would I do that?'

'What do you think you'd find?'

'I don't know.'

This time Beth hoicked her eyebrow. 'Well, what do you think?' Almost immediately she recognised she was imitating her mother. She blinked the expression away. 'This country has an obsession with,' she lowered her voice to a whisper, 'child murderers. The papers would still pay for any information about...' she lowered her voice even further, looked about, '...me.'

'I just want to see my daughter occasionally. Is that too much to ask?'

'And that's without Callum trying to track me down. After what I did, how his life's turned out? Do you think he wants to kiss and make up?'

In the silence that followed Beth heard Ryan take a deep breath. He spoke as if his words were falling on a minefield. 'That's what we were discussing when you arrived. Should we frighten him off, ignore him, or what?'

'And what did you decide? Without me.'

'Dad offered to go and talk to him, and see what he wanted.'

Beth glanced at her father, who shrugged, as if he didn't have feelings either way. He said: 'Your mum thought it really wasn't a good idea.'

'Ryan,' continued Mum, 'was rather more inclined to let Callum know, in no uncertain terms, that he wasn't going to get near you.'

'You're my little sister. He needs warning off. In a way he'll understand. Let him know we mean business. No one, *no one*, threatens my little sister.' Ryan thumped the table with his fist. The ice in Beth's drink clinked. His words had an edge that Beth hadn't heard for years. Similarly, she couldn't recall the last time Mum had given him *that* stare. Beth glanced around, scared he might have attracted attention.

After a second's pause, Mum spoke. 'I really don't think, this family should be advocating any more violence, do you?'

Ryan shook his head. 'What else is someone like him going to understand?'

'And how's he going to respond to threats of violence?'

Dad piped up. 'What about a restraining order?'

It was Beth's turn to shake her head. 'Well, I know he's been inside, but—'

Dad shook his head. 'I heard it was a mistake. That—'

'God, Dad, he's been inside for assaulting women. That's what he did to his girlfriends. Even put one in hospital. Have you really not Googled him?'

'Well,…' Mum and Dad glanced at each other, gave each other the sort of 'that was your job' look that couples use.

Beth ignored them. 'And how exactly,' she asked, 'would a restraining order work? Without giving away where I'm living?

The name I'm using? The papers would find out. They would love it.'

'I'm telling you, Pudge...' Ryan squared his broad shoulders, the T-shirt tightening over his chest, the polar bears seeming to grow, '...something needs to be done. What if he doesn't go away?'

A shiver shuddered through Beth. She'd spent over half her life trying to keep everyone – including herself – safe from her temper whilst simultaneously being ready to flee should the past catch up. The first few years after the murder there had been the predictable problems – excrement through her parents' letterbox, rocks through the windows, spray paint on the walls – but then the past had mostly, *mostly*, settled into an existential danger; fear of an accidental recognition, a slip of the tongue or, as happened in Caterham, a combination of unlucky events that gave enough clues to who she was and what she had done. Then it had been petrol through the letterbox and poor Jackie scarred for life. Beth always maintained it was Callum, but there was no real proof. She never trusted the period of quiet that followed – now she knew it pretty much coincided with Callum's incarceration. The realisation that he was now free to hunt her again produced a new kind of dread. Prickles ran across her neck, as though someone had brushed her with a static-charged balloon. She couldn't help it; she looked behind her. No one was there, of course.

Not this time.

She went to pick up her drink but the moment the glass left the table the rattle of ice she didn't want revealed her trembling. She coughed and put the glass back down, bringing her fist up to her mouth, pressing it there.

'He will go away,' Mum spoke with such conviction Beth wanted to believe her. 'He'll get bored eventually. He's only back for Mary's funeral. I understand he's planning to sell the house.

What else has he got to stay for?'

Ryan shook his head, the way he would if someone were claiming all the traffic outside was good for the planet. 'It depends on how desperate he is to find Pudge.'

'But he can't, can he, dear?' Dad leaned over the table towards her, smiling, nodding. 'No one will help him and, besides, even we don't know where you're living.'

'No, we don't,' her mother harrumphed. 'It would be—'

'Hang on.' At that moment, Beth didn't care she'd interrupted her mother, and ignored the pointed look at her temerity. 'He's selling their old house?'

There was a moment of silence, as Beth looked across the table at Mum then Dad, who, glancing across and seeing that Mum was still tight-lipped at being interrupted, decided it was his job to speak.

'That's as we understand it,' he said. He glanced again at Mum, this time for agreement. 'He mentioned it, or so we've been told. We check every day, online, to see whether the place is listed. You know, estate agent sites and what have you. Your mum checks. Why?'

Beth looked at the three faces staring at her, the same question written on each of them. They hadn't worked it out yet. They hadn't thought it through. For all their words, they clearly weren't as invested as she was. But then why would they be?

'No matter,' she said, shaking her head, trying to keep her voice natural.

If Callum sold the house he grew up in, the one his brother – thanks to her – never had a chance to, then he was going to get an awful lot of cash. These days it was almost impossible to go completely off-grid yet still be part of society and make a living. She had done her best, but had no doubt someone with the right skills, a good private detective, say, would be able to find her. An expensive one, she was sure, would succeed. The tabloids, she knew, were willing to pay for the adult identities of child murderers, but most were too lazy and cheap to fund proper investigative journalism; they had more important stories to manufacture, more famous and contemporary lives to ruin. Apart from the occasional fishing phone calls to Mum and Dad from a bored or newbie reporter, she always figured they were waiting for a tip-off. Besides, there were more recent and infamous child murderers than her now, ones the tabloids cynically used to get their readers frothing at the state of today's society. They didn't care if someone got hounded or their house firebombed. In fact, the tabloids used such news to get their readers spluttering yet again over their breakfasts. What she found both horribly fascinating and frustrating was the double standards: somehow it was deemed more horrific, more *evil*, for girls to commit murder than boys. This even projected into adulthood. The media deemed it more shocking, more deserving of comment and retribution, if a women killed rather than a man. 'She was crazy, hysterical!' compared with 'Well, he was a man, what did you expect?'

She looked out of the window once more. The traffic still moved in pulses, as if it could never be permanently halted – paused maybe, but never stopped. Destinations would always be reached.

Unless there was a fatal accident.

Nodding, lips tight, she looked back to her family. 'I don't want anyone to contact Callum. Not in any way. If someone goes to see him, there's more chance he can use that meeting to find me.'

A fatal accident.

She looked at her brother. 'I mean it, Ryan. I know you. Don't go in heavy-handed. One way or another, it'll only cause further trouble. Violence breeds violence.'

Fatal.

As if requesting permission to speak, Dad raised his hand. 'But I could just talk to him.'

'No, Dad. Let's not have any contact with him at all. Just keep me informed if you hear anything, if he…'

A thought came out of nowhere and hit Beth. 'You drove up here today?'

'Yes, why.'

'You weren't followed?' She looked around the top floor of the Rodboro Buildings. Looking at all the male faces she could see. Investigating them, looking for a face familiar from her online searches. For features she hadn't seen in the flesh for over a decade. Not since his attack.

'No. I don't think… I mean, no we weren't. We're used to this now.'

Her family also began looking at the other customers. They soon got bored and returned their attention to Beth. She, however, felt a pressure around her chest, as if someone were tightening straps around her. The background chatter and clatter of the place faded. A man, two tables over, had just been served a plate of what looked like gammon, egg and chips, but instead of looking at his food, his attention was – Beth would have sworn – on her. He hadn't picked up his cutlery. Her breathing became difficult. She didn't recognise the man, at least she didn't think so. He was sitting at a table on his own, which was what had first drawn her attention, but he looked older than Callum would be, at least fifteen years older. She looked away, scared of catching his eye.

'Besides,' Dad was saying, 'we've moved a couple of times since… then. He wouldn't know where we live now.'

'Are you all right,' she heard Ryan ask.

'Oh, she's fine,' her mum said, 'and I'm getting hungry,' and delicately picked up a menu.

Beth glanced back at the man on his own. She caught him in the process of looking around, then he returned his gaze to her. She saw him take a deep breath, look at his still untouched meal, and push his chair back and stand.

Oh God, he's coming for me.

Beth pushed her own chair back; it caught on the carpet. She shifted her weight, putting her legs fully under her, soles flat on the ground, ready to spring up and flee.

'What's the matter?' Ryan tried to give her a menu, waving it in front of her. 'Are you sure…' She tried to look around the large card as the man got closer. He was behind Mum's shoulder. Within touching distance.

His gaze flicked between all four of them, coming to rest on Beth. 'Excuse me,' he said. 'Umm, could I borrow the ketchup?'

Beth couldn't speak, couldn't swallow, could only exhale – which she tried to do silently.

'Of course.' Mum picked the plastic bottle from the centre of the table. 'Anything else.'

'Just the ketchup. Thanks.'

He gave them all a nod, and Beth thought his smile lingered a fraction of a second more on her, a hint of confusion narrowing his eyes, as if he was wondering what this strange woman's problem was. Then her turned and walked back to his table.

Beth relaxed at the same moment as Ryan dropped the menu into her lap. With her attention still on the retreating man's back, she made no attempt to catch it, and it slipped onto the floor.

'Oh, Bethany. Do pay attention.'

Beth responded on instinct, 'Sorry, Mum,' and, slipping from her chair to pick it up, found herself kneeling by her mum's feet. She looked up, and found her mum looking down at her. Beth felt like a five-year-old, reading in her mum's expressionless face everything from confirmation of her daughter's hopelessness to disdain and scorn. Beth wanted to scream, to shout, to grab her mother and shake her, but she knew from bitter, bitter experience, it would only corroborate her mother's unexpressed views. Besides, they both might both lose their tempers. Then no one would be safe.

She grabbed the menu, bending it and almost piercing it with her fingernails.

She hated feeling like this; and what made it infinitely worse was that she could never tell if what she was reading in her mother's face was really there or was just a projection of her own insecurities. And, if she was projecting, what did that say about her?

'All right then,' Dad said, aiming for good cheer, 'I'll go and order. What do we all want? Now that we're all happy.'

CHAPTER 7

Inevitably, when Dad announced he was going to have a burger, with bacon, cheese and chips, Mum's immediate response was to oppose the idea. 'Des, you know that's not a good idea.' She added, 'Think of your cholesterol.'

'Tell you what,' he offered Mum an innocent smile, 'I'll pay for us all. Okay?' His tone was pitched to show he was only being fair. 'And if I'm treating everyone, then I might as well have what I want.'

Mum replied with a stony-faced silence; Beth and Ryan glanced at each other. They'd been here before. Sometimes it seemed Dad only said things to wind Mum up. And, of course, no prisoners were taken on her part. Beth always wondered whether, now she and Ryan had moved out and they didn't have an audience, they still acted like this at home. Maybe it was done for their own benefit.

'And you two?' Dad looked from Ryan to Beth. 'I'm paying, so have what you want. And the two of you are young enough not to have to worry about cholesterol. Not like some of us. It seems.' Mum tutted and looked away.

Beth and Ryan glanced at their menus, looked at their father and said, simultaneously, 'fish and chips'. They laughed together. Beth remembered how good it felt, and a flood of warmth washed any residual anger away.

Mum glared at them, then at her own menu, as if trying to burn through it with her stare.

When she did look up and speak, and just to make her point, she announced she would just have the chicken salad. With slow deliberation she ran her gaze over Beth's bare arms and creased blue blouse. 'Not many calories in a salad,' she said. 'Are you sure you don't want one?'

Beth tried to hug her sudden good mood, and not let Mum rip it from her.

Dad went off to order the food and, the moment he was out of earshot, Mum leaned towards Beth.

'I don't suppose you're seeing anyone yet, Bethany.' Before Beth could respond, she added, 'But if you ever do, take my advice.' She twitched her head towards her husband. 'Don't let him get ideas above his station. It'll only lead to trouble.'

'Mum,' Beth spoke as if to a child, and felt guilty that she was doing so, 'he's treating us to lunch. Let him have what he wants.' Accompanying the guilt, though, was irritation. Had Ryan been asked whether he had a girlfriend? He was five years older, surely he should be the first to get asked about his love life and whether he was planning to settle down. He never got those questions though, not at Christmas and not when the family gathered for birthdays. Different rules, it seemed, for sons and daughters.

Mum twisted in her chair, looking over her shoulder at her husband. He was, Beth could see, ordering their food, standing with one foot resting on a brass bar. Above the bar was what looked like a genuine sign for 'Dennis Bros Ltd', whose old factory had been converted into this pub. Pictures of the factory in its hey-day and various leading members of the Dennis family, men of course, adorned the brick walls. White pipework that looked big enough to crawl through ran under thick black metal beams that held up the ceiling. 'Of course he's paying,' Mum said, as if it was an irrelevance. 'He's your father.'

Beth and Ryan shrugged simultaneously.

'Don't be like that, you two.' Mum sounded huffy. Not a good sign. She turned to Beth. 'Well?'

'Well what?'

Mum let out a sigh. She couldn't have sounded more exasperated. 'Are you seeing anybody?'

'Mum!' For a second Beth thought of Jake, in the flat downstairs. But she'd refused his party invitation. She could, she supposed, lie about him.

'I'm just asking because I care about you. After all we've done for you, is it a crime to want you to be happy?'

'I am happy, Mum.' Beth tried to calm herself. She hated to admit it, but Mum had a point. Her parents had done a lot for her. Beyond what parents should have to do for their children. Not least the promises they'd made – and kept – to the police and the authorities so that she could remain with them, her family. And, of course, there was the money they gave her when she first moved out. Enough for a stake and the first few years' rent. Without that head start…

'You promise you're happy? I don't want to think of you on your own, unhappy. If there's anything we can—'

Dad returned clutching a bottle of ketchup. Whether it was the same one that had been borrowed or a new one, Beth couldn't tell.

'Salad's off, so I ordered you some chips,' he said. 'If you don't want them, I'll have them.'

'What?' Mum spun round, anger reddening her features until she saw Dad's grin. 'Oh, very funny. Your father's a comedian.'

He bowed. 'Thank you very much. I'm here all night.'

'A comedian who's about as funny as a clogged artery.'

Dad looked around, as if seeing the pub for the first time. 'You know this place is a Grade II listed building? A factory—'

'Yes,' Mum said, 'Ryan mentioned it in—'

'—for motor vehicles.' It was as if Dad had never heard. 'Started back in 1901.'

Beth had never been able to tell whether needling each other was how they expressed their love.

They let Dad talk about the cars and the history of the building until a waiter arrived carrying two plates. One with a burger so tall the bun was beginning to slide off the top and one piled with a salad.

Mum took one look at her salad and – Beth winced, knowing what was about to happen – turned to the waiter. She stated, loud enough so other customers could hear: 'Oh, that's far too much. I can't eat all that.'

Beth and Ryan exchanged almost imperceptible nods: expectations met.

'Mum.'

'I'm just saying, Bethany.'

'Just leave what you don't want.'

'I'll have what you don't want.' Dad grinned. '*I'd* complain if there was too little,' he said, quickly picking up a chip, 'not if there was too much.' He ate the chip in two bites, sucking in air to cool his mouth, then licked his fingers.

Mum harrumphed again and looked down at her full plate – her expression the one she reserved for charity collectors who dared rattle a tin too close – then looked up to her husband. 'Des, why are you always so impatient? Wait for the other meals to arrive.'

It was a family joke that Dad was a fast eater. He came from a large family and Beth had always assumed if he hadn't eaten his meals fast he'd lose them to his brothers and sisters.

'I don't want it to get cold. Besides,' he winked at Beth and

Ryan, a mischievous grin plastered across his face, 'I like my food like I like my women.'

'Yes, we know,' said Mum, resigned, 'hot.'

'No.' He winked at Beth and Ryan again. 'Covered in grease.'

'Dad.'

'Ignore him, Bethany. He's just being silly. Fancy ordering a meal like that.'

'Get it while you can, that's what I say. This is one of my rare chances.'

The waiter arrived again, holding the two plates of fish and chips.

Mum looked at Ryan and her expression softened. 'How's work going then?' she asked. At that moment Beth could see how her mother would appear at work: a pleasant, smiley, middle-aged lady, beginning to go grey yet secure enough in herself not to bother hiding the fact.

'Yeah,' said Ryan, 'All right.' He hadn't had a chance to eat anything yet. 'I know you weren't happy with me dropping out of uni, but I still think it was the best thing I've done. It just wasn't getting me anywhere. I didn't feel I was doing any good. At the WWF I feel part of a team that's achieving something. Something useful. I feel I'm doing something worthwhile. You know what I mean?'

Beth almost dropped her fork. She glanced at her mother, saw her rapt expression, and felt a mixture of irritation and surprise. Ryan had never expressed any particular interest in nature before. And Mum certainly hadn't. They'd never even been allowed pets when they were children.

'The World Wildlife Fund? I didn't know you were working for them. You never mentioned it.' Beth thought about making a crack regarding the World Wrestling Federation but decided Ryan would have heard all such jokes and almost certainly made a few himself.

'Well, Worldwide Fund for Nature as it is now.'

'That explains the T-shirt,' she said, nodding at the family of polar bears stretched across Ryan's chest. 'You work in Guildford?'

'Nah, Guildford's where I live. Share a two-bedroomed flat with a mate. WWF's in Woking. It's not far. Frankly, I'd rather live in Guildford than Woking, so I cycle there. Saves on the expense of having a car. And it's pollution free of course. An easy commute. In fact Paul, my flatmate, also works there. He's got a car, but we both cycle.'

'You mean you race?' Beth knew what her brother was like.

'As if.'

'You will be careful on a bike, won't you, dear.'

'Yes, Mum.'

Beth nodded at their plates, breaking into an impish grin. 'Are you sure you should be eating an animal? What would they say at work?'

In fact, he hadn't eaten anything yet.

'There are a lot of vegans there, but I like my food.'

'That's my boy,' said Dad, swallowing a mouthful of burger, then, with lowered eyes, glancing at Mum as if expecting yet another reprimand.

Ryan nodded his acceptance at Dad's comment. 'I may be many things but I'm not a hypocrite.' He ostentatiously picked up his cutlery: he wanted to eat now. 'So, Pudge. What are you—'

'Me?' she said, 'no, I'm not a hypocrite either.'

Dad laughed. Ryan laughed. Mum looked annoyed.

Ryan speared a chip. 'You know what I mean. What are you doing now? The same?'

'Still working from home. I—'

'Ryan,' Mum leant towards her son, 'what is it you actually do? For work. I want to know.'

Beth felt a flash of anger and looked away, at the relentless traffic outside. It's not as if she wanted to talk about herself, but neither did she like the way the opportunity was snatched from her. The fact she should be relieved that attention had been diverted elsewhere only made her irritation worse. It felt as if she'd been shown a gift with her name on it, only to have it taken away. If she and Mum ever lost their temper with each other, there was no telling what would happen. It would certainly involve broken plates. She counted passing cars, reaching seventeen before the traffic stopped again and she no longer felt like shouting at her mother. Although turmoil still churned deep inside, she felt calmer. Then she thought of Callum, and wondered where he was.

'What I do,' Ryan shrugged, 'is nothing special.' His knife and fork were beside his plate again, the cooling chip still impaled on his fork. He leaned on his elbows. 'I'm involved with the supporter publications, trying to improve WWF's profile, get more people to adopt endangered animals, raise more money, that sort of thing.'

'Sounds like a lot of responsibility.'

'Yes, Mum.' He paused a second and, when there was no follow-up, plucked his cutlery from the tabletop. 'Now, Beth,' he stabbed another chip to warm up the first, 'you were saying. You're still working from home?' He took a bite and began chewing.

Beth remembered Jake asking her something similar. In her reply she hadn't told him the entire truth. 'It's for the best,' she said. 'I see no one. No one need know my name. I just set up an email account and work gets sent to me and I send it back. No one is any the wiser. I'm still editing, so if you want any help Ryan…'

'You have a whole new identity? A new passport? With a different name?' Beth couldn't tell whether her mum with disgusted or impressed with the idea.

'No, I just keep my head down. I don't want to do anything
… anything else illegal.'

In the silence that followed, Beth regretted her words; they
were just another reminder that this wasn't a normal family get-
together, that thanks to her they weren't a normal family.

She waited for Ryan to comment on the similarity of their
jobs, ask for advice or maybe, maybe, offer her some work, But
Mum spoke first.

'I know how it's done, you know. Getting a new passport. I
read about it.'

Beth sighed, shook her head. 'I've read about it too. But… I'm
not sure… I mean, like, I don't really need a passport. It's not as if
I've got anywhere to go.'

'You really haven't got a passport?'

'No, Mum.'

'I'm only trying to help, Bethany.' Mum skewered a piece of
chicken with her fork and raised it. 'In your position *I* would have
considered it, so I could leave the country if I had to.' The chicken
disappeared into her mouth and she began chewing. Her eyes
never left her daughter. 'You need to go around a graveyard, find
a girl born about the same year as you, then apply for a passport
in her name, and—'

'Taking a dead girl's name,' Beth shook her head at the
thought, 'that's just not who I am. How would that girl's family
feel?'

'Ah, now she thinks of family.'

'That…' Ryan put his fork down hard; it made a dull *thud* on
the wooden table, '…is unfair, Mum.'

'I'm only trying to help. When we lose everything, we've still
got family. You do know, Bethany, we will always be there for you.'

'Hear, hear.' Dad nodded in agreement, arranging his cutlery on his empty plate.

Beth looked at her fish and chips, unable to meet the eyes of her well-meaning family. A swell of emotion surged inside her, a mixture of gratitude and responsibility.

'Thanks,' she said, knowing it sounded weak.

When she looked up, Dad was holding his napkin, ready to wipe his lips. 'It's what families do,' he said.

His tone, his sincerity, reminded Beth of one of his favourite comments, one he'd made repeatedly when she and Ryan were growing up: 'God makes your family, but you make your friends.' It had taken her a long time to realise that she and Dad had interpreted this aphorism in different ways. She now understood that to Dad it meant that family bonds were divine and could never be broken; family was everything. To her, it meant that she had no control over who she was related to, but it was her choice of friends that reflected who she really was.

Which was ironic, because she didn't have any friends.

Jake, she wondered. Could Jake a friend?

No. She couldn't afford to have anyone too close. For their sake.

The thought constricted her throat.

She looked at her meal again; she'd lost her appetite. She pushed it away with her right hand, her left hand rubbing her scabs and scars through her jeans.

'Don't want that?' Dad asked already reaching for her plate. 'I'll have it.'

'I told you, you should have had a salad,' said Mum.

CHAPTER 8

Watching Dad finish his apple pie and custard was somehow mesmerising. He had been the only one of the family to have dessert and Beth knew he was amused they were all waiting for him.

She felt Ryan's nudge. 'Want company?' he said, almost a whisper. 'Walking back to the train station?'

'Yeah. That'll be good.' Beth gave an appreciative smile to her brother. He replied with a knowing nod.

There had been a hollow worry in Beth's stomach. She and Ryan spent so little time together now that she had feared they would be strangers, that he would no longer understand her or her worries. But it seemed they weren't and he did.

It would be a relief to spend time with Ryan, without Mum and Dad. Maybe, she thought, supressing a smile, they'd laugh as they once did, anticipating each other's responses, setting up a punchline for the other to deliver. Despite her and Ryan's differences, their sibling fights and rows, they simply understood each other in ways others didn't. And when they didn't have to worry about someone else misconstruing their comments and in-jokes, things felt looser, more relaxed, freer. Mum and Dad had never got their humour. Maybe it was a generational thing.

She glanced at her watch: it was a few minutes before three o'clock. She had noted the train times back to Reading: two an hour, at six and forty-four minutes past the hour. As was usual though, connections didn't work out in a helpful way. Whichever train she got would arrive four minutes after the train to Leamington had departed, giving her about a half-hour wait. Time to hide in the toilets again, avoiding the people and the CCTV.

'See,' said Mum, eyeing the last of Dad's custard as he scooped it up, 'your greed has made her late now.'

'No, Mum. I'm—'

'See, she says she's all right. There's no rush. Why won't you let me enjoy myself?'

'Because I know your cholesterol level. You want a heart attack?'

'You worry too much.' He swallowed, smacked his lips together and, just as ostentatiously, dropped the spoon into the bowl. Its clatter made Beth wince and look around. 'Besides,' Dad said, his voice now muffled behind his napkin, 'you know what effect you going on about it will have. Maybe,' he winked at Beth and Ryan, 'you want to get rid of me. Got a fancy man?'

Beth and Ryan exchanged rolled-eyed glances,

Mum harrumphed again and Beth sniggered, resulting in one of Mum's special stares; those reserved just for her.

In the silence that followed, Beth composed herself. She took a deep breath and didn't look at her brother. 'Just so I am certain. Whatever you agreed before I arrived—'

'We—'

Beth held up her finger to her mother, impressed with her own bravery. 'Whatever you agreed,' she repeated, 'I don't want anybody doing anything. If you contact Callum, it's bound to make it easier for him to find me. I need him to decide it's too difficult to find me. It should be so hard that he gives up and goes away. Of his own accord. Never to be seen again.'

'Well, okay.' Ryan didn't sound convinced.

'Agreed.'

'If that's what you want, Bethany. If you're sure.'

After that, the conversation became fitful and, as if they knew there was little more to say, they began making noises about leaving.

'Come on then,' said Dad, looking at his watch and standing. 'We'd better get going. It was nice to see you two again. You will stay in touch, won't you?' This last was said nodding at Beth.

'Yes, Dad.'

Mum picked up her handbag and stood. 'If you won't give us your address, Bethany, at least call occasionally. Let us know you're all right.'

Beth felt a blush of shame on her cheeks; that her Mum had to ask this. She nodded, cleared her throat, and when she felt able, said: 'If that's want you want, Mum.'

Mum gave the slightest of nods, as if evaluating her daughter's answer. 'Yes,' she said with reluctance. 'Good.'

Over the years, Beth had seen the way other families part after meeting, with hugs and handshakes and kisses. Her family didn't go in for touchy-feely emotions, for which she was grateful.

Mum and Dad simply said their goodbyes and walked away.

She figured they were bickering by the time they reached the bottom of the stairs.

'They mean well, you know.' Ryan sounded as relieved at their departure as Beth felt. She'd always gone to Ryan for strength, had assumed his five-year superiority had given him limitless supplies, so it was interesting he was now also finding them exhausting.

'They have a funny way of showing it.' Beth couldn't keep the sadness from her voice.

'They just want the best for you.'

'Second best.'

He smiled. 'Here we go again.'

Beth pointed at her brother. 'Well, they know you're the best.'

'Not true, Pudge.'

'We both know it is.'

'I wouldn't say that.'

'In their eyes.'

'Who knows what they see.'

They stood together and made their way out of the pub, without glancing back at the detritus on the table. Someone else could clear it up.

Outside, they joined a crowd at the traffic lights, ready to cross the road. A similar crowd grew on the opposite side.

Beth watched the traffic passing. 'You've really sold your car?' she asked.

'It was too big, too polluting, too unnecessary. I decided I could do without it.'

'You loved that big beast.'

'I did, but then it occurred to me. Why do I need a 4×4? Really? In Guildford? In fact...'

The lights changed and they found themselves separated as they tried to weave a way through the oncoming crowd; two groups, crossing in opposite directions, and getting in each other's way. Beth thought there couldn't have been more blocking if they had been opposing American football teams.

Before they reached the opposite pavement, Beth and Ryan were side by side again. Beth continued as if they'd never been separated. 'And now,' she said, 'you're working to protect wild animals? I never thought of you as an animal lover.' As she stepped up on to the pavement, an older man in a suit, in a hurry to beat the lights, pushed her aside. With sudden fury she turned to swear at him, but her foot missed the kerb and she stumbled.

In an instant Ryan's hand wrapped itself around her arm. 'Careful,' he said, releasing his grip as she recovered and calmed herself. He positioned himself between her and the traffic, which was just beginning to move.

She felt a swell inside, an ache, a pride not only that he was her brother, but also that she'd managed to douse the flash of temper.

Ryan continued. '... believe it or not, I've even adopted a polar bear.' He pointed to the picture on his T-shirt.

'You keep it at home?'

'We've bought a bigger freezer.'

'What does your flatmate think of that?'

'Paul? What's he gonna say? He's got a panda in the living room.'

'My money's on the polar bear. They can look cute, but they'll tear your head off as soon as look at you.'

Ryan laughed. 'Maybe that's why I like them. What about you, Pudge? You want to support a good charity? WWF?'

'I've always thought wildlife was best seen from behind glass. Red in tooth and claw and all that. A bit like me.' As they crossed the bridge over the river, Beth found herself thinking, for the first time, of pets. Ryan's comment had been a joke, but how would it feel to have a cat or dog or something – nothing large (not a polar bear) – that was actually pleased to see you when you opened the front door? Could she get a pet?

No, she thought, of course not.

There were times – most of the time, in fact – when she felt she couldn't take care of herself, let alone take responsibility for another living creature. She needed a pet that would look after her. She thought of the guide dogs she seen, those being trained.

'If I was to support a charity,' she said, 'it would be guide dogs.' She laughed without knowing why.

'Really?'

'Really.'

'For the blind?'

'I think they're fantastic. Think about what they do, the help they give. The lives they improve. I'm always seeing people training them. Sorry, but if I had any spare money, that's who I'd support.'

They do some good, she thought. They help people. Whereas pandas…?

'Yeah.' Ryan nodded. 'That's a good cause.'

'As is yours,' she said feeling guilty. 'Mankind's got a lot to answer for. Good luck with saving the planet. If anyone can…'

He was laughing when they entered the station concourse. Beth looked at the monitors displaying departures.

'Oh, not bad. Not bad at all. Only four minutes late.' She delved into her bag for her tickets.

'Are you on Facebook, Pudge? Social media?'

'What do you think?'

'Don't you miss it?'

'No,' she lied. She often saw others on their phones, and wondered: what would it be like to have friends she could…? She forced the thought from her mind. 'Never had it,' she added, 'so can't miss it.'

Ryan stepped in front of her. When he spoke, his good humour had vanished. His voice was hard, precise. He held out a slip of paper. 'Here's my mobile number. You only have to phone. Any time. Day or night. Tell me where you are. I'll come to you.'

He paused, staring into her eyes, to make sure she understood, then added: 'Don't let Callum get anywhere near you.'

CHAPTER 9

With a hiss the train doors juddered shut beside her as Beth knelt on Platform 2 of Leamington Spa station, pretending to search through her handbag. She glanced at her watch and let out a sigh that seemed to her just as loud as the doors. For want anything better to do, she pulled out her phone and checked the time: just past six o'clock. The train was only twenty or so minutes late. Not bad. These days, anything under about forty minutes and she could keep her temper. Resignation and lowered expectations when using the trains defused her anger. Maybe that was British Rail's plan.

She looked up, relieved to see the few others who had stepped from the train were already walking away, down the stairs to the exit, paying her no attention. As soon as the train began to pull out, she replaced her phone in her handbag, which she picked up as she stood. She made her way out of the station.

While home was about two miles away, it never occurred to her to wait for a bus or even take one of the many taxis queueing in the station forecourt. She was so accustomed to walking that a couple of miles meant little. Besides, she needed the time, not only to get her mother's voice out of her head, but also to come to terms with Callum looking for her. The word *hunted* appeared in her mind and, as she tried to push it away, her jaw tightened.

She concentrated on picking up her pace, but it felt as though the surrounding hot air was heavy, pressing against her. Or maybe it was the voices of her family, colliding chaotically, splitting, forever doubling inside her. Either way, it made her feel self-conscious, certain that everyone was aware of her. More than once – as she walked from the station to the Parade, Leamington's high street – she looked around, becoming convinced she could feel eyes on her, certain someone was watching, stalking her. Nobody though, no matter how hard she stared at them, seemed interested in her.

Just the usual common-or-garden paranoia she tried to convince herself, maybe exacerbated by talk of Callum and by seeing her parents. Surely that was it. She pursed her lips.

Once again she looked behind her, then back to the Parade, needing something to distract her mind from her circling, prickling fears. A few years ago, she had edited an architecture book, which had mentioned Royal Leamington Spa. She tried to recall what it had said and to link what she could see to what she had edited. The place was a Royal Spa town and proud of it. Looking up the incline that was the Parade, doing her best to ignore the growing, burning itch between her shoulder blades, she noted the regency architecture above all the shopfronts. The council, she thought while fighting the urge to look again behind her, must have an ordinance that all the stuccoed buildings were painted the same shade of cream. It could have made the town centre dull and samey, but Beth thought it gave the whole town a sense of character. She'd once overheard someone explain that, because of the town's distinctive look, one of the local squares had been used for the exteriors of the *Upstairs Downstairs* TV series. It was ironic, then, that the only major building on the Parade that wasn't in the regency style, defiantly so, was the Town Hall. The red brick and limestone building, Beth thought, just looked uncomfortable and out of place. It would have been more appropriate somewhere else, Venice maybe. It even had a renaissance-style campanile – a square bell tower with a clock on each side. Beth looked up at it, compared the time with that on her watch. It was twenty past six.

That's okay, she thought, home about seven.

Despite the warmth of the summer evening, a shiver ran through her. Jake had said, eight o'clock for his party: she would be in her flat, safe, by then. No danger of seeing Jake and the embarrassment of having to find another excuse to turn down his invitation. Kind as it was.

Looking up the Parade, Beth was surprised how few people she could see, with most of them in a hurry. Probably just staff heading for home after having shut up their shops.

Not too crowded, she thought. Should be safe.

For some reason, possibly because she couldn't shake the sensation of being watched, a less obvious route felt more appealing. She looked behind her once more, checking for approaching traffic and anyone following her. She saw neither and so crossed the Parade. Here. to her left was the Town Hall, in front of which stood a statue of Queen Victoria.

For a few months after arriving in Leamington, Beth had found the statue to be disconcerting in a vague way, like looking at an optical illusion. Eventually she had noticed the small plaque, its three lines explaining that, during the Second World War, a bomb – probably intended for Coventry – had landed nearby. The blast had shifted the statue and its plinth by an inch, while leaving the base untouched. The off-centre statute was now part of the town's history. Beth knew she had a good eye for page design, for symmetry and balance, so was relieved that this was why she found the thing troubling.

It amused her to think that no one had found it fit to return the monarch – the sovereign who had liked the town so much she had granted it a 'Royal' prefix – back to her original place. It was almost as if they were embarrassed by the patronage. Certainly, few of the locals ever bothered to use the 'Royal' when referring to Leamington, and some not even the 'Spa'.

The route Beth took passed through the centre of what was, in effect, an elongated roundabout, about a third of a mile long. She liked it because of the broad tree-lined footpath, wide enough for six people to walk abreast. On each side of the footpath ran grass strips – of about equal width to the path – so that the roads either side felt a long, long way away. With all this space, Beth was surprised no developer had bought it up and built a small 'prestigious' housing estate here. She always felt safe walking on this path, with the thick trees either side like muscular bodyguards, a protective roof above made from intertwining branches.

Walking on the path, she waited for the expected sense of security. Nothing. She frowned, frustrated, and found herself unable to resist looking behind her. There were very few pedestrians in view, five she counted. Three were behind her: one man, in knee-length shorts, had joined the path Beth was taking, he had a phone in one hand and a takeaway coffee in the other. Behind him, a girl, a teenager, in a short scarlet skirt was crossing the road, apparently talking to herself; her earbuds explained she was on the phone. Beth was amused at the – in comparison – overdressed man behind the girl, in thick jeans and lumberjack shirt, who glanced guiltily from his own telephone to the girl's legs. Beth didn't recall seeing any of them at the station, and felt that all three – the two men and the girl – were so involved with their phones that, even if she stood directly in front of them, they wouldn't notice her.

Seeing others on their phones, Beth felt of stab of sadness and an ache of isolation. With her history she had never dared investigate social media. As she understood it, her peers were infatuated with exhibiting themselves and criticising others, it didn't sound fun but she couldn't help feeling she was missing out. It was one of the many things, she thought, dejected, that increased her separation from the rest of humanity.

She sniffed at her stupid sense of self-indulgence and looked ahead, to the left of the path, where a young couple sat on a bench. The feeling of being viewed vanished, washed away by a flood of guilt at her awareness that now she was the one doing the surreptitious watching. The couple had to be in their late teens or early twenties, in love but, with nowhere else to go, even this council bench with its cracked and flaking green paint seemed attractive. The man had one arm around his lover's shoulders, his fingers caressing, smoothing her hair. Beth couldn't hear what was being said, but every now and then the couple would giggle and the girl would snuggle further into the boy's encircling arm and kiss his cheek with loving gentleness.

Beth looked away, first feeling embarrassed at such exhibitionism, then curious at why. The couple looked at complete peace with the world and blissfully content with each other. So why, Beth pondered, did the sight of them make her feel like flinching. She almost stumbled, as if the ground had dropped a fraction, when the answer came to her: she had no idea what either of those emotions, peace and contentment, felt like. Let alone a combination of the two. She sniffed and blinked away the stinging in her eyes. Would she – she speculated, and not for the first time – now be in a stable relationship if she'd had a normal childhood? Married maybe, with kids? The warm idea of embracing someone, and them not recoiling at who she was, at what she'd done, made something inside her melt. For a brief moment she squeezed her eyes shut, trying to re-freeze the thaw inside before it became a dangerous flood.

You don't deserve a normal life.

How many times had she heard that?

Neither of the couple looked up or took any notice as she passed. And why should they? They were together, safe, sharing each other's warmth, while she was way, way outside their world. A sad smile fluttered on Beth's lips. She felt no animosity towards the couple – wished them good luck, in fact – but that didn't stop a stab of self-pity and, she was ashamed to admit, more than hint of jealousy.

She pulled in a deep breath, the warm air getting caught in her throat in a way that, even to her, sounded like a sob. She increased her pace, still feeling dark envy swirling like ink in her blood.

If Ryan were here…

She shook her head. She just wasn't going to be one of those women who rely on a man. She'd survived this long on her own, she didn't need anyone's protection.

Company would be nice though.

Blinking away the prickling behind her eyes, she strode on, increasing her pace, making for the safety of home.

Her key was already in her hand as she approached the main door to Regency Court. Instinct made her look around. While there were people passing, none seemed to be paying her any attention. A man in a mobility scooter hummed passed on the other side of the road; on this side, a woman looked into her pushchair, smiled and adjusted the canopy, protecting the pushchair's occupant from the low sun. Beth turned away, feeling the threatening sting of tears again; the mother's expression just seemed too genuine.

The main door to the flats comprised alternate vertical strips of dark wood and reinforced glass. On the left-hand wall was the doorbell unit: six buttons and an intercom to ask the resident for entry. The buttons were numbered; no names. She liked that. She inserted the key in the lock, twisted and pushed open the door. Stepping into the lobby she let the heavy spring shut the door behind her. When she heard the loud *clunk* of the lock reverberate around the stairwell, she felt safer. With no carpet on the concrete floor and bare cream-coloured walls, the lobby echoed Beth's long exhalation. To her right was Jake's front door, painted a dull orange. She mentally wished him luck with tonight's party, while hoping that he hadn't heard her arrive. If his door opened right now, she wasn't sure how she'd get out of another invitation. Ahead on the right were the stairs that led up to her flat, and then on up to Shreeya's. To the left and behind the stairs was the door that led to the car park. She could see through the window that, despite her offer to Jake, no one had parked in her space. She felt a little disappointed.

Still early, of course.

To her left, opposite Jake's door, was Mr Lottan's flat. Her landlord's door was painted a colour somewhere between blue and purple; Beth could never quite decide whether it was deliberate or whether the original colour had aged.

She began climbing the stairs, hurrying in case Jake appeared.

She reached her landing and saw the drooping peace lily on the windowsill – she must remember to water the flower, in fact she would go and get some water now. Movement outside the grimy window caught her attention: in the car park, a man walked towards Jake's car, the polished red beast with its unnecessary bull bars. As she watched, curious, her phone chimed; an email had arrived.

Close enough to my home router, she thought, distracted, while watching the stranger approach the vehicle, as if inspecting it on a forecourt. She frowned and without taking her eyes off the tall, well-built man, opened her handbag, which was slung over her shoulder, to pull out her phone. This, she could do by instinct.

The man shielded his eyes and peered inside the car, moving from its front to the rear windows. He stepped back, squatted on his haunches by the rear door, reached out and touched the bodywork, then appeared to use his fingernail to scratch the paint.

Even at this distance, she could tell the man was muscular. His jeans stretched over his thick legs while his black T-shirt strained over his broad shoulders then gripped the bulges of his biceps. There was a complicated design on the front of the T-shirt that she couldn't quite make out. His hair was very short, looking as if it were only a week or two's growth after it had been shaved off.

Using her phone as an excuse to take a moment, she pulled her eyes from the stranger and what he was up to. She glanced at the screen of her phone, part of her mind wondering who would be emailing her on a Saturday, hoping it was new work, knowing it wasn't.

It was Mum. It was marked 'Urgent'.

Subject: 'Break in?'

First line: 'When we got back home today, we…'

She looked up, the words taking their time to register as her eyes re-focused through the grimy window. She gasped.

The guy in the car park was staring up at her.

Smiling.

CHAPTER 10

'Jake! Jake! Your car.'

Beth slammed her palm against Jake's front door.

Silence, then a metallic clattering, then silence again; not even a muffled curse.

It hadn't been a conscious decision to warn Jake someone was checking his car. It was instinctive; one injustice that she could prevent. Beth realised her mistake, however, the moment her palm made contact with the orange door. She hadn't wanted him to know she was home and yet here she was banging on his door. Still…

'Jake!' Was that a mumbled reply? It was difficult to hear over the blood pounding in her ears, a result of the limb-threatening leaps downstairs, phone still in one hand and her handbag swinging dangerously, threatening her balance.

Come on, Jake.

She looked around. There was no one to help her.

Oh, for.... Shit. Shit.

She ran to the rear door of the flats, twisted the lock, yanked the door open and dashed into the car park. Then halted so suddenly she stumbled, her momentum carrying her forward even when her legs had stopped moving. Her handbag swung one more time, threatening to pull her over.

The guy had opened the driver's door of Jake's Mitsubishi and had his hand on the steering wheel.

How…?

'Hey,' she shouted in the absence of any plan. Her left hand clutched her mobile; her right was snaking into her handbag, still open from when she had removed the phone.

The thief had one hand on top of the door and, instead of getting in, had turned to face her. That annoying smile appeared again, his eyebrows rose, and she got the impression he was daring her to push the confrontation.

Stall. Wait for Jake.

For once Beth *wanted* to feel anger, something to give her strength, the confidence she could confront this man; instead, she felt a liquid fear, a presentiment that this would not end well. She had never considered herself brave.

She fought to catch her breath, not taking her eyes from the man, her right hand moving with stealth in her handbag, her fingers knowing where to go, slipping into the side pocket. They wrapped themselves around the smooth plastic of her rape alarm. Clutching it seemed to give her strength. It felt as if all today's anxieties were solidifying, become jagged and hard.

She stared at the man, trying to return his challenging, amused expression, while, inch by inch, she began to remove the alarm. She realised she still held the phone in her left hand, and she wondered whether she could be quick enough to take the thief's picture if he decided to do a runner. He was, however, showing no inclination to run. Quite the opposite; it was as if he were enjoying the show. Just as well, because there was no way she was going to introduce herself to the police, even if presenting them with a picture of a car thief. Although both hands were full – one gripping her phone, the other her rape alarm, now free of the bag slung over her shoulder – she placed the knuckles of both hands on her hips. Somewhere at the back of her mind she recognised her stance as the one her mother took when laying down the law. Whatever was inside Beth solidified even further; if it worked for Mum…

She pitched her voice like a teacher's. 'Can I help you?'

The man's smile broadened further. 'I don't know,' he said. 'Can you?' His grin seemed to fill the car park; the brick walls with their black railings barely containing it.

The fact that he was not bothering to hide his amusement added a new level of concern to Beth. Did he see her as just a weak woman? Well, she'd show him. She hoped.

She clutched the rape alarm tighter.

Beth felt the man run his eyes, with deliberate pauses, over her body. It made her itch, as if spiders were scuttling over her flesh. He didn't even disguise what he was doing. She wanted to turn away or cross her arms, but didn't move.

He tucked his thumbs into his trouser pockets, which seemed to accentuate the black T-shirt over his chest. It carried the logo of a skull, with snakes writhing from its eye sockets, between two phallic-looking candles.

Jake. Where are you?

Unable to resist the urge any longer, she glanced behind her. It was the quickest look ever, but still enough to glimpse Mr Lottan, the landlord, in the hallway talking to Jake, preventing him from getting outside.

Beth returned her attention to the stranger. 'What are you doing?' She nodded her head at the entrance to the car park. 'This is private property.' He had walked in from that direction, passing the sign that proclaimed this fact. In case he couldn't read she added, 'Residents parking only.'

He didn't look behind him, so he missed the movement at the entrance. It caught Beth's eye: a man sauntering past, wearing a lumberjack shirt and skinny black jeans. A phone held to his face.

Beth frowned, opened her mouth to speak but he beat her to it.

'Residents parking?' He nodded to himself, as if contemplating this piece of information. 'Well then, it's a good job it was parked by a resident. I'm sure we'd all hate rules to be broken.'

He stepped forward – Beth resisted the urge to step back – and without looking he swung the car door shut behind him. It closed with a concise *clunk.*

The guy didn't seem perturbed to be caught breaking into a car. He was, Beth thought, one of those men so self-confident that life's vicissitudes just cause them amusement. For some reason she thought of the couple smooching on the bench. This guy would have no problem with such exhibitionism.

Then understanding flooded through her with such force she staggered. Soggy embarrassment remained in its wake. She squeezed her eyes shut. When she opened them, he was still standing there, expectant, and she knew the answer to her next question.

'It's your car. Isn't it?'

Give him credit, he didn't say anything, just let his grin grow even further. He gave a single nod.

There was a particular look of disappointment that used to appear on her brother's face the moment Beth, as a kid, realised she was being teased, when Ryan knew his friendly tormenting was over for that day. She was surprised: the man's face showed no sign of that expression. If anything, he seemed impressed.

'Hey!' Jake at last.

Beth turned to face him, her right hand slipping back into her handbag, dropping the rape alarm inside.

Although Jake was midway through a wave, there confusion in his eyes as he tried to work out what face-off he'd interrupted. His T-shirt hung as if it had lost its elasticity and while it may have once been white, now it was an over-washed grey with strange dark specks. Protruding from beige cargo shorts were pale legs that contrasted with his sunburnt arms and face.

Beth tried to turn her cringe into a shrug, feeling a blush rise up her neck. 'Sorry, Jake. I saw him. I thought it was your car and…'

Laughter from behind her, although it didn't sound mean. 'You've got good neighbours, Jake. Not necessarily welcoming, but they look after you.'

'Sorry,' Beth shrugged again. 'I saw him, and …'

A grin unfolded over Jake's face reflecting his growing understanding. 'Thanks,' he said, and relief filled Beth. He wasn't angry. She felt her shoulders slump as tension dissipated. 'You did the right thing,' Jake said, and then to his friend: 'Mikey, this is Liz, my neighbour. And Liz, this is Mikey. A lazy bastard from work.'

'Who're you calling lazy?'

'All right, a bastard from work.'

'That's better.'

Jake smiled. 'Mikey leant me his car to help me move my stuff in. What a time for the suspension on my old wreck to go. Talk about a bumpy ride. What are you doing here, Mikey?'

'I was checking to see what damage you'd done.'

Jake's shrug was one of amusement. 'I guess he doesn't trust my driving.'

'I've seen the way you work, mate. Slapdash.'

Jake pointed at his friend. 'And how many points have you got on your licence?'

'Shut up.'

'And you've come to help me prepare for the party? That's very kind of you.'

'You think?' Mikey's tone showed what he thought of the idea. 'I know who's coming. Wanted to count the dents on my car before they start parking.'

'Ah, but this is private parking in here.'

'So I've just been informed.'

By now Mikey was standing before Beth, hands deep in his pockets. He was taller than she was, taller than Jake even. His skin tanned, as if he spent a lot of time outside.

'So,' Mikey asked, 'you coming to this party?'

'Well...'

Jake turned to her. 'I thought... Can you make it, now?' Beth could see puzzlement in his blue eyes. But was there also hope there? She felt a swirl of confusion. Did he really want her company? He wasn't just being polite? And did she want to go? An image of the loving couple on the bench came to her.

'I... I was, like, supposed to be seeing my family, but I got back earlier than expected.' She couldn't tell if he believed her.

'So you can come?'

'Well.' She wasn't mistaken, there was enthusiasm there. 'How many are you expecting?'

'Dunno. Fifteen, maybe twenty. People from work and their partners, some other friends. It'll be very low key.'

'And,' Mikey added, 'we promise not to talk about work. Well, not all the time.'

Jake nodded. 'So, you coming?'

Beth thought of going upstairs, opening the door on her silent, empty flat, opening a bottle and drinking solo while the sound of a party reverberated through the floor. For the first time in a very, very long time, she didn't fancy being alone. A combination of seeing her family, Callum hunting her and the couple cuddling on the bench made her yearn to live like a normal person. Besides, now that the confusion with the car had been explained, she was surprised she felt, well, comfortable. It had taken her a moment to place the emotion. She wasn't used to feeling relaxed, especially in company.

'In fact,' Jake said, glancing behind him, at the flat, 'I'm just getting things ready now.'

Beth spoke before she could change her mind. 'Need any help?'

'Really?'

'Really.'

'Sure?'

'Sure.'

'Well, yeah. But you don't have to.'

'Please.'

Jake blinked. 'Okay. If you put it like that. This way.'

'Hang on.' Mikey pulled his hand from his pocket, waved it at his car. It bleeped, and flashed its lights as it locked itself. 'Lead on,' he said.

So Jake did, unlocking the door back into the stairwell. In his hurry, Jake had left his own front door open and already the stairwell was filling with the smell of baking. Some supermarkets, Beth thought, would pay a fortune to be able to pump that aroma around their aisles.

Being directly beneath hers, Jake's flat had the same layout as Beth's. It wasn't dirty, but it did look as if it had seen more guests. Beth thought the colour combinations of her carpet and wallpaper were nicer. She glanced behind her when Mikey shut the flat's front door; he didn't lock it, just left it on the latch. She stamped on any more relaxation by reminding herself she was in a new place with two unknown men.

Jake led them to the kitchen. He'd been busy: pans were on the hob, a saucepan and lid in the sink, bottles of spices and ingredients lined upon the work surface. Fascinated, Beth looked around. It wasn't tidy but it felt ordered, with many shelves and hooks: a kitchen in use by someone who knew what they were doing. Even when she made the most basic of meals – which was most of the time – her kitchen ended up looking as if it had been raided by ravenous students. Looking closer, she saw a shiny saucepan lid sitting in the sink that no longer gave a perfect reflection. She wondered if it would fit anything circular anymore.

'Oh God,' she said. 'Sorry. Did I do that? When I knocked?'

Jake shook his head, waved his hand as if wafting smoke. 'It's okay. It wasn't my favourite.'

At the entrance to the kitchen, Mikey snorted. 'Favourite? Who has a favourite saucepan?'

Jake picked the lid from the sink and inspected it. 'Someone who cares about cooking, maybe?'

Mikey looked at Beth. 'Ha, I bet he likes *Bake Off* as well.'

Beth ignored him. 'Sorry, again,' she said to Jake, knowing it was insufficient.

'S'okay.' He replaced the lid in the sink, leant down, opened a low, wide drawer, a pan drawer, and pulled out a new saucepan and lid. Beth almost gasped. Not only did he have more pans than she had plates, but they also shone, as if brand new. Recipe books filled the shelves above the worksurface, and more were stacked on top of the freezer.

'So, tonight,' Jake said, 'we've got my special homemade leak and stilton quiche, sausage rolls with my own famous cheesy pastry, spicy sausage rolls,...' He pointed at the oven door window. The light inside revealed two baking trays on a lower shelf. Beth was intrigued to know what was going to fill the upper shelf.

'We need some dips,' he muttered.

Beth nodded, impressed. 'What can I do to help?'

'Can you peel and chop up some carrots, for dipping?'

'Course.'

He handed her a bag of organic carrots, a peeler, a scarred

chopping board and indicated some space on the worksurface by the door. Turning to a knife rack, he tapped his finger first on one black handle, then another, then pulled the second knife free. The way the blade slid from the wooden block made Beth flinch. She put her hand on the worksurface, feeling as though she were on a boat in choppy waters.

As if unaware how lethal a blade could be, Jake casually turned the knife around, offering her the handle. She stared at the serrated blade; a delicate stinging at the top of her legs reminded her of the last time she'd held anything so sharp. When she held it out, her palm trembled. Jake placed the knife in her hand and then – she was astonished – turned back to his task of chopping a red onion. Beth tried to remember the last time someone had handed her such a weapon, had trusted her. She felt the weight of the knife, then wrapped her fingers around the cool, smooth handle, took a deep breath then turned to the bag of carrots.

'Are you all right?' Mikey leaned against the doorframe. 'I thought you were going to practise your knife throwing skills then.'

Beth forced a smile.

Before she could answer, Jake spoke. There was no pause in his dicing. 'Are you gonna help, Mikey? Or just watch and heckle?'

'Oh, I love hard work. I could watch it all day.'

'Well, thank you for your contribution.'

'Actually, I was going to take the car to get some booze. Well, I was, before I was accused of being a car thief.'

His grin, Beth was sure, was intended to show there were no hard feelings. But was there something else behind it? Or was she imagining it?

'It's your car,' she said with an answering smile and a shrug.

Mikey turned his attention to Jake. 'Is there anything else you need?'

'A bit of luck that tonight goes well.'

'Which aisle is that in?'

'The aisle marked "stop wasting time and get going".'

Before Jake could answer, Beth spoke. 'I've got a couple of bottles of wine. I'll bring them.' It felt important to her that they didn't think she was freeloading. Glancing at Jake, the way he moved with confidence around his kitchen, his ease with ingredients, she felt a flutter of panic. 'It's only cheap stuff,' she muttered. 'I don't know if it's any good.'

Jake's smile was reassuring. 'It's wine. It'll be fine.'

Mikey laughed. 'Thank you, Dr Seuss. If you think of anything else you need, text me.'

'Some juices for the cocktails. I think I'm low on vodka, so a bottle of that. And whatever beers or lagers you think are appropriate for tonight's guests. You know 'em better than I do.'

Mikey nodded and, with a knowing smile, said, 'Be back soon then,' and left. Beth watched him go. Sure enough, he left the door open, so that anyone could walk in. Beth had put a security chain on her door. Jake hadn't, despite being on ground floor. Men just didn't think like that. They didn't need to.

She began work on the carrots, while Jake began deseeding a green chilli.

Without looking up, Jake spoke, his tone neutral. 'Be careful of him.'

'Sorry?' Beth realised Jake had seen her watch Mikey leave and had misunderstood.

'He's got a reputation you know. At work. Bit of a womaniser.'

'Really?'

'Well, he thinks he is. The stories he tells. Probably just stories. But... you know.'

'Thanks for warning me.'

Jake nodded and returned to his chilli. He began chopping

with quick, practised strokes of his knife.

While he had his back to her, Beth took the opportunity to study him. His fine fair hair, long enough to brush the frayed collar of his T-shirt, and his clear, smooth skin – despite being pink from the sun – gave the impression of someone who didn't spend time grooming, but never went anywhere where he might get weather-beaten.

She marvelled at the unhurried way he criss-crossed the kitchen, occasionally checking the oven clock, and his effortless ease at preparing, mixing and keeping everything cooking to time. She thought he looked in complete control, and not just because this was his own space; she felt he'd look the same in any kitchen. She'd never cooked for a party, had never let enough people get close to her, but if she did, she imagined there would be significant signs of panic. In fact, she'd probably be overwhelmed by everything, and she'd be a danger to be around, especially with a knife in her hand.

The kitchens in the flats weren't spacious, but neither were they tiny. There was just enough space for two people to work and to move around, without brushing against each other. If they concentrated.

'How did you learn to cook?' Beth continued filling a bowl with carrot sticks.

'Taught myself.'

'That's impressive.'

'Not really. Before Mum and Dad split my family used to love going camping and being, well, outdoorsy. Trust me, that's not for me. So as soon as I could I told them, I'd rather be warm and dry. Once the shouting had stopped, they relented and I used to stay home and look after myself while they were off enjoying their battles with the elements. Then my parents split.'

'Sorry to hear that.'

'I was of an age where I could decide who to stay with. My older brother and sister had already left home. I had to live with one of my parents.'

'Must have been hard.'

'Choosing a favourite? Yeah.'

Beth paused, gripping the knife, cringing at the ramifications of picking a favourite.

Jake didn't seem to notice. 'When it came down to it,' he said, 'I really, really wanted to stay with my mum. But I knew, if I did, my dad would either starve to death or OD on Kendall Mint Cake. He could put up a tent half-way up a mountain in a force ten gale, but couldn't be bothered to turn on an oven. He just wasn't interested in food. Mum used to have to remind him to eat. That was something else that used to annoy her.'

The silence was filled by the sound of Beth's knife slicing through the carrot onto the chopping board. Eventually, even that finished.

'Here. Done,' she said.

'Excellent job.'

'I thought we'd have some salsa. Can you chop up some tomatoes and onions and stuff? I prefer it a bit chunky rather than use a food processor.'

'Just give them to me.' She spoke with a confidence she didn't feel, but felt he wanted to hear.

'Here.' He took a couple of red onions and tomatoes from a vegetable rack, then some coriander and jalapeño peppers he had on the side.

'So, you enjoy cooking then?' Beth asked.

'It's a way to be creative. You can try a recipe once and then experiment with it all you want before getting something interesting enough to inflict on others. What about you?

'Ah.' Beth shook her shoulders as if she had an itch in the

middle of her back. Not only did she feel uncomfortable being the centre of the conversation, but the arguments were still sharp and clear in her head – the clashes and explosions and shouting matches when her childish attempts at cooking hadn't met Mum's expectations. 'I'm not a big foody,' she said, aware it sounded weak.

'Okay.'

She continued chopping, still surprised he wasn't looking over her shoulder or criticising her technique or telling her how to do it better. Instead, he was slicing avocados in half and then, with deftness, using a spoon to scoop out the stones. Guacamole, it seemed, was also on the menu.

'So,' he asked, 'how long have you lived here?'

Please. Stop asking questions.

'Just over a year. I—'

'Where'd you move from? Locally?'

'I've chopped the tomatoes and onions. What's next?'

'That's great. I'll have some of those now, could you do the peppers and a clove of garlic? I've got some coriander. And there's some lemon and lime juice over there. Put all in that big bowl when you've finished.' He pulled a pestle and mortar off a shelf and began turning a mixture of chopped chillies, coriander, tomatoes and onion into a paste.

'I thought,' he said, without looking up, 'for those with a sweet tooth, I'd do a baked Austrian cheesecake, as well.'

'Made with real Austrians, no doubt.'

'There're not easy to source around here. The most important thing is not to take the cheesecake out of the oven when it's cooked, but to turn the oven off and leave the door ajar. Let it cool that way. It stops it sinking.'

'Clever.'

'I'd like to claim credit for it, but it's something I read.'

Beth laughed. 'You know,' she said, amazed at what she was feeling, 'I'm enjoying this.' She was also astonished she'd said it out loud.

With her work, it often felt like she'd make someone's submitted paper understandable, improve it, send it off and it that would be it. No feedback, no nothing. Here, she not only felt as though she were being useful, but there was a visible end product and – an unexpected, not to say unusual, emotion – she was enjoying the company. A long way from relaxed, but nowhere hear as tense as she expected.

'I have just the thing to make all this work we're doing more fun.' He took an opened bottle of red wine, merlot, from the windowsill, two glasses from a shelf and poured them each a drink.

'Cheers.'

'Thanks, cheers.'

They clinked glasses, took a couple of sips, held up their glasses in a toast to each and returned to work, chatting about nothing in particular, the atmosphere drifting towards mellow thanks to the wine and the thick scents of cooking. When the doorbell rang to announce Mikey's return, Jake buzzed him into the flats.

He arrived wearing a new T-shirt, black again but with a new logo – two crossed guns with improbably long barrels – and carrying an open cardboard box that clinked as he walked.

'Well, you two have been busy.'

Jake shrugged. 'Amazing what they can deliver these days.'

Beth looked into the box. 'Just how many people are you expecting?'

'Anything left over,' said Jake, 'will allow me to experiment with cocktail recipes. Trust me, nothing will be wasted.'

'Where should I put this?' Mikey shifted the weight of the box. He couldn't have done it any better if he was trying to show off his muscles.

'In the other room. I'll deal with it in a minute.'

'The receipt's on top.'

'Thanks.'

Mikey took the box into the living room, reappearing seconds later.

'Jake, mate, can I have a hand getting stuff out of the car?'

Jake looked around at the ingredients on the worktop, the several dishes he was simultaneously putting together 'Er…'

Beth stopped her chopping. 'Maybe I can help?'

Mikey gave her an apologetic smile. 'I don't think so, love. Some of it's quite heavy.'

Nodding, Beth turned her whole body towards him. 'A word of advice.' She offered him a demure smile. 'You know, it's probably best not to patronise a woman,' her tone hardened, 'when she's holding a *knife*.'

'Ouch.' Jake winced.

Inwardly, Beth did the same. The words had just come out without her thinking. In her unaccustomed enjoyment she'd lost concentration. She held her breath.

Mikey held his hands up in acceptance. 'You drive a hard bargain, Liz.'

In silence, Beth let out her breath, impressed – and shocked – at her own bravery.

'You'd better believe it,' she nodded, matching his grin.

Beth followed him out to the car park, still amazed at herself. And confused: it was as if these two men had accepted her as a normal human being.

Everything about Mikey's car seemed to Beth unnecessary. It was unnecessarily tall, unnecessarily wide, with bull bars on the front, and an unnecessarily vivid shade of red. It couldn't avoid bringing attention to itself. She couldn't believe, now, she had ever thought it was Jake's.

Just before Mikey opened the rear door of the car, Beth saw the model name: it was a Mitsubishi Warrior.

Could there be a more macho name? she thought, amused.

The door rose, revealing boxes of German lager, British bitter and an open cardboard box filled with various spirits and cartons of mixers and fruit juices.

He took two boxes of bitter, held them out for Beth. 'They're quite heavy,' he said with mock concern.

'I'd better not drop 'em on your foot then,' she replied, shocked at her daring.

She took them, hefted them until the weight was as comfortable as it was going to get, and then watched while Mikey placed the cardboard box on top of the two boxes of lager and. straightening his legs, lifted everything from the boot. With his elbow he closed the boot and, to Beth's surprise, he turned away from the flats, to the car park entrance.

'What's up?'

'Nothing,' he said, although it seemed to take him more effort to pull his eyes from the road than it did to hold the drink. 'Come on.'

They'd propped the rear door to the stairwell open with the wooden wedge that lived there, and Beth waited for Mikey to enter before kicking the wedge to one side, allowing the door to swing closed and click shut. Despite all her fine words, she was finding the beer heavy and was struggling, the boxes leaving marks on her arms. There was no way she was going to let either man know that, though. She followed Mikey into Jake's place and managed to place the beer in the hall before her strength gave out.

Mikey walked into the kitchen, stepping around Jake, who continued with his preparations.

'Jake, mate?' Mikey walked to the sink, leant over it and pulled the net curtain to one side. He looked out the kitchen window, to the left, to the right.

'What?'

'I think you've got a stalker.'

Ice formed in Beth's veins. Goosebumps rippled up her arms.

'Or maybe someone who's desperate to come to the party.'

'Come again?' Jake looked up.

'There's some strange bloke outside. Seems to be watching these flats. I saw him when I went to get the drink. And he was still walking around when I returned. I'm sure he tried to hide when he saw me.'

'Where?'

'Can't see him now.'

'What… what'd he look like?' Beth asked. 'Tell me he wasn't wearing a lumberjack shirt.'

Both men turned to face her. The same question written on their faces.

CHAPTER 11

It was only when Beth reached her front door that she realised she should have been more careful. She should have kept away from the window on the landing, the one behind the peace lily (which she really ought to water). If someone were watching the flats, looking for her, her progress up the stairs would have been obvious. Annoyed at letting her guard down, she twisted her key in the door lock so hard she was scared she might it break off. Her temper had broken keys before.

She hurried into her flat,

Was this what happens? First you make friends; then you make mistakes?

Typical, typical bloody man: when she'd asked Mikey what he'd noticed about the person loitering outside, all he could come up with was, 'just some guy'. He could not even be drawn on what this 'some guy' was wearing.

What was it about men that they never noticed such things? She wanted to thump the wall.

One. Two.

The three of them, she and Jake and Mikey, had peered out of the windows of Jake's flat, while trying not to move his net curtains. They'd seen nothing untoward. Being a ground-floor flat, they had a good view at the front, up and down the main road, all the way to the crossroads. At the rear though, there was only a limited view of the car park and its entrance. No one suspicious passed on the road beyond.

'You really can't remember what he looked like?' Standing in Jake's living room, Beth tried to make the question casual; ask it without grabbing Mikey by the neck. Her fists were on her hips, but that felt too confrontational. Yet when she moved them she didn't know what to do with her hands.

Mikey shook his head. 'Didn't know it was important. What's it worth? He was just some guy.' He shrugged. 'Hang on, you mentioned his shirt, did you see him as well?'

Beth couldn't prevent a sigh. 'How would I know? You haven't exactly given a good description.'

Mikey laughed. 'Fair comment.' Beth felt there was calculation behind the humour.

Jake glanced at his watch. 'Look, I'd better get on, I've a party to prepare, I'm running late and there's bound to be someone who arrives early. You will let me know if this guy turns up at my door and tries to get in.'

'Yes.' Beth and Mikey spoke together, but Beth thought only her tone carried conviction. Jake left for the kitchen, and Mikey turned to stare at her, his eyes narrowing. It made her think of someone sizing up a potential business partner. She noted that, unlike Jake, with his smooth cheeks, Mikey's looked pitted and rough, as if he didn't so much shave and use a sanding tool. While Jake's hair was fine, fair and wispy, Mikey's was dark, almost black, with each short strand so thick she wondered if whatever had cut it had been blunted.

Mikey was still staring at her, now wearing a half smile that suggested he was either close to understanding something or enjoying his ignorance.

Beth felt the heat of a blush rise from under her creased cotton blouse.

She cleared her throat. 'Jake's right,' she said. 'I'd better go and get ready as well.'

Without waiting for a response, she left the room, knowing she was being studied made her skin burn. She poked her head into the kitchen, attempting a smile. 'I'm going to pop upstairs to get ready. That okay?'

Jake had the oven open and was putting in a baking tin filled with his cheesecake mixture. He glanced at her. 'I'll try to manage. You've been a great help, Liz, thanks. See you in a bit.'

She rushed from his flat, bounded up the stairs and entered her flat as fast as possible, aware she'd been careless.

She slipped on the security chain, then went from room to room closing the curtains, the blind in the kitchen, and keeping as far back from the windows as possible. Unlike Jake's ground-floor flat, she had no net curtains to hide her. She would have to do something about that.

Only after she switched on the light in the kitchen did she let out the breath she was holding. The sigh surprised her in its duration. It was as if she were exhaling some of her strength as well, so much so that she slumped against the wall.

Her thoughts were as confused as her emotions. Now she had escaped from Jake's flat, she could consider what had happened and her participation in it. This wasn't how she had expected the day to turn out.

And it's not over yet, she thought. Her hands trembled and she licked dry lips.

Now free from the distractions of the party preparations, her doubts, like creatures surrounding wounded prey, began to gather.

She tried to shoo them away, when that failed she tried new distractions; she thought of the couple she'd seen as she'd walked home, kissing, finding happiness in each other, oblivious to the outside world. She knew she didn't deserve that, but sometimes –

more often than not, it seemed – it didn't matter what anyone deserved. Some people complained life was unfair. It wasn't. She knew that. Life didn't keep a scorecard. Things just happened.

Right now she had two choices. Get ready for tonight and return downstairs. Or hide away up here. Really though, it was too late for the latter. If she didn't re-appear, Jake would come looking. He knew where she lived. For ever after things would be awkward if they met, and so she would have to move again. And yet... yet... the thought of Jake coming upstairs, searching for her, wanting her presence, produced an unexpected but not unpleasant tickle inside her.

No. It was a party. She could enjoy herself.

And...

She strolled, affecting nonchalance, to her bedroom, trying to contemplate the day's events rather than acknowledge what she was doing.

She stood in the doorway, taking in the room, dropping her handbag. Wardrobes to her immediate right, bed with its disarrayed duvet against the far right-hand wall, and the window opposite her. If she hadn't closed the curtains, it would give a view of the car park. A wooden chair sat in the far left corner, still draped with clothes intended for the washing basket.

She tried to see the room through someone else's eyes. Someone who maybe accompanied her home tonight. Moving with haste, before she changed her mind, she took the old clothes from the chair, dumped them in a pile in the hall, studied the bed, pulled back the duvet, re-tucked the sheet, folded back the duvet and smoothed it down, then plumped up the pillows. Finally, from the end of the bed she picked up the two soft toys which had been with her forever. Pickle and Rascal had lost their fluffiness and their colours, but they still held a place in her heart; they had never deserted her. 'Sorry, boys,' she muttered, as she gave them a hug then placed them in the wardrobe. She looked around the room again.

Yes, that's better.

She was about the leave when she stopped.

One final thing.

She went to her bedside cabinet, pulled it away from the wall, traced the lead from the light down to the socket, unplugged it and then pushed the cabinet back. Her scars: darkness would be best to hide them. Her breaths were shallow now.

Better.

She took the clothes from the hall to the bathroom, put them in the plastic basket she used for dirty washing, and this she hid in the airing cupboard. She looked at herself in the only mirror in her flat. Staring back was such a familiar face that she had no conception of how others saw it; whether they could see or sense who she really was. Did anyone ever really know anyone else? She often wondered how others coped and whether, because of who she was and her unique childhood, she had missed something everyone else took for granted. Was that another sign of being neurodiverse?

Frowning, she stripped and inspected the patchwork of fine white dashes on her upper thighs; the newest scars the colour of Jake's sun-pinked forehead. She sucked through her teeth, wanting to touch the scabs, to get a fingernail under them. She'd had a good time downstairs, something she knew she didn't deserve. Jake's knife had felt good in her hand; it had had a razor-sharp blade.

Would he let her borrow it?

She let out a humourless laugh, straightened, took another look at her reflection, felt disgust, and began washing then drying herself with unnecessary violence. She put on a nice pair of three-quarter length shorts, with a subtle pattern of climbing roses around the outer seams, and found a pastel yellow blouse she thought complemented the shorts. She'd never worn either of these garments, always feeling she should, as Mum would say, 'save them for best'.

She was certain she had some lippy somewhere that would be suitable.

Next was her make-up. Looking in the mirror once again, she grimaced and started taking pots and pencils and brushes from the bathroom cabinet, lining them up on the shelf behind the sink. With more care than usual, she began what she thought of as 'putting on her face'. She didn't care whose face it was, as long as it wasn't her own.

She was halfway through, when she heard her phone chime and remembered the email from her mum that had arrived when she'd first seen Mikey.

Oh, shit. Yes.

She put down the brush with which she was applying her blusher, blew out her cheeks and went to find her handbag.

The most recent email was also from Mum, wondering why she hadn't replied to the first one.

The first email read:

It was odd, when we got back home today, we both thought someone had been in the house. Nothing appears to have been stolen, nothing is missing, nothing damaged. At first I thought we'd caught your paranoia. Yet the more I thought about it the more it felt some things were just slightly out of place. Your father agreed. Neither of us wanted to report it to the police. What can we tell them? Besides, we don't want the police involved with us again, for your sake if nothing else. If someone was looking for your address,

then it's a good job we don't have it. So perhaps you may have been right on that point. Alternatively, maybe it's nothing. Maybe we are just feeling paranoid after spending time with you.
Keep safe and keep in touch.
Mum

The strength leaked from Beth's legs, and she found herself sitting on her bed, re-reading the email, and again, and again. Each time trying to focus harder on the individual words, as if their meaning was becoming obscured.

Eventually, she tapped on 'Reply' and typed,

Don't involve the police.

She hit send.

Mum and Dad just couldn't go to the police. Mum was right, nothing illegal appeared to have happened. They couldn't accuse Callum, couldn't even mention him. And they couldn't tell the police who they were. That could lead the police to search for her. And then what? She knew from experience that it would only require one officer – whose need for extra money was greater than his fear of being caught and punished – to sell her address to the tabloids. She could see the headline, 'Island Killer Kid Caught near Coventry'. It would run above the famous picture of her – nine years old, confused, bewildered, wearing a police-provided grubby T-shirt that was too large, with her hair tangled and knotted. The deep shadows around her eyes, combined with her half-amused expression – simply because she'd always been told to smile at the camera – resulted in a malevolent, calculating, appearance. Even the adult Beth thought her younger self looked like an evil presence. She'd always assumed that picture had been leaked to the press either by a greedy cop or a police friend of Owen's – her victim's – father. Maybe one and the same guy.

She stared at her phone, as if an answer her problems was going to appear.

Anyone going to the police, she had no doubt, would start a trail that would lead Callum to these flats. Too many burly, angry men had loomed over her, snarling that, because of her age, she had escaped justice, and that, one day – they swore – she would pay. Oh, yes she would.

Eventually, she sat up straighter, pursed her lips and forced herself to stand. Whatever had happened to Mum and Dad's house, if anything, she was pretty sure she still couldn't be found, and certainly not so quickly.

So who was that loitering outside?

She went to the front door and confirmed the security chain was still in its slot. Mum used to keep a can of fly spray by the front door – as pepper spray was illegal – and use it whenever a tabloid journalist would peer through the letterbox demanding a quote. 'For pests', Mum used to say, shaking the can after she'd used it. Looking back, Beth was surprised the hacks hadn't sued. Different times.

Maybe now she should get a can?

She returned to the bathroom, and found her hands were trembling again. Concentrating, she attempted to add an extra layer of make-up.

CHAPTER 12

With its well-chosen music, dancing for those who wished, tasty food, engaging conversation and much laughter, Jake's party was a huge success... right up until Beth slapped Mikey.

Once she had applied her make-up, smoothed down her blouse, and decided that the face in the mirror was just about acceptable, Beth returned to Jake's flat. She took two bottles of wine with her and kept as far from the stairwell window as possible. Attending the party was the right thing to do, she reassured herself. If there was someone outside looking for her then, for once, being amongst others was the safest place.

Jake's front door was open, revealing Jake, standing in his hall, talking to a woman who cradled a bottle wine like a baby. Jake saw Beth, beckoned her in, and pointed to the other woman. 'This is Sue,' he said. 'The best Office Manager in the country.' He indicated Beth, 'And this is Liz, one of my neighbours. She's been a great help today.'

Beth took the compliment with a nod. 'I don't know about that,' she said, 'Jake seems to have done it all, he's had everything under control in a way I couldn't manage.' Jake had changed into a pale yellow short-sleeved shirt, which appeared to have been freshly ironed, and lightweight tan chinos. Beth thought the colours suited him.

'Speaking of which,' Jake glanced back to the kitchen, 'things to do. Excuse me. I'm sure Mikey will take those bottles from you.'

'Oh, thank God,' Sue whispered once Jake had returned to the kitchen and Mikey had taken their bottles to add to the drinks collection. 'I knew I was going to be early, one of my faults, but I thought I was going to be the only woman here.'

'That bad? These two are all right, aren't they? Jake and Mikey.'

'Oh, yes.' Sue nodded. 'Well, Jake is. Mikey can be a bit… you know.'

Beth didn't, but before she could enquire, Mikey returned. 'Drinks, girls?'

'Glass of red.' Sue spoke as if she were used to being listened to. And obeyed.

'Me too.' Following Sue's lead seemed a good idea. She gave the impression of being a manager you didn't want to get the wrong side of.

'Coming right up.'

Sue raised her eyes to the ceiling. 'Me, a girl. I ask you.'

It was difficult to be sure, but Beth decided Sue was probably in her late forties. If she was actually in her fifties then, Beth thought, she knew how to look after herself. She was blonde, although probably out of a bottle, and what some fashion magazines would politely call curvy. She wore a plain white top under a navy jacket and from the way she stood, the precise way she spoke, she had an aura of efficiency. Beth could believe the office was very well managed, and that not many were brave enough to argue once Sue had made a decision.

Beth led the way to the living room. The furniture had been pushed to the edges, the curtains closed, and the table lamps positioned to provide soft lighting without the room being too dim. One could read, but would probably choose not to. Someone's phone had been plugged into a sound system and was playing something bland that Beth didn't recognise. She guessed it wasn't the band on Mikey's T-shirt. Whoever it was, it was at a volume such that she and Sue could talk without shouting. Looking around, they chose a high-backed sofa that was long enough to lie on. Beth sat at one end, put her handbag on the floor and pushed it back, sliding it out of the way, almost to the wall behind the furniture.

Mikey walked over and handed them their wine.

'Here you go, girls.'

'Thanks,' said Beth.

Sue snorted but Mikey didn't seem to notice. He sauntered to the kitchen. Beth was sure there was a swagger in his step.

'Do you think he knows he's being patronising?' Sue asked.

'Do you think he cares?'

'Probably not.'

Beth held up the glass. Looked at it. 'That,' she said, 'is not so much a glass as a goblet.'

'Good job we didn't ask for large one.'

'He'd have given us the bottle.'

'More likely he'd have leapt on the innuendo.' Sue tasted her drink, nodded. 'So, you're one of Jake's new neighbours? And not the one with the baby; he's told us about her. He's only just moved in so you can't have known him long. And here you are.'

Beth took her time, kept her glass to her lips, shifted in her seat, then took another, larger, sip. She didn't want to be rude, but neither did she want to be the subject of questions.

'Just a few days,' she said then asked, before Sue could speak: 'How many in the office then? How many coming tonight?'

'I think Jake said about ten or so from work. Some with their partners. So, Liz, tell me—'

'And it's a computer games company?'

'That's right. Do you play?'

'Ah, well…'

'It's okay.'

'Maybe if I had more free time.'

'Take my advice,' Sue leaned closer. 'Don't get into a conversation about it with anyone here.'

'They take it seriously then?'

'Some do.' Sue shook her head, and her tone became one of incredulity. 'Like you wouldn't believe.' She raised her glass.

'Thanks for the warning.' Beth took another large sip, more of a gulp. Before Sue could bring the conversation back to 'Liz', Beth spoke again. 'How do you cope? At work?' In Beth's experience, most people are more than happy to talk to a good listener about their own work, their own lives, rather than ask questions.

'At work? I treat 'em like kids. I've got two kids of my own – well, they're not kids anymore, they're grown up now – but I can still remember what they were like as teenagers. How, let's be honest,' Sue said, leaning towards Beth, 'horrible they could be. Even my lovely girl. I'm sure we were just as bad at that age. But I didn't go through all that, raising kids, without learning some tricks. *That's* how I deal with 'em at work.'

Beth thought of her own mother and wanted to ask Sue whether she treated both her children the same, but before she could formulate the question, Sue cocked her head, studying Beth's face. 'But, you… do…' Beth felt her heart jolt then plummet, like an acrobat who misses the trapeze. She knew Sue's expression; she'd seen it before. It never ended well.

'…do… I recognise you from somewhere. You look vaguely familiar, but I can't place you. We haven't met before, I don't think. Are you from around here? Have you been in the news?'

Beth shook her head, but Sue wasn't to be stopped.

'Liz? Liz who? My ex would know. He was journalist on the local paper, always kept cuttings ready for his big scoop. It never came of course. He spent more time waiting for that than he spent on our marriage. Men, huh? But you do look familiar. Have you—'

'I've been told, many times,' Beth couldn't stop the words tumbling out, 'that I look like that girl, you know, who used to be in that old advert, for... you know. Can't see it myself,' she shrugged, 'but there you go.' It was the best story she and the appointed psychiatrist had come up with: it encouraged people to fill in the gaps with their own images, or to blame their own hazy memories for not bringing anything to mind. It always surprised her how many people just agreed and accepted that explanation. If they didn't, it allowed Beth to add suitable details, following the questioner's lead. It was why, if someone did know her nine-year-old face from TV or the papers, they could be convinced it was from somewhere else in the misty past. Not from her police photograph that should never have been released in the first place.

'Hmm, yes. Advert for what? It might be on YouTube.'

Before Beth could answer, the doorbell rang, and out of the corner of her eyes she saw Jake rush from the kitchen to the hall to buzz the newcomers in from outside.

'Oh,' Beth said, 'new guests.'

Beth went to take another drink of wine to save her from having to deal with Sue's inquisitive stare, and wasn't surprised to see she'd already emptied the glass.

She knew she ought to take it easy, but then she also knew she ought to leave, but leaving would draw attention to herself, making Sue even more curious.

She held up her empty glass. 'Another?'

Sue pulled a face and shook her head. 'Driving.'

'Okay.'

Over the next hour, more people arrived, and Beth was

introduced to them. She attempted to remember their names and faces while hoping they forgot hers. Beth reckoned it was seventy: thirty, men to women, and that Sue may have had ten years on the next oldest. Not that she acted like it. It was clear she enjoyed dancing.

Watching others enjoy themselves was exhausting. Some folks were clearly energised by meeting others, by such gatherings. Beth felt drained, despite – much to her own surprise – enjoying the party. Eventually, after finding herself weary of happy people, Beth found herself in the kitchen helping Jake. He was washing glasses and she was drying them.

'Told you,' he said, with an attempt at a grin. 'You'll always find me in the kitchen at parties.'

Feeling the effects of the wine, Beth placed, with exaggerated care, a dried highball glass on the counter; breaking a glass at someone else's party was never a good idea, especially if trying to keep a low profile. She wasn't sure how many glasses of wine and cocktails she'd had by now, but was feeling a little too mellow. Picking up a wet wine glass from the draining board, she let the suds slip from it. Drunkenness she was used to, but this was different. In the soft enveloping atmosphere, everything felt fuzzy and friendly, her acceptance by these strangers, and her mutual response, felt almost sensuous. She had forgotten how it good relaxed felt. A diminishing part of her was aware she was in that sweet spot of inebriation, where more drinks would be a mistake, but also that there any willpower to refuse another cocktail was fading fast.

'Safest place, the kitchen,' she agreed, standing so near to Jake as she dried the glass that she could feel his warmth. 'Away from everyone.'

Jake's grin was cute and lopsided, but vanished as the glass in his hand slipped from his grip. It hit the water with a splash, drips landing on the front his shirt. 'Lucky,' he said letting out a long breath. He picked up the glass, inspected it, and put it on the drainer. He looked out of the window. The net curtain had been pulled aside and someone had opened the window in a vain attempt at ventilation. Beth was sure the air was just as heavy and humid outside; these summer evenings held on to the day's warmth like a child clutching its comfort blanket. Beyond the reflection of the two of them, a cone of light from a streetlamp illuminated its own strip of pavement. Beth wanted the curtains closed, but didn't know how to ask without it seeming an odd request.

'Well?' Jake's voice had become soft. Beth had to lean closer to hear him over the music thumping from the living room. He didn't turn to her. 'How do you think it's going?'

'Good, I think.' Beth added the dried glass to the others.

'Really?' He turned to face her.

'Yeah. Of course.'

'This is important to me. I'm coming to end of my probation with the company, and I want to do well there.'

'Don't worry. Everyone's enjoying themselves.'

'It's not that my job depends on it, or anything, but I want to make friends. Just a shame Shreeya couldn't come.'

'It's going fine. You'll be fine.' Before she could stop herself, she patted his arm, reassuring. His thin forearm was wet and spotted with peaks of washing-up foam.

'Oh,' came a voice from the doorway and Beth pulled her hand back as if it were burnt. 'Sorry to interrupt, mate,' said Mikey. The harsh light of the kitchen revealed old acne pockmarks on his cheeks. The pint glass held in his hand was almost empty. If he had been going for an amused tone, Beth thought, he had overshot and landed in gloating. 'You doing the washing up? And all that cooking? You know, mate, you'll make a wonderful mother.' He said it as if it were an insult.

Beth felt rather than saw Jake stiffen at the comment.

Mikey looked at Beth, raising his eyebrows as if expecting a giggle or agreement. Beth gave him neither. She liked Jake, liked him too much to hurt him. Besides, she had had too much wine to judge whether this was intended as an insult. It also brought to her cotton-wool-filled mind her own mother.

Jake picked up a towel and wiped his hands. 'What do you want, Mikey?'

Mikey's head twitched toward Beth. 'Liz, here. If I can borrow her for a bit.'

Furrows appear in Jake's forehead, as if he were trying to follow Mikey's answer but found the sentence had consisted of random words.

'Sorry.' He shook his head and glanced at Beth, confused. He looked as if he needed help deciphering Mikey's meaning. 'What are you asking me for? She's right here.'

Beth could have hugged him.

Mikey squeezed his eyes shut. He opened them and sighed. 'All right. Yeah.' He looked at Beth, then finished his drink in a single gulp. 'Sue could do with some support.'

'What? How?' Now she noticed the music – a guitar-based indie band who were big last year, but which she couldn't name – had decreased in volume, unlike the voices, which were louder, although not yet shouting.

'Oh, don't tell me,' Jake looked as if he'd lasted to the end of a particularly long shaggy dog story, only to find the punchline wasn't worth it, 'they're winding each other up again.'

Mikey raised his eyebrows. 'You know what they're like. They're as bad as—'

'Be careful how you finish that sentence.' Sue appeared behind Mikey, empty glass in her hand. 'Some people seem to think there was a golden age of computer gaming. No, scratch that, that somehow the wondrous golden age was ended by, get this, women.'

'It's Lewis, isn't it?' Jake spoke as if it wasn't a question.

'He's convinced that,' Sue made angry quotes in the air, 'the "good old days",' those days of tasteless, misogynist, macho violence were forced to come to an end because of some feminist agenda. I told him, we'd have made a better job of it if that had been true. It's hardly the case that there are no games out there now pandering to adolescent boy's fantasies, about big men having big guns and shooting everything. With women whose clothes are two sizes too small and —'

'Come on, Sue,' Jake made a calming gesture with his hands. 'You know what he's like. He's just being provocative.'

'He claims women haven't got the reactions, or the temperament to cope with the stress, pressure and tension of the games. I ask you, as if we don't go around every day with stress. We know what men – men like *him* – are like. You think we need to be reminded that we could be victims, at any time? And you,' Sue pointed at Mikey. 'You. You were no help at all. What you said?'

'It was just a joke.'

'You set him off.'

'Yeah,' Mikey nodded and bowed, as if accepting applause. 'I did, didn't I. No need to thank me.' He threw a proud glance at Beth.

Sue looked from Jake to Beth. The bright kitchen light caught her eyes, causing them to sparkle. She was enjoying herself.

'Tell them what you said.'

'Ah, now come on, Sue.'

Beth was beginning to understand the dynamics of the office. Sue was mother. Wonder if she has any favourites?

Beth shoved the thought away. 'No, Mikey.' Beth tried for commanding to match Sue's tone. 'Tell us what you said.'

Mikey shrugged, and in that moment Beth thought she could see how he'd looked as a teenager. He stared at Sue with defiance; it was the expression he'd used when Beth had confronted him by his car. 'It was a joke. All right?' He shrugged and, as if it were nothing, looked down. 'All it was, Lewis was talking about why there aren't many women in the business, and I just said that,' his voice hardened a fraction, 'a woman's place in the kitchen facing the sink or in the bedroom facing the ceiling.' He looked up, proud of himself and daring contradiction.

At first Beth couldn't tell from Mikey's expression whether he meant it as a joke or not, then she decided it didn't matter. She couldn't stop herself. 'Facing the ceiling?' she laughed. 'Oh, ye of little imagination.' Sue's snigger and the look of surprise on Mikey's face, encouraged her. Her own bravery had been a shock, a surprise, and she was going to use it. 'Besides, we all know,' her own voice hardened in imitation of Mikey's, 'that a woman's place,' she paused for effect, 'is *in control.*'

'Yes!' Sue punched the air and Jake nodded in approval. Mikey blinked.

A mixture of pride and embarrassment warmed Beth as she watched grins appear and heard the sound of growing laughter. She felt she was glowing.

Did I do that? Really?

'I want a T-shirt with that on,' Sue said. 'Good neighbours you've got here, Jake. And a good party.'

'Well, credit where credit's due. Liz has been a great help, and with the preparations as well.'

Beth found herself both the centre of attention and staring at the fridge. It appeared to be the safest place to look while her cheeks burnt. She felt if she got any closer to the fridge she'd melt its contents.

'Hey,' said Mikey, tone light, trying to change the subject. Out of the corner of her eye Beth saw him dig in his pocket. 'How about a team picture?'

She shook her head, unable to speak. Her blush disappeared in an instant.

'Yeah. Good idea,' said Jake. 'The team that made it happen. Come on, Liz.'

Beth shook her head again, and turned to watch Mikey pass his phone to Sue. Suddenly, the two men were shuffling either side of her — Jake to her left, Mikey on the right — attempting to find a position that faced Sue but didn't invade anyone's space, any more than could be avoided in the kitchen.

'Okay, smile.' Sue said, holding up the camera.

Beth found her voice. 'No.'

'Oh, come on,' said Mikey, already grinning at the camera. 'Just a picture.'

'No.' Beth felt fear and fire explode within her. The music had been turned up again in the living room. It was deafening her. Making it difficult to think straight. The kitchen was suddenly too small and still contracting. Too bright.

'It's just a picture.' Mikey sounded insistent.

Beth swallowed, trying to force down her anger. To control herself.

One. Two.

'What are you going to do with it?' she asked with care.

Three. Four.

Mikey turned from posing for Sue to look at Beth, curious. 'I don't know. Put it on Instagram, Facebook. I—'

'No!' Beth shouted. The light in the shrinking kitchen was dazzling. The mixed aromas in the room became almost physical. If her face was on the web, on social media, she could be seen, she'd have no control over it, it could end up anywhere on the internet, someone might have set up an image search, might recognise her, whatever name she was tagged with. All her hard work...

'No!' she shouted again, loud enough for them to hear in the next room. Furious. Scared.

Sue lowered the camera.

Mikey's eyes narrowed, uncertainty writ large on his face. 'But...'

In the restricted space, something inside Beth detonated. She twisted, her anger erupting, beyond her control. She slapped Mikey. Open palmed. 'Ow!' he cried. 'You little—'

'Don't you get it?' she screamed, 'No means no!'

Rage surged across Mikey's features. Beth thought he would retaliate. Welcomed it.

Come on, give me what I deserve.

He didn't though. Maddeningly, he controlled his desire to strike back.

Beth went to push her way out of the kitchen, now desperate to escape. To somewhere with fresh air.

Sue, of course, was still blocking the doorway, phone in her hand, frozen with shock. 'L...Liz,...' Sue stammered, 'Who are you? Where do I know...' but got no further as Beth threw her shoulder forward ready to shove aside any obstruction.

'Out of my—'

Beth saw Sue's white face, wide eyes and mouth forming a large O. But it was the fear she saw in Sue's eyes that drained her own fury, as if a large plughole had been opened. Sue's clear horror reflected Beth's own, of what might have happened if she had been holding a weapon, one of Jake's kitchen knives, for example. Beth felt herself sag, her strength flooding from her, felt Jake catch her, hold her up. It was always the same, whenever she lost her temper – a massive chain reaction with its inevitable explosion, immediately followed by deflation and empty remorse. And terror that what happened when she was nine, and for which she was still paying, could happen again.

'Sorry,' she shut her eyes, unable to meet the concerned expressions of those around her. 'Mikey, I'm sorry, I…'

The music had been turned down in the living room. Her yell had been heard.

She tried to find some strength in her legs. She needed to stand up. Jake was still taking her weight. She couldn't have that. Just couldn't. Not Jake. She stumbled, opened her eyes and found a wall to lean on.

Through the blur of incipient tears she saw Mikey touching his face, confusion and anger also reddening his face. Crazily she wanted to laugh; his cheek was already the colour of Jake's sunburn.

'Really,' she managed to say, shaking her head both in sorrow and in apology and as a way of trying to find the strength to string words together, 'I'm sorry. I don't know… It's… Oh, God… let me go.'

Sue stepped aside and Beth staggered, jelly-legged, along the hallway to the front door. It felt never-ending. Her flesh burnt where everyone's gaze touched her. At first she thought she wanted to die, but then realised that would be too quick. She didn't warrant anything so easy. Her mother was right. All the dreams Beth had had for this evening, all the fantasies that had followed from seeing the happy and content couple on the bench were useless. The notion that she might feel a protective arm around her tonight, be embraced, was laughable. Like the stupid girl she was, she'd laid her plans, knew who she wanted, knew it had to be her place or not at all. She needed to control events. Not just to stop any secret phone/laptop recording of what they got up to, no, she needed to be in darkness so the man she took to her bed wouldn't see her scars and realise just how worthless she was. She had even unplugged her bedside light.

Head bowed, shamed, she reached the front door, opened it, only to have it slammed shut. The crash of it closing echoed down the hall. Mikey stood behind her, his arm outstretched, his palm flat against the door, holding it shut.

'Why don't you want your picture on social media?' His face was frozen, expressionless. 'Who are you?'

Beth turned to look at him. Behind him, in the kitchen doorway she could see Jake, his face now pale. He thought his party was falling apart, she realised. She had done this.

Her stomach lurched and she felt sick. She'd had thoughts of ending the evening, not with tender loving care – she knew she'd never merit that – but shielded by strong, tough, muscled arms. Just for one night. Just – now she knew Callum was searching for her – to help her get through a single night.

'I'm no one,' she said, and meant it.

It was never going to be Jake. She couldn't bring herself to hurt him. He was too nice. Besides, he'd be gentle and considerate. Not at all what she deserved. And it was only to be for one night, so with Jake it would be awkward after that. Being neighbours and all. Also, most important, she liked him too much to lead him on for a one-night stand and then dump him. Mikey though…

Mikey stared at her, face hard. He would, she was certain, never apologise for ignoring her request about the picture. It was something he'd try to turn to his advantage. He spoke with repressed violence, pushing his face close to hers. 'I don't believe you.'

She took her chance.

Reaching up, she put both hands behind his head, feeling the prickles of his short hair and pulled his face to hers. She kissed him, hard, passionate, vicious. Their teeth clashed. She continued. To her surprise he responded. His arms going around her, pulling her tighter to his body.

When she eventually let their bodies pull apart, breathless, she looked him in the eyes. She could see their undisguised excitement, anger and bewilderment. 'Come back to mine,' even to herself she sounded throaty, as she caught her breath. 'Give me what I deserve.'

She opened the door and this time he didn't stop her. What did halt her though was the realisation of why it is so much more difficult for women to make a dramatic exit than men.

'Oh, I…'

She looked down the hall to see Jake walking towards them, holding out her handbag. His lips were so tightly compressed they had disappeared.

Beth took the bag, unable to bring herself to speak, upset by his expression.

Didn't he get it? It was because she liked him and didn't want to hurt him that it was Mikey she was now pushing out of the door.

CHAPTER 13

Early next morning, and keeping as quiet as possible, Beth slipped out from under the duvet. She hadn't slept well despite the night's exertions. Her worries had waved at her from the edges of her shallow dreams, called her and leapt out. They had kept her aware that – amongst many other things – she'd have to get up before Mikey to keep her hyphened thighs secret in daylight. Once she was standing, she looked back at him and wondered why she was being careful. He was dead to the world. He wasn't snoring as such, rather his breathing was so deep it sounded as if he had some mechanical means of inhaling and exhaling. On her way around the bed, she peeked through the gap between the curtains. Although the sun had risen and was readying itself for yet another hot day, the shadows were still elongated misshapes.

She collected some clean clothes from the wardrobe, all the time listening for any changes in Mikey's heavy breathing, then crossed the hall to the bathroom, where she closed the door and let out the breath she had been holding. It made a noise equal to that emanating from the man in her bed.

Taking care not to slip, she stepped into the bath, closed the shower screen, and turned on the shower. She felt she needed something warmer than normal, scalding even. She also wanted high power sprays pounding her skin, but the water pressure, she knew, just wasn't strong enough to sting.

I must investigate a power shower, she thought stepping under the shower head, sucking in her breath as the steaming water flowed over her skin. Turning a full three-sixty she found she could see, past the clear plastic shower screen, all the way to the sink and the cabinet above. Its mirrored door was ajar.

'Shit.'

She tried to look away, but found it impossible. Her eyes were always pulled back to her reflection.

'No, please.' It came out as a wail.

She squeezed her eyes shut her once more, so tight she could feel the wrinkles. It didn't matter, she knew she'd have to look eventually. And there she'd be, in all her shame.

Taking a deep breath, she found some willpower and forced herself to step out of the bath. Water dripped on the floor as she picked up a hand towel, draped it over the mirror, and weighed it down with eye-shadow palettes and face moisturiser pots.

With greater care now everything was wet, she stepped back under the shower. Even with the towel over the cabinet, she stood with her back to the mirror while she checked herself. No bruises, but a number of tender spots that complained when she pressed them – which she was unable to stop doing. She winced, and winced again, until she let out a muffled groan and was surprised to find she was crying.

She was no good, she was useless – everything her mother insinuated about her was right. She was no benefit to humanity. After all the pain she'd caused others, she should suffer, she deserved to. She found a tender spot on her neck, pressed it, and let out a moan. And then again, harder. The spot would become a bruise soon.

She was pathetic.

Great wracking sobs shook her until she could no longer stand, and she sank down into the bath, water landing on her body like unending tears.

She curled up, and cried and cried and…

No.

She clenched her jaw, sniffed, wiped the snot from her nose, and – fighting against the falling the water – forced herself to her feet.

Strong. She was going to be strong. She'd survived this long. She wouldn't go to pieces now.

It didn't matter that she'd made herself this promise many times in the past. Each promise was new, not dependent on vows that had gone before. Yes, what she'd done as a child was the ultimate crime, but she wasn't a bad person. She just wasn't. She always tried to be considerate and helpful. To atone.

Picking up her flannel, she washed herself, all the time fighting the compulsion to rub her skin raw. She fought the same urge when she used her bath towel. After dressing she removed the hand towel from the cabinet and inspected her face in the mirror.

A bit puffy, but that'll fade. All in all, acceptable. Considering.

After applying enough make-up to make her feel presentable, she went to the living room and switched on her laptop. While it booted, she went to find some lemonade. She was craving something refreshing and fizzy. There was nothing in the fridge. Even the tonic bottles were empty and waiting to be taken to the recycling bin. She had just enough milk for a single cup of tea. She smiled at the thought of a trip to the local shop and shook her head. She had a strange man in her flat. Yes, she'd let him sleep in her home, encouraged him even, but she wasn't about to leave him alone here.

That reminded her, yesterday she'd dropped her rape alarm into her handbag. She needed to retrieve it and put it in its proper place, the side pocket where she could find it in an instant.

Using the last of the milk, she made herself a mug of tea and carried it into the living room. She had no bread for toast either. Her routine was to replenish milk and bread from the local shop on a Saturday, but the trip to Guildford to see her family meant she hadn't had time. It wasn't that she didn't trust Mikey to behave while she went to the shop, but… actually no, that was it – she did have trust issues. She placed the mug on her notebook beside the laptop. Digging into her handbag, she found her rape alarm and slipped it in its proper place in the bag's side pocket.

Right, let's do some work until Mikey gets up.

Beth immersed herself in editing. The first paper was for an Asian cultural studies journal and written by a Malaysian speaker, the next by someone from India. While sometimes frustrated by the lack of feedback on her work, she took pride and pleasure in that fact that she was, although invisible, helping others. Without her, such academic papers might not be published or, if they were, might not be understood or appreciated in the way they should be. She was confident many authors looked at their published work and took pride in their particularly good phrases – the ones she had improved or even written.

Once she had finished the Malaysian author's paper she checked the time. Mid-morning and still no movement from Mikey.

What did he think this was, a hotel?

She started the next paper but, now irritation had taken root, she found it difficult to concentrate. She was becoming more aware of her situation, finding it difficult to ignore the time and that she felt imprisoned in her own flat, unable to leave, with the curtains closed and the front door locked.

She made herself a black coffee, this time making as much noise as possible. Still nothing.

As she was nearing the end of editing the second paper, checking its references matched the *Australian Journal of Forensic*

Sciences house style, she heard a noise. A padding to the bathroom, followed a flushing toilet and then running water. She finished the references and took the cursor back to the beginning, ready for the final spell check.

Mikey appeared in the doorway, dressed only in his underpants. Navy blue trunks.

She didn't know whether to shout at him for keeping her waiting or laugh at how ridiculous he looked. Neither option would feed his ego; in her experience that was one of things men craved. Besides, the way he stood there, chest puffed out, legs slightly apart, reminded her of a boy in his swimming cossie on a beach.

The thought didn't help her mood.

'Hey,' he said, an unembarrassed smile plastered to his face. 'Fancy coming back to bed?'

Careful.

She looked from him to her laptop and used the time it took to save her document to choose her words. She wished she'd left out her rape alarm and it was within reach. What was it Sue had said last night? 'You think we need to be reminded that we could be victims?"

All men can be violent if pushed. It was why there were so many wars. So the trick was knowing when to stop pushing. Mikey, she knew, could be rough. It was what she had needed last night. But not today. Her rejection had to be worded with care.

She took a deep breath. 'I don't think so. Last night was great, thanks. But unfortunately I've got things to do today.' The implication, 'otherwise...', was left hanging.

His expression managed to hit what Beth thought of as the three Cs of male rejection: crestfallen, confused and cross.

'Oh,' he said. Then, although his mouth moved, no words came out. His hands clenched into tight fists, just for a second, before he crossed his arms over his chest and looked down, as if suddenly aware of what he was wearing.

'I'll... I'll get dressed then.'

'I've no milk so if you want tea or coffee, it'll have to be black.'

He looked at her. 'Oh, for God's sake,' he said and stalked off back to the bedroom.

She smiled at the thought of shouting 'Manners' after him, but decided this wasn't the time to push her luck.

When he returned, he appeared to have calmed down, although his lips were compressed so tight she didn't think he would have been able to drink anything anyway.

Without a change of clothes, he was wearing the same black T-shirt as yesterday, with its adolescent, imitation gothic logo. Beth still didn't know what rock band or game it advertised. She didn't care.

'Not gonna open the curtains?'

Beth thought of the man in the lumberjack shirt she'd seen yesterday. Seen twice. Might be coincidence. Might not. 'Maybe later,' she said.

Mikey nodded at the laptop. 'What ya playing?'

'I'm not. I'm working.'

'On a Sunday?'

'I was waiting for you.'

'Never liked working from home. Difficult to get started.'

You'd never get out of bed.

'Well, I find it's a choice. Start working, or starve.'

'I'd still spend all my time gaming.'

Beth shrugged. There didn't seem to be much she could say to that other than, 'your choice'. She waited, sure Mikey was about to ask what she did for a living.

He took a step towards her, then another, as if trying to see her screen. 'No gaming for you, then?'

143

She looked up at him. Maybe Jake told you? Or maybe you just don't care?

She shook her head. 'Never found something that really got me hooked. Mostly, I haven't got time. I'd rather earn money at home. While I can.'

But what if the work dries up? She felt a flare of anger.

Mikey nodded, as if understanding everything. He was so close now, Beth could extend a finger and touch him – something she wasn't about to do. He stood, looking down on her. 'Yeah, right,' he said.

'What's that supposed to mean?'

'Well, what Lewis was saying last night. Women don't really get games, do they? I mean proper games.'

'Proper games?'

'They're quite therapeutic, you know. Old people do gardening. People our age, they like playing games. MMOFPS or—'

'Sorry?'

For a second it was clear he didn't understand her question. 'Oh,' he said, with a sudden nod, 'Massively multi-player online first-person shooter. Although if you don't want to play online we created a successful first-person shooter. I shouldn't, of course, but I can get you a free copy if you want.'

'Thanks, but no.'

'Free. I know I shouldn't, but for you...'

'Again. Thanks, but no.'

'There's research been done. Gaming, it improves your reactions and mental flexibility, and—'

'I don't think so.'

He laughed. To Beth it sounded patronising. 'It's not real violence, you know.'

Real violence? If only you knew.

Beth's reply was lost as Mikey spoke over her. 'It's stress relief. It's good for you.'

Why was it, Beth wondered, that when some people had a hobby – whether it was playing the piano or running marathons – they always thought it was the cure for other's ills.

Mikey continued. 'It'll take your mind off your troubles.'

'My troubles?'

'Your troubles,' he said, and rubbed a hand over his cheek, the one Beth had slapped. He hadn't shaved this morning, so his palm made a sound that reminded Beth of a wave on pebbles. An unpleasant shiver ran through her. Mikey didn't seem to notice.

'My troubles…' Beth began, then stopped when it became clear Mikey wasn't listening. He was staring at the text on her laptop screen, at the title and authors of the article she was editing, as if confused as to why someone from Mumbai would be investigating 'the use of infra-red techniques to discover signs of human remains in partially decomposed fabrics'. Then his face brightened. It was, Beth thought, with a hint of jealousy, as if clouds had parted, letting the sun cleanse all shadows from his face and dark thoughts from his mind. She wished she could work miracles like that.

'I know,' he said, grinning, 'let's go somewhere. For breakfast, lunch, whatever. Let's go for a drive.'

'No, I—'

'It'll be good. You don't want to work. We could go to Stratford, or Bourton-on-the-Water, or… wherever you want.'

'Thanks.' Beth located her best you-know-what-it's-like smile and spoke with forced gentleness. 'But I've got work I'd better do. Sorry. You know.' She shrugged, looking regretful. It was, she thought, unfair. They'd spent the night together, in her bed, at her insistence, and yet *she* was the one having to treat *him* gently. There was no way a woman could get up the morning after, try to take over a man's life, and not expect repercussions. And yet here she was, having to tread with care, trying not to hurt *his* feelings. She doubted the reverse had even occurred to him.

'It's a Sunday,' he said. 'No one works on Sunday. Come on, enjoy yourself. That…' he indicated the laptop, '…will wait. And who knows, when we get back,' he raised his eyebrows, smiled and lowered his voice, attempting to be suggestive, 'we may be tired and need to go to bed.'

'It's tempting,' she lied, 'but—'

'It's okay,' he laughed as if he understood her reticence, 'I'm a good driver. You'll be perfectly safe. Well,…' he raised his eyebrows once again, '…until we get back and resume our bedroom activities.'

Beth felt a dark stain of anger begin to swirl in her blood. She wanted to stand, to tell him to go away. They'd had their fun. It was time for him to leave.

She swallowed, trying to keep calm. This was yet another of those times men needed to be handled with care. She knew, *every* woman knew, that there were two things no man would ever admit to being bad at: sex and driving. And if you were alone with a man and valued your safety, you just didn't challenge their prowess at either.

And frankly Mikey, you weren't all that good in bed.

Taking a deep breath, still presenting what she hoped was her most contrite smile, she shook her head. 'Forgive me, Mikey, but—'

The scream seemed to fall from the ceiling. They both looked up as if expecting to see the howl's owner.

Beth spoke first. 'That'll be Dashee. Kid upstairs.'

'What the hell? Christ. Come on, you can't work here, with this.'

There was a moment of silence while Dashee gathered

himself, then he let out another pained cry.

'Who'd be a kid, huh? Trying to make sense of the world.' Beth tried to lighten the mood.

Dashee let rip with another scream.

'Please, Liz,' Mikey said, 'let's get out of here.' His eyes were shut in a wince, as if someone had scraped nails down a blackboard, and then, in a brief lull from Dashee, he opened them and Beth could see pleading. He reached out and touched Beth's arm. His fingers encircled her wrist and, from his look of distress at the crying toddler, she half expected him to drag her to her feet. She braced herself, ready to resist.

Another cry and Mikey's fingers tightened. It occurred to Beth he was grabbing on for his own benefit rather than to dominate her. She wasn't sure how she felt about that.

'All right,' she said, 'Give me a moment.' She twisted her wrist and, with reluctance, he let go. Beth knew she couldn't work well like this, but also knew she shouldn't leave the flat, especially if lumberjack-man was still outside. There again, leaving with Mikey would be preferable to leaving on her own. And she couldn't stay inside with the curtains closed for the rest of her life. At the very least she needed some milk and bread. Besides, maybe she was being paranoid about lumberjack-man. Maybe he lived nearby and had just been passing? Yeah, right.

She saved her work and closed the laptop, and picked up her handbag. Mikey was already at the front door, wincing at each of Dashee's pitiful wails and looking as if he was enduring a migraine. Beth glanced into her bedroom as she passed. It looked a mess, the duvet scrumpled, with half of it hanging on the floor. Mikey had made no effort to tidy or make it look enticing, and yet he wanted them to return there later. Beth toyed with the idea of straightening things, but realised she couldn't face it and what it represented. It was a reminder of how she had acted last night and, from somewhere in her mind, she heard her mother's tones, dripping with disappointment, "I hoped my daughter was better than this."

Mikey was first out the door and onto the landing, his muscles relaxing as he realised Dashee was no longer immediately above and so the baby's cries were slightly more muffled. Beth locked the door behind her.

'All right, then,' she said. 'Where are you going to take me?'

'How can you work at home, with… that.' Mikey looked up as if expecting the ceiling to cave in.

Beth started down the stairs. 'What choice do I have? He'll grow out of it.'

On the ground floor, as if by agreement, they both sped up as they passed Jake's door and exited into the car park. The sun, high in the cloudless blue sky, produced shadows with precise sharp edges.

'Right,' said Mikey. 'Let's… oh…'

'Hello, you two,' Jake said, pulling the peak of his baseball cap down to shield his eyes. 'Good night last night?' He didn't slow as he returned from the fenced off corner where the recycling and refuse wheelie bins lived, and where Beth could see a saucepan with a dented lid sitting on the ground. He walked past Beth and Mikey, looking about as happy to see them as he would seeing the spilled contents of one of the wheelie bins. Beth squinted; his white T-shirt seemed too bright in the harsh sunlight. It wasn't until Jake had one hand on the door to the flats that he turned to face them. No, Beth realised, that wasn't quite true. Jake's attention was only on Mikey; he couldn't bring himself to look at her at all.

'Oh, yeah,' Mikey said. His elongated smile contained triumph rather than amusement. 'We had a great time. Great. Didn't we Liz? Tell him how good.'

Shit. What have I got myself into?

She not only couldn't answer, but she found herself looking at the worn concrete underfoot.

When it was apparent she wasn't about to say anything, let alone agree with Mikey, he reached for her, grabbing her wrist with an unexpected roughness. 'Tell him,' he said. Beth thought he had intended to hold her hand, but because she had clenched it into a fist, he had grabbed whatever he could. His fingers felt rough around the soft skin of her wrist.

Beth looked up, at Jake, who still wouldn't meet her eye. 'Your party was good, Jake.' She muttered. 'Really good. I had a great time. Thanks.' She recalled the two of them preparing snacks in the kitchen. She'd had a good time then. Now though, the memory was overshadowed by what happened after.

She looked down. Mikey's grip tightened. It was going to leave a mark.

'But…' she tried to shake off Mikey's grip, '…I know I need to apologise for how it ended.' She took a step towards Jake, putting herself between the two men, but her arm was twisted as Mikey tried to pull her back. 'I'm sorry. Really sorry. I—'

'Come on!' Mikey yanked her wrist, and it felt as though his rough skin had left a graze. As if the ground had shifted, she felt her balance go and she staggered. His grip slipped up her arm and she was reminded of Chinese burns given at school. Anger flared, mixed with fear.

'No,' she said, flat and commanding.

'Leave her alone,' Jake said. 'Come on, be—'

Once again, she shook off Mikey's grip, difficult but she managed, yet it was Jake she spun to face. 'I can fight my own battles.'

'Liz,' commanded Mikey, his voice hard enough to leave bruises. 'We're going.'

She turned to confront him and stepped away as she did so. It put her closer to Jake. When she saw the expression on Mikey's face she took yet another pace away. Anger and confusion fought for supremacy on his features: he was being disobeyed and he didn't know why. He stood on the balls of his feet, his fists by his hips, bunched like a boxer waiting for Round 1 to start.

'No,' she stated again.

'Yes,' he said, almost a shout, raising one fist, jerking it up and down as if hitting an imaginary table. 'Now.'

She looked him in the eyes, recognising the red anger she saw there. She chose her words with care. 'I slapped you once; I'll do it again.'

Mikey blinked, and Beth could see confusion overwhelming his anger, smothering his fury. 'But…' he held his hands out in a help-me-out-here gesture, '…you said… I thought…'

Her anger at his behaviour, however, was already alight; she could feel it being fanned.

One.

Two.

Three.

As she counted, Beth saw herself as if from a distance, between the two men, having to make a choice. As if a switch had been flicked, the image changed to a similar one: her mother between her and Ryan. Choosing her favourite child was not a difficult choice for Mum. Beth was quite aware of her place, knew that everything revolved around her brother. If Mum thought of her at all it was as Ryan's disappointing sister. Parents who say they don't have a favourite, they lie.

Four.

Beth looked up, squinting. The open sky passed from bright white around the sun to a deep blue near the horizon. She reached a count of five before she felt under control. Maybe being outside – not having a close, claustrophobic ceiling confining her – helped in controlling her temper. Maybe today. Not in the past.

'I've changed my mind,' she said. 'I've got things to do. I'm sure you have as well.'

'Liz,' Mikey stepped towards her, his face flushed and contorted. She held her ground. He jabbed a finger towards her. 'You… oh, fuck you.' He spun and strode to his car, repressed violence making him walk stiff-legged, as if his knees could not bend.

When he reached his car and its lights flashed, he turned and stared at Jake. 'I'll see you at work tomorrow.' It sounded as if at least one of them should not be looking forward it. Mikey opened the door and climbed in.

Beth and Jake watched him get into his car. He revved the engine but the car park was too small to do anything like take off with a spray of gravel. Even so, he shot for the exit only to have to brake hard in order to avoid pulling into the side of a passing car. Beth held her breath, waiting for road rage from at least one of the drivers. There was silence for a moment and, although the driver was obscured by a reflection, she saw a hand move, but not in the gesture she was expecting. The driver waved Mikey out.

'That was very polite,' Jake muttered, now standing beside Beth.

'Yes,' Beth said absently, her breath still being held. She stared at the other car, an SUV – blue, the colour of a tropical sea – trying to see the driver inside, just in case it was lumberjack man. She just couldn't see, no matter how hard she squinted.

'Look, I'm sorry about that,' said Jake, indicating the space where Mikey had parked.

Beth nodded, releasing her breath. 'I'm glad to see you're wearing a hat.'

A smile lit Jake's face. He attempted a nonchalant shrug. 'It seemed a good idea.'

Beth found herself beginning to relax. 'Surprised no one mentioned it to you before.'

'I probably wouldn't have listened if they had. You know what men are like.'

'They ignore good advice from others, then claim it was their own idea.'

'Like I said, it seemed a good idea of mine to wear a hat. A person could get sunburnt otherwise.'

'Wouldn't want that.' Beth felt the beginnings of a grin. Jake was refreshingly open. Maybe today wouldn't be so bad after all.

There was a pause and Beth noticed his tone had changed, as if picking his words with care. 'I've been thinking,' he said. 'I reckon I've figured it out. Why you don't want your picture on Facebook. You're hiding, aren't you? You don't want anyone to find you.'

And then things got worse.

'I realised it,' he said, staring at her the way a police detective would, 'when I was taking out a load of party rubbish this morning. And some guy appeared, asking about you.'

CHAPTER 14

It was like falling into a deep icy lake. Beth's lungs clenched to the size of her fists; try as she might, it was impossible to suck in air. As if searching for safety, her blood vessels had sunk deep inside, leaving her skin cold and pale.

'I…. God, are you all right? You look like you've seen a ghost.'

Beth tried to speak but, with no air, it was beyond her. Guttural sounds escaped from her throat.

'It's all right,' Jake said, his hands raised in an apologetic and defensive gesture, as if he wanted to touch and calm her but was afraid to. 'I didn't tell him anything. Nothing. In fact, I denied you lived here. Now breathe, that's it. Slow. Deep, that's it.'

Beth found herself becoming lightheaded. She put her hand out for support and, after a moment, Jake grasped it. She held on as if it were a lifebelt.

After a dizzy few minutes, Beth's frantic shallow breaths deepened; the constellations in her vision slowed their eruptions and faded.

'What… what happened?' If she'd had the strength she would have shaken Jake. 'What did he say?'

'Liz? Liz. You want to come inside? Looks like you could do with a sit down. A drink. I'll get you a tea. Something stronger.'

'Who…' She gripped his hand tighter, saw him wince.

'I don't know. He was just some guy,' Jake shrugged. 'What can

I say? Clean shaven; short, dark hair. Average looking. Nothing exceptional. About my age, possibly a little older. Sorry, I'm no judge. He was just … some guy. He asked after you. No...' Jake shook his head, desperate to get it right. '...he didn't. He described you. And he asked if you lived in these flats. I said I didn't recognise the description, that no one like that lived around here. Was that okay? Did I do the right thing?'

Beth released his hand, and nodded. The ground didn't feel solid beneath her, but she wanted to stand on her own. She swayed as relief swept through her body.

'That's when it occurred to me,' Jake continued, serious, but unable to disguise both his pride and the quality of his deductions. 'You didn't want to be tagged on Facebook, because you're hiding. It's… he's…' He stared at her. 'It's an abusive ex-boyfriend, isn't it? You got away from him. That's it, isn't it?'

Beth pulled in the biggest gulp of air she could, getting a sudden image of her lungs re-inflating like balloons. 'Something like that,' she croaked, surprised at how dry her mouth was.

'I knew it. I knew I was right. I did the right thing didn't I?'

'Yes. The right thing. Can I get that drink now?'

'Of course, come on.'

He led her back towards the flats, used his key to open the rear door to the stairwell, and let her enter first, making sure the door was shut behind him.

'What time was this?' Beth asked, once inside. To her left were the stairs up to her flat, and safety. Just beyond the banisters she could see Jake's orange door. It stood ajar so that one edge was lined with darkness.

'Probably about half-past nine, maybe ten, something like that.'

'What was he wearing?' Beth grabbed hold of the handrail, as if to swing herself up the stairs, but instead just waited.

Jake stepped around her. He pushed open his front door. From up the stairs there was a clunk, then another, getting closer, then another two.

Holding his door open, Jake looked from Beth, up the stairs, then back to Beth. 'Um…' he began.

'What was he wearing?' Beth repeated with more force. This was important. She needed an answer.

Was it lumberjack man?

Jake blinked and looked up the stairs again at the sound of another clunk. He was bouncing on his toes.

'Jeans,' Jake said, 'and a T-shirt. No. No, maybe it was a polo shirt. A black polo shirt, possibly navy. Or perhaps it was a T-shirt. Dark anyway.' An apologetic smile touched his lips. 'Sorry. I promised myself I'd remember but now I'm beginning to doubt myself.'

'Have you seen him before?'

'No. Can you just hang on a moment? Go in, make yourself at home. I'll be with you in a moment. First…,'

Jake bounded towards the stairs, looking up, shouting: 'Do you need a hand? Just coming, Shreeya.' He glanced at Beth. 'It's difficult with the pushchair.' And then he was leaping up the stairs two at a time.

For the second time in a matter of minutes Beth felt the ground shift under her. She thought she had Jake's attention, was thinking of him as a friend, but when it had come to a choice between her and Shreeya, Jake had chosen the woman with the baby. The sour taste of disappointment coated Beth's dry mouth, followed by the familiar pangs of guilt and self-loathing. She was being selfish. Of course a young mother with a baby in a pushchair, trying to negotiate several flights of stairs, was more deserving of attention than she was.

And yet.

And yet it felt like her mother always tending to Ryan's

demands and wishes, rather than hers.

From above, echoing down the stairwell, she heard Jake's voice. 'Hel-oh little man.' Beth could imagine Jake, bending over, smiling happily at a silent and now shy Dashee. She tried to swallow the sourness in her throat but found it difficult. She needed a drink.

Beth glanced into Jake's flat, but decided to wait for him at the bottom of the stairs. It would serve her self-centred self right to see him helping someone else.

The clunking stopped and she heard their voices.

'Here, let me help.'

'That's very kind of you.'

'It's no trouble. Well, little man, how are you?'

'Trouble.'

'Don't believe that.'

Beth's eyes widened and her face froze as she realised that, with the ceilings as thin as they were, it was possible that last night's drunken lust with Mikey could have been heard both in Shreeya's flat and – more importantly – in Jake's.

Oh, no. Please, no.

She looked up just as the two of them turned the corner: Jake bending, walking backwards, holding the front of the pushchair; Shreeya holding the back, with a bulging tote bag over her shoulder. It looked as if she had stuffed a double duvet into it.

They descended with ease, as if they were practised at the task. 'Here we are,' Jake said as they reached the bottom. He lowered the wheels of the pushchair to the ground and straightened.

Dashee was looking up at him, silent and wide-eyed, worshipping, gurgling tiny bubbles.

'That's very kind of you, Jake.' Shreeya hadn't had time to think about make-up or to do anything with her shoulder-length chestnut hair, which looked as if a tornado had just swept through it. However, it was the smile of gratitude she gave Jake that revealed to Beth how Shreeya had attracted Dash's father. Whoever he was.

Jake gave a little bow. 'You're very welcome.'

Watching Jake, Beth wondered: *is he one of those guys who gets off on helping everyone? Being the hero? He is, isn't he?*

Shreeya's eyes flicked to Beth, but she spoke to Jake. 'Are you settling in all right?'

'Fine thanks.'

'And your party? How did that go? Did everyone enjoy it?'

Jake never missed a beat and didn't even glance at Beth. 'I think people had a good time. I hope so.'

'Good. Sure they did.' Shreeya shrugged her bag further up her shoulder and nodded at Beth. 'Hello, Liz. How are you?' She sounded curt and Beth wondered again, inwardly cringing, just how much noise she and Mikey had made last night, and how far it had travelled.

Beth nodded back, keeping her voice neutral. 'Fine. You?'

'Good, thanks.'

'And Dash?'

'Yeah,' Shreeya looked down at her son, her stiff expression melting. Dashee managed to gurgle and giggle and dribble simultaneously. From somewhere Shreeya produced a cloth and bent down to wipe his mouth. The sight rocked Beth for, at that moment, Shreeya's expression was one that Beth couldn't remember seeing close up before. It was a smile, a simple smile, but one utterly pure and genuine: one filled with unconditional love. After hearing Shreeya's understandable frustration and anger with Dashee and his unstoppable howling, Beth didn't think such love was possible, but clearly it was.

Shreeya wiped her son's chin. 'Yeah,' she spoke with a gentleness to the boy that still provoked amazement in Beth, 'you're all right, aren't you.' Beth watched, fascinated, unbelieving, as if it were a performance – compassionate, understanding and forgiving – put on for her benefit. Still beaming at her child, Shreeya said, 'I don't think the soundproofing is up to much in these flats, so I do apologise if you can hear him. You said you work from home, I hope it's not been a problem. It won't last for ever.'

Again, Beth cringed inside. She went to speak but only a desiccated croak came out.

'Ahh,' Jake said, waving his fingers at Dash, 'have you been poorly? Not well? Poor little man.'

More gurgling. Dashee couldn't take his eyes off Jake.

Jake grinned and held up his hand. He moved his extended fingers from vertical to horizontal and back, several times.

Eventually he stepped backwards to the front door, which he held open while Shreeya negotiated the pushchair through it.

'Bye.'

'Bye.'

He shut the door once he was certain she was safe on the path and, after a moment, returned his attention to Beth. 'Sorry about that. A single mother, we must do what we can for her. Now, where were we? Yes, you need a drink. Come on in. I did the right thing, didn't I? Telling your ex… that guy… you didn't live here.'

Beth didn't move. She stared at him, trying to order her thoughts. Someone had been asking about her. Jake had lied to protect her. He couldn't identify who he had spoken to; it might not have been Callum. In fact, it couldn't have been Callum. No way could Callum have found her. More important, though, much more important at that moment, given a choice between Beth and Shreeya, Jake had gone to help Shreeya.

Beth winced and shook her head. The familiar knowledge of

being second best flowed through her body like a poison. She began counting, hoping to stop her irritation sparking into something worse while also trying to convince herself that Jake was a good guy and was just helping someone who needed assistance. That it wasn't a value judgement on her.

Except it was.

'Liz? I did, didn't I? The right thing?' Jake gave her a curious look.

She reached a count of six before she could trust herself to answer. 'Yeah,' she said in a flat tone. 'Thanks.'

'Are you all right? Anything I can do? That drink?'

'You've done enough,' she croaked, 'Look, it's been a bit of a shock. I need to…' She began to walk up the stairs to her flat.

Hide. Get away from everyone.

'Liz?

She didn't turn around, just kept walking. 'I've got stuff I need to do. I'll see you around.'

'Liz? Liz? Let me know if there's anything I can do. I want to help.'

She turned the corner, looked out of the window at the car park. It looked the same. There were no odd movements, no one peering around corners to find her. She glanced at the dehydrated peace lily on the windowsill and reminded herself once again to water the plant. It was hers, she really ought to care for it. She didn't want to be responsible for something else dying.

Once in her flat, she went to her bedroom and, with blood pounding in her ears, opened the window to allow in some fresh air. The curtains she left closed. She hadn't seen anyone outside, but, if what Jake said was true, then someone was close. With Jake's denial, and no sighting of her, Beth hoped whoever it was would move on. Sue had been trying to identify her last night, had found her familiar, maybe she'd got someone – her ex? – to investigate.

Sue knew 'Liz' was a neighbour, but Beth couldn't remember telling her which flat.

She looked at the bed and grimaced. Grabbing the duvet, she jerked it off the bed, pulled at the poppers at the bottom of the cover and yanked the duvet out. She flung the cover into a corner; the duvet she dumped on the floor. Her nose wrinkled when she looked at the bedsheet. Tugging free one corner, she yanked at the sheet and heard a tear as one of the other corners caught on the white wooden bedframe. *Good*, she thought. The sheet was a reminder of last night and now could be chucked away rather than cleaned. Screwing up the sheet, she threw it towards the door. Take it out to the rubbish later. If she could burn it, she would. The pillowcases and the duvet cover she stuffed into the washing machine, selecting a hot cotton wash. She also switched the kettle on, before switching it off again.

No milk.

And when she looked, she remembered there was no lemonade either.

And gin was not a good idea when she was in this mood.

Sighing, she settled for two glasses of tap water. She remade the bed with clean linen then vacuumed. It was only when she'd switched off the vacuum cleaner that she noticed how quiet the flat was. Just the gentle whir of the washing machine. She returned her two stuffed toys to the end of the bed, 'There you are, boys', she stroked them. These two toys had been with her almost all her life; they'd given her comfort whenever she needed it and expected nothing in return. They'd put up with tight hugs and been dampened with tears. Between the two soft toys and herself, she didn't know which was more battered. She looked around, only now feeling at ease.

Okay, while Dashee is out…

She fired up her laptop and set about doing some more work.

Get it done and invoiced while she had it, she figured. There were another two papers submitted to a Chinese accountancy journal that she could tell had been poorly translated into English. What would happen once the publishers implemented their decision that such articles didn't need copy-editing she didn't know. The journal would suffer a loss in quality along with a consequent loss in trust from its readership – and she would have to find work elsewhere. She couldn't face a job interview and the inevitable checking that would be involved.

Halfway through her work on the first article, the washing/dryer finished its cycle, so she emptied the machine, draped the linen over her airing rack, then returned to her work, giving it total concentration. If she had thought about it, she was happy and comforted by being unaware of the time or her surroundings.

Two hours later, and she had almost finished the second, longer, article when yelling yanked her from her work. At first she thought, madly, it was Dashee returned, the volume was the same, but then she realised it couldn't be the baby. While Dashee could scream for his country, he didn't use profanities. Besides, the shouting, the screaming and the sickening sounds of a fight, were coming from below.

From Jake's flat.

CHAPTER 15

Beth was on her feet and running for her door before she knew it. The shouting and screaming hadn't subsided. *Was that Jake? Mikey?* She unchained and yanked open the front door to her flat, and for the first time wondered what she was doing and whether she needed a weapon. Too late. She leapt down the stairs, grabbing hold of the banister and swinging herself around it, taking the next flight in three leaps until she skidded to a stop outside Jake's door, heart pounding and not just from the sudden exertion. If Jake was in trouble, he deserved her help.

His orange door stood ajar, as if he'd just stepped out, but she could hear him inside – his swearing muffled, as if so ashamed of his language he'd covered his mouth. It was the other voice though, the one shouting and screaming, that worried her more. It sounded like Mikey. There was a dull thump followed by a muted groan, then a louder impact and associated scream of pain and rage. Someone punching a wall?

Beth froze and contemplated running back to her flat, pretending she had heard nothing. No one would believe that though. Besides, these were two men she knew, who she liked. She didn't feel she could desert them now. She wasn't brave, and for most of her life she'd been taught – and had learnt – never to put herself, or anyone else, in danger, to run away, to avoid strange men, especially those who could turn violent (although, if she was honest, she sometimes ran towards those rather than away). Yet, she also wanted to think of herself as a peacemaker. Ryan would have told her to run. Just run. Her mother would have demanded to know what she had done to get herself into this situation. Beth's overriding feeling was of being overwhelmed by circumstances, unable to think through them. Rightly or wrongly, she was acting on instinct.

She hadn't had time to put her shoes on, but that didn't stop her pushing Jake's door open with her toe. She shouted the first thing that came to mind: 'Hello?' Even to her it sounded ridiculous. Asking whether anyone was at home was a stupid question, but it brought a moment of silence.

The first thing that caught her eye were the new dots on the hall floor. Three splashes of blood, fresh and glistening, each about the size of a five pence coin, soaking into the fibres of the matted carpet.

'Hello?' she said again, stronger. 'Jake? Are you all right?'

'Go away. Fuck off.'

'Mikey? Is that you? What's going on?'

Taking a deep breath, wishing she'd taken the time to slip on some shoes, Beth stepped into Jake's hall. She avoided the spots of fresh blood on the floor. In her head the hallway became a tunnel, far longer than the length of the flats; walking along it felt like wading into deep water. Another two blood spots dotted the carpet by the door to the kitchen. She could see part of the worksurface. It was clean. As far as she could tell the room was empty. She could hear heavy breathing – two people, she thought, one of whom was making a whistling noise with each breath.

'My fucking car.' It was Mikey's voice, coming from the living room. She took another step. 'He fucked my fucking car. My car!' A thump again, sickening; Beth's stomach, already fluttery, turned over. 'This is your fucking fault, Liz.'

At the bottom of the doorway to the living room, a blood-splattered hand flopped into sight. It left another mark on the carpet.

'Mikey!' she called, 'what are you doing? Jake? Jake? Are you all right?'

Keeping her back to the wall opposite, she inched to the door, as far out of reach as possible while trying to see what she could.

What she saw was Jake slumped on the floor, leaning against the wall, one leg outstretched, the other under him; one hand – the one Beth had seen – flapping limply by his side trying to get purchase, the other he held to his face as if to stifle a sneeze. Blood leaked from his cupped nose, slicked his mouth and dripped onto his white T-shirt.

'My. Fucking. Car.' With each word Mikey took a kick at Jake's outstretched leg and, although Jake grunted with each impact, Beth could see there wasn't the force that all three of them were expecting. She thought – hoped – her arrival had taken some of the anger out of the situation. Thoughts tumbled over themselves like jigsaw pieces in a tumble dryer. She tried to piece events together. One thought that blazed for a moment was how wrong this scene was: it was normally her anger causing the violence.

'Mikey,' she didn't raise her voice, and tried not to sound accusative or severe, 'you can stop now. Come here and tell me what happened.'

Mikey caught his balance, turned from the body on the floor and, chest heaving, looked at Beth. In that moment Beth thought he'd caught some dreadful disease, his features were swollen, suffused with fury. At that moment she couldn't believe she'd found him attractive enough to sleep with. His skin was taut and blotchy, white in some places, maroon in others.

God, do I look like that when—

'Liz.' Mikey glanced at her and took a step back. It enabled her to step forward, putting herself between the two men.

She squatted. 'Jake, are you all right?'

He blinked, taking more than few seconds to focus on her. When he did, his attempt at a smile was even worse than Mikey's expression. Beth controlled her impulse to vomit.

'Been,' he wheezed through blood-coated teeth, 'better.'

'Silly question, sorry.'

He nodded, and more drips fell onto his T-shirt.

'Let's get you on your feet and cleaned up.' Hooking a hand under one arm, she helped him to his feet. 'What happened?' she asked, pitching the question more to the room than either man. 'What's going on?'

Silence reigned for a second too long. Mikey was the one to break it. 'He fucked my car. My car!' There was still seething anger there, but Beth could tell it was suppressed now, mostly under control. 'Scratched it. He's gonna pay to have it repaired.'

Jake shook his head, managing to fling blood on the clean parts of his T-shirt. One bloody hand was splayed across his chest, the other cupped over his nose.

'Oh yes you are, you—'

'Din't do it.' Scarlet bubbles burst from his nose.

'Yeah right. Who—'

'Din't.' Jake looked down at his shirt and winced, whether from the movement or what he saw, Beth couldn't tell. 'Gonna have 'rouble gettin' this out.'

'No!' Mikey exploded. 'You're gonna fucking pay to get it repaired.'

Beth turned to him. 'He was talking about his T-shirt, you idiot.'

'I don't care about his fucking T-shirt. My car—'

'Yes, you've said. Let's get Jake cleaned up and then discuss it. After that, if you think kicking a man when he's down will fix it then...' Beth threw up her hands, '...what can I say?'

She helped Jake to the bathroom, where he looked into the mirror and winced again. Her own reflection stood tall beside his bent and bloodied one; she was amazed at how self-assured she looked.

A woman's place is in control.

A sick joke. She'd hadn't felt less self-possessed in her life, but she knew she couldn't let either of these men see how utterly adrift and ill-equipped she really was.

She ran some water, soaked his flannel and left him to it. She wasn't going to dab his face. He was old enough to do that himself.

Mikey was pacing around the living room when she returned. His movements were stiff, as if his joints had fused. His hands repeatedly clenched into fists as he muttered: 'he's gonna pay, he better pay. He'd better, I'll make him. My car. After all I've done.'

Beth tried to look nonchalant and competent, in that moment understanding what a mother must feel when her kids fight. Not her own mother, obviously, but one trying to maintain balance, peace and her own equanimity.

For lack of anything else to do, she decided to maintain the tradition of English mothers throughout the ages: make some tea.

By the time she had boiled the kettle, found the tea bags and milk, and filled three mugs – she didn't know or care how either of them took their drinks – Jake had peered out from the bathroom and taking a cautious step into the hall.

Leaving the hot drinks, she went to him. He had swapped his bloody T-shirt for a clean white one, across which his left hand still pressed against his chest. Beth suspected there were bruises under his palm.

He'd got most of the blood off his face, but Beth was neither about to tell him there were a few crusty marks under his chin, nor about to lick her own handkerchief and wipe them off. As far as she could tell, she didn't think his nose was broken, but the flesh under his eyes looked as if it was already beginning to swell. He was going to have two magnificent black eyes.

'Is he still here?' he whispered.

Beth nodded.

'I didn't do anything. I didn't.'

Beth nodded again, in acknowledgement rather than agreement.

'Right,' she said, her voice raised so that Mikey would hear. 'I've made everyone a cuppa. I don't know what's happened but we're going to get it sorted.'

Who was this confident person talking?

She returned to the teas, leaving Jake in the hall, waiting for her. She gave one mug to Jake, and picking up the other two she led the way into the living room. Mikey paused in his pacing and welcomed Jake's reappearance with a look so malevolent that Jake froze in the doorway.

'Stop that, now,' Beth commanded, still surprising herself. She placed the mugs on the dining table. 'Right, tell me what happened.'

Mikey jabbed a finger at Jake. 'He wrecked my car. He's gonna pay for repairs.'

'I didn't... I never... I...'

'It was all right when you left earlier.' Beth tried to sound reasonable.

'He followed me, scratched it, dented it then smashed a window.'

'What? How...?' Jake's voice had increased in pitch, to Beth it sounded like a whine. 'I haven't got my car back from the garage. Was I going to walk to your place?' Jake looked to Beth for confirmation.

167

Much to her surprise, Beth found herself agreeing. In fact, lying. 'It's true,' she said, nodding emphatically, 'he's been here all the time.'

She didn't dare look at Jake. For all she knew he could have caught a bus or called a taxi or maybe he did walk to wherever Mikey lived. But then, he was Jake, he was nice. Between him and Mikey, she knew who she'd put money on when it came to damaging a car.

'I can vouch for that. He's been here,' she said.

'You expect me to fucking believe that? You and him… You're just as much to blame.'

'Me?' Beth jerked, taking a step back.

'Oh, come on. Miss fucking innocent.'

Now Beth looked at Jake and was relieved to see him look as confused as she felt. He held his hands out in a 'don't-ask-me' gesture.

'Oh, for fuck's sake.' Mikey's features were regaining their crimson hue; the skin over his knuckles was bone-white.

Beth knew how dangerous, lethal, a loss of temper could be. And enough damage had already been done to Jake.

'Okay, okay, let's calm down.' Her palms pushed down empty air. 'You could have broken Jake's nose.'

'And my ribs.'

'After what he did to my car, he's lucky I didn't fucking kill him.'

'Trust me,' Beth spoke before she could stop herself, 'you don't want to do that. You'd have to live with it.'

She felt more than saw Jake turn his head to her. Even Mikey paused; his eyes narrowed, reminding Beth of someone focusing on the 'Magic Eye' pictures popular in her childhood.

'Well,' she said, her hand flicking towards the front door, 'Go on, show us what the problem is.'

Mikey chewed his bottom lip and for a moment Beth thought he was going to draw blood. She'd seen more than enough of that today.

'Right. Okay. But one of you…' he thrust his finger at each in turn, '…is gonna pay for this. To have it repaired. Like new. Or fucking else.'

He spun so sharply Beth was certain she heard the carpet creak and complain.

'It's gonna need a new window and whole new panel,' Mikey muttered as he strode to the front door, not checking whether Beth and Jake were following. 'That ain't gonna come cheap. And the colour better fucking match.'

They followed him into the car park, Jake with one protective arm still pressed across his chest while the other hand kept touching his nose, as if hoping each contact would be less painful than the last. From the way he winced that didn't appear to be the case. Beth wanted to tell him to stop, but knew it would do no good. Besides, it would be hypocritical: she always picked at her scabs.

Mikey's car stood tall and proud in Jake's parking place, as it had yesterday: a bright red Mitsubishi with polished bull bars on the front. The driver's side was facing them and, with the sun glinting off the gleaming paintwork, Beth couldn't see a problem.

'What…?'

'Other side.'

Mikey stood, statue-like, and Beth couldn't tell what was clenched tighter – his fists on his hips, or his jaw.

She and Jake walked around the car. And stopped.

'Oh, fuck.'

'Christ.'

It wasn't the line of dents in the bodywork, which looked as if someone had attacked it with a hammer. It was the three words, in capital letters, carved so deep even the exposed metal had been scarred.

LEAVE HER ALONE

Chapter 16

Beth stared at the words scored into the paintwork until the letters whirled, circled, spiralled into a single realisation.

I've been found.

She didn't move, barely breathed, could think of nothing beyond the fact that her life was no longer a secret. It felt like forever before the next thought swirled round and almost floored her.

How?

It struck her hard enough to make her flinch.

Beside her, Jake looked, open-mouthed, from the damaged car, then to Mikey and finally to Beth, on whom his wide eyes remained. She could feel his stare, like a bully's knuckles, grinding into her. He was the first to speak.

'Liz...' he whispered, 'you... you know who did this.' It wasn't a question.

Beth shook her head, unable to pull her own eyes from the scored command in the bodywork. 'No,' she lied. 'I... What?' The motionless air, warmed by the heat of the day, was becoming hard to breathe.

'Who?' demanded Mikey, taking a step closer, leaning towards her. 'Give me the bastard's name. I want to know who did this. I *deserve* to know.'

When Beth didn't respond, Jake spoke, his voice controlled, as if explaining something to a volatile child. 'It's like last night,' he said to Mikey. 'You know, the photo business. Liz didn't want her picture on Facebook—'

'Shut up, Jake.' Beth's words came out in a croak, and Jake either didn't hear or didn't understand.

'—because she's, well, hiding from her ex. An abusive relationship, I reckon. He must, must have…' he turned to Beth, his pride in his deductions vanishing when he saw her expression, '…found you.'

Beth shook her head, trying to stall her thoughts so they'd fall together in a different combination, one that fitted what she was seeing, and what Jake was saying – and what she knew to be true. She searched for possible scenarios to explain how this could have happened.

How?

She spun, scanning the car park, its entrance, the windows in the flats and nearby buildings. Nothing moved. Nothing out of place. No one watching. Even so, she felt exposed and vulnerable. The hot summer air lay thick and heavy on her shoulders, stagnant. When she turned back, Jake was talking.

'…police. Let them deal with it.'

Mikey thrust a finger at him. '*Whoever* did this,' he said, staring at Jake, 'I don't want them fucking *fined*. I don't want him,…' he jabbed a finger at Jake again, this time making contact, forcing Jake back a step, '…being fucking protected from me. I want my car fixed and I want him *here*.' His finger thrust downwards this time, point to the ground before him. 'Where I can show him what I think and what I do to—'

'But the police—'

'You're not listening,' Mikey leaned in until his fury-suffused face was an inch from Jake's. 'I want to show him what happens to people who do this. *It's my* fucking *car*.' He turned his head, shot a look at Beth, 'You get it, don't you. A coward did this. And now we have another fucking coward telling me I shouldn't seek revenge. Hmm. The same coward d'ya reckon?'

'Oh come on, you know it wasn't me.'

Mikey snarled. 'Do I?'

'Yeah, you do. Besides, you attack whoever did this, he'll have you for assault.'

'Is that a threat?'

For an instant Beth thought she a saw smile behind Mikey's twisted lips.

'Christ.' Jake put his hands out in a gesture that was both defensive and exasperated. 'No, I'm just saying, the police—'

'No,' Beth said softly, then with more strength, 'No.'

'Liz,' Jake began, 'if you know who—'

'I can't. I just can't, all right?' She looked at each of them, daring them to challenge her. They returned her stare but said nothing. Mikey looked as if he were enjoying his glowering. The semicircles beneath Jake's eyes were swelling and darkening by the minute. Despite the heat Beth felt a shiver run though her. 'Let's go inside,' she said, and without waiting for an answer marched back into the flats. She thought she'd feel more secure indoors, but didn't, not even when she pushed open the front door to Jake's flat, the nearest place of safety, and stepped inside. Jake and Mikey followed,

'Tell me.' Mikey said once they were in the living room. He thrust his hands into the pockets of his jeans, as if needing somewhere to confine his fists.

Beth looked at him, keeping her gaze steady. 'I'll pay for repairs,' she stated. 'You get a quote, or get it fixed. Give me the bill.' In her head she contemplated her finances and meagre savings. She tried to keep her face neutral as she remembered Wednesday's email. Losing one of her journals, a significant proportion of her income, would mean there was no way she could afford to cover the repairs on such an expensive car. One that was so masculine it wouldn't demean itself by being cheap to fix. 'I will pay,' she added for emphasis, partly to convince herself.

One way or another, the thought came to her, unexpected but obvious, *I'm going to have to pay.*

She shook the notion away.

'Liz,' Jake's tone was that of a man aiming to be reasonable but hitting paternalistic dead on. 'Really, I get that you don't want to tell us who did this. I do.' Beside him, Mikey swore and looked away with a movement so violent Beth was surprised it didn't pull any muscles. 'But don't you think it would be better if the police handled this?'

'I can't involve the police. It's… too…' she shook her head, '… complicated.'

'Then don't. Don't involve the police. Just give *me* his fucking name and address.'

'Oh yeah.' Jake touched his swelling nose, glanced at Beth. 'That's a good idea. Violence always solves problems. This isn't a game you know. Not one of your computer games. Besides—'

'It'll make me feel better.'

'Will it fix the car?'

'It'll tell us who's best.' This time Mikey glanced Beth's way, his lips curled into what could be a grin or grimace. He switched his stare to Jake. 'And if I do find out it was *you* who did it, if I do, I'll—'

'Mikey. Listen, you dummy. You're missing something. Liz. She needs protecting.'

Mikey took a step forward. 'Don't call me…' He blinked then glanced back at Beth, then returned his attention to Jake. 'Well, you're fucking useless. Look at you. Weak. Afraid. Scared to do anything. Wanting to rely on the police. What she needs is a real man.' He thumped his own chest. Beth couldn't believe it: he hit his own chest the way a gorilla would.

For a second she shut her eyes, as if such an action would remove the raised voices as well as the sight of the two men. It was hard to believe this was the same room that had hosted yesterday's party. Now, it seemed to have shrunk, was nowhere big enough for the three of them. 'No,' she said, intending to sound assured and put an end to all this bickering, instead the word came out a weak plea, more of a question.

Mikey stared at her, his head thrust forward, but his gaze baffled. 'Why are you protecting Jake? I thought... After last night... We... I mean, why are you defending *him*? I know he can't defend himself, but...'

'Oh, really.' Jake looked at Mikey, defiant, then at the floor.

Mikey continued: '...but if I do find out *he* fucked my car...'

'I didn't.'

'He didn't.'

'You're sure?'

'Yes.'

'Positive?'

'Yes.'

'How do you know?'

'I know.'

'You really know who did it?'

'I do. Yes.'

'So tell me.'

'No.'

'An abusive ex? Violent? It seems *I'm* the only one here who's able to protect you.'

Beth shook her head.

'Jesus fucking Christ. What a day.' Mikey raised an arm and for a moment Beth thought he was going to lash out and hit one of them. Instead, he swiped his palm down the back of his neck, wiping away imaginary sweat with unnecessary ferocity. 'No breakfast and now my car's fucked.' He stared at Beth, his rigid lips moving as if he were attempting to chew something. 'Thanks to you,' he eventually managed.

She met his stare. There were many things that scared her; at this moment he wasn't one of them. 'I told you,' she kept eye contact, 'I'll pay for your car. And sorry,' she shrugged, 'but I'm out of bread and milk.' She decided not to tell him that if he'd risen earlier they could have both visited the shop for supplies.

'You.' Mikey pointed at Beth. 'You're gonna be getting the bill.' His laugh was no more than a humourless snort. 'You know, one day you're gonna get what you deserve. And you,' he spun to face Jake, his tone harder, even more threatening, 'You,' he nodded, 'I'm gonna be seeing you at work tomorrow.'

He strode out the flat, not even bothering to slam the door. Somehow that made the silence that remained deeper and more difficult to break.

Beth and Jake stared at each other, with Beth seeing in Jake's face a reflection of the chaos and confusion of her own thoughts. She attempted a smile, knowing it was thin. Jake returned the same expression.

They spoke in unison: 'Sorry.' Their use of the same word at the same instant broke the moment.

They smiled and both went to speak again, only to pause, seeing the other about to utter something.

Their subsequent laughter had, Beth thought, the familiar sound of nervous release.

Jake held his palm out. 'After you,' he said. His smile now relieved, genuine.

'Sorry for putting you through that,' said Beth. 'And thanks for, well, taking the flak.'

He nodded acceptance of her gratitude. 'Likewise,' he said, 'and thanks for backing me up. I didn't do it, you know.'

'I know.'

Jake tentatively touched his nose, winced. His narrowed eyes only emphasised the darkening swellings beneath them. 'I don't know how I'm supposed to show this face at work tomorrow.'

'Take a sickie?'

'Then what? Mikey's bound to tell them his version of today. Then what happens when I go in on Tuesday? Or next week? Or whenever these bruises have faded? How long's that gonna take? I'm not sure I can face going in.'

'I'm sure it'll be all right.' It was quite clear Jake didn't agree, and Beth didn't believe it herself. This was yet another entry on her growing list of things to feel guilty about.

How can my life ruin so many others? she wondered.

'If there's anything I can do.' She made an ineffectual gesture with her hands, not knowing what else she could say or do. She had enjoyed Jake's company and their preparations for the party. He didn't deserve this. None of it. She liked him. Was this what happens when you like someone?

Jake went to shake his head, but winced instead.

'You can give your ex a message from me. Just two words. And the second one's *off.*'

Beth let out another laugh, surprised that she could, and also how good it felt. And was relieved to see her response had pleased Jake.

'I'll do that,' she said. 'I'll call him right now. You're sure you're okay?'

'I'll survive.'

She waited a second, then left Jake's flat, climbing the stairs to her own, her anger growing with each step as she thought about what must have happened. How her own stupidity had brought it on. Her rage swelled, expanding outwards like a shockwave. She jabbed her key in the lock, flung open the door then grabbed it before it smashed into the wall. She had a sudden vision of herself furiously banging the door into the wall, knocking out great chunks of plaster, the door handle gouging a huge hole. So tempting. It would feel so good. She tensed about to do it, anticipating the explosion, the release, but from somewhere a sliver of cool sanity cut through. No. Get the rage out of her system. She shut her eyes and reached a count of fifteen before she felt she could close the door without breaking any hinges. Stiff with suppressed rage, she went straight to her handbag, rummaged viciously through it until she found what she was looking for. Any longer and she might have flung the bag across the room. She yanked the strip of paper out so fast it tore. 'Fuck it.'

Putting the two pieces together, the number written in ballpoint was still legible. 'Thank...'

She paused again, using every anger management technique she could, in her current state, bring to mind. That small, cold part of her brain flashed again, like sunlight reflecting off ice, warning against making this call while furious. Controlled anger. That's what she needed. Controlled. Not frenzied and unrestrained.

After a couple of minutes she grabbed her phone from beside her computer and punched in the number written on the torn slip of paper. She feared the mobile's plastic case would shatter if she it gripped any harder.

Her call was answered before the second ring.

He's been waiting for me.

CHAPTER 17

'What the fuck,' she shouted into the phone, 'do you think you're doing?'

'I don't know.' Ryan sounded sad and lost. Beth was convinced she could hear him shaking his head. 'I just lost control. I just... You know. *You* know.' His confusion was as clear to Beth as her own raw and blistering fury. She wanted to scream at him, scream until her throat ripped, and then scream some more. Except... Except..., as always, just hearing Ryan's voice did what a medieval bloodletting was supposed to do: her rage – despite it being righteous and deserved – just drained away. He had always been her calming influence.

Ryan's words were now hurried but clear. 'I lost it, like, you know... when I saw what he did. No one treats my little sister like that. Not when I'm around. Not my sister.'

Beth looked about, not seeing her living room, not seeing anything except the wispy tendrils of red mist that had been her rage. 'What he did? Who?'

'In the car park. I saw him grab your wrist. I saw. Don't tell me I didn't. I did. It was,... he was violent. He looked like he was going to hit you. I was too far away to... He shouted at you, dammit.' Ryan was winding himself up now. 'Grabbed you. Hurt you. You! My little sister. He's lucky I just keyed his car. Next time I'll score the goddamn message into his chest. He—'

'Hurt me? He didn't hurt me.' Beth tried to remember. She tried to picture the car park. Mikey. He had been annoyed, yes, but nothing more than a frustrated bloke. What he had done was no more – less, even – than women anticipate every day. He hadn't hit her. Christ, he hadn't even come close. 'Fuck sake, Ryan. You think I can't handle something like that? After all these years, that I can't look after myself? I... Where are you? Are you driving? Sounds like you're driving.'

'Hands free.'

'Oh, I don't believe it. You're running away. You are, aren't you? From what you did. You put me in the shit and you can't wait to get away. You—'

'How dare you. I stand by what I did. If he wants to make something of it...'

Beth could hear his anger, recognised a burning, raging reflection of her own – a family trait. Another thought hit her, rocking her. 'Wait a minute. You told me you didn't have a car. You lied about that? As well as putting me in the shit with my friend, you lied to me? You bastard.'

'I wouldn't lie to you, Beth.' Ryan's voice became unnaturally calm. 'It's Paul's car. But seems he's gone and got the huff for some reason since I borrowed it this morning. He's deliberately not answering my calls. And as for putting you in the shit with your "friend", you need to get better friends.'

'My friends're none of your business. And how'd you find...' With an almost audible click, her fractured thoughts slotted into place with precision. They formed an instant and complete picture. She let out a long breath and slumped into her work chair. 'It was the dogs, wasn't it? Training the guide dogs.'

''Fraid so. You mentioned them at Guildford station. A quick Google search to find that the Guide Dog for the Blind Association has a centre in Leamington. It was that, coupled with how long your train was delayed. You mentioned it. The only train on the screen delayed that long was to Reading.'

'From where I have to change trains to get to Leamington.'

'Yeah. I called Paul, my flatmate, and he picked me up, we barrelled straight up the M40 and had just arrived in the station car park, at Leamington, taking a gamble that's where you'd get off. When you did, Paul followed you.'

'He wear a checked lumberjack shirt?'

'I… dunno. Think so. Probably. He followed you to those flats. Keeping me informed by phone. Couldn't be certain if you actually lived there, of course. And if you did, which flat.' Ryan sounded pleased with himself, his smugness oozing down the line. 'That's why I borrowed Paul's car and drove back this morning.'

'Why?'

'Why what?'

Beth stood, despite feeling shaky, and let out a long exhale, one she was sure her brother could hear. She felt as though something had been taken from her, and realised it was the power to keep her family and her life separate. An urge to reclaim what had been stolen, to regain control for her own sense of self, burnt through her. One hand scratched a familiar itch at the top of her leg. She kept the phone to her ear as she strode to the kitchen. A sharp blade was required. 'Why,' she asked, her voice flat, 'are you so desperate to know where I live?'

'Callum's trying to find you.'

'God, you think I don't know that?'

'I just thought, I dunno, If I knew where you were it'd be easier. I could come to you, should you need me. Or be around. Besides, I… I was curious. About your life. Where you were living. For all we knew, you were homeless. Living in a tent or something. You're my little sister, of course I care about you.'

'You really think I can't look after myself?' Standing in the kitchen, she swapped her phone to her left hand and pulled open a drawer with her right. She a slid out her favourite knife, black-handled with a serrated blade. Looking at her distorted reflection in the blade, feeling the thrill of anticipation, she realised she had missed what Ryan was now saying.

'What?'

She heard his heavy sigh. 'Beth, there're people who care for you. You shouldn't cut yourself off. Or cut them out.'

The blade turned fuzzy as Beth blinked due to the sudden stinging in her eyes.

She swallowed, fighting for control. 'I—'

Knocks, loud, three of them, on her front door. 'Got to go, Ryan,' she sniffed, both thankful for the interruption and angry with herself for letting him off so lightly. 'I'll be ringing you back, trust me. We need to talk. You need to pay for repairs to that car. I can't. You will.'

She cut the call before he could reply, now aware there was someone outside her front door, who was already in the flats, who hadn't rung the intercom outside and asked to be let in. Because there was this intercom entry system, the architect had decided there were no need for windows or spyholes in the front doors. Just a letterbox. There was no way of knowing who was outside.

She swore under her breath, then remembered she was still holding the knife in her right hand and her phone in her left.

'Yes?' She tried to make her voice sound strong.

'Liz. It's Jake.'

She shut her eyes and let out a loud exhale. She slumped against the hall wall before a burst of anger coursed through her, forcing her upright.

He knew I was making a call, she thought, enraged, *so why the hell is he knocking now?*

'Jake?' She didn't remember putting on the security chain

when she'd returned, but she must have done. Second nature.

She transferred the knife to join the phone in her left hand and with some clumsy effort managed to hold both by her side. 'What do you want?'

'Yeah,' he called, as she opened the door to the extent of the security chain, and checked he was on his own. 'I just,... oh,' he said, surprised at the welcome.

'Hang on.' She closed the door again, slipped off the chain and opened the door further but not wide. She needed to keep her left hand and what it was holding obscured.

'Oh, sorry, You okay?' he said, seeing her irritation.

'What? You knew I would be on the phone. I told you.'

'Oh, yeah. Apologies.' His pale skin flushed and he looked flustered, as if attempting a foreign language.

He'd put on a new T-shirt, orange with bronze horizontal stripes. And even though he was wearing a baseball cap with the peak pulled low and glasses that were so dark they wouldn't look out of place on a ski slope, she just knew his swelling eyes were narrowed with confusion. She decided, with an attack of pique, not to confront his unasked questions.

'Well?' she snapped, unable to stop herself. The knowledge that her justified anger towards Ryan was being aimed at an innocent neighbour made her feel awful. Worse, she knew her guilt at her own unjust behaviour and lack of control was also getting projected at Jake.

He took a step back, as if she had pushed him.

What did you expect? You knew I would be on the phone.

'Umm,' he shook his head. 'I was... I was on my way out to throw this away.' He held up a bloody crumpled rag – the once-white T-shirt he had been wearing. 'And I remembered you saying you had no milk or bread. And after last night, as you can imagine, I need some stuff as well, so I thought I'd pop to the corner shop and get us some supplies.'

'What?'

Oh yes, you do like to be the hero, don't you?

'Sorry, but you said you were out of bread and milk. I thought I'd get you some.'

'What? No. Yes. Look, you knew I would be on the phone. I told you.'

'I just thought...'

'Semi-skimmed. Any type of bread.' She stared at him, intimidating him, as if daring him to waste more of her time. Her thoughts were still a writhing mass of all the things she still desperately wanted to say to Ryan. Didn't Jake understand that bread and milk were the least of her worries?

'Sure. Want to...'

Her attention was on her phone before the door shut. She juggled with the knife as she re-dialled her brother.

'Hey,' Ryan answered immediately. Again, his voice was a balm on her exposed anger.

'Still running away?'

'Something's up with Paul. Dunno. Maybe I upset him. He's not talking to me. Need to apologise.'

'For fuck's sake Ryan. You're going to apologise to Paul, but not me?'

'Why should I apologise to you?'

'Well, how about putting me in the shit with my friends?'

In the pause that followed, she was certain she could hear him chewing his lip over the noise of the car.

Ryan's voice was soft when he spoke. 'Does he mean that much to you?'

'No. Yes. That's got nothing to do with it. You shouldn't have done it. He could quite legitimately call the police.'

'But you stopped him.'

'Course I did. But someone's got to pay for the repair. One of us two. And it's not gonna be me.'

For what felt a very long time, the sound of the car and surrounding burr of traffic was the only noise Beth could hear.

She heard him sigh. 'Come on,' he said, 'you've lost your temper before. We all know you have.' There was pleading in his voice. She didn't know which of the many, many occasions in their childhood Ryan was alluding to. There were countless options. In the last few days she had smashed a glass and slapped Mikey.

'But I always accept the consequences,' she said, looking at the front door.

'Yeah, consequences. Look, I'm about to hit the M25. I'll call you back when I can. Bye.'

'Wait.'

But he'd disconnected.

She stared at the phone, the blade of the knife poking out from behind it, glinting.

It occurred to her that Jake had apologised more than Ryan. In fact, the word 'sorry' hadn't even passed her brother's lips.

At least I feel contrite when I lose my shit. For fuck's sake, look at how I atoned to Mikey for a slap.

Her hand shook, causing her to blink as sharp reflections from the blade slashed across her vision. A laugh erupted from her; soon there would be a reassuring sting, one that proved she was alive and in control. And another hyphen added to her collection.

This is your fault, Ryan. I need this. And I'm bloody well going to enjoy it.

Her lips drew back into something she could feel was neither a grimace nor grin, but something unattractive in between.

At least Jake isn't here to see...

Jake!

Shit. Shit. Shit.

He would be returning, he would be knocking on her door again, expecting her to open it. He couldn't see her shameful secret.

Shit!

She raised her arm like a baseball pitcher, a guttering cry erupting from her throat as violent visions burnt themselves into her mind – the phone exploding against the wall and the knife embedding itself in the door – but at the last moment she stopped, not through self-control bur because she simply couldn't decide which would be more satisfying – the phone or the knife?

'Oh, hell.' A sudden deflation, as if all her energy had escaped from her body, made her sag. For support she put her hand onto the front door which, a moment before, had almost had a knife stabbed into it. Bile rose in her throat at the thought. It was too reminiscent of what she had done to Owen. What had altered her life.

With care, avoiding sudden movements, she made her way to the bathroom, spat out the sharp tang in her mouth, rinsed with mouthwash and spat that out. All the time she tried to avoid her reflection in the mirror. Her lungs hurt and her chest heaved, as if she'd just skidded from an all-out eyes-bulging sprint, to a stop.

She returned to the kitchen with reluctance. The knife felt reassuring – at home in her hand, as if made to fit her palm. In the same way that the internet always has the answer so, she felt, did a sharp blade. But then also just like the internet, the answer wasn't always correct. Despite her craving, she just couldn't enjoy the sharp blade, not with Jake returning soon. She didn't know whether she should be thankful or resentful that he was making her feel like this. Either way, she wasn't about to let him in on her secret.

Once she'd returned to the living room, she turned her laptop on, and sat down to kill time. YouTube was her occasional solution to waiting. Over the years she had become an avid watcher of DIY videos. They had shown how to wallpaper this room, including the important preparations she needed to do beforehand. If she was going to spend the rest of her life on her own, and was never going to earn enough to pay for professionals, then learning DIY would be essential. More important was learning to keep her temper when things went wrong. Yes, she'd done the wallpapering, but more than one sheet had been screwed up in an explosion of anger when it had stuck to itself like Sellotape. Watching unflappable experts was somehow calming; she marvelled at how they kept their composure when things went wrong. If only she could be like that.

She searched on how to install a power shower, and watched a dozen clips, a few of them over and over, pausing over details, jotting observations in her notebook, following links, contemplating the difficulty involved, wondering whether she was capable of the plumbing and wiring. Her concentration became total, so much so that it didn't occur to her to be grateful to the uploaders for taking her mind off her hyphens.

When she first noticed the noise, she thought it was something on the soundtrack. On her screen, a confident man wearing a T-shirt that emphasised his gut, and a beard that emphasised his baldness, was standing in a bath pulling wires through a hole in a recently tiled plasterboard wall. He was talking to the camera and ignoring the knocking, unfazed by it. Then it came again, and Beth realised it had been in the background for longer than she had thought. And still the man ignored it.

'Liz? Liz? Are you there? Are you all right? Liz?'

Jake.

She pulled herself from the screen, started for the front door, stopped, returned to the laptop and paused the video, then rushed to welcome her downstairs neighbour.

He's taken his time. What took so long?

She took a step back when she opened the door and saw him. 'Jake, what? What's wrong?'

His face was paler than she'd seen it before. No trace of a tan or sunburn. The dark glasses were gone too, being held in his hand. The bulging sickles under his eyes were more purplish than she remembered. His eyes flicked from side to side, trying to see around her.

'Liz, are you all right?' His chest was fluttering as if he were hyperventilating.

'Yes, what—'

He pushed his way in, slamming the door shut and leaning on it, as if trying to get his breath. His hands were clenched, Beth noted, and free of shopping.

When he could, he spoke. 'Who... are you?' He stared deep into her eyes as if searching were clues there.

Oh, God.

Beth's stomach flipped, then fell. 'What... what do you mean?'

'There was another one. He stopped me. Outside.' He shook his head, but never lost eye contact. 'Just how many violent ex-boyfriends do you have?

CHAPTER 18

'What...' Beth placed her palm on Jake's chest; he needed to know this was important. 'What did this man say?' She was sure he must feel the thumping of her heart through her hand. She could feel his.

Jake stared at her, calculating. The purple crescents beneath his bruised, narrowing eyes still darkening as they slowly filled with blood. When he broke eye contact, he looked down at her hand with, Beth suspected, the same expression he would use when inspecting a stain on his shirt. Beth's fear almost overwhelmed her guilt.

Jake raised his eyes. 'He... he asked after you.' He levered himself from her front door, standing straighter, pushing against her palm until she removed it from his chest. 'He described you. It was definitely you, he got your hair wrong, and the wrong colour. But it was definitely you. And he didn't call you Liz. He used another name.'

He spoke as if he couldn't recall the name that had been used, but it was obvious to Beth that he could remember perfectly well – it would have been repeated in his head and memorised. Beth swallowed a rising wave of nausea. Did Jake recognise the name? Oh God, did he *know*?

Her hallway felt very small, dark and airless.

'This way,' she said, and without waiting walked away. She

needed to get to her living room, to her laptop and printer. 'What did you tell him?' she asked without looking back. She had to stop herself from shouting.

'That I didn't recognise the description, or the name, and that no one like that lived around here anyway. That was right, wasn't it?'

Beth closed her eyes in thanks, grateful that Jake couldn't see her face. He'd know though, she realised, just from the involuntary relaxation of her shoulders.

'He also asked,' Jake continued, confusion colouring his voice, 'if these were one-bedroomed flats. That's an odd thing to ask isn't it? What did he want to know that for?'

Her phone rang, but she didn't touch it. She had more important things to do.

'Sit down.' Beth indicated her sofa and without looking at whether Jake had complied, went to her printer, turned it on, and then sat in front of her laptop.

'I waited.' Jake said behind her. She was sure he was nodding. 'I waited downstairs, watching him. I waited until I was absolutely sure he'd gone before coming up here. That was right wasn't it? I didn't want him seeing me come straight up to see you. That would've been a bit of a giveaway, wouldn't it?'

Her phone stopped ringing.

Beth nodded but her attention was on her laptop. She tapped Callum Calbourne's name into her web browser, retrieved the reports she'd found from Isle of Wight newspapers, picked what looked like the most recent picture of Callum, right clicked and selected 'Print Target'. Her printer juddered into life and began chattering.

She was so intent on watching Callum emerge from the black mouth of the printer, each revealed line ratcheting up her unease, that she didn't even look at her phone when it rang again. With most of Callum's face visible, the printer paused as if trying to catch up with itself, or frightened of what it was creating. And in the brief silence she grabbed the phone. Glancing at the display, she remembered dialling the number shown there. It was Ryan.

'Yeah?' She put one hand over her ear as the printer shuddered again and finished its work. It ejected the image, chuttered a bit more and fell silent.

'Pudge? You're okay?'

'Yeah, hang on.' She took the sheet from the printer's tray, looked at it and a shiver shook her. It was still difficult to believe that this muscled thug had once been a sweet and gentle friend. The image though, was as she wanted. Just a picture, no names or text.

'Are you all right?' Ryan sounded insistent.

'Yeah. Why?' She handed the sheet to Jake, mouthing 'This him?'

Ryan was almost shouting in her ear. 'Paul... Paul's in hospital. Callum... Callum put him there. Tortured him. You've got to get away. He—'

'What?'

She was listening to her brother but looking at Jake, who didn't need to stare at the picture. One glance. Just one. And he nodded.

Beth felt the floor of her flat tilt, then drop away. She found herself sitting at an angle in her office chair a second before her stomach resumed its normal position. She suspected she'd fallen. It was easier to focus on wondering where her strength had gone than anything else.

Ryan was still speaking, almost shouting, but she could only just hear him. Everything was muffled. She felt disconnected, separated from reality, as if everything were happening the other side of scratched Perspex. She looked up. Jake was on his feet,

191

standing over her, and when she focused she could see an expression of genuine concern. His hands flapped as if he didn't know what to do with them. He still held his sunglasses, one arm of which made a clicking sound as it flipped open and shut in time with the movement of his hand.

She waved her own trembling hand at Jake, but he didn't seem to understand its 'wait' message. He remained standing, looming over her, the way policemen once had. She shrank back in her chair, trying to wheel it away from him. She'd been expecting his confirmation of Callum, but it hadn't diluted the shock. Jake noticed her movement, and must have misunderstood it, because his expression changed from concerned to wounded.

She tried to speak, but her mouth felt as dusty, as if it were ancient. She tried to get some saliva going.

'Wait,' she finally croaked into the phone, which felt too heavy.

Strong. She must be strong, in all senses. Right, concentrate. She tried to make sense of what Ryan had just said. 'Wait. Start again. Callum's attacked your flatmate?'

'He must have broken into Mum and Dad's – while we were in Guildford – looking for your address. Mum and Dad said they'd felt there'd been a break in. He must have, well, found my address instead of yours. And he arrived there while I was ..., I was with you. He made Paul... He tortured... He made him say where we'd followed you too. This... it was a couple of hours ago. He could be there by now. Oh, Pudge, *Beth*, if you see him, run. He's clever. Don't let him talk to you. Don't let him get anywhere near you.'

Beth tried to swallow some oxygen, but the room was airless and she needed to breathe, needed a clear head, needed to think. 'He's here,' she said.

'There? Now? With you? Oh, shit. Shit. Are you all right? Don't listen to him, don't let him...'

'No, no. I mean he's here in Leamington. He was outside. I

think he's gone now.' She looked up at Jake, who nodded.

'Run, Pudge. Run.'

'But...'

'If you knew what he'd done to Paul...'

Beth began to compress her fear, push it down to where it wasn't debilitating, and to calculate. She'd prepared for this. She knew where to find her Fleebag, knew it was up to date. It was a mystery to her why more people didn't have one for emergencies. What else did she need? Her laptop. Phone. Money. She glanced at her watch. It was after four on a Sunday. She doubted she could organise new accommodation now. A hotel, B&B maybe. She could get on first train out, get off somewhere new, start again. But she'd have to get to the station. If Callum was watching...

'Pudge?'

'Okay.'

'You have somewhere to go?'

Her first thought was of Mikey; strong Mikey; Mikey who could look after himself; who, she figured, owed her for a night spent in her bed. But then, thanks to Ryan's temper and a sharp key she was also in his debt. She looked up, surprised to see Jake still standing nearby, waiting to help, wanting to, but unsure how. 'I'll let you know,' she said into the phone.

Ryan's voice was loud in her ear. 'I'm coming right back.' She had a vision of him breaking every speed limit on his frantic return, tired, desperate, worrying about her, about Paul, losing control, crashing, taking out other vehicles, claiming more lives. She was responsible for more than enough tragedy. She couldn't take any more.

'No,' she snapped, 'No. You make sure Paul's okay. I'll be all right. I'll phone you tomorrow. Tell you where I am and what's happening. Let's all keep calm. Besides, if you're up here you're just another person Callum could recognise. I don't want anyone leading him to me.'

'But—'

'Just make sure Paul's okay.'

She disconnected and looked up at Jake. The sincere worry that was written on his face caused something deep within her to swell. It brought a flash of memory, one of gratitude to her brother for those occasions when, despite her being nothing but an annoying baby sister, he had sacrificed his own time to help her, to join in her play. What she felt now though was so, so much stronger. It was painful, actually painful.

She forced a couple of deep breaths to get herself together, flooding the ache within her.

'Right,' she said. 'Don't take this the wrong way,' she tried to emphasise with her tone that this was not a come-on, 'but can I stay at your place tonight?' She didn't want to be on her own and knew that, 'Can you stay with me tonight' was always going to be open to misunderstandings. Also, she wanted to be elsewhere.

'What's happened? Who is he?' Jake flapped the picture he still held, making Callum's glowering features appear and disappear. At that moment it reminded Beth of a wild-west Wanted poster; it was an association she thought she should find funny, but didn't.

She stood, forcing Jake to take another step back.

'He's someone who wants...' she had trouble forming the words, '...to hurt me. And now it seems he's found me.'

'And no police?'

'No police.'

'Can I ask why?'

'Is your help dependent on me answering that?'

'Of course not.'

'Then I may tell you.'

But not everything.

'I was supposed to get you some stuff from the shop. Have you eaten anything today?'

Beth tried to remember. 'What with one thing and another, no.'

'You know, neither have I. Come downstairs and I'll throw something together.'

'That's... this is really kind of you. First though, I've got to collect some things.'

'I'll wait.'

'Trust me, it won't take two minutes.'

CHAPTER 19

'So?' Jake asked.

Once again they were in Jake's kitchen. Beth had been afraid he would actually confront her, do the full hands on hips, parent-type thing. Instead, he busied himself taking food from his fridge, a frying pan and saucepan from cupboards, pulling a chopping board, a rolling pin, a sharp knife, ingredients from various places. He was in constant movement; confident, decisive steps in the limited space. It meant he was neither looking at Beth nor not looking at her, just listening while he pottered. She wanted to thank him for that, for making it easier for her, but didn't know how.

She felt she should help, to return to yesterday when she had enjoyed participating in the party preparations, and Callum hadn't found her. That was impossible, though. Standing straighter, as if about to give a presentation, she began. 'That picture I just showed you. That was Callum Calbourne.'

'Okay. Who's he?' Jake placed a sealed plastic tray that held a single chicken breast beside a chopping board, and picked up a knife. The blade was the length of his hand.

'His brother was Owen Calbourne.'

Jake paused, the blade hovering. 'That name rings a bell. It's... that's a name I haven't heard in long time. My childhood. Wha... woah, it was you?'

He spun towards her – in the moment their eyes met, she saw him focus, then re-focus, on her features, saw recognition, but then nothing else – and then he continued the spin as if he was always intending to get something from the spice rack. He transferred the knife to his left hand and pulled some unlabelled seasoning from the rack. He looked at the glass bottle as if to confirm it was exactly what we wanted. Its contents were the deep golden colour of a beach at sunset.

Beth swallowed, then forced herself to nod. 'It was me. Yes.'

His hand moved as if weighing the spice bottle. 'You're Beth Garway? You were, you were too young to face trial; that right? Should have been anonymous. I remember, now. Your picture... and, yes, your name, your name as well, got leaked to the press. It was... big news at the time. The TV, the papers. For... both for what happened and because of the breach of confidentiality. And the arguments, some supporting you, some not.'

'Most not.'

He turned back to the chicken breast, trapped in its container, catching her eye again as he did so. Now there wasn't just recognition, there was curiosity. She winced but there was no follow-up, leaving her exposed to a wave of surprise and a rush of relief: yes, he still held a knife in his left hand but there was no sign of fear. She felt a need to let something take her weight, to lean against the doorframe, but felt it would appear too nonchalant, inappropriate for her story.

She continued. 'We could only think someone in the police station knew or liked the Calbournes. They certainly didn't like me. The investigation didn't turn up anything or anyone. No one thought it would.'

Jake nodded, moved to the sink. Beth saw him look through the net curtain, out of the window as he washed his hands, craning his head left and right.

He looked to her as he dried his hands. 'Okay, what I don't understand... No, among the many things I don't understand, is what this brother... Callum... wants with you. And why now, after all these years, and who was that I saw earlier – who I assume is the git I should thank for the message on Mikey's car?'

In the bright, clean and well-ordered kitchen, the bruises under his eyes appeared even more livid, more shocking.

To think I'd been worried about his skin going a little bit pink, thought Beth. *And then I caused this to happen to him.*

'That was my brother.'

'Your *brother*? What—'

'He was watching. He didn't like the way Mickey,... what he thought he saw... Mikey's behaviour to me.'

'Christ, I don't know who's more dangerous.' He shook his head then looked straight at her; his raised eyebrows and knowing smile told her there was no malice. 'And you, you haven't killed anyone else recently, have you?'

Despite the conversation being the first of its type she had ever had, she couldn't supress a little laugh. 'Not recently.'

A cloud flickered over his face. She could only think he was remembering the way she had slapped Mikey.

'You're safe,' she added, trying to return his knowing smile.

'Thought so.' He indicated the single chicken breast. ''Fraid I wasn't expecting company tonight, but I'll try to get something for two out of this. That okay?'

'More than I deserve.'

He nodded, returned to the ingredients he'd placed on the work surface, picked up the knife, stabbed a hole in the film on top of the container, then slit it open. He let the lump of white meat flop onto the chopping board. 'So,' he said, picking up the breast and turning it in hands, 'tell me about this Callum. Who, and why now?'

As she watched him pull the knife along the edge of the meat – the way it sliced into the flesh the blade had to be razor sharp – she began to tell him about her memories of young Callum.

She could tell he was listening as he cut edgeways almost through the chicken breast, allowing him to open it up like a book. He placed it between two sheets of greaseproof paper and picked up the rolling pin, which he flipped through the air, catching it with ease. It was an automatic, unconscious, gesture; one he'd must have spent a lifetime doing. Beth was surprised once again at how comfortable and assured Jake looked when in his own kitchen.

'Sorry,' he interrupted her description of the polite, delicate boy that used to be Callum, 'this could be a bit loud.'

He began pounding the meat, taking care to get it an even flatness. The noise of each impact reverberated through the worksurface, through the kitchen and through the flat. Beth wondered if she'd have heard this if she were upstairs. Probably. But would she have recognised it for what it was, or would she have come down to investigate? More to the point, she still didn't know whether Jake had heard her and Mikey last night. She knew from Dashee's screams that there was little sound proofing in the ceilings of these flats. And she and Mikey had both been drunk and definitely uninhibited. Oh, God. Poor Jake.

She watched him judge the thickness of the flattened meat that now covered almost the entire surface of the chopping board. He said: 'Sorry, about the noise. Necessary for my version of a cordon bleu. Now, carry on.'

'What? Oh, yes.' She continued, explaining how Callum's life had gone off the rails; how first the departure of his father from his life and then the murder of his brother had turned Callum hateful and violent, especially – it appeared – towards women. Jake listened as he pulled some ham and gruyere from the fridge and placed a slice of each on the right-hand side of the flattened chicken. He folded the flesh over.

'Again,' he said when Beth had finished. 'I return to my question, of why now?'

Beth sucked her lips and shook her head. 'His mum's funeral's tomorrow. For all I know he was let out of prison on compassionate grounds to deal with the arrangements. I don't think there was anyone else in the family. Can't believe, after all these years, his father would come back for that.'

'Hmmm.' He began sprinkling the contents of the spice bottle onto a plate 'This is my own special recipe. Breadcrumbs and a selection of spices.' Beth could see him calculating. 'Yes, I reckon, by the time this is cooked, it'll feed two, with some mash, peas and carrots.'

Beth watched him brush the chicken with beaten egg, then roll it in the spices. 'This is very kind of you,' she said.

'Here,' he passed Beth a knife. It was the one she had used last night. 'Carrots are in the fridge, chop up a couple, will you?' For a fraction of a second he caught her eye, then returned to inspecting the chicken to ensure the coating was even. His back was to her.

She glanced down. If it were possible to hold a knife so tight it broke, she would have broken it. The kitchen seemed to spin around her. Her thoughts with it. It reminded her of being drunk.

When she looked up, steadying the image, his back was still towards her, although she couldn't help thinking it looked braced. She didn't know whether to hug him or tell him how mad he was.

'Bravery above and beyond the call of duty,' she said, swallowing. 'And you even know who I am now. What I've done.'

He turned to face her, leaning back on the work surface. 'You told me you hadn't killed anyone recently.'

'Well, no. I haven't. Just the one person, Owen. But one is too many.'

He raised his eyebrows. 'You were holding that knife last night. Could have had me then. You didn't. Could've stuck Mikey. You slapped him, sure. But I understand that now. I reckon... well, I hope... no, I figure... I'm safe enough. Besides, you know that if something happens to me, with your fingerprints everywhere, and with enough witnesses from last night, you'd definitely be a suspect. Your secret would be out.'

'But if I lose my temper, if I can't control myself?'

'Then don't lose it. The carrots are still in the fridge.'

She swallowed again, and turned to the fridge, feeling as though her movements were robotic.

'Here,' he said, putting the vegetable chopping board on the work surface beside her, along with a peeler. 'Is that what happened then?'

'What?'

'When... you know. Did you lose your temper?'

She pulled the bag of carrots from the fridge, removed a couple, put them on the chopping board and placed the knife beside them. The sound of the handle against the scored plastic sounded loud to Beth. She took another deep breath. 'Are we gonna do this now?'

'Not if you don't want to.' He turned back to the chicken.

'I don't know. It's all a bit confused. Yes,' she said. 'I....' deep breath, '...must have lost my temper. Everyone said so. He... I...' She looked at the window. Even with the net curtain, the light entering seemed too bright. It reminded her of what the police called 'the interviews', but what felt more like an interrogation. And then, when she had finally been allowed to go home, in borrowed clothes that were far, far too large, there had been another interrogation. Mum and Dad were trying to make the pieces of her story fit with the facts as they knew them. It must have been so hard for them, trying to understand. Like the police, they kept proposing different scenarios, so many that even now, Beth wasn't always sure she was remembering what really happened. Was she remembering what the police told her, what Mum and Dad asked her, or – maybe – she sometimes wondered, was she was just blocking the memory? One clear recollection though, was of Dad pulling Mum from the living room, before Mum lost her temper at Beth's inarticulate sobbing. Another sharp image was of Owen's blood on her hand. She could still see it. Sometimes she could still feel its heat, feel the plastic handle of the knife in her hand, punching her hand forwards in time with her screams, the look of utter surprise on Owen's face, his eyes somehow – in her memory – both wide and narrowed, his mouth a big O as he staggered backwards while she shoved the knife in further, harder, him slipping, falling, the cry, the splash.

'I stabbed him. I murdered him.' Beth used the words she had been encouraged to say in the sessions that followed. When she focused, Jake was looking at her.

'I thought,' he said, forehead creasing into lines, 'that he drowned. Have I got that wrong? Am I misremembering? It was a long time ago.'

Beth shook her head. 'No. He... After I... He fell in paddling pool, but after I stabbed... he wasn't getting out.' She couldn't seem to stop shaking her head. 'I was responsible. I stabbed him. I didn't pull him out. I let him... His... they said his wounds would have been enough.' Beth was aware she was sounding like a robot, emotionless.

'Okay,' Jake rubbed his chin, as if he had a beard. 'But why?'

'Why what?'

'Why'd you lose your temper? What happened? I seem to remember there were some folks who were on your side. Said he must have deserved it.'

'Does it matter? Probably something trivial. Why does anyone lose their temper? Why do married couples argue? Why does Dashee cry? It's always something trivial. We... our families, mine and his, were on holiday together again, on the Island – sorry, the Isle of Wight, we always call it the Island – and maybe he criticised my swimming costume or called me fat or something.'

'You were, like, nine years old. In fact, weren't there some folks who tried to defend you? Said he must have deserved it? Yes, I remember some of the papers really going for those folks. It was a much better story if you were the monster. I have to say, you don't look like a monster to me.'

'There are times it feels like it wasn't real.' Beth looked around the kitchen, as if the words she wanted could be found written on the clean, shiny tiles. 'You know how sometimes you have an image or something in your head, and it's from a movie you saw as a kid, or an old dream? It feels real but you're watching it, like, from the outside? Sometimes it feels like that. Other times I have a very clear memory of me...' she felt her hand making involuntary stabbing movements, '...of what happened. Now, Can we stop this?'

'But—'

Are you mad?

'Enough. Please.'

Looking down, she was amazed to see the knife was back in her hand. She didn't recall picking it up. For a second the contrast between her whitening knuckles and the black handle mesmerised her. Then, with an effort of will she felt was almost superhuman, she unclenched each finger and managed once again to place the knife on the chopping board. She even managed to withdraw her hand. It must look, she thought, like an addict going cold turkey and making one final effort to step away from their stash. The hyphens at the top of her legs began itching.

'Enough,' she repeated.

'Okay then,' Jake said, with a smile, as if nothing had happened. 'No probs. You go and set the table, I'll peel and cut the carrots and potatoes and get this lot going. You want to open a bottle of wine? White's in the fridge. Red's in the rack.'

It was only when he turned her back on her again to continue his preparations that Beth noticed, throughout the conversation, his hand had never been far from the rolling pin.

A good enough weapon.

Not completely mad then.

CHAPTER 20

Beth found Jake's version of cordon bleu to be excellent and just what she needed; the conversation less so.

She and Jake sat at adjoining edges of Jake's dining table. Its smooth surface showed it had been polished that day. There was no indication of the debris that had accumulated on it during last night's party. Their placemats matched the drinks coasters, the former showing a list of ingredients and steps to make a pasta dish, the latter showing an illustration of the meal. Beth's placemats had carbonara; Jake's a bolognaise. Both sets of mats looked new and Beth couldn't help but wonder whether someone had bought them as a moving-in present. On the mats sat their white plates, now cleaned of Jake's cooking. If it had been a restaurant Beth would have happily paid for the meal and added a big tip.

It was the thought of payment that drew her attention to the centre of the table. It worried her that Jake had placed a candle there. The evening light wasn't yet weak enough for him to attempt to light it, but it wouldn't be long. Some soft music played from Jake's phone. It was a film soundtrack Beth recognised but couldn't name. She didn't want this to be a romantic evening. She was dreading any attempt to ask her to bed.

'More wine?' Jake held up the bottle.

Oh, God yes.

Beth placed her hand over her glass. 'No, better not.' It was her second glass of merlot and only a few sips remained.

'Really?' Jake shrugged, unsmiling. 'Okay. I just thought after the day you've had...' He filled his own glass. Beth watched him take a gulp. Sometime after his third glass he had stopped wincing from his black eyes.

It wasn't the day she'd had that was bothering her – for that she deserved the numbness of alcohol – but the night that was still to come. The bedroom arrangements. She'd slept with this man's mate last night, imposed herself on his goodwill today and had asked to stay the night, yet – for some reason she wasn't keen on investigating – she didn't want him to think she was easy. Ironic, she knew, considering how she'd left last night. More than that, and this surprised her, she wanted his respect. It was important to her. With the exception of her brother, a desire for male respect was not something she'd often experienced before. She not only cared about Jake's opinion, but she also wanted him to like her, despite her past.

'I bet,' she said, her face set in an expression of sadness, 'you wish you'd never met me now.' She raised her eyebrows. 'You wouldn't be the first.'

He blinked several times, as if concentrating on an intractable problem, then shook his head. 'Why?'

'Well...' she indicated his eyes. 'Sorry.'

He put his glass down. 'First of all, it wasn't you that hit me. Punched me... I think he punched me.' He frowned, which emphasised the discoloured swellings. 'It could have been a head-butt, thinking about it. You know, I can't really remember. How strange is that?' He focused on Beth again. 'Second, it doesn't matter. Like, we are where we are. We have to start from here. We can't go back and change things. Let's move on. In ways that we can.'

Beth remembered the conversation they'd had, when he'd

given her a lift in what turned out to be Mikey's car. She still didn't understand how someone could ignore the pertinence of the past on their place in the present.

Jake went to speak again, then stopped, took a gulp from his glass. A pained expression flashed across his face. Beth thought he winced as he swallowed. He looked into his glass, as if trying to see what was leaving a bad taste in his mouth.

It was a moment before he looked up and it was as if a mask had fallen away, leaving behind a wounded expression. 'There is one thing though,' he spoke as if unwilling to form the words. 'Something I'm finding hard to put behind me.' He had trouble swallowing, yet Beth knew his mouth couldn't be dry. She waited, because she had no choice.

'You lied to me,' he said.

'But...' For a second Beth was speechless. Did he not understand? 'Can you blame me?' she spoke before her thoughts were in order. 'You know my story now.'

'But... I trusted you. I don't even know what to call you?'

Beth found she couldn't blame him for looking hurt and offended, as though he'd just been told that his cooking stank and that he was ugly and shouldn't be allowed in a kitchen. Just about everything Beth had told him had been lies. And here she was begging a favour, to stay in his flat, for safety, for at least a night. With no reward.

'Beth. Only my mum calls me Bethany.' She supressed a shiver and attempted a smile.

'But what do you want *me* to call you? Do I have to keep calling you Liz, especially if someone else is around? That's gonna feel odd. Too odd. I'm not a good actor, so I'm not sure I can pull that off. I'm not sure I can do that.'

'My brother calls me "Pudge". And he's the only one who does. You could try that.'

'Pudge?' He tried the word as if it were new flavour, and she saw his eyes flicker to her legs and back. 'Pudge? That sounds a bit, I don't know, insulting.'

'On account of my pudgy cheeks when I was a baby.'

'Not sure I can call you that either.' He spoke with a seriousness Beth wasn't expecting.

'Beth then. Or Liz. Whatever you want. Look, I know I've been a lying cow, but surely you can see why?'

He began chewing his lip. Only stopping to pour, then swallow, some more wine. Beth didn't think he tasted it, or that it even touched the sides. Then he resumed his lip bothering.

When it became clear he wasn't about to answer, Beth tried another tack, immediately hating herself and wishing she hadn't resorted to her underhand tactic. 'Besides,' she said, 'I'm asking for your help, pleading if necessary. I can't stay in my flat tonight, not if Callum suspects where I live. I need someone to...' She tailed off, the unsaid words 'look after me' hung in the air. She knew that appealing to him to act like a hero wouldn't fail, and she added it to her mounting pile of self-loathing.

He stopped chewing his lip and looked at her with a suddenness she found surprising. 'Did you tell Mikey who you are? You know, last night, when...' He looked away.

'No.' She shook her head even though he wasn't looking at her. 'No. In fact...' the truth of what she was saying hit her hard enough to rock her in her chair, '...you are the only person I've ever confided in. The first, believe it or not. No one else.' Her heart was thumping so hard she was certain even Shreeya, two floors up, could hear it.

Despite her sudden realisation, which left Beth with wide eyes and open mouth, the import of what she had just told him didn't seem to register with Jake. 'Good,' he said, 'If Mikey thought there was money to be made or... well, let's not find out shall we? I don't think he's good with secrets.'

For a moment Beth wanted to reach out and shake him. *Did you not hear? You are the only one I've ever told about my past. The only one!*

To hide her turmoil Beth reached for her almost-empty glass; at the same time he leaned forward and took his. She knew she was using her movement as a distraction, an excuse to give her time to order her thoughts. Jake, she assumed, was doing the same.

She still couldn't believe his reaction – or his lack of reaction. She had always wondered, never believing she would ever find out, what would happen if she revealed her secrets. Her imagination had supplied scenarios ranging from explosions of disgust, coupled with orders to leave, to words of reassurance and protective hugs. She hadn't anticipated indifference. Likewise, her own emotions were not what she expected; she figured there would be a rush of either fear or relief. Instead, it was like waiting for exam results.

She watched him swallow another large gulp of wine. She'd seen guys fill themselves with drink, confusing reduced inhibitions with courage. It never ended well. Her experience in such matters was, of course, limited – limited to those men who would have their fun and (she hoped) forget her. She didn't think that was Jake, but was well aware that you could never tell. Sometimes it's the quiet ones you need to watch out for. Case in point: Callum Calbourne used to be a quiet one. She felt she could trust Jake. But then, if it really was a matter of trust, she'd already proven herself to be the liar, the untrustworthy one. How could he rely on anything she said anymore?

She watched him empty his glass in one gulp: a man drinking as if wanting to ask something yet fearful of the response. It made her desire more alcohol while knowing it wouldn't help. She wondered how she would cope with what was coming, and how he would deal with rejection of his drunken advances.

Jake's bruised eyes were focused on somewhere that wasn't this room as he again refilled his glass and knocked back yet another slug. Beth hoped he was processing everything she'd told him, but eventually she could take the silence no longer.

'So,' she said, hoping she sounded perky, 'you know my secrets now. What about you? What brought you here?' For both their sakes she wanted to slow his alcohol intake; it was the only neutral question she could think of.

She watched him try to focus on her, his eyes now mere slits. Beth thought there was sadness behind his tentative smile, but that could have been the wine.

'I'm the one that got away,' he said, but sounded neither triumphant nor proud. 'My family comes from Derby. Even though Mum and Dad have split up they still live within ten miles of each other. In fact, my grandparents, parents, my brother and my sister, still live around there. I must be, like, the black sheep of the family.'

'I can relate to that,' Beth nodded and went to run her hand through her hair, stopping herself at the last moment. Such gestures can be misread.

If Jake noticed he didn't react. 'Well,' he continued, 'not so much the black sheep, more the pale one.'

'Pale sheep?'

'They're all very outdoorsy. Love hiking, climbing, cycling, swimming. When I was young, before Mum and Dad split, their idea of a good family holiday was to go camping in the rain half-way up a mountain. I hated it.' He let out a humourless laugh and looked into his glass. 'A hardy lot. They've always got scrapes and grazes from coming off their bikes or sliding down some mountain slope. Didn't save the marriage though.' He looked up at her, his eyebrows raised. 'And then there's me. You can always tell when you're not your parent's favourite child.'

Beth's laugh was devoid of humour. 'Tell me about it.'

'There's a saying that, however hard parents try to be fair, their kids know which of them is the favourite. And if you don't know... it's you.'

Beth thought of Ryan, and nodded. 'As I say, I can relate to that.'

Jake didn't seem to register her understanding or agreement. 'You know, I'm the only one of the family not to have broken a bone, an arm or a leg or something. Not even sprained an ankle. I don't even know if that's a good thing or a bad thing. Sometimes...' He shrugged. 'It looks like it hurts. So I try to avoid... I'm happiest indoors, you know, reading or experimenting with my cooking. They'd laugh at these.' He indicated the livid crescents beneath his eyes. 'I'm such a disappointment.'

Beth spoke before she could stop herself. 'No. And I think you're a good cook. I...' She mentally kicked herself again. She didn't want anything to be misconstrued as flirting. She wanted to stay in his flat tonight, not his bed.

A vague nod of acceptance showed he heard the compliment, but it was obvious his mind was still elsewhere.

Eventually he looked at her, 'What do you reckon,' he raised his eyebrows, but his eyes remained slits above puffy purple flesh, 'can I go into work tomorrow?' He gave another humourless snort. 'I was hoping I'd make an impact with my party, but not like this. Mikey will, I'm certain, have already boasted about what he's done, to me, to everything.' He made an expansive gesture. Beth was glad his glass was empty, but she knew what he meant. There was a dent in the wall from Mikey's fist. It would take major plastering and painting to hide it. And, when she'd arrived this evening, Beth couldn't help but glance at the bloodstains on the hall carpet from Jake's earlier bloody nose. Although he had tried to clean them, they were still visible. She knew all too well that the consequences of violence cannot be scrubbed away so easily.

Jake continued. 'And Mikey will have told everyone why, and they'll all think I deserve what I got. They'll all believe what he says I did to his car.' The breath he took shuddered through him. 'Dare I show,' he twirled a finger at himself before dropping his hand back to the table, 'this face?'

Beth wanted to reach out and squeeze his hand, to tell him everything would be all right. And she wanted him to do the same to her, but she also didn't want to do anything that could be misunderstood. It felt like she was standing on a cliff edge looking at the drop below and feeling an urge to jump. A compulsion she was not only resisting, but also resisting investigating. In fact, she didn't even want to question the reason behind the resistance.

'I think...' she began, meaning to be reassuring about his bruised face, before realising almost anything she said could be misinterpreted as flirting. Was that why he had asked it? Was she over-thinking things? How did normal people cope?

'... er...I don't think I've any make-up to cover those bruises, but you'll be...' She froze. A sound, a clunk. The front door to the flats. Fear took her ability to move.

'I'll check,' Jake said, stood and almost ran to his front door, which she heard unlatch.

Beth wanted to scream at him to stop but, as in a night-terror, was unable to speak. Half a second later she heard the door close, and she held her breath until Jake returned.

'It's all right,' he said. 'Mr Lottan, Mr Grumpy you called him, returning from somewhere. Looks like he's been to a pub.'

Beth took some deep breaths, trying to slow her speeding heart rate. She stared at her hands as they moved from rigid to trembling to under control. 'I've only just about got used to the noises I can hear in my flat. I'd forgotten we're on the ground floor.' She took a breath so deep it turned into a sigh. 'Sorry,' she whispered. She'd never thought of herself as brave, but at that moment, when it mattered, it wasn't a case of fight or flight. She'd simply frozen.

'You can relax. No need to worry. You're safe with me.' He suppressed another yawn in – thought Beth – a very theatrical manner. 'Now,' he leaned back putting his hands behind his head, 'about tonight's sleeping arrangements.'

CHAPTER 21

Outside, the streetlight switched off. Dark. Eerie.

Midnight. It's only Midnight.

Beth couldn't stop herself huffing with frustration, then feeling angry with herself for the noise she'd made.

Compared with the curtains in her own flat, which were thick and double-layered, Jake's were no more thin cotton; the illumination from the streetlight had been able to creep into the living room almost undimmed. Hence, to Beth, lying on her side on the sofa, facing the window, the sudden and silent switch off was obvious. It also confirmed just how painfully protracted was each night-time second.

Forced to save money, Leamington council had been reduced to switching off streetlights in certain areas at midnight during the week, and at one-thirty Fridays and Saturdays. Anger flashed through Beth at the thought of those being forced to walk home in darkness, at the choice forced on the council: cost savings versus women's safety. Her fists clenched tighter.

Might as well have a curfew for women.

She'd read of a fatal accident, a pedestrian hit by a car, where the police and ambulance crew had spent over an hour searching, in the dark, through the undergrowth beside the road for the body. Thoughts of this tragedy joined all the other fears swirling inside her skull.

She turned from lying on her side to her back. It made no difference. It didn't matter how tired she was, there was just too much going on in her head. Images collided with ideas which collided with phrases which created new thoughts, new associations, all spinning off in new directions and colliding again, forming new images, ideas, phrases, ad nauseam. She wondered why, as with a bad cold, things were always worse at night. And that became yet another question dropped into the maelstrom in her mind. It was as if, without light, the air around her were being filled by her doubts and fears; all her worries expanding to fill the dark empty space.

It's going to be a long night.

This was the sofa where Sue had almost recognised her, had wondered where she'd seen Beth's image before. She squeezed her eyes shut, and Callum's face appeared. She knew it was him even though she had no idea of what he looked like these days. It was some monstrous morphing of her memories and the online pictures she'd found. In her teeming head, the words that accompanied those pictures – ABH, violence, pain, prison – circled his face, creating their own associations, each creating new worries and fears. And then Jake appeared in her mixed-up thoughts. Considering the short time she'd known him, he was filling more than his fair share of space in her overwrought mind. She knew she shouldn't be constantly investigating his words and actions but, like an addict, was unable to stop.

He had offered her his bed, and claimed he was happy to take the sofa. He had explained that thanks to his late-finishing party, his inability to sleep last night (was that her fault? she wondered), his early morning spent cleaning, along with the excitements of today, he was exhausted and reckoned he could sleep anywhere. So, the sofa would be fine. She had told him, in no uncertain terms, that that just wasn't going to happen. She would take the sofa. He deserved both his own bed and a good night's sleep. It hadn't been an argument as such, but it did remind Beth of her mum and dad. And of course, she'd won.

Jake had tried to hide his yawns while clearing up of the plates, but one final jaw-breaker had made him admit defeat. She had made him lock the front door and watched while he turned the key. He didn't have a chain on the door like she did, but she thought it prudent not to comment on it. He was doing his best, but men just didn't need to think of security. He had taken a pillow and blanket from his airing cupboard and passed them to her. As her arms had encircled them, he had said 'goodnight' and given her a look she just couldn't fathom. It had been an attempt at a smile, but it was clear there was something else behind it. It felt like she'd spent days trying to decide whether there was malicious desire, sadness, regret, loneliness or something else lurking there. Her mind expanded then focused upon what she may have seen, and then twisted and distorted it until she was no longer sure of anything except that she wasn't asleep. Now the streetlight outside had switched off, and the gloom around her instantly thickened, she realised it wasn't yet an hour since she'd first lain on the sofa. It felt like half the night.

She let out another soft sigh and turned again onto her side, her spine pressed against the padded back of the sofa. She pictured herself, aware that across the hall was Jake's bedroom. Her gaze passed across granular gloom, noting that, even without streetlights, in a conurbation such as Leamington, the nights were never pitch black. Dangerously dark, but never so dark you couldn't see anything. And tonight, there were few clouds to absorb or soften the harsh moonlight. Another few days, she thought, and it would be a full moon. Silvery-white shapes lay, sharp-edged, on the floor beneath the curtains. A car passed and Beth watched its headlights move shadows across the room.

Her brain tried to counter her inability to read Jake's tired, inebriated, stressed mind. Try as she might, she couldn't hear him. A snore or snort echoing through the flat would have been a relief. As it was, she could hear nothing through the wall. Was he awake? Thinking of her? For all she knew he was lying in bed, contemplating the idea of her, possibly naked, in the next room. She wondered if he also had his eyes open, frustrated at finding the blessed comfort of sleep impossible. New doubts and fears took root and flourished. Was he waiting until he was sure she was no longer awake? Would she hear the creak of his bed as he rose? Was it really the quiet ones you had to watch out for? She shook her head.

To give herself a sense of security she hadn't removed her clothes, just unbuttoned her shorts, untucked her blouse, and loosened everything before plumping the seat cushions. It wasn't down to discomfort that sleep refused to find her.

After another hour or so, which felt like an entire night, she rolled onto her back and tried to focus on the ceiling, hoping its invisibility in the darkness would calm her mind. Her empty flat sat above her. She began to go through a list of things to do tomorrow. Find a map of the country, choose somewhere else to live, look for flats there. Talk to Mr Grumpy, her landlord. Dare she go back to her own flat in the daylight? Maybe with both Mikey and Jake as guards. And yes, there was Mikey; she'd have to do something about his car before she disappeared. She couldn't very well...

What was that?

A noise, the slightest of clicks outside Jake's front door. Had she imagined it? She hadn't heard the lock on either the front door or the door to the car park. She knew from Mr Grumpy's arrival earlier that she would have, especially in this silence. Although her eyes were open, all her concentration was focused

217

on what she could hear.

There it was again.

A soft click, metallic. A pause and then again, this time it wasn't so much a click as an extended susurrate of metal on metal.

Oh God, someone's breaking in.

CHAPTER 22

Beth knew she wasn't brave. After all, she'd spent almost all her life running away. She'd never even had the courage to visit Jackie to see how she was coping with her burns. She had always hoped, however, that when the time came, she'd prove herself capable and proactive.

Lying in the dark now, hearing the almost imperceptible swish of the bottom of Jake's front door brushing the doormat, she discovered the dreadful truth. Sub-zero terror forced itself into her throat, cutting off her breath. Even if she'd wanted to call out, she couldn't. She had been dropped into icy water. Her muscles froze. Only her heart managed to keep working; it had plummeted, sickeningly, but somehow still thumped in her ears. Far too loud. It was as if it were trying to call for help, to escape her numb body. She wanted to sink silently into the sofa and disappear.

Above the pounding in her head she heard the door shutting. It seemed to take an age. Someone was taking great care.

She thought she heard soft footfalls, but wasn't sure. It could just have been her imagination. Then came another elongated shush, this time Jake's bedroom door over a carpet.

Then silence.

Her muscles didn't work, refusing to take any message from her brain. All she could do was listen. And imagine.

'Oi!'

Beth jumped at the sudden shout, and just managed to swallow her gasp. Callum. It was Callum. Just from the single syllable, she knew. She hadn't heard him in fourteen years, but she knew.

'Oi!' again, and a fraction of a second later a light was switched on. It only illuminated the transom window above the lounge door, but it made Beth blink and blink until tears rolled down her ice-cold cheeks.

'Shit. What ...?' Jake. Confused.

She didn't know whether it was Jake and Callum who had turned on the bedside lamp. It didn't matter.

'I don't think, you little prick, you told me the truth earlier.' Callum's tone was flat, controlled. 'No, don't move.' He wasn't bothering to whisper. He knew had no need.

A muffled creak. Beth guessed Callum had sat on the bed.

'Who...? How'd the fuck you get in? Get out of my... ow.'

'I told you not to move.'

'You're...'

'She told you who I am then? And where I've been? You can learn a lot in fucking prison. More practical skills than any sodding university. There's stuff I know now. Lock picking, for instance. And my speciality: how to hurt without leaving any fucking marks.'

'Ow..., Jesus fuck.'

'See? Seems to me though, someone's already left their mark on you. Pretty crude though.'

'Ow, Christ...'

'What was it, a head butt? Yeah, pretty crude. Believe me, I can do worse. A *lot* fucking worse. Oh, what I've seen done. You're lucky, at least this blade is sharp.'

'Ungh.'

'See? Sharp. Now... Fuck's sake, stop moving. That's better.'

'...scars.'

'Yeah well, maybe today leaving marks ain't so important. After all, really, what do I care? Now, tell me where the fuck she is. Tell me and you'll never see me again.'

In the silence that followed, Beth became aware she was getting light-headed, ready to faint. She thought it was the tension, then realised she had no idea when she last inhaled. She tried to breathe. Her breathing was rapid and shallow, as if she were hyperventilating. A fraction of her concentration went on slowing her breaths and keeping them silent, the rest on straining to hear. Terror welded her to the sofa.

'Last warning...'

'All right, all right.' Jake's voice was louder than it needed to be. Beth's pounding heart gave a double beat at she realised he wanted her to hear his words, to warn her. 'What... what are you going to do to her?'

'Fuck's sake, you think you're going to protect her? You?'

'What're going to do?'

'She killed my bother. You know that? You know who she is? What she is?'

'Killing her won't bring him back.'

Beth shut her eyes; more tears squeezed out.

'It'd be fucking fair though.'

'No... Not fair.'

There was a snort that could have been a laugh. 'I know stuff now. Stuff I didn't know before. How much I hurt her depends on how she answers a few simple fucking questions.'

Jake's voice grew louder still. 'What questions?'

Careful, pleaded Beth in her head. *Don't make it obvious you're talking to me. Don't make him come looking.*

'Just tell me which flat is hers.'

'What—'

'I've a need to have a word with her fucking brother as well, all right?'

In the pause that followed, which Beth figured was Jake deciding whether to mention that her brother had been here, she finally begin to control her terror. She found she could move, even though she didn't sit up; she started to think about protecting herself. She had a rape alarm in her handbag. Could she get that without attracting attention? She didn't believe she could get to the kitchen where knives were available. Certainly not silently.

'Ow, Jeez.'

'Which fucking flat? Not asking again.'

Beth went through the same thoughts she reckoned were passing through Jake's mind. He couldn't send Callum up to Shreeya's. Or to Mr Lottan's, or to the two families above Lottan. There was only one flat he knew for certain was empty.

'Directly upstairs. Number Four'

'There. That didn't hurt, did it?'

'Fuck, yes.'

'If you're lying, I *will* come back. You know I can get in now. Into your flat. Into your fucking life. You can never lock me out. Not fucking ever. You call the fucking police? Trust me, not only will I be gone by the time the bastards arrive, but then I'm *really* gonna come for you. Fuck you up. You understand?'

'Ow. Yes, yes, I understand.'

'Now, stay there. Safe in bed.'

Beth heard movement, then a long, long pause, then the front door opening and shutting.

CHAPTER 23

It was like a sudden spring thaw: Beth's energy flooded back. She could move, finally she could move. And she needed to move fast.

Ignoring the light-headedness from holding her breath, she rolled off the sofa and leapt to her feet. Too quick. A wave of dizziness washed through her, almost sweeping her off her feet. She grabbed the arm of the sofa for support. Bright flashes burst before her eyes as though she were under fire. There was no time to compose herself though; she was out of the room and into Jake's bedroom before she was confident of her balance or had even tucked in her blouse.

'Get up.' It may have been whispered but it was an order. 'Now.'

In the light from his bedside lamp, Jake appeared corpse pale. His suntan had vanished and the purple crescents under his sunken wide eyes accentuated his death's-head appearance. He hadn't even had the strength to wipe away the trickle of blood that was drying, tear-like, on his cheek. Its origin a pinprick under his left eye, as if someone had tried to pop the bruise.

'Come on. Before he returns.' She said it louder than intended and went to clap her hands: a sudden noise might shock Jake into movement. At the last moment she changed her mind, incensed by her own stupidity. She had always wondered whether, in an emergency – and if nothing else – she'd survive by losing her temper. That her unrestrained violent self would be her saviour. The discovery that, when it became necessary, she was cowardly – unable to fight or even stand her ground – shocked, shamed and hurt her. Furious with herself now, she grabbed a fistful of Jake's duvet and flung the whole thing aside. He lay there, arms by his side, naked apart from a pair of shorts, odd-looking boxers whose thick cotton had bunched in his groin.

She hissed through clenched teeth. 'Let's go.'

He blinked, as though just coming round from anaesthetic. 'But...'

'Now.' She kept her voice as low as possible and she looked about, saw a pile of clothes on the floor. She grabbed them and threw everything at him. 'We're leaving. Now. Get your phone, anything else you need, and *come on.* You can dress on the way.'

'But...'

She turned and ran. She knew to the centimetre where her fleebag was. All that was missing was her washbag, still in Jake's bathroom. She'd have to live without that. She reckoned they had a few minutes, but not many. Callum had to get upstairs. He wouldn't run, being in no hurry and not wanting to make a noise, but he wouldn't dawdle either. He had to pick a lock and, as he had just done, enter slow and quiet. And it wouldn't take him long to realise she wasn't at home – she thought she'd left the curtains open, that would give him a clue – but she figured he would still have to check every room. She and Jake had to be out of here, out of the entire building, out of sight, before he came back downstairs.

She met Jake by the front door; she was carrying her fleebag, he was holding his jeans, T-shirt and pair of trainers, and struggling to keep his balance as he pulled on a sock one-handed. He looked ridiculous, one pale leg cut short by a dark sock, the other in mid-air as he dragged the sock up its thin shin. He raised himself, breathless after the exertion, saw her and tugged at the top of his baggy shorts, clearly nervous in case they slipped down. Beth noticed that they weren't boxers; probably part of a pyjama set.

'Ready?' she whispered.

He shifted the weight of his clothing, and again pulled at the loose waistband of his shorts. 'Do I look ready?'

'Good enough.'

'But—'

Beth opened the door as quietly as possible and stepped out into the ground floor of the stairwell. The lights were on a timer, but Callum hadn't bothered to hit the button to switch them on. It was dark, but Beth had lived here long enough to picture her surroundings: the stairs up to her flat to her right; Mr Lottan's door opposite. To her left was the door out to the main road, and between the stairs and Mr Lottan's door, the route to the exit that led to the car park. She froze, straining to listen so hard she was surprised it didn't hurt. She thought she could hear noises from above, from her flat, but it might just have been her imagination. She wondered what he would do once he found the flat empty. Would he wreck it?

Please don't let him do anything to Pickle and Rascal...

She shook the thought away. As far away as she could get it. 'Right,' she said, 'come on.'

She stepped to her left, to the glass-panelled front door. Behind her, Jake used his key to shut his front door, keeping as quiet as possible. It seemed to take an age.

Come on. Why are you locking it?

Impatient, she waited for him to join her before twisting the knob on the front door's Yale lock. It made a soft click, loud in the dark silence, and for a second they both froze. Yet again Beth strained to hear something – anything – other than her heart pounding, her blood pulsing in her ears. Taking a deep breath, she pulled open the door. She'd never noticed before that it squeaked. They both slipped through and before the heavy spring pulled the door shut, Jake put his hand on the glass. She was aware of him shaking his head. In the moonlight, she saw the faint glint of the keys he still held. Beth winced at another sharp sting of self-directed anger. She would have let the heavy spring do its job and shut the door, accompanied by a loud *clunk* from the electronic lock. She watched, impatience and anger both growing as Jake struggled to find the right key. She fought the urge to rip the bunch of keys out of his hands and do it herself.

'Come on, Jake. Come on.'

'I'm trying. Got it. Here. This one.'

He gripped the key the way a drowning man would an offered hand. He held it up, the moonlight betraying how much his hand was trembling. That's when they heard it: the echo of a door being slammed one floor up. There was no subtlety about it. Callum was angry. And he was returning.

The key missed the slot. 'Shit.' His shaking worsened and he missed the slot again.

Beth yanked the key from him, surprised at the weakness of his grip.

'Run,' she whispered in his ear, as loud as she dare. 'Behind the library.'

Jake didn't need telling twice.

Taking the deepest breath she'd taken in what felt like days, Beth held it for a fraction of a second, and slid the key into the lock. Through the textured glass panels in the door she could make out the various shades of darkness that comprised the stairwell. She twisted her hand, using the key to draw back the bolt, and pulled the door shut, using all her willpower not to slam it and run. She released the lock as slow and as quiet as she dared.

The moment it clicked – soft, but still louder than she was

expecting, louder than she hoped – her world burst into light. She almost cried out as she blinked and blinked trying to reclaim her vision. Callum had hit the timer on the stairwell lights. He was no longer being cautious. Now he didn't care.

Through her blurred vision she saw a movement. Callum's feet on the stairs. The uneven glass made the descending figure appear distorted and monstrous. She pulled the key from the lock and threw herself to the side, out of sight of the man descending the stairs.

The rucksack on her back scraped the wall and she held her breath again. She tried to squeeze away the after-burn in her vision from the explosion of light. She was sure she'd moved before Callum's face had come into view. He couldn't have seen her. He couldn't.

She turned and tried to look down the road, her eyes watering, smearing the view. It wasn't as dark as she expected. Movement at the crossroads: Jake. Great, the only streetlights the council paid to use throughout the night were those at major junctions, like the crossroads where Jake was now clearly in view. He was almost at the library. Considering he was only wearing socks, he'd done well. She wondered about his feet, whether they would be as bruised or as bloody as his eyes. Better that than whatever Callum would do to him.

A shout and a thump from inside the flats, a heavy fist against wood. Callum must be back at Jake's door.

She ran. And as she did she realised why it was not as dark as she'd expected: Callum had switched all the lights on in her own flat. With her curtains open, it was her living room and kitchen lights that were illuminating her, threatening to reveal her escape.

Immediately, she realised a problem: running was harder than expected. With no sports bra and the rucksack flinging itself about on her back, she felt like she was lurching through a dream, horrifically slow and ungainly. So much for her fleebag. The library felt like it was receding, it was...

The night suddenly lightened even more. Callum must have switched on Jake's lights. She tried to increase her speed, but the movement of her rucksack kept threatening her balance, knocking the breath out of her with every pace. She had to get away. Her panic increased a notch with each step. Callum was going to appear at the main entrance, she just knew it. He was going to see her. Would overtake her with ease. She was sure she could feel his eyes on her, like lasers burning into her back. She tried to accelerate. Her lungs and legs began to shriek.

Then she was pounding up the steps, then the slope to the library. Just before she was under the portico she turned right, following the path around the building, To her left were the windows into the children's library area, to her right a hedge that only came up to her knees. Useless, no concealment there. Anyway, the sound of her laboured painful breaths would be enough to alert Callum. At the corner of the building she turned left, waning to cry out in angry frustration that she couldn't keep up her speed. Not only had she discovered she wasn't as brave as she'd hoped, she wasn't as fit either. She didn't want to think what other revelations this night could bring. Feeling every step, as if her legs had been wrapped with lead weights, she stumbled the width of the building, each breath knocked out of her by her fleebag. She turned left again, halted with gratitude and leant with her hands pressed against her knee-length shorts, scarred thighs beneath, as she fought for breath. When she looked up, she could see Jake in the gloom. She grinned like a lunatic, barely believing they had made it, they were now out of sight of the flats. There was no way Callum could know where they were: a hidden courtyard, edged by the children's library to the left, the door to the staff rooms ahead, to the right were trees, shrubs and the side wall of the Lillington Community centre. Behind her, more shrubs and trees, easily taller she was, separated her from a grassy bank which led down to the road. Apart from the path she had followed, there was one other, which wound through the thick foliage. This was how the library staff arrived, she realised. It occurred to her that even in this hidden area it wasn't as dark she she'd expected. A glance behind told her why: through the branches and leaves came light across the crossroads, and from the Fourways care home. A single sodium bulb cast its yellow light over the home's car park and a vertical line of windows revealed a well-lit staircase. One room had its curtains open and a light on. Beth hoped the resident was all right.

She turned back to Jake. He had his back to her, his shirt and shoes lay on the ground beside him, and he was trying to pull his jeans up over his pyjama shorts. His balance appeared to be all over the place and, in the shadows, he looked all gawky arms and legs. She thought he was lucky to remain on his feet, and wondered what a stranger would have made of the sight. Bubbles of hysteria began to expand inside her.

Before she could stop them, giggles burst from her lips. She clamped her hand across her mouth.

'Wha...' Jake wobbled, putting his hand out for support that wasn't there. Beth stepped forward, grabbed his hand, holding him up. He wasn't expecting it, and jumped. She felt further laughter bubbling inside, a release.

'Jeez,' he said, trying to regain some manly composure. Failing. His pyjama shorts bunched, preventing him from pulling up his trousers. 'Scared the life out of me.' He put one hand on his chest as if to feel his breathing. 'And don't laugh at me.'

'Sorry. It just occurred to me,' she whispered. 'What's wrong with this picture? If this was a film it would be a woman running about in her underwear. It always is.'

'Thanks. Shit, you're as bad as Mikey.' He finally tucked himself in and pulled his belt tight, harder – Beth thought – than was necessary.

'Sorry,' she said again, trying not to laugh. She didn't want to upset him, he'd been through enough, but the sight of him now... Another giggle escaped. 'I didn't mean anything,' she said and swallowed. She tried to focus on something serious. 'Are your feet all right?' Her thoughts were all over the place, unable to settle. She needed to focus. He should be as jubilant at their escape as she was.

'I think I found every sharp stone.' He picked up his shirt, thrust his arms into it and began furiously buttoning.

Beth bit her lip. The thought that in his anger he might rip open his shirt, tearing off the buttons, suddenly seemed amusing. She felt as though she were drunk; she didn't dare open her mouth to speak.

'You think that's funny?' Jake spoke too loudly, but she couldn't bring herself to hush him. He misinterpreted her silence. 'I don't even know what I'm doing here,' he said. 'Or what just happened.'

Beth stared at his face, squinting, trying to concentrate. She knew from his tone he was angry, but in the gloom, and with his bruises, she could only see deep shadows instead of his eyes. She couldn't judge the level of his rage.

The thin trail of dried blood, like a scar, still marked his left cheek.

She stepped towards him, swallowed again. 'Sorry,' she repeated, this time hoping it sounded more genuine. She pulled a tissue from her pocket, licked it, took another step forward and began wiping at his cheek. He'd feel better without his own blood on his face.

To her surprise he jumped back, vehemence in his voice

'What the... What the fuck are you doing?'

'Just trying to—'

'Don't. Just don't. I'm okay.' He wiped the back of his hand across his cheek, smearing the trail where Beth had wetted it. He held his hand up, close to his eyes and stared at it.

'Yeah. And this was my fault as well,' he muttered. Beth leant forward to hear. He looked at her. 'I moved, jerked, when he put the... the... knife on me. I shouldn't have moved. I shouldn't. Jeez, everything's my fault.' He ran his fingertips down his cheek, as if feeling for a message in the drying blood, then followed the line again, then again.

Beth spoke, scared his repetitive movements would become somehow unstoppable. 'Jake. Come on, we've got to move. To get away.' The courtyard no longer felt as safe as when she arrived. The dark walls were beginning to loom over them, feeling less protective and more like a trap.

Jake's hand stopped moving, and she saw his forehead crease as though he was squinting at her. 'Where? Where can we...? No.' He shook his head. 'No, please. Don't ask me to do that.'

'Have you any better ideas?'

'The police.'

'No police. You know why.'

'But—'

'Remember what they did to me last time.'

'A hotel, then? What about a hotel?'

'At this time?' She glanced at her watch. 'It's well after two. Would you let us in? Besides, how many nearby hotels are there? With your...' she indicated his bruised eyes and bloodied cheek, '...you're not exactly unnoticeable. It wouldn't take Callum long to phone up local hotels and track us down. Plus there's the cost.'

'Yeah. But Mikey?'

'I thought he was a friend of yours.'

231

His fingertips found the swelling under one eye. 'So did I.'

'Anybody else from work?'

'Don't know their phone numbers.'

'You've just had a party, you don't know their numbers?'

'I asked them at work.'

'It's got to be Mikey, then.'

'Please, no.'

'What choice do we have?'

'But not Mikey. No. He already thinks I'm... he's got no respect for me.' He shook his head with increasing intensity. 'What's he gonna think? He's gonna say I can't look after myself, let alone you?'

Beth stared at him. *Who said you were supposed to be looking after me?*

'No. Not Mikey. I...'

'What?'

He stopped shaking his head and looked away, mumbling something.

'What?'

He looked back, face hard, stiff jaw moving as if trying to speak.

'What?'

'I'm afraid you'll sleep with him again. All right?'

'Oh, for...' She had a sudden desire to shake him, to give him a slap, to knock such thoughts from him. How could he be so stupid?

She placed her hands on his shoulders, this time he didn't flinch, and her palms felt his warmth. It was as if something passed between them, some reassurance.

Did he feel it?

She couldn't give him a shake. He'd been through enough, and had the cuts and bruises to prove it. He stopped moving his head, looked at her and put his hands on top hers. It was difficult to see his face in the gloom, but she thought he looked confused, torn.

'Where does he live?' she asked with gentleness.

'Please don't ask me to do this?'

'What choice do we have? Can we walk? Is it close? Get an Uber?'

'He lives not far from the Tesco superstore. Where he picked up the beer yesterday. Two maybe three miles away.'

'Ring him. Tell him we're on our way.'

His head started moving from side to side again. 'No, please. I just can't.'

'Who else? Your Dad? Your family? Mine's too far away.'

'My...? No. No.'

She felt his hands grip hers. She said nothing. Let him work it out. Who would be best in this situation? Him or Mikey?

She pulled her hands from his shoulders, rougher than she intended, angry with herself at making such an unfair comparison. It was the sort of thing her mother would do, picking a favourite. And in that moment, she hated herself even more than usual. If Jake had slapped or shaken her it would have been what she deserved. She felt a sudden desire to get a knife and add to the hyphens on her leg.

Jake took a hurried step back, holding up his hands in apology and looking at them as if they had taken it upon themselves to touch Beth.

'Sorry,' he said. 'I didn't...'

It was Beth's turn to shake her head. She knew he didn't like confrontation, and his ego didn't want to appear weak to Mikey. She needed to convince him. 'Jake,' she said, not raising her voice but filling it with strength, 'Mikey owes you. What he did to you, he owes you. Big time. Now's the time to call it in. Make him earn your forgiveness.'

When he didn't respond, she added, with emphasis: 'For me.'

She couldn't see his eyes, hidden in the shadows, but she could tell he had squeezed them shut.

With a loud dramatic sigh, he pulled out his phone, tapped the screen a few times and, with a finger held above the screen, looked up at her. 'He might not even be up at this time. Might have his phone set to silent overnight, might be playing a game. Probably that.' Without waiting for Beth's response, he touched the screen and held up the phone. They could both hear the repeated double buzz of Mikey's phone ringing. And ringing. And ringing.

'Hi...'

Beth's hand clenched into a fist at the success.

'...Too busy doin' what I'm doin'. Leave a message.'

Beth's fist pounded her leg in frustration. Of course, it was too much to expect.

'Mikey,' Jake spoke into the phone. 'It's me Jake. I... We... Liz and I need your help. Now. Liz has... The guy who did your car...' he looked up at Beth, as if wanting approval for the lie, but was speaking again before she could nod. 'Look, there's been some violence. We'll explain when we see you. We're on our way to you now. Know it's late, but we'll be knocking on your door soon. We need...' a moment's hesitation, 'somewhere safe.'

His thumb tapped the screen.

He raised his head, as if still contemplating what he'd done. 'Uber?'

Beth held up her hands. 'Only if you've got the App. I can't have anything like that on my phone.'

'Of course,' Jake said, resigned. 'Might as well pick us up from here.' He looked at Beth and smiled. For the first time since she'd lain out on the sofa, she felt reassured.

'Now,' he said, 'all we have to do is...' Music burst from his phone, a jangly unrecognisable tune. His thumb answered it.

'Mikey!' he said holding the phone up again. 'It's—'

'Mikey? Who the fuck is Mikey? Trust me, whoever the fuck he is, he won't save you.'

Callum.

CHAPTER 24

Callum.

Beth slumped. Her strength drained while the ground fell away beneath her.

It was as if she were looking the wrong way through a grimy plastic telescope. A blurred version of Jake's left hand drifted into her tunnel vision. She managed to clutch it on the second attempt and felt his fingers slip down her hand to grip her wrist. She did the same to him, wrist to wrist, and held on tight as she could, trying not to topple. With one hand he held her wrist, the other the phone, which he held out between them, as if presenting a gift. Its light betrayed his trembling.

A sigh emanated from the mobile. 'Jacob. I know you're there.' Callum sounded impatient.

In the glow from the screen she could see Jake's gaze dart from side to side. Then his eyes found her, stopped, and he stood up straighter. He cleared his throat. She could see his legs shaking but the strength in his voice surprised her. 'How did you get this number?' He spoke every syllable with a hardness Beth wasn't expecting. Cold. It didn't sound at all like him. His iciness acted as a plug, and she managed to retain the last of her strength.

'Fuck's sake, Jacob,' Callum sounded amused. 'I've got the run of your flat. How long did you think it would take me to find your business cards? Really?' Beth could imagine him, sitting on

Jacob's bed, smiling, enjoying himself, basking in his power.

The screen light illuminated Jake's face from below, giving him an unnatural look and highlighting the swelling beneath his eyes – eyes that were fixed on Beth yet not seeing her. Thanks to the quivering of his hand, he looked as if he were underwater.

'What do you want?' Jake's voice may have been emotionless but his face wasn't. Beth could see the effort involved in acting tough. Muscles clenched and relaxed, trembled then clenched again.

'What I want is Beth Garway and that bastard brother of hers. Fucker Ryan's proving difficult to find. So I figured – I mean, really – if anyone knows where the bastard is, it'd be his sweet little sister. His murderous fucking sister. So, yeah, before you say anything, I'm gonna want to see her. Just a little friendly chat. Unfinished business, you might say.'

As if she had sped over a hump-back bridge, Beth's stomach dropped again, and a sharp bile flooded into the void. She tried to swallow great gulps of air without making a noise. This wasn't a time for fainting or vomiting. Jake twitched his head to attract her attention. She'd missed something. He mouthed, 'Ryan?' She nodded and found herself wishing her brother were here. He'd look after her. He always had.

Steel reinforced Jake's voice, but he shook his head pointlessly. 'I don't know where either of them are.'

'Tell me where she is.'

'I don't know—'

'Don't fuckin' lie to me.'

'And if I did know, you think I would tell you?'

'Yes.' Callum's laugh was rough edged. 'Eventually.'

'I've called the police.'

'Fuck's sake. No, you haven't.'

'Yes, I—'

'What d'ya think'll happen then? Eh? I'd be outta here, first sign. So many exits. Which'll leave you to explain what's happened. How you gonna do that without telling 'em who she really is? Fuck's sake, you expect me to believe she'll let you do that?' Callum paused to let the message sink in. When he spoke again, his voice had taken on a chatty tone, 'Jacob, Jacob, just tell me where she is. You can come back home then, to this lovely flat – it's nice here – and you'll never see or hear from me again.'

Jake shook his head. The phone in his palm still shook, as if – despite the night's residual warmth – he was shivering. Beth could feel him grip her wrist tighter than was necessary. She wasn't sure who was supporting who now. Any tighter and it would be painful.

'What,' Jake's voice still didn't expose his feelings, which were obvious to Beth, 'if she doesn't want to see you?'

Callum's sigh was clear. 'The fuck's it's got to with you? Just tell me where the fuck she is.'

'I told you—'

'Don't fuck with me.'

Beth felt night air brush her wrist as Jake released his grip. He smiled at her then looked back to the screen. She felt a sudden awareness of what he was about to say. She leant forward, eyes wide, mouthed 'no' and shook her head, desperate to catch his attention. Too late.

Jake thought he was being clever. But his tone gave him away. 'Okay,' he said. 'If I see her, I'll tell her you're looking for her.'

No!

In the silent seconds that followed, Jake raised his eyes from the phone to see Beth's response, and Beth saw his mask fall, leaving an expression of confusion.

Too obvious, she wanted to shout. *Too obvious.*

The voice that emanated from the phone sounded different.

Wiser, more adult. 'She's there, isn't she. With you.' It wasn't a question.

'No...' Jake shook his head again, his acting skills finally failing. 'No..., she's—'

'Yes. Thought it was her I saw.'

'No—'

'Shut the fuck up, Jacob. Beth? Beth, you there?'

Jake squeezed his eyes shut, swelling the bruises beneath. 'Sorry', he mouthed. 'Sorry. Sorry. Sorry.'

'Okay, Beth. I know you're there. Right. You've been gone, what, five, ten minutes? You can't be further than ten minutes away. You got ten minutes to get back here. Just Beth. Or both of you, I don't fucking care.'

There was pause while Jake tried to find the ice in his voice once again. 'Or what?' he demanded. It should have come out confrontational. It just sounded weak.

'Fuck all to do with you Jacob.'

'No.'

'Fuck's sake, Jacob. Beth, Beth, I know you're there. Wanna catch up on old times? We ain't seen each other in years. It's about time we caught up. Stuff I could tell you.'

Beth kept silent. She didn't know what to say. Jacob kept his head turned, his eyes on the ground.

'Jesus. Right. If you're not here by... what, two thirty – see can't say I'm not generous – then I'll be forced to investigate how *fuckin' flame retardant* the cladding is on these flats. Guess what? I can't see no fuckin' sprinklers. Two thirty, Beth, or Jacob's cooker accidently catches fire.'

The line went dead.

CHAPTER 25

Beth and Jake stared at each other. Before the light from his phone died, she saw his mouth moving, as if trying various words for taste, finding them unpleasant, and discarding them. His eyes were now deep in shadow, looking like empty sockets. She was also trying to form the right sentence. Something other than a prayer for her brother to appear. She needed something inspiring, some perfect plan or clever idea. But everything apart from Ryan seemed to drop from her head, following her stomach into a sickening abyss. She felt nauseous and empty. And what was worse was the familiarity, as if this feeling had always been lurking deep inside her, like a predator waiting for its chance.

I remember now. This is what real fear feels like. Oh, Ryan. Where are you?

She and Jake broke the silence together.

'Right...'

'Okay...'

There was a pause and Jake turned to his phone while Beth got hers out. Double the illumination.

As she tried to tap on the screen, she heard him leave another message. 'Mikey, Mikey. Answer the damn phone. Where the hell are you? This is urgent. Now.'

Beth's call was also going to voicemail. She couldn't help but copy Jake. 'Ryan. Ryan. It's me. Answer the phone. Please.

Callum's here. He's, like, here now. Come quick. Wherever you are. He... he says he's looking for you too. He...' She looked up into the surrounding gloom, finding it difficult to focus on the library wall; tangled shapes, the deep shadows from unmoving branches made it difficult to know what was a pattern and what wasn't. She needed time to think, but that was something else she didn't have. Callum's deadline had seen to that. She looked back at her phone, Ryan's voicemail still recording. 'Why does he want you?' she asked, pulling the phone closer to her mouth. 'Have you contacted him? What have you told him? Don't risk yourself to protect me.' She found she was standing straighter as she finished her message. 'It was my crime. It's about time I faced the consequences.'

She looked at Jake as she ended the call. Jake kept his gaze on her phone. She thought she saw him blink just before wiping the back of one hand across his eyes.

'Sorry,' he said. It may have only been a single word, but it was clearly a huge effort to say.

But she wasn't feeling forgiving. She was feeling scared about what Callum would do, and beneath that she felt a familiar stab of guilt at having brought Jake into this, but that was all. She couldn't bring herself to feel angry at Jake, let alone forgive him for his stupidity. His tone, his words had been an obvious giveaway, and said to someone who had already injured him and put Ryan's flatmate in hospital. 'It was a dumb thing to say,' she said flatly.

'No. Yes. You think I don't know that?' Now he looked up at her. 'But that's not what I meant. I can see it in you. You're wishing you had Mikey here or your brother. Anyone but me. You can't hide it, it's obvious. Well, sorry, but it's me you've got. Not Mikey. Not your brother. Me.'

Beth stopped her denial before it reached her lips. They both knew he was right.

'Well,' she said, thinking through their options, 'We are where we are. It doesn't matter how we got here. We have to deal with this with what we've got. Shall we go?'

'And see the angry man with the big knife?' Jake stepped forward, into a patch of light. Beth couldn't tell whether the yellow tinge to his very pale face was down to the sodium lamp in the car park opposite or his fear. The smeared trace of blood down his cheek and the bulging bruises beneath his eyes were ink black. He took a breath so deep it made his shoulders rise. 'We can do this,' he said.

They re-traced their steps, following the path around the library, and were side by side as they walked down the steps. They didn't pause at the bottom, didn't dare, and together they marched back to Regency Court. Beth pushed her rising fear down, trying to suffocate it. The fact she and Jake were moving with purpose and in step somehow increased her confidence.

There should be music swelling, she thought. *The march towards a showdown.*

Jake was the first to speak. 'What d'ya think he wants?'

'I killed his brother, ruined his life. I doubt it's a social call.'

'Yeah, but *what* does he want? How does he think this is going to end? If we knew that we might be able to put a stop to this.'

'After me, he wants get Ryan.'

'Who you won't give up.'

'I don't even know where he is. I know Callum went to his place in Guildford. If Ryan isn't there, then… And no, I won't give him up. He's my brother.'

'So…'

'Look,' Beth tried to picture what was awaiting them and their options. 'Callum's in your flat, right? What about if, before we confront him, I sneak back to mine. Pick up some weapons. I've got knives.'

In thinking about her suggestion, Jake's foot scraped over a lump in the pavement and almost stumbled. 'You don't think,' he whispered, hurrying to get back into step with her, 'that might be, I don't know, provocative or something? And not just as a threat.'

Beth nodded.

'You could really… use it on him? He's got a fuck-off sharp blade.' He touched the dried blood on his cheek. 'I don't think he's the type to take kindly to threats. You might have….'

'I could.' She had stabbed Callum's brother, so quickly and violently that when she had pulled the blade out for another thrust, he had stumbled and fell into the paddling pool, too wounded to pull himself out. There were times when she could still feel his blood as she rammed the blade as deep as it would go. Could still see his surprise when she pulled back and the blood-streaked blade slipped free. It had made a strange, soft, almost imperceptible hushing sound; even now, in her memory, she didn't know whether it was his flesh or his T-shirt on the blade. 'I could,' she repeated, more to herself than Jake.

'And then what?'

The question stopped her.

She tried to see any way this could end well. Ideally without anyone getting hurt or identified. She couldn't. Callum had proven himself to be a man used to getting his way through violence. It was ironic that this was something she – through violence – was responsible for. She didn't think he was someone who could be warned off, or even bribed. He wanted something. Simply, if he was left alive, she would always be running from him. She knew now he would always find her. And yet the alternative wasn't any better. It was clear to her that violence always had consequences, spreading ripple-like from the original impact. She knew all too well – *had experienced* – what would happen if, in the extreme, she used a knife on him. Whether he lived or not, there goes the rest of her life. Prison. No being saved this time by being under-aged, by family coming together to support her, by help from the Youth Offending Team. Everything everyone accused her of would be true. The papers would claim they had been right all along, that she was a monster, the baby-faced butcher, the Island's Killer Kid, who should have been put away when they had the chance. And how would Ryan, and Mum and Dad, cope? The press would still be hounding them, only with renewed vindictiveness.

She became aware Jake had stopped a pace ahead and was staring back at her.

'You know what?' she said, trying for a smile, even a weak one. They were almost at Regency Court. 'I'm glad it's you here, not Ryan. Or Mikey. Both of them are likely to go in fists flying. Or worse. You. You, however, are more likely to defuse the situation.'

'Is that a compliment?'

'Yeah.'

'Funny,' he said, wiping his forehead. 'I was just thinking, you were right about getting a weapon. I've never been in a real fight before. Not even at school, not in the playground. Nowhere. Always managed to get out of it somehow. Even this,' he touched the bridge of his nose and winced, 'it wasn't a fight, more of a massacre. So what the hell, if now's my time, then now's my time. I'm not going to run anymore. If I'm going to stand up and be a man — as my dad always said I should. I'm ready. I'll finally make him proud.'

'No,' Beth shook her head. 'You were right first time. It'll only make matters worse.'

Jake continued as if she hadn't spoken.

'One of those things, they say, isn't it? Ignore bullies and they'll go away. Except that's not true. I've seen it, I remember at school. They only pick on the weak ones. I remember the school bully looking around for someone to torment. Only it wasn't just someone weaker, was it, it was some poor kid who he was positive wouldn't fight back.' He took a heaving breath. 'Maybe now is the time to fight back.'

'Jake. He's got a knife. You know that.'

'I'll be ready for him.'

'And he knows how to handle himself. He's been in prison, for God's sake.'

Jake felt the bridge of his nose again. 'I'm not gonna back down, this time. I've had enough.'

Up ahead was the door to Regency Court, light flooding out, illuminating the path, revealing tufts of grass between its concrete slabs. Beth could see all lights were on in her flat and also in Jake's.

Callum must have been moving between flats.

She wanted to feel angry, to feel that familiar flare of fraying temper. Now, at this moment, it would have been comforting. All she felt though was scared, a curling fear, deep inside, huddled in somewhere cold, hollow and echoing, like a lost child in a cathedral.

Jake continued his striding, as if desperate to arrive.

She needed Jake to see sense, and fast. 'This isn't like the movies, you know,' she said. 'Where violence solves all problems. Trust me, it only makes matters worse. Violence is...' Images, thoughts, questions cascaded through her, tumbling into one another faster than she could find the words. Things she had been warned about when in therapy.

Teeth kicked out? They're gone forever. Broken limbs? Crushed fingers? They might never work properly again. Jake was worried about black eyes at work? What about no teeth? A cracked rib? A punctured lung? She knew from when Callum had last attacked her: agonising.

'Violence is horrible,' was the best she could say, aware of just how weak that was. 'Look,' she wanted to stop him striding ahead. 'You can't just knock someone out by hitting them on the head. There's fractured skulls, brain damage. Murder. It's... it's not like the movies,' she repeated.

'What do you suggest then?'

She thought again of going up to her flat first, before entering Jake's, to find something defensive. No knives, but he had a spare rape alarm in her fleebag. Would that help?

'I... oh.'

Through the narrow strip of textured and reinforced glass, she could just make out the stairwell, with Mr Lottan's strangely coloured door on the left and Jake's orange one on the right, near the stairs up to Beth's flat. On the steps, something moved. This close, the lumpy glass made the body look bulbous. Then it moved again, the shape rippled.

One misshapen arm was raised, beckoning them in.

Chapter 26

Beth froze. Wide-eyed, she stared through the reinforced-glass panel. She'd thought Callum would be in Jake's flat. Seeing him sitting on the stairs was so unexpected it knocked the breath from her. She knew it was him, even though she struggled to recognise him, especially through the textured glass; she could *feel* it was him.

Twelve years, she thought. *Twelve years since we last saw each other. Since he attacked me. Have I changed as much as he has?*

'Right. I've got this.' Jake inserted himself between her and the door. His key was already in his hand and Beth noticed he had no trouble finding the lock. Not a shake. Not a tremble.

The *clunk* of the lock sounded so loud it was almost physical; it jerked Beth into breathing again. She sucked in the warm, night air, conscious that she didn't want to appear gasping, looking like a fish yanked from the safety of water.

Jake stepped into Regency Court, holding the door open, but keeping himself between Beth and Callum. She felt a spark of irritation that he believed she needed his protection; she inwardly scowled. At that moment she had to restrain herself from putting her hand on his back and shoving him.

Once inside, they both stopped to let the heavy spring do its job and swing the door shut. The lock gave another clunk. It sounded loud, echoing up and down the stairwell. Beth took a step to the left to make it clear she wasn't hiding behind Jake. She'd always thought her terror when seeing Callum would be overwhelming, and was impressed at how well she was controlling her fear. Her imagination had made this meeting so much worse. Seeing Callum here though, he was just a man. *Only* a man, she reminded herself.

In control. A woman's place is in control, she remembered. *That's what I told Mikey.*

But where is Mikey when we need him? And Ryan?

She stared at the man sitting on the stairs, leaning back on his elbows. A stocky man. Barrel-chested, with arms so thick she doubted her two hands could encircle one of his biceps. No neck as such, just a shaven head atop wide, muscled shoulders. He had, thought Beth, the expression of disdain that comes from the complete certainty that he's better than both of them. A knife rested on the step beside him, within easy reach.

Her jaw clenched until the muscles ached. The bastard thinks he's untouchable.

She looked for the boy she'd once known, anything recognisable she could grab for support, but there was no sign of the slight, gawky boy she'd spent her early holidays with.

Callum was also staring at her. She guessed he was looking for the girl she used to be. Then he moved, glanced at his watch, sat up straighter and – for several heartbeats – his features softened. While a smile wasn't a total stranger to his face, Beth thought it wasn't a frequent visitor. Callum appeared just as surprised at its arrival, and – even though there was no true humour there – he stamped on it. Too late though, in those seconds she saw the boy she remembered. She thought of an X-ray, or maybe a ghost: one figure just about visible within the other. There was no doubt.

'Hello, Beth.' Callum hauled himself to his feet, picking up the knife on his way. Light glinted from a blade at least as long as his hand, fingertips to wrist. He stood two steps up, looking at her.

The lights went out.

'Wha...' from Jake.

Beth tensed, but then with a click, the lights came on again and Callum's left hand was on the light button, a timer. She could hear its faint buzzing. In a few minutes the stairwell would be in darkness again.

It was so disorientating, switching from bright light to sudden darkness and then back again, that Beth blinked back tears and then felt angry with herself. She didn't want Callum to think she was crying. She clenched one hand, pressing her fingernails into her palm, enjoying the sting, taking comfort that only she could stop the pain – or make it worse. Still blinking, Beth became aware of the stairwell as if seeing it through someone else's eyes; how enclosed it felt, how the floor needed sweeping, how dustballs lurked in the corners like frightened animals and how stale the air tasted.

'Callum,' she returned her attention to the big man on the stairs. 'You're looking... different.'

Jake cleared his throat and shifted his weight. Beth clenched her jaws together again at being forced to take another a step to look around him, to see Callum. Jake thinks he's protecting her, but actions were beginning to irritate.

'What do you want?' Jake's voice was still cold and hard, but now, Beth thought, compared with Callum, he sounded like someone doing an impression, someone who'd seen too many movie enforcers.

Callum ignored him and remained focused on Beth. 'Fuck it, I'm not the boy I once was. Thanks to you. How long—?'

'Twelve.'

His nod was sharp and precise. 'Yeah, twelve fucking years. I'd still know it was you though. Don't know about anyone else but

249

I still fucking recognise you.'

So much for age changing my appearance, she thought. And a new hairstyle and colour. She wondered if he was seeing a double image as she was, the younger version visible inside the older.

Maybe he was still seeing her lying on the ground, blooded and bruised and sobbing while he continued kicking. Maybe that was his memory of her.

Jake tried again, his voice raised so that it echoed around the enclosed space. 'You got us. We're here. What do you want?'

As if taking a great effort of will, Callum forced his attention from Beth to Jake. He pulled a face that was half wince, half something Beth couldn't interpret.

'Yeah. Look… fuck it. I just wanna talk.'

'Go on then.' Jake folded his arms over his chest, waiting.

'In fucking private, you prick.'

'That ain't gonna happen.' Jake shook his head and in doing so took another half-step to his left. Once again Beth had to peer around him to see Callum. What did he think he was doing? She didn't want this. The buzzing of the light timer sounded louder. None too gently, she put the back of hand against Jake's arm. Pushed. He glanced over his shoulder at her, and she saw confusion flood his face.

What did he expect?

Callum spoke to Beth, once again ignoring Jake. 'I've learnt a lot since we last met.' His expression reminded Beth of her brother when he was teasing her with a secret. That same smug male superiority, confidence, and untouchability. Supercilious git. She hated it. It angered her when she was a girl; it irritated her now.

Beth pitched her voice to that of bored rather than scared. 'Oh, fuck off, Callum. I don't care.'

'You heard her,' Jake added. 'Fuck off.'

Beth saw Callum clench his fists, one set of knuckles whitening around the long-bladed knife, the muscles in his arms expanding, stretching the cotton of his T-shirt. She couldn't tell if the gesture was for show, to intimidate, or if he really wasn't used to disobedience.

'Fuck's sake—'

'No.' Jake's voice went up another notch in volume.

The lights went out. Beth heard the thump as Callum hit the timer and the buzzing started again. Together with the explosion of light, the noise seemed to fill the world.

When Beth had stopped blinking, she was aware Callum was staring at her; he nodded towards Jake but aimed his words at her. 'He mean that much to you?'

How could she explain her feelings towards Jake? She knew he was trying his best, was just as scared as she was, attempting to act tough, yet the way he kept pushing in front of her was just so bloody irritating.

She knew she'd hesitated too long when she saw Jake's shoulders sag, just a fraction but noticeable – much the same as Callum's nod. They both thought they understood. Jake twisted his head so that he could look at her again.

Oh, grow up, Jake.

Knowing Jake would see it, she briefly raised her eyes to the ceiling. Then, ignoring the look on Jake's face, she turned all her attention to the man, the threat, on the stairs. 'For God's sake Callum. You've found me. Now what?' Beth looked into his eyes, deep into a face that she found unsettling – not quite a stranger and not quite familiar. 'We can have you sent back inside. You broke into my mum and dad's place to get Ryan's address, beat up his flatmate until he told you Ryan was here looking for me, broke into Jake's flat, attacked him with a knife, and have now threatened to burn down a building. Having a good day? What is

251

it you want? Really?'

'I... what?'

Beth took a sliver of delight in Callum's surprise. He wouldn't expect her to make herself public property again. 'Yeah. You think I wouldn't tell the police? Really?'

He shook his head, as if he hadn't made himself clear. 'Fuck's sake. Look, I don't know what..., ah, fuck it. I don't know how to play nicely, all right?' The last few words tumbled from him as if rushing to escape. 'It's prison. Fucking prison.' His lips went tight and thin. In the second that followed Beth could see him consciously trying to relax. It appeared to be hard work. 'Inside, in prison, you want something...' He swallowed. Tried again. 'Asking "nicely" is a sign of weakness, it'll get you fucking killed. Threats and violence: that's what works. That's what I learned. That's what I'm used to. Fuck it.' He glared at her, as if she were responsible for the penal system.

'Don't blame me. Your crimes.'

'You think my fucking life'd be the same if you hadn't murdered my brother?'

Beth had no answer to that.

'You just don't fucking get it do you?' Callum's colouring was darkening, a livid rash rising from the neck of his T-shirt. 'How much damage you did? The shrinks explained it to me. Made it all fucking clear. Owen may have been a jerk, but he was the only fucking role model I had. Dad fucked off just before I was born. Thanks, you old bastard, wherever you are. So all I was left with was Owen. I looked up to him. Jerk or not, he was all I fucking had. *My* role model. After you fucking killed him, I had no one. Mum didn't wanna know me, didn't wanna know anything. The only one...' The words got caught and Callum sniffed and swallowed. The knife glinted as he wiped the back of his right hand over his tight glistening forehead. 'Only your dad, *your fucking dad!* could see.' He took a step down, closer, and the point of the knife jabbed towards Beth again. 'He tried. I know he tried, but, fucking hell, a second-hand role model, out of *charity*? Fuck off.' Spittle flew from his lips and sweat flicked from his face just before the light went out again.

In the utter darkness, Callum's heavy breaths sounded like explosions in the otherwise silent stairwell.

The button was punched, light exploded, and the buzzing started again. Beth felt it was now in her brain, like a trapped biting insect.

She waited, watching Callum's colour recede as he fought to gain control. He had more control over his temper than she had over hers. Despite everything, despite the loud buzzing in her head, the over-bright lighting, one small part of her brain was impressed.

Eventually, Callum managed to speak. 'You,' he managed to say, with a jaw that was only just beginning to unclench, 'did that to me. Fucked up my life.'

Beth took a deep breath. This was getting out of control: the light, the sound, it was getting difficult to think clearly. She tried to concentrate on the hyphens scarring her thighs, and the sharp and delicious pain that was under *her* control, no one else's. It caused a break in the fog suffocating her thoughts. She pressed on, and held out her hands, wide as if presenting herself. For a moment her thinking was clear. 'Well, you wanted to see me, Callum. Here I am.' Jake stepped in front her. She was ready, and after slapping his arm and a quick shimmy and sidestep, she was beside him, shoulders not quite touching.

If he'd carried on, she thought, *he'd have pushed me into Mr Grumpy's front door.*

'You going to attack me again, Callum? Like last time? Is that what you want?'

He stared at her for a moment, chewing the inside of his mouth, before speaking. 'Who would blame me for wanting revenge? On you, and your fucking brother. Where is he? Where's Ryan. I know he was here. Where is he now?' He raised his voice as if trying to reach the back row of an auditorium.

'Ryan? What do you want Ryan for?'

Callum opened his mouth, Beth was certain he was going to say something, then he stopped and pursed his lips. He stared at Beth. There was condescension in his gaze. She could almost see cogs turning as he calculated whether to speak or not, whether his thoughts would become diluted if he shared them, whether they were more valuable if it was only he who owned them, or whether speaking them would prove his superiority.

Oh, for God's sake. Tell me.

'Well?'

Callum glanced at his watch, then back to Beth. 'What the fuck do you think I want him for?' he said.

Beth's fought to keep silent. She didn't want to put ideas into his head.

The stairwell was becoming too bright again, too full of the buzzing timer. Counting down. Concentrate. She needed to concentrate.

Callum nodded, as if only just understanding some confusing maths. 'You don't know? You really don't...' His snort of laughter echoed up and down the stairwell. 'Just tell me where the little shit is.'

Beth clamped her mouth shut. Squinted against the harsh light.

'Where is he?'

Beth let out the tiniest laugh before she could swallow it. Composed herself, attempted to control her fear. 'You're right. I really don't know,' she said. 'I don't know where he is. I've just tried to ring him, to warn him. No answer. Believe it or not, you know as much as I do. He was in Guildford, as you know. Then he drove up here, as you know. Where he is now,' she said with a shrug, 'none of us know.'

'Don't fuck with me.' He stepped off the final stair on to the concrete floor. The point of the knife was jabbed at Beth once again. It felt a lot closer, but she impressed herself by not moving, and noted that Jake turned his fractional flinch into a half-shrug before speaking, using the tone of someone dealing with a recalcitrant child.

'Oh, come on,' he said. 'What did you think was going to happen? If we knew we wouldn't tell you. As it happens we don't know, so *we can't tell you.*' The fact there wasn't a tremor in his voice filled Beth with pride. And also brought a realisation. This brightly lit stairwell, the way they stood, facing each other, the sharp echoes – this was no more than a stage. She was trying to act confident, Jake – even with his black eyes – was trying to act tough, and Callum, well, he was also acting, trying to reprise his role as prison hard man. The dominant, alpha male.

Oh God, this was almost funny.

Jake took out his phone, holding it up, turning it as if it were an exhibit in court. 'I've had enough,' he said, his voice raised to a louder volume than Callum's, as if it were a competition. 'I'm calling the police. This has gone on long enough. I don't care anymore.'

The lights went out, only this time there was illumination from Jake's phone. Callum swore and punched the button. Everyone was getting annoyed with this.

Beth turned to Jake, but could see only his profile. His attention was fixed on Callum. It was as though she wasn't there, or he was ignoring her. She went to say something, pulled her hand back to slap him, to prevent him from making a call that could further ruin the lives of her and her family, then stopped. Her hand hovered between them, moving towards him, then retreating. For once, everything, everything she could hear – the buzzing, the squeak of Callum's trainers – and everything she could see under the harsh, too bright lights, faded.

God, maybe he was right, maybe this was how it had to end. With the police, again unwilling or unable or too greedy to keep her identity a secret. The papers stalking her, and Ryan, and Mum, and Dad; journalists waiting behind every corner for them, provoking them, desperate for quotes – which if they didn't get they would make up anyway. And more petrol through the letterbox. More graffiti on doors and walls, more being spat on in the street, more attacks, more hatred. *No!* Bile rose in her throat. She wasn't going to go through all that. Not again. She just wasn't. Couldn't. She attempted to swallow the sharp sour taste filling her throat and in doing so her sound and vision returned. And as if someone had tweaked her world's settings, they were louder and brighter than before.

Through narrowed eyes she saw Callum shake his head, saw fine lines on his shaved scalp. 'I told you, Jacob,' Callum said, 'you won't call the fucking police. You want everyone to know where Bethany Garway is fucking living?' Callum pointed his knife and looked down the edge of the blade at Jake. 'Sure as fuck she don't. Look at her. You won't fucking call the—'

Beth jumped and swore at the sudden noises behind her. The clunk of a lock, a door jerking open.

'He doesn't need to. I have.' The clipped words transmitting barely suppressed rage.

Mr Lottan. Shit.

They all turned to look at the new actor in their drama. His grey hair hadn't been combed – it pointed angrily in all directions – and somehow his features looked as if they'd grown more pointy. Over his midnight-blue pyjamas he'd thrown a long coat, one side of which was still caught up under itself. He was jerking a shoulder trying to get the material loose. He was also holding a phone near his ear, as if he'd just finished a call.

'You know what time it is?' His voice was raised, as loud as the others. 'You know how much noise you were making?' He glanced at Jake. 'I told you before. Last night. Your party. And then that racket this morning. I told you then it was your last chance. You've only been here a week. You're trouble in my flats.' His gaze swept from Jake to Callum, as if he'd just noticed him, and he scowled. 'You lot want to fight? Have it somewhere else. Quietly.' He turned back to Jake. 'You can't say I didn't I warn you. Anyone keeps me awake gets a visit from the police. And you...' He was close enough to tap Beth on the shoulder with his phone, but there was no need to get her attention, she was already glaring at him, her insides alight, ready to explode. He stared into her face, searching, and her stomach punched upwards the moment she saw his flash of recognition.

'It *is* you,' he said, 'Bethany Garway. Well, well. I remember...' He shook his head as if, in fact, he didn't quite have the memory he claimed. Beth knew whatever he recalled was going to be too much. She felt a terrible urge to scream herself out of this nightmare.

'Oh, threatening behaviour?' Lottan asked. He took a quick, frantic, step back. Out of reach. 'You haven't killed anyone? Anyone else? I...' Beth saw him lose focus for a faction of a second, his thoughts obscuring what he could see. 'Me,' he said suddenly, with an unexpected smile and raised eyebrows. 'Me. I'm the one who found Bethany Garway, the Island's Killer Kid. Me.'

'No!' she yelled, anger erupting, and her hand pulled back to slap him with all her strength.

Jake grabbed her arm a fraction of a second before the lights went out.

Beth heard steps behind her, but she was transfixed by the afterimage of Mr Lottan's expression, his greedy mind clearly presenting him with images of fame, fortune and celebrity.

She tried to jerk her arm free. She needed the release of violence, but felt Jake's arms go around her. 'Come on,' Jake said in her ear. She struggled against him, kicking his shins, and then – as instantaneous as had been her explosion of temper – her anger vanished, carried away in a waterfall of emotions. It was only Jake's grip stopping her from falling to the floor and howling.

The lights exploded on, again – Mr Lottan was pressing the nearest light button – just as she heard Callum's voice from the door to the car park. 'I'm coming for the two of you, you and your fucking brother. Unfinished fucking business.'

He opened the rear door of the flats, looked back, said, 'Tell your fucking brother my mum kept Owen's diaries', then jogged away just as Jake moved, almost pulling Beth off her feet. He managed to open the other door, the front entrance to the flats, and pushed her through, shouting over his shoulder to Mr Lottan, 'Tell the press, and see what happens.'

She heard Mr Lottan's plaintive, 'Wait.'

They didn't.

They fled.

CHAPTER 27

They didn't speak. Beth didn't think she could even if she wanted to. They ran the first hundred metres or so, then slowed. Not only was Beth finding breathing hard – her rucksack knocking air out of her with each step, a hot band of iron tightening around her chest and broken glass lining her throat – but she'd left her strength in the stairwell. As always, immediately after an explosive loss of temper, she felt emptied. It was as if all her energy had been consumed in the detonation. All that remained was the charred dust of guilt and self-directed anger. She was amazed she could keep moving at all. Her legs felt as though their bones had been removed. She'd seen on TV people staggering over the finish line of the London Marathon, on legs that appeared weak and wobbly. She thought that was how she looked now.

Jake led, but she figured she knew where they were heading, even if neither of them wanted to get there. They may have been leaving the flats, and hopefully Callum, behind them, but they still had to be careful.

Every now and then one of them scraped a sole on a raised bit of pavement and stumbled, the other put out their arm for support. Tree-lined avenues were all very nice, but the trees had hidden roots, ruining the pavements, causing bumps that were invisible in the darkness. Very quickly, the danger of tripping became too great, and they were forced to slow to a walk. Beth didn't want to fall: she feared she'd never get up again. And the thought of hitting her head, of glorious unconsciousness, felt like the best option at the moment. Walking allowed her heart to return to something like normal and the pounding in her ears to fade. Now, though, she was aware of every car she could hear in the distance. Callum was out here somewhere.

When they had run to the library she had experienced elation. Now it was just grim acceptance.

'Are you okay?' Jake placed his hand on her arm with such lightness it felt like a caress. Despite them being on a darkened and deserted suburban street, he was whispering.

She found she couldn't produce words. 'Uh huh,' she nodded, using everything she had to gather herself. To keep going.

After several rough, grating breaths she managed to say, 'You?'

'Think so. I... I stood up him, didn't I?'

Whatever she said, Beth knew it would sound patronising (*Yeah, you were very brave, a real hero*), so she remained silent, concentrating on putting one foot in front of the other while waiting for her internal battery to recharge.

'Would've made Dad proud,' Jake whispered, then shook his head. 'No, probably not.' He was speaking more to himself than Beth. 'He'd have wanted more. He used to say, if the other guy could walk away, it wasn't good enough.'

The far end of the road was suddenly illuminated. As the car turned the corner, shadows moved in formation like a battalion of ghosts. A scraggly fox, caught in the headlights, shot across the road and across a lawn.

'Here, quick,' Beth said, taking a few quick steps into someone's garden and dropping behind a hedge. Jake followed and they sat on their haunches waiting for the vehicle to pass.

'That him?' Jake whispered.

For God's sake, how do I know?

Irritation at Jake still niggled. Knowing that he'd done his best, that he really had shown courage, didn't help her mood. If anything, her unreasonable attitude just made her feel worse about herself. He'd be better off without her. In fact, he'd have been better off if he'd never met her.

The car seemed to pass too slowly, and Beth couldn't decide whether it was someone taking extra care because the streetlights were out or someone searching for them. She had no idea what car Callum drove.

They waited until their eyes had adjusted to the dark again and they couldn't hear the car's engine before stepping out.

Beth was aware of Jake glancing at her as they began walking again.

'What?' she snapped, and immediately wished she hadn't.

'You sure you're okay?'

'Are you?'

'I'm not the one that guy wanted. Or the one who almost punched our landlord.'

Beth managed a tiny cough of a laugh. 'He, like, needs to look at the security of his flats. Anyone, it seems, can get in.'

'Do you think he will go to the press?'

'Would you?'

'For some reason I seem to be on your team now. I'm not sure how that happened, but it did.'

'But would you?'

'Course not. You're in a team, you stick with it. We seem to have chosen each other. For my sins, I trust you.'

'Really?'

'Loyalty between friends,' he said, the words sounding rough and loud, 'means more than between family.' He touched the bridge of his nose. Beth figured he was thinking about Mikey. They both knew that was where they were heading.

'You going to be okay seeing Mikey?'

'Dunno.' It was several steps before he spoke again. 'It'll depend on what he does.'

They moved from terraced houses built in the 1970s, to much more modern compact buildings. Ahead were bungalows and a community centre. Beth always thought this area was sheltered accommodation for the elderly. She had once thought they looked safe, reassuring. Now, in the dark, she wasn't so sure.

'I think he probably will,' Jake said, echoing Beth's own thoughts. 'Go to the papers.'

'So do I.'

'What will you do?'

'The usual.'

'You've been here before?'

'Too often. This'll give my parents yet another reason to despise me, but I've got to warn 'em though; they're, like, gonna get inundated again. You ever seen a press pack camped outside, howling for your attention?' A wave of nausea passed through her at the memory. 'Pray you don't. It's worse than you can imagine. God, Mum hates me enough as it is.'

Jake looked at her, as if deciding how to respond, then looked at his watch. 'You gonna ring them? Now?'

'I reckon we've got at least until the morning. Mum'll only blame me more if I disturb their night. The deserve one last night of good sleep.'

They walked on, listening for traffic, watching for headlights. Jake led them to a footpath connecting two roads.

'A short cut,' he said.

'I wish I'd known about this before.'

After a few minutes, Beth could see streetlights ahead, illuminating the Midland Oak roundabout. Despite their necessity to save money, not even Leamington council would leave such a junction without lighting. To their right, the Midland Oak Park was filled with long foreboding shadows thrown by the streetlights.

The closer they got to the roundabout, the faster they walked, the more they checked for traffic. When it was clear nothing was imminent, they both broke into a run, attempting to cross into the darkened road on the other side as quickly as possible.

As she passed it, Beth stole a glance at the plaque commemorating the Midland Oak. It was what had brought her to Leamington – to this very moment. A sudden and overwhelming feeling hit her that she would never again see the plaque or the tree. She glanced at them, then couldn't stop herself looking once more. It was suddenly important she committed the image of the plaque and tree to memory.

She stumbled and Jake put out a hand, but she caught her balance without his help.

They crossed the wide road, and continued moving fast, all senses alert for approaching vehicles.

'How far did you say?' she asked as they approached the Kenilworth Road. It was a major traffic-light controlled junction, and again well lit. They looked around as if expecting a sniper to open fire.

'Maybe a mile more.'

'Was there anything in your flat that had Mikey's address on it?'

Jake halted.

'Come on, keep moving.'

He started again, but Beth could tell he wasn't looking at where they were going.

'No,' he said eventually.' No, I don't think so. Nothing that could lead him to Mikey. I can't think of anything.'

It took them another twenty minutes before Jake turned right off a road that was lit, into a cul-de-sac that wasn't. Squat terraced houses made a wall of brickwork on the left, semi-detacheds with small front gardens and cars parked on short drives lined the other side. From what she could see, Beth thought the brickwork looked modern, built in the last thirty years or so. She couldn't tell how far the road went, or what was at its end. It disappeared into darkness.

'There,' Beth said, pointing to the left, to the second car lined up along the kerb. Parking was clearly at a premium here as there wasn't much room between it and the cars parked in front and behind.

There was no doubt it was Mikey's Mitsubishi. The metal exposed by the scratched letters glinted.

'Yeah, his place is a bit further on. Hah, probably the only parking spot he could find.'

They kept to the left-hand side of the street, passing doors and darkened, curtained windows, until Jake stopped. In the gloom Beth couldn't tell what colour the door was other than dark. Could have been black, could have been navy or brown. Near the top was a semi-circular frosted glass window. No lights were on inside the house. Beth didn't expect there to be. In the gloom, she could just see a white plastic security camera, nestling like a shy animal, in the corner below the lintel. She wasn't surprised. Mikey probably wanted the camera trained on his beloved car.

She raised her eyes, taking in the front of the house: downstairs were two paned windows, one either side of the front door; two similar windows upstairs. It didn't look a huge place, but even so, these days, in this location, and for someone of Mikey's age...

'Pay must be good in computer gaming' she muttered.

'I've already been warned,' Jake said, 'it's best not to ask where he gets his money from. Speculation around the office, however...' he shrugged, then asked: 'You ready for this?'

'Where else can we go? Can't stay in our flats. Callum could be back at any time. Probably expecting us to return and he's waiting there for us.'

'Let's hope so. Mind you, I thought he kept, like, looking at his watch. As if he had somewhere else to be.'

'Someone else to terrorise, probably.' She glanced at Jake, the paleness of his face accentuated by the dark, bloody bags hanging under his eyes and the still visible smear of blood down his cheek. Once again, she felt an urge to wipe it for him; once again knew she didn't dare. 'Don't forget,' she said. 'I'm Liz.'

'What?'

'Mikey doesn't know who I am. Bad enough with Mr Grumpy knowing.' Her stomach somersaulted at the prospect of the whole country knowing her identity.

'Good point, Liz.'

'With, like, the abusive ex-boyfriend.'

He rubbed the back of his hand, over the smear of dried blood on his cheek. 'Tell me about it.'

Beth stared at him in the gloom. 'Are *you* ready for this?'

'What more can he do to me? Here we go, then.' Jake pressed the doorbell, and kept it pressed. The soft sound of chimes from deep with the house surprised Beth. She had been expecting something louder, more raucous. The chimes pealed. And pealed. And pealed. Jake kept his finger on the button, and the chimes kept chiming. For a moment Beth wondered whether, if the doorbell was battery powered, the battery would run out before Mikey roused himself.

Then the spiral pattern in the small semi-circular window revealed itself, illuminated from the other side. Almost immediately they were lit by an exterior light. Beth felt exposed and vulnerable, as if frozen in a spotlight while attempting a prison escape.

265

There'd been too many lights going on and off, this night.

'That's done it,' muttered Jake. He removed his finger from the button and, in silence, under the light, they waited.

CHAPTER 28

Mikey raised his eyebrows at the sight of Beth. 'Talk of the devil. This could be difficult.'

She was puzzled by his lack of surprise, but then remembered the camera. He had known exactly who was calling. He stood in the doorway, one hand holding the door open, naked apart from his blue briefs. Beth remembered how he had paraded around her flat in his underwear that very morning (*was that less than twenty-four hours ago*, she thought. *Really?*) She stared at him. He must relish such exhibitionism.

He looked as if he'd had another hard evening. His eyes were bloodshot and bleary. A dark shadow of stubble coated his cheeks. Looking at him now, she couldn't believe she had ever found him attractive. Deep down though, she knew it wasn't his looks that had taken him into her bed.

'And...' Mikey turned his attention to Jake. 'Christ, what happened to you?'

'What? Apart from you head-butting me?'

Mikey didn't respond, instead put his finger to his own cheek, indicating the dried blood still on Jake's.

'Yeah, you've not been answering your phone.'

'You've come here, at this time, to tell me that? What's going on?'

'You owe me, after what you did. And now we need help. It's,

267

er…, Liz's ex-boyfriend turned up, again. Well, broke in. He's got a knife.'

'I don't owe you. What about my car?' He turned to Beth. 'And weren't you hiding from this ex?'

'What can I say? He found me. Can we come in?'

Mikey glanced down the road, took half a step back into his hall. Enough to be indoors, not enough to let them pass. 'Were you followed?' His eyes were clear and focused now. 'Could he have followed you here?'

Jake shook his head.

'You're sure? You better be sure. There's nothing to lead him here? Nothing he could use to follow you?'

Beth felt her colour rising along with her anger. It had been dormant since she'd tried to lash out at Mr Lottan. 'Actually, Mikey, we're okay. Thanks for asking.'

'That's all I bloody need, you to bring me a present of a knife-wielding maniac.'

'Christ, Mikey,' she said, remembering how good it had felt to slap him. 'I thought you were brave. Someone we could trust. We came here for your help.'

'From your ex?'

There was something about the way he said it Beth didn't like, an emphasis on the last syllable. As if he knew it wasn't true.

'Can we at least come in?' She shuffled forwards and nodded at the hallway. 'We'll explain what's happened?'

Mikey glanced behind him. The light was on and revealed a hall with a closed door on the left and a matching door on the right. Beyond this door, also on the right, were the stairs. A series of framed pictures ran up the wall. Beth was surprised: they appeared to be decent photographs of idyllic country scenes. Not what she expected of Mikey at all. Darkness hid the top of the staircase where it made a left turn.

'Well,' Mikey turned back, his eyes fixed on Beth. 'This *is* a little awkward.'

'Just for the rest of the night,' she said. 'Tomorrow, Jake can get a new lock. I'll find somewhere else to live. We'll be gone. We're tired. So just a few hours. Please.' She hoisted her rucksack off her shoulders, as if that would prove what she was saying. Then she felt her colour deepen as, in an unexpected moment of comprehension, she realised her misunderstanding. His familiar bleariness, his reticence – of course. 'Oh, you've got someone… with you? S'okay.'

He stared at her, doubt in his eyes.

She held out a hand to show there was no sense of betrayal. 'I don't care. Trust me, I don't. Last night was, well, it was last night. A one-night stand. What you do, like, tonight… I really don't care. I really don't. You don't care either, do you Jake.'

Before Jake could speak, Mikey leaned forward, looking deep into Beth's eyes. 'You been lying to me?' he asked.

'What? Let us in and I'll explain.'

'Explain what? You've an ex-boyfriend? And you're name's Liz? *Really?*'

The emphasis pierced Beth through the chest like an icicle. Cold and sharp.

He knows, her brain shouted. *Run.*

Jake spoke before Beth could. 'Mikey, mate. We've been attacked. Can we at least come in and sit down. We need to work out what we're gonna do and—'

'Well,' a voice asked from the top of the stairs, '*is* she? Was I right?'

They all stared. The woman had appeared, apparition-like, in the darkness at the top of the stairs. Her legs were bare and she was barefoot. Her bleached-blonde hair badly patted down. She had one hand on the banister and was wearing a sleeveless, loose-fitting dress, floral. It was the sort of thing, Beth thought, sold by Cath Kidston or Laura Ashley. Not something she herself would contemplate.

'Well,' the woman repeated. 'Was I right? Is she who I said?'

'Sue?' Beth stared, trying to remember Sue's words at Jake's party. A warning, surely. About Mikey. And she had to be twice Mikey's age.

She could be his mother.

Beside her, she felt Jake stiffen 'Sue?' His exclamation matched Beth's, but was followed by, 'Fucking hell, Mikey. Sue? You... no. Tell me you....'

Beth looked at Jake. His mouth remained opened from his unfinished sentence, his eyes similarly wide. Beth could understand the disbelief she saw there, but was there envy as well? Jake thrust his hands in his pockets, as if he wouldn't be able to control them otherwise.

Mikey shrugged as Sue, as if unsure of her footing, came slowly down the stairs. He didn't look back at her, but stared at Jake, his chin raised. A challenge in his expression. 'Sue came round this afternoon,' he said. 'She had a theory about Liz. Or is it Bethany Garway? She wanted to know if I'd noticed anything last night that might conform her idea. She bought some wine and well, you know, one thing led to another.'

He didn't even have the good grace to look embarrassed, thought Beth. And neither did Sue, after all her warnings. Mikey did, however, wear the expression of a man daring a woman to challenge him. Men seemed to find that face easy to slip on.

By this time. Sue had reached the bottom step. Without taking her eyes of Beth, she crossed her arms over her chest, hugging herself.

'You *are* Bethany Garway, aren't you?' She didn't wait for an answer. She was certain. 'My ex-husband, oh, he would kill for this scoop. He spoke all the time about such things, dreamt of finding infamous murderers given new identities, such as the Island's Killer Kid. The files he kept. They took up so much space…'

Beth shook her head, trying to wake from this nightmare. She felt spacey, uncertain that what she was hearing and seeing was real. It was almost four o'clock in the morning. Was this some sort of insomnia-fuelled hallucination? It felt like it.

Sue took a step forwards and scanned Beth's face with the intensity of someone reading a small-print novel. She nodded. 'Don't deny it. I can see you are. I remembered Dan's clippings and notes. Spent the afternoon online. I thought you looked familiar.'

'Sue…' Jake managed, 'You. Mikey? Why? How could…'

Beth wanted to nudge him – *Focus on something important!* – but didn't dare move.

Sue looked at Jake and tilted her head. 'The vigour of youth,' she said, with a non-committal shrug.

'You don't think it might make things at work, like, I don't know, difficult?' said Jake.

'Actually,' Mikey said, with a smile Beth thought was deliberately provocative, 'that wasn't top of the things we were thinking about.'

Beth didn't know who she wanted to slap the most, and that included Jake – who was missing the big picture. She had been identified twice in a couple of hours.

'Can we come in? Talk about it?' she asked again. 'Please?'

'You won't,' said Sue, 'change my mind. I *know* you're Bethany Garway.'

'And I don't think it's a good idea.' Mikey moved closer to Sue.

Beth wondered if he noticed Sue's fractional lean away from

him.

'So, what are you going to do?' Beth didn't want to know, but was certain she had to ask. Everything felt distant, as if she were light-headed and floating... or maybe drowning and lacking oxygen.

'What do you think I'm going to do?' Sue unfolded her arms, put her hands on her hips, as if the whole of the upper part of her body were asking the question.

'Just to get back at your ex-husband?'

Jake spoke, 'You'd better be quick as—' This time Beth did nudge him. There was no need for them to know they weren't the first to identify her tonight.

If Sue saw the nudge, she didn't acknowledge it. 'You don't understand,' she said.

Mikey grinned. Smug. 'Nothing personal, Liz – sorry, *Bethany*.' His expression made up for its lack of humour by an excess of taunting, as if daring her to contradict him. 'But there's money to be made here.'

'Not by you.' Sue looked at Mikey for the first time.

'What?' he said.

'Or me.'

'What?' Mikey said again, louder. His expression now one of shock.

'It's the least I can do for Dan. After everything I've put him through... he deserves this at least.'

'Now, wait a minute.' Mikey was blinking as if looking at a strobe light.

'No. This is Dan's big story.'

'But...'

'He's waited all his life for it.'

'But, Sue...'

Jake nudged Beth with his elbow, his hands still deep in his trouser pockets. 'Let's go,' he said, wearing a strange smile. 'Leave them to it,'

'But—'

'Come on,' he turned and began walking back the way they had come. With one last look at the couple now arguing in the hallway, she followed.

'I need—'

'Look what I've just found.' Jake brought his right hand out of his pocket, opened it. 'I forgot I still had this.' He pressed a button on the car key and ahead of them Mikey's Mitsubishi flashed its lights and emitted a soft welcoming bleep.

CHAPTER 29

'Your parents?' Jake's finger was poised over the satnav in the dashboard.

Beth wiped her hand over her tired eyes and tried to think of a better place to go. She had to warn Mum and Dad about Callum, about the press, about everything she feared was about happen, and face to face would be courteous. She told Jake their postcode. Ryan, damn him, still wasn't answering his phone so she didn't know where he was or his address. She knew she should have asked. Stupid not to.

Jake input the postcode, gave the system a few seconds to calculate the route, then began trying to extricate the car from a space that, Beth was convinced, did not allow any room for manoeuvre. Were they to be here all night? Jake backed up the vehicle, centimetre by centimetre. 'Best not to hit the car behind,' he said, eyes on the rear-view mirror. Then he looked ahead as they began moving forward. 'Or the car in front.'

'This car's already been damaged enough.'

'I was thinking of car alarms.' Reverse then forward, then again, and again, until Jake turned the wheel to full lock and managed to guide the car into the road. From her angle Beth thought they'd missed the rear bumper of the car in front by the thickness of paper. Not being a driver, she didn't know whether to comment or not, or whether he would find it insulting.

'He'll remember you've still got his keys, right?' she said.

'He's been walking to work the last few days. He'll survive.'

'No, but he's not going to think his car's been stolen, is he? By us. He won't call the police?'

She saw Jake's grin reflected in the windshield. 'I'll ring him when we get there. Or you can try him now if you want?'

'That'll go down well. If we get him out of bed again he'll call the police out of spite.'

The voice of the satnav – female, Beth noted – guided them to the M40.

'God,' said Jake, once they were on the motorway. 'If only it was always this empty.'

Beth leant forward and turned on the radio, keeping the volume low, and glanced at the speedo as she did so. Eighty.

'No rush,' she said over the honey-smooth DJ, thinking of what she was going to say to her mother, and already dreading the response. Her heart rate increased and she felt her breathing becoming shallower. She forced herself to take slower, deeper breaths. 'There's no point in getting there too early,' she said, 'before Mum and Dad get up. And let's not get pulled over or draw attention to ourselves. Any more than we already are.'

'What? Oh yes. It's hardly an unmarked car is it?'

'Not thanks to my brother. I'm still going to make him pay.'

A car – the first they'd seen – appeared from nowhere and shot past as if they were dawdling.

Eventually, ahead and to their left, Beth could see the sky lightening, changing from a deep red to orange above the horizon. The sun was beginning yet again to muscle its way into yet another cloudless sky. According to the satnav they were due to arrive about seven.

'Going to be yet another hot day,' she said, and a few moments later, after a song had finished, the DJ announced that today was

275

going to be the hottest day of the year so far.

'Oh. Good.' Jake said. 'God.'

'I've got a theory,' said Beth. 'Our weather's normally so changeable that if the weather stays the same for more than four days people get antsy. No matter whether it's sun or rain or snow or just grey and overcast. Four days of the same, and if it doesn't change people don't like it. They complain it's too hot or too cold or too wet or too dry. It's the one time people want change for change's sake.'

Jake nodded, and then they sat not speaking as something too cheerful for this time in the morning played on the radio. It wasn't even six o'clock. Beth watched the road pass through the headlight beams to disappear beneath them. To her, in this light, the M40 appeared featureless, unchanging; it felt if they weren't getting anywhere. They'd be here forever. Even the drone of the car didn't vary, and as she thought about this she felt her eyelids become heavier and begin to droop. She forced herself to sit up straighter, aware that she hadn't had a good night's sleep in several days, and that it would be unfair to snooze while Jake was driving.

She tried to moisten her dry stinging eyes by blinking. 'So really, why are you doing this?' she asked, partly to make conversation, partly because she was curious. She had Jake down as relishing his hero complex, always wanting to feel good about himself, but was sure there was more.

'Seemed like you needed someone to help you.' He didn't take his eyes from the road. 'At the time I thought it was an abusive ex you were running from.'

'But after that?'

'When I knew you were the Island's Killer Kid?'

'Always hated that name.'

'I bet.'

'The papers couldn't even be consistent with it. They tried all sorts of variations.'

'I remember.'

'Take my advice, if you're ever going to commit a crime, especially if you're going to get caught, don't do it in a slow news week. And definitely not a slow news month – the silly season they call it. They've all got front covers to fill, each of which needs to be more lurid than its competitors.'

'It caused arguments in my family.'

'Yeah?'

'But then quite a lot of things did.'

His silence was filled by another overly cheerful song. Eventually, Jake leaned forward and switched the radio off.

It was a few moments before he spoke again. 'Mum was never one for believing the papers. She'd lost a mountaineering friend. Some of the papers made it sound like it was a suicidal climb, that she'd brought it on herself. As if Mum's friend had deserved it. Dad, however, would read the papers and then repeat what they said, uncritically parroting what was being shouted in the headlines.' He glanced at Beth. 'For example, that you should be strung up or at least go to prison.'

'I was nine.'

'Yeah. Mum didn't believe all the hysteria about the Island's Killer Kid. She thought there was more to it. She reckoned there was something we weren't being told. There was a reason for what you did. Justification. Not just – as the papers put it –"pure evil". I remember, when my school term started, how the arguments split my friends, pretty much along gender lines. Most of the boys were "how dare she get away with killing a guy", most of the girls – probably from their mums – also claimed there was stuff we weren't being told, that it must have been self-defence or something. The papers never said whether he – Owen – had done anything to provoke you. Dad, and some of the other kids, said it didn't matter. Nothing could justify what you… what happened.'

'Sorry? What?' Dumbfounded, Beth twisted her head to look at him. He was staring at the road ahead and, with his pale face illuminated by the dashboard, the reflection of their headlights and the sun's first rays, she thought he looked like an apparition. A ghost from the past.

She'd heard of it, but never believed that there might actually be people who had consumed the reporting of her crime but didn't wish her ill. She tried to consider the concept, but her mind found it as difficult to focus on as the blurred scenery outside.

'Yeah,' Jake spoke louder. 'The arguments were mostly split along gender lines. There was a lot of speculation whether he had provoked you.'

The idea that there were some people to whom she wasn't altogether evil and maybe, just maybe, shouldn't be made to suffer continual punishment, ricocheted inside her head, never coming to rest long enough to investigate it. Moreover, she wasn't sure she wanted to look at the concept. After what she did – and there was no argument that she did it – did she deserve such understanding and consideration?

'Well?' Jake still didn't look at her.

When she didn't answer, he tried again. 'Had he? Provoked you?'

Beth winced. Jake was the first person to ask this in over a decade. As she'd been instructed, she'd accepted what she'd done. There was no point in reliving things. She was a murderer who hadn't even been punished by prison. And whenever her thoughts did escape and begin examining events, there was always a knife and more hyphens to carve into her legs. She clutched the armrest with her left hand while the fingers of her right gripped the car seat so tight she feared it might burst. 'It was all confusing, scary. The police, the ambulance, all the shouting, the blood. Everyone telling me what I'd done. How I'd done it. I... I'm not sure anyone asked me why. They must have done, of course. But I just did it. I don't why. It was all so bewildering. They had me in custody, that was all they were interested in until they knew my age, and then they got angry I wouldn't be punished. And my parents...' She trailed off, looking for her thoughts.

'But had he provoked you?'

'No. I mean, I don't think so. Not that I can remember. But I don't remember much. It's all confused. Images, blood, screaming, noise. And something about a vase.' She shook her head as if to shake things into new positions. 'No. He had, I remember, been helping me all day. We'd had a barbeque, and I was in put charge of laying the table in the garden and, afterwards, of clearing up. I... he had helped. He used to tease me. He and Ryan. Ryan always acted differently when Owen was around. Trying to act older. Owen was a year or two older than Ryan. At that age, Ryan was fourteen, and I guess Owen almost sixteen. He...' Beth breathed deep. 'Thanks to me he never saw his sixteenth birthday. It's true, I never liked him. I thought he was bully. But that day in Aunt Mary's garden, he seemed to be acting, well, nice. She wasn't a real Auntie, but a friend of Mum's. Aunt Mary's husband had done a runner just before Callum was born, or just after, and our family used to go on holiday with them and visit them over the summer. It always seemed an adventure visiting the Isle of Wight. I can remember wondering if Owen was helping me that day because he was sucking up to his mum for some reason. He was trying to be seen as being helpful. He didn't deserve...'

Beth shuddered as she took another deep breath. She managed to unclench her right hand and looked at it for signs of Owen's blood that she swore she could still feel, before wiping the back of her hand across her mouth, feeling how dry her lips were. She should have brought a bottle of water with her.

'Where'd the knife come from?'

'What?' Her fingers ached but they returned to the edge of the seat and began clutching once more, as if she were scared of being thrown off. 'Oh... I... think it must have been left over from the barbeque. We were clearing up.' Beth thought for a moment, her forehead wrinkling.

'And what did you actually do?'

When Beth didn't respond, Jake tried again. 'Sorry, forgive me for asking, but I mean, I know what the papers said you did. But, like, what actually happened?'

Breathing was painful. She needed to lighten the atmosphere. 'You really want to know?'

'Just curious.'

'This from the man who says he doesn't believe in looking back.'

'Well, I seem to be involved now.'

'You've got a murderer in your car and you're asking them about their crimes. Aren't you scared?'

'Well. I wasn't.'

Even to herself, Beth's laugh sounded hollow, but she was relieved that, after a pause, Jake also laughed.

Even the satnav thought it was time to join in; the female voice telling them to take the A34.

Jake indicated left and took the slip road at Junction 10. Once they were on the slope approaching the traffic lights at the top of the hill, Jake indicated right. The lights turned green as they approached and they followed the road, circling the roundabout over the M40 until they joined the A34. There were taillights ahead in the distance, pulling away from them until they disappeared. After that they were alone. Beth felt they could have been the soul survivors of an apocalypse.

'So...?' Jake asked, far too casual. 'What did actually happen?'

Beth felt her muscles relax, the ache in her fingers beginning to fade. This was better. She knew the words.

Looking straight ahead, she began. 'We were staying at Auntie Mary's – Mary Calbourne's. As it was the school holidays and as Ryan and I were sleeping on camp beds in the sitting room, I was allowed to stay up late. I did not have to go to bed before the grown-ups. It had been a hot day and Aunt Mary had set up an inflatable paddling pool in the garden which I'd been playing in all day while the grownups had their barbeque. About nine o'clock in the evening – it was not quite dark – Mum asked me to go and empty the paddling pool. Owen offered to help. Ryan was fifteen and Callum was fourteen. I went into the garden…'

She felt Jake look at her, and when she turned to him, she saw his expression. It was as if he didn't know her.

'What?' She said, annoyed at being stopped mid-flow. She knew the order of things was important.

'You're not giving evidence, you know.' He kept his eyes on her.

Look at the road, please.

'But…'

'You sound like you're reading a script. There's no need,' he gave her a big smile, reassuring. 'Just tell me.'

Beth looked into her lap. 'I'm not sure how.' A wave of anger swept through her. How dare he make her do this? Couldn't he see it was difficult?

He shrugged. 'Or not, if you don't want to.' He returned his attention to the road.

Make up your mind. Don't make me go through this, and then tell me you're not interested!

She counted to ten, tapping with her fingers, regulating her breaths, before daring to speak. 'Do you want to hear or not?'

'Yes, but only if it's okay, only if you want to tell me.'

Beth clamped her lips shut to stop herself swearing.

After a minute of silence, which felt a long time, she took deep breaths and began again, piecing together everything she had been told, everything she had learnt off by heart, and everything she could recall. Those three things had always been hard to reconcile thanks to the chaos, the screaming and the accusations. She always thought of the events like a jigsaw, but with gaps where some pieces were missing and other spots where there were too many pieces.

'Thinking back, Owen hadn't been annoying all day. Normally he was teasing me, splashing me, giggling, taunting me with his water pistol. He always managed to make it look like he was being helpful or just playing, so the grown-ups thought I was making a fuss. You know what it's like trying to convince your parents of something they can't see and so don't believe.

'But that day he'd been helpful and attentive. I thought he'd done something wrong and was trying to make up for it. So, when we were sent outside to clear up the table after the barbeque and to put away the paddling pool, and he tried to push me in it, it was a shock, and I guess I lost my temper. I remember stabbing him. I can't remember how many times. And then I shoved him and he fell into the pool. I can remember hearing the splash, and looking at the blood on my hand. It felt so hot in the cool of the evening.

'And then I ran. Mum found me on Culver Down. I was standing on the edge of a cliff. Owen drowned, but they said I did such a good job that, if he hadn't drowned, he would have died of his wounds. Where I stabbed him.'

CHAPTER 30

By the time they took the M3 around Winchester, the sun was high enough for Jake to turn off the headlights but low enough to be in their eyes. Neither Beth nor Jake had spoken since Beth's recollections. She had hoped telling someone might make her feel better. It didn't. She felt worse – a churning, a writhing, roiled in her stomach. It reminded her of the travel sickness she used to experience when very young, but this was so much worse. She thought of asking Jake to pull over, so she could get some fresh air, but knew that would make no difference. Something unpleasant had made its home inside her.

They both jumped when the satnav erupted into life. Its sudden and loud instructions guiding them on to the M27 just before they reached Southampton. The unexpected commands, sounding like a shout after the quiet, seemed to break the ice.

'Wanna stop somewhere for some breakfast? There must be somewhere around.'

To Beth, Jake's jollity sounded false. His silence over the last forty or so minutes had made her wonder what he had expected to hear from her. Not what he had, evidently.

She tried to speak, but her mouth was too dry. Not only didn't she seem to be able to moisten it, but she wasn't convinced that if she drank some water she would be able to keep it down. 'Let's get there first,' she managed to croak.

The thought of seeing her mother and explaining this weekend's events didn't help her anxiety.

Eventually, she found enough saliva to lick her lips. 'Mum and Dad,' she said, still raspy, 'have been slowly moving towards this bit of the south coast, thanks to me. They started off in Liphook, were forced to move, so the went to Petersfield, then to Horndean, now in Havant. I guess that now I'm back in the news, they'll have to move again. They're, like, not going to be happy.'

'Maybe it won't come to that.'

'Yeah, right.'

Beth kept quiet as the satnav took them through the backroads of Havant until they were almost at their destination.

'Keep going,' Beth said. 'Slow. Turn left at the end of the road. There. That's their house. First one on the left. Oh, thank God.'

There was no pack of journalists, no photographers waiting for prey, and relief washed through her, sweeping away some of her tension.

They drove until they found an empty space, into which Jake managed to reverse park the Mitsubishi. Beth would have sworn the gap was too small. Like Guildford, the streets here felt much narrower than in Leamington and, with cars parked both sides, more claustrophobic. It had taken an effort of will not to squeeze her elbows to her sides.

She opened the door to get out, and almost fell over.

Jake ran around the car to her. 'Are you all right?'

She nodded. Even at seven o'clock the heat of the sun could already be felt. It wasn't, however, the temperature that had knocked her off balance, it was air itself, saturated with the metallic and salty tang of the sea. It reminded Beth of blood. And, of course, there was the cawing of too many gulls, who wheeled overhead. All this, coupled with her memories on the journey, transported Beth back to Mary Calbourne's back garden.

She shook her head.

I shouldn't be here. I don't want to do this.

Standing up straight, stretching her back after the journey, she slammed the car door, and began striding to her parents' house. Jake fell into step beside her.

It was an end-of-terrace house, built early last century. The end wall had always been covered with ivy, but Beth was shocked at how it had grown since her last visit. Half the front of the house had been invaded. Ivy now encircled windows, both upstairs and down, its tendrils had even reached the edge of front door. It reminded her of some creature, and she told herself, yet again, that if she lived here, she's have killed the plant and ripped it down – no matter what that did to the brickwork.

The front door opened as they approached, and Dad stepped out, looking behind him as he did so, a navy-blue bag – one for a suit – draped over his right arm. He hurried up the short garden path. His white short-sleeved shirt seemed to Beth to be the brightest thing in the street.

'Dad,' Beth called before she could stop herself.

He turned, saw her, blinked twice then grinned. 'Beth? Oh, Beth. How lovely to…' His grin froze as he looked her over. 'Are you okay? What's happened? Are you all right?'

'I'm fine, Dad. I…' Beth couldn't bring herself to explain everything now, knowing she'd have to do it all again for her mother. Instead, she indicated the man walking beside her. 'This is Jake, he's been helping me.'

'Jesus, what happened to you?'

Jake put his hand up to his bruises. Beth thought the swelling had reduced, which was surprising considering he'd barely slept, but a yellow brown tinge had appeared at the edges of the purple crescents. It was as if they'd been smudged by someone's thumb.

Jake gave an embarrassed smile. 'I'd like to say, "you should see the other guy"',' he said, 'but actually he's fine.'

'But you're okay? Both of you?'

'Yes, Dad.'

'Just give me a second.' He put a finger to his lips and whispered: 'Doing this while your mum's in the shower.' He opened the boot of the nearest car. It was the green Nissan Micra Beth could remember them getting at least ten years ago. It had been second- or third-hand then. In places, specks of rust bubbled under the paintwork.

He lay the bag in the boot, smoothed it, then turned to Beth. 'Don't tell your mother. I'm getting my suit cleaned. She always says I never take her anywhere nice. You know her.' He raised his eyes to the cloudless sky. 'So I thought I'd make the effort and take her somewhere posh.' He gave her a conspiratorial smile. 'You know, as a surprise. Anything to stop her complaining. Just don't tell her, okay?' He shut the boot. 'Now, come on, before she notices I'm outside. Let's go in, get you some breakfast and a cup of tea. Oh, it's good to see you.'

Beth found herself engulfed in a hug she didn't want to end, crushed against a shirt that felt as if it had been freshly pressed just for her. But the hug did end, and Dad released her to shake Jake's hand. 'Very pleased to meet you.'

He led them into the house, and shouted up the stairs. 'Bel, got a surprise for you.'

'Oh, what have you done now?' When Beth heard her mouther's shout she felt the urge to turn and run, but Jake was behind her, blocking her exit. She turned to him, whispered, 'Like, sorry about my mum.'

Her mum appeared at the top of the stairs, one hand fumbling with her glasses, the other patting down her damp greying hair. Once her glasses were on and she saw Beth, her hand fell to the top of her chest, as if she were having trouble breathing. It was a gesture Beth recognised, an over-dramatic expression of shock and sadness: it had never led anywhere good.

She stared down at Beth; her shoulders fell, just a fraction. 'Bethany,' she said, her voice pitched as though she'd been anticipating this but was disappointed that her expectations had come true. 'What have you done, now? What's happened? Why are you here?' She took a few steps down, stopping when Jake came into view. 'Who're you? Did she do that to you?'

'Mum—'

'Why are you here? What do you want? What have you done?'

Beth felt a spark. 'Well, you always make a fuss about me not visiting,' she snapped. 'So here I am. What a welcome.'

'At this time in the morning? What do you expect? What's happened? Where's Ryan? Does he know you're here?'

'Woah.' Dad held up his hand, saw the look on Mum's face and immediately dropped it. 'Give her a chance,' he whispered, 'she's only just arrived. Let's get some breakfast and a cup of tea.' He turned and smiled at Beth. 'And then you can tell us all about it. Have you eaten? I'm starving.'

'You're always starving,' Mum continued her descent to the ground floor. 'You eat too much.'

'Can't help it if I've got an appetite. You know what I always say: get it when you can. And as much as possible.'

Beth and Jake followed Dad into the kitchen, where he filled the kettle and switched it on. 'Tea? Coffee?'

'Tea, please,' said Jake.

Beth didn't need to think about it. 'Nothing for me.' She didn't think she could swallow anything, let alone keep it down.

'Breakfast? Toast? Cereal? Something else?'

'Toast would be nice. That's very kind of you, thank you.' Jake smiled.

Beth glared at him. He was acting like a teenager meeting his girlfriend's parents for the first time.

'Go and sit in the dining room.' Dad nodded in its direction. 'I'll bring everything in, and then you tell us all about it. Oh, and Beth?'

'Yeah?'

'Good to see you.'

She led Jake into the dining room. A wooden table, large enough that six people could sit comfortably around it, dominated the space. Cabinets and cupboards flanked it on two walls, with French windows at one end letting in the low, slanted sunshine. The angle of the morning rays threw into relief gouges, like scars, disfiguring the far end of the table – evidence of a time mum had lost her temper, broken a plate against the table and then embedded a fork in its surface. Beth couldn't remember what the argument was about now, or who had started it. It wasn't the infamous sausages row, of that she was certain. She sat at the end furthest from the damage.

The sound of whispering came from the kitchen, but she couldn't make out words. Jake, she was acutely aware, could hear the same. When she looked at him, to offer a non-verbal expression of apology, she saw his attention was elsewhere. He had walked around the table to a pine cabinet and was studying the framed photographs standing on its polished top. A few pictures of her parents, their wedding – one of these showed the biggest smile Beth had ever seen on Mum's face – and some more recent ones. There were many of Ryan – as a baby, a boy, in his teenage years, older, and – the most recent – posing and grinning under a glorious blue sky, snowy peaks and ski-runs in the background. He was bundled up in a dull green jacket holding a snowboard. Anger and jealousy flared in Beth: she didn't know Ryan had ever been snowboarding. She managed to control her urge to leap across the room and sweep the picture to the floor. Jake picked up the only picture of Beth. A photograph of when she was a month or so old, and being hugged protectively by a five-year-old Ryan who couldn't disguise his pride.

Jake looked at her and raised his eyebrows.

She shrugged, glowered, and shook her head.

Tell me about it.

He replaced the photograph and sat in the chair next to hers, opened his mouth to speak but Dad arrived carrying a tray of tea-filled but mismatched cups, sugar, milk and a pile of plates. Beth didn't know what Jake was about to say but was relieved anyway.

'Here we are,' Dad said, placing the tray on the table. 'I made you a cuppa, Beth. Just leave it if you don't want it.'

Her mother followed with another tray, which she plonked down before them. This one held butter, jam and several rounds of toast.

'Okay,' she commanded. 'Tell me.' She dragged out her chair at the far end of the table, sat with her back to the windows, folded her arms, and waited.

Feeling as though she were being interrogated, Beth took a deep breath. 'Callum found me,' she said. 'And now others, like, know who I am. And will probably sell their story to the papers.'

'Oh no.' Dad put his head in his hands. 'Not again.'

'Sorry,' said Beth. She knew it sounded weak.

She looked at her mother, who stared back, expressionless. After a too many long seconds, Mum spoke. 'How?'

Beth began and, where necessary, Jake joined in between mouthfuls of toast. She explained how, on Saturday, while Mum and Dad had been with her and Ryan in the pub in Guildford, Callum must have broken into this house and found Ryan's address. She told them she'd been living in Leamington Spa, and about how Ryan and his flatmate, Paul, had followed her there after the meeting in Guildford. Once Paul had followed her from the station and discovered where she lived, and with nowhere to stay overnight, Ryan and Paul had returned to Guildford. Yesterday (*was it only yesterday?*), Ryan had returned to Leamington to check on her and had damaged Mikey's car. While he was doing that, Callum had visited Ryan's address in Guildford and had tortured Paul to tell him where Ryan was. And so Callum had turned up in Leamington. Neither Beth nor Jake mentioned the night she spent with Mikey.

When they were done, Beth sat back, drained. She didn't feel any better and still didn't feel like eating. She looked at her mum who remained stiff-lipped and impassive.

If it hadn't been for Dad buttering his third slice of toast — embarrassed and wincing at the sound but not stopping — there would have been absolute silence. Mum was the first to speak. 'Are you sure it was Ryan who wrote on the car? It seems—'

'Mum!' Beth's irritation didn't know who it should be its recipient: Mum for focusing on the wrong bit of the story, or herself for — after all her experience — not expecting this.

'I'm just asking. It doesn't sound like something Ryan would do.'

'Mum, he admitted it. And you know his temper's as bad as mine. Or yours. Especially if he lets it stew.'

'I was only asking.'

'And he didn't write on it, he gouged it with a screwdriver or something. Something sharp.'

Mum's lips tightened again.

Dad looked at his watch. 'Look,' he said, 'I've got to get to work. There's important stuff I've got to do today. We'll discuss this when I get home. I'll try to get away early. But Callum didn't hurt you, did he?'

'No. In fact, thinking about it, I'm not sure what he wanted. I thought he'd want revenge for Owen and for how his life had turned out. Now, I think he wants Ryan as well as me.'

Mum stared at her. 'Ryan?'

Dad shook his head. 'I don't think he would have hurt you. Or Ryan.'

'With respect.' Jake held up an apologetic hand. 'You weren't there. He had a knife. I for one believe he'd have used it. I can vouch for how sharp it was.' He indicated the trace of blood still encrusting his cheek. He should wash that off, thought Beth. It's doing him no favours.

Dad continued shaking his head. 'But…? It was only a threat. I can't believe… No. After all, he'd have ended up prison again, and—'

'Dad, remember what he did to me last time.'

Dad stared at Beth, his unwillingness to accept her interpretation quite clear in his expression. But it was Mum who spoke first.

'Have you told Ryan?' she asked as if dealing with a child. 'Ryan needs to know. He's got to be warned.'

'I've tried phoning him on his mobile, but I can't get through. I thought I'd phone him at work, or at least leave a message for him.'

Mum went to say something, then stopped, just nodded once again.

'That reminds me.' Jake pulled out his phone. 'I suppose I'd better call Mikey and tell him we have his car.' He looked at the people around the table, offered an embarrassed smile and touched the dried blood on his cheek. 'And can I use the bathroom to wash this off?'

Mum told him where he could find the bathroom and he left, closing the door behind him, already dialling. They could hear him in the hall. Beth couldn't hear the words but, despite the tone of pleading, she was pleased there was no shouting, none of the ice in his voice.

Mum spoke, dragging Beth's attention back to her. 'He seems nice.' Beth heard the fractional emphasis on the first word – she clutched the edge of her chair so tight her knuckles hurt again – she understood the subtext.

Too nice for you.

Beth clamped her mouth shut. The only thing stopping her from exploding was the fact she thought Mum was right. Her anger turned in on herself and, in that moment of hesitation, she saw satisfaction in her mum's eyes. Beth felt a terrible itch at the top of her left leg, and clenched her fingers so she wouldn't scratch her scars and scabs. What she wanted though, was a sharp blade.

Dad coughed and made a show of looking at his watch again. 'Look, I've really got to go. I'll be back as soon as I can. I'm sure by the time I get back it'll all be sorted. It's great to see you, Beth. Everything will be all right, you'll see.' Beth knew him well enough to recognise when he was trying to sound confident.

'Yes. You go to work, dear.' Mum had her arms folded. 'And let me deal with this. I'll take the day off, shall I? It's okay. It's only the end of this academic year. Nothing important.'

Both Beth and Dad opened their mouths to speak, then snapped them shut. They shrugged at each other, recognising the other's expression. They both knew when saying something would be worse than saying nothing.

Jake returned to the room, and Beth thought he looked paler and shamefaced. 'Told Mikey,' he said to Beth. 'He's not happy, but there's not a lot he can do about it. According to him, Sue's going to see her ex-husband tonight. It seems they still go for a meal occasionally. She's going tell him about you then.'

Even with her eyes on Jake, Beth felt her mother's irritation. Mum stood and clattered the plates onto one tray, the cups onto the other with as much noise as possible. 'Did you hear that, Des?' she said, sounding so reasonable it was scary. 'They're divorced and yet he still takes her out somewhere nice.' She headed for the kitchen taking the tray of plates with her.

Beth went to speak, but her dad put his finger to his lips again and shook his head.

'Once would be nice,' they heard Mum mutter.

'Dad...' Beth whispered.

He grinned at Beth and Jake. 'It'll be a surprise. Let her enjoy her fury now. You know how much it makes her day.' He stood, Beth stood, and they hugged. 'Maybe Callum just needs talking to,' he said. 'I'm sure he's good at heart. He used to be a nice boy.'

'You didn't see him. How he looks now. Not the same guy.'

'Okay, if you say so. It'll be all right. You'll see. Promise you.'

Dad shook hands with Jake. 'Nice to meet you. See you later, I hope.'

After Dad left, Mum left to phone her school and tell them she wouldn't be in today.

Using her mobile, Beth found the number of WWF in Woking, where Ryan worked, and, just after nine o'clock, she called.

'WWF. Can I help you?' A female receptionist. Her voice friendly and efficient. Reassuring.

'Can I speak to Ryan Garway, please?'

'Sorry?'

'Ryan Garway.'

'Hold on please.' Beth could hear tapping.

'Ryan Garway. It's urgent.'

'I don't have anyone of that name on my system. Is he new?'

'No. He's been working there for a year or so, I think.'

'Who does he work for?'

'I... Oh, for the publicity department. Dealing with

publications.'

'I'll put you through there. Please hold.'

'Hello?' A man's voice.

'Can I speak with Ryan Garway, please?'

'Who?'

Beth looked up, her hand shaking. Jake was scrolling through something on his phone. Her mum was in the kitchen, also on the phone.

'Ryan Garway,' she said again, louder, but couldn't hide the quiver in her voice. She was aware she had barely slept and felt spaced, as if this could be a hallucination.

'There's no one here of that name. Hang on.' Despite the sound being suddenly muffled, Beth could still hear the man on the other end. 'Paul...? Paul...? Isn't your flatmate Ryan someone? Didn't he work here briefly? Yeah. Someone calling for him.'

A pause, then: 'Sorry. It seems he worked here, but then... uh... there was an altercation, and he left.'

'Paul,' Beth said. Jake was now staring at her. 'Paul, his flatmate. Let me talk to him.'

'Can I tell him who's calling?'

'It's Ryan's sister.'

'Hang on.'

A new voice. 'Hello.'

'Paul? Paul. Are you okay?'

'Ryan's sister?'

'Yes. Ryan said you'd been taken to hospital. That... someone...'

'Hospital? Me? No. I'm fine.' Beth could hear the confusion in his voice. 'What about you? You're in Leamington Spa.'

'Yes. No. You followed me from the station, I know. But Ryan said... said that Callum put you in hospital. That he... hurt you until you told him where Ryan was.'

'No. Well, it wasn't quite like that. Yes, he asked in, shall we say, quite a forceful way. But he never hurt me. Never even touched me. At the time I didn't know where you were living was such a secret. How was I to know I wasn't supposed to tell him? How was I to know that? Ryan never said it was supposed to be top secret. Typical Ryan. You only ever get half the story with him. I…'

'Where's Ryan now?'

'He's not with you?'

'I can't contact him. He's not answering his phone.'

'Ah. He came back last night. Yeah. Typical Ryan, He lost his temper when he found I'd told that bloke, Callum was it? You know what Ryan's like. Threw his phone at the wall. Think he smashed it.'

Beth knew exactly what Ryan was like. She and Mum suffered sudden explosions of temper, after which everything was calm. Ryan, however, could compress his anger, letting it ferment and mature until it became too volatile to contain.

'So where is he now?'

'Definitely not with you?'

'I told you.'

'Oh, hell. He must have… he said he'd had enough and was going to finish things once and for all. If he's not with you, I think he's… he's gone after that Callum guy. That's what he said. He was going to finish things. After the way Ryan acted last night, I thought he was just… Oh, God, I hope he doesn't do anything stupid and get himself hurt. Or hurt anyone else for that matter. Not again. You know what he's like. Frankly, though, I thought that Callum guy was a nasty piece of work.'

Beth stared at the phone and ended the call without saying goodbye. She looked up at Jake.

'What?' Jake said. 'What's happened?'

'It's Ryan, he's—'

Mum re-entered the room, as if she'd been waiting to hear her son's name, and strode to the opposite end of the table, beside the pine cabinet. 'Ryan?' She stared at Beth. Challenging. 'What about Ryan?'

'He's been lying to us. He doesn't work at the WWF.'

'Of course he does. He said so.'

'Not for a long time.'

'You've got it wrong again, Bethany.'

She shook her head. 'His flatmate thinks he's, like,...' Beth paused, but knew there was no way to avoid telling her mum, '...going after Callum.'

'What?'

'How?' Jake stood. 'How's he going to find Callum? We don't know where Callum is.' He looked from Beth, to Mum, and back.

Beth shook her head. Jake hadn't thought this through. 'But we do. At least we know where he will be.'

Jake's forehead creased, then a wash of realisation smoothed his features. It made the bruises under eyes more pronounced. 'The funeral,' he whispered.

'The funeral,' Beth nodded.

Mum shook her head. 'No. Ryan wouldn't confront Callum. And certainly not at his mum's funeral. What would people... No. I can't believe...' She picked up one of the metal-framed photographs of Ryan as a teenager and stared at it. 'Not Ryan. Besides, he knows how nasty Callum can be. He's too dangerous. No. Ryan wouldn't do that. No.'

Beth thought of the gouges along the side of Mikey's car. Wounds deep enough to score the metal beneath. And premeditated. She remembered all the times he'd got into fights, often to protect her. The times he'd come home from school with bruises and scraped knuckles.

'Mum, when he's angry, you know he's likely to do anything. When his blood's up and he's let things stew...' Beth suddenly saw Callum last night, threatening her and Jake with a knife. 'We've got to stop him,' she said, 'otherwise...

Blood.

'...someone could get hurt. And possibly badly. We don't want it to be Ryan.' Another thought occurred to her. 'And then the police would get involved.'

Mum's eyes widened and Beth could see fury taking over her body, her lips tightening, turning into a grimace, her colour first fading and then rising as blood suffused her face. For a millisecond, Beth thought she recognised herself, then Mum's scream filled the room.

'You!' yelled Mum. 'This is all your fault. You did this! You!' She flung the picture she'd been holding. On instinct Beth put her hands out. The corner of the metal frame hit her left hand, and she winced. The impact took the momentum out of the flying frame, which fell to the floor, landing on its edge with a loud *crack!* The glass had fractured but there was no subsequent tinkling.

For a second there was silence, and Beth looked at the growing red mark on her palm. Then her mum screamed again.

'Now look what you've done!' Mum went to step forward, but the table stopped her.

From the depth of shock, Beth felt her own temper explode and burst through.

'Me? *You* threw it. How is it my fault? Why is it always my fault?'

'Because—'

'*Stop this. Now.*'

Beth turned to Jake, ready to yell at him, only for her anger to be smothered as if with a fire blanket. Mystification filled the space left by her fury. Jake had raised his voice, but his expression was one of total control.

How does that happen? How on earth could he remain so calm with all this going on? Just how is it possible for someone to keep such control?

He held out his hands, one palm facing Beth, the other Mum.

'Now,' he said in a long exhale. 'Can we all just stop shouting?' Beth noticed the slightest of shakes in his fingertips, and remembered what he said about avoiding confrontation and the arguments between his parents. Guilt washed through her. She went to apologise, looked from Jake to Mum, who was still glaring at her – and the words just got stuck in her throat. She looked back to Jake, and still found herself unable to say what she knew she ought, what she actually wanted to.

When no one spoke, Jake – with a slight shake of his head, stepped towards Beth and, with care, picked the photo frame from the floor. When no glass fell out, he turned it over to reveal a crack running diagonally from corner to corner, crossing Ryan's grinning face. It gave him a hideous scar.

Jake placed the photo, face up, on the dining table. 'Right,' he said. 'What time and where is the funeral?'

'Hold your horses. I've got to make a phone call.'

'Mum.'

'I told you to wait.' It was the tone she used when there was to be no debate.

'Mum. We don't have time.'

'I'm calling your father to tell him. He needs to know.'

'He's driving, Mum. Call him once he's at work.'

'I'll call now, if you don't mind. I'll leave a message for him at work. Don't pull that face, Bethany.'

Mum left the room, leaving the door open.

What can you do, huh? Beth shrugged at Jake.

'Your hand all right?'

She looked at the line on her palm. 'Yeah.'

From the hall they heard Mum. 'Can I leave a message for Des? Oh, when…? All day? No, this is his wife. What? When? No, I don't… Okay, yes, thank you.'

When Mum staggered back into the room, she looked as if she'd been punched. All her anger-filled energy had been knocked from her. For the first time in Beth's life, she thought Mum appeared truly old. And at that moment, this felt the most upsetting thing that had happened in the last few days. Mum sat, almost fell, onto one of the dining table chairs.

'Mum? What is it?'

'He's not at work. Your father. He's… He's on leave, they said. Taken a day's annual leave today. He's… he's had today booked as holiday for at least a week. He lied. He told me it was important he was at work today. He lied to me. Lied… Where is he?'

Beth glanced at Jake, knowing they were both thinking the same thing. The suit Dad had put in the car. The freshly pressed shirt.

Jake spoke with deliberation. 'I think he's also going to the Isle of Wight…'

'…to the funeral,' Beth finished for him, and stared at Mum.

CHAPTER 31

Once again, Mum was ready to explode.

Despite all the years Beth had lived on her own, away from her parents, she had never forgotten the signals. They were etched into her very core – Mum's stiff shoulders, the darting wide eyes, the clipped words, the barely repressed violence with which her disobedient glasses were shoved back onto the bridge of her nose. And, above all, the dark, thunderous cloud that seemed to hover just above her head. The signs were all so clear that Beth used to wonder why no one else saw them. She, at least, recognised them as a warning to take cover. She used to watch, with growing disbelief, as Dad and Ryan continued doing whatever they were doing, oblivious to the approaching hurricane. Ryan she could understand, everything was all sunshine for him; but she often wondered whether Dad could see what was coming and just didn't care, or whether he welcomed it. It had taken Beth too many years before she'd realised that, more often than not, she was the one the storm sought out. Whoever said lightening never strikes twice had never experienced her mum in a temper.

While Ryan, of course, could do no wrong and so never suffered the full force of the tempest, Beth had learned – again after a shamefully long time – that whatever she did was, at best, simply not good enough. In fact, she was always – she'd been forcefully informed – being deliberately difficult and trying to fail. As if. Mum prided herself on her cooking and so had decided to show a young Beth her way around a kitchen. It hadn't gone well. The only things created were double-decker shouting matches, drizzled with tears and garnished with broken crockery.

'This is all your fault.' Mum jabbed a finger at Beth, a thrust that could have penetrated steel. Crimson rose from the collar of Mum's blouse like the glow from a volcano.

Mum's anger was understandable; Dad had lied and, worse, at this very moment was doing what he knew he shouldn't. However, understandable anger was still anger and so, Beth knew, would doubtless soon be heading in her direction. This morning, more than ever, Beth wanted to avoid the oncoming tornado. She pulled out her phone, and her fingers flicked at the screen as possibilities scrolled though her mind.

'Mum,' she said, 'if Ryan and Callum meet, then… it won't go well. At least one of them will be hurt. Possibly both. Probably badly. And then the police… We need to hurry. You—'

'I just knew this would happen.' Mum's words were abrupt and tight. 'I told your dad. I did. I told him, one day your daughter's—'

'Mum!'

Her left hand held the picture, with her right Mum grabbed the topmost dirty cup from the tray on the table and flung it at the wall. 'Don't shout at me, Bethany,' she screamed as the cup exploded.

That quiet that followed was broken by Mum's laboured breathing, sounding as if she'd just sprinted a marathon.

The few seconds Beth waited felt long and full. Jake stood as silently as he could then went to pick up the pieces of broken crockery. It was no wonder they never had a matching tea set. Finally, Beth spoke, picking a tone as even as possible, as if nothing had happened. 'Look Mum, Ryan needs to be stopped. For his sake. You need to call Dad. On his mobile. Leave a message. Tell him what's going on and that he's got to get to Ryan, and stop him from confronting Callum. If those two meet…' Images of the knife in Callum's hand, and the letters scored deep into the side of Mikey's car flashed across her brain. Her fingers twitched at the memory of Owen's blood flowing through them, and her fingertips missed their targets on the screen. At least she could see the time: nine fifteen. She ran her tongue around her mouth to get rid of a sudden sourness. 'Call Dad.'

Mum had lost her high colour; she now looked pale. 'If you think I'm—'

'Mum. You can bicker with Dad later. Right now we've got Ryan to think of. We've got to hurry. Ryan must have driven down early this morning. He could have got the first ferry across. He'd have taken the car ferry. Probably from Portsmouth.'

Beth's trembling fingers finally managed to scroll through pages on her phone, and Jake cleared his throat, holding broken crockery in his palm. 'Callum was checking his watch when we saw him,' he said. His words accelerated as they tumbled out. 'He probably had an early ferry to catch as well. What are the chances they were on the same ferry?'

'Then we'll be too late. At least one of them will be overboard. I think there's, like, one ferry an hour early in the morning. Yes.' She looked up from her screen. 'Hopefully one of them's on the six o'clock ferry, one's on the seven, or even eight o'clock. Callum will be in no rush. He might have stopped for breakfast somewhere. What time did you say the cremation was, Mum? Two-thirty?'

A single nod from Mum, her lips so tight they had disappeared.

'Dad will be in no hurry either. I reckon the earliest ferry he could get will be the nine-thirty, most likely the ten o'clock. Depends if he pre-booked.'

302

'Pre-booked!' Mum didn't have the energy to truly explode at the thought of him doing this.

Beth continued, trying to keep up with her speeding thoughts. 'It's a – what? – from what I remember, like, about an hour on the car ferry? To cross to the Island?'

Mum nodded, her mouth opening and closing like a stranded fish.

'Callum wasn't dressed for a funeral,' Jake said, excited. 'So he'd have to go home to get changed.'

'Mum, tell Dad to go there. To Aunt Mary's. No, wait.' Her fingers flew over her phone.

'I'll go and get the car,' Jake said, and in his impatience dumped the remains of the cup on the table. 'Do you reckon we can catch them?' Beth could understand the fear and excitement in Jake's voice. Finally, a plan that didn't involve running away.

'Hovercraft,' said Beth, staring at the screen. 'It's closer. It's like a ten-minute crossing. We probably can't catch the nine thirty, but if we get the ten o'clock...'

'And at the other end?'

'Taxi. Car hire, or something. Depends where Dad is. If he managed to get an earlier ferry, he might be able to pick us up. Go. Go and get the car. I'll book a taxi just in case. Mum, do we still have Aunt Mary's phone number?'

Mum shook her head. She moved as if her neck was stiff. 'I don't think so. Maybe, Somewhere. But it was more than ten years ago.'

'Okay. Callum withheld his number when he phoned Jake, so we can't call him directly. But you mentioned a lot of names on Saturday, when we were in the pub. Your friends. You said they'd told you Callum was, like, looking for me. Are they on the Island? These friends? Ring them, get one of them to go to Aunt Mary's and try to keep Ryan and Callum apart.'

She saw her mistake at once: the flicker of guilt across Mum's face. Mum may have mentioned all those people but, despite her claims, she wasn't still friends with them.

Jake must have seen it as well. 'Do you want to come with me to get the car?' Beth was unsure whether she felt relieved or not that Jake didn't want to leave her alone with Mum.

Still shaking her head, Mum stared at the picture of Ryan under the cracked pane, gripping the frame so hard Beth feared it might snap and shower everyone with broken glass. 'I'm not sure...' Mum muttered.

'It's okay, Mum.' When she herself wasn't in the grip of anger, Beth could recognise situations that needed calming. She just wasn't good at defusing them. 'If you can think of anyone. Only if you've, like, got their number. A neighbour or someone.' She turned to Jake, nodded her thanks at his understanding. 'I'll stay here with Mum. You go and get the car.' Mum was having problems with all this, and Beth didn't want Jake to return with the car and find the house wrecked. Dad was going to have enough trouble as it was.

Jake left and, while Mum gripped the picture frame – a new black cloud thickening above her by the second – Beth found the dustpan and brush, cleared up the last of broken crockery, sweeping the carpet and table clean of shards, and returned to the kitchen to deposit the remains of the cup in the bin. She returned to the dining room to collect the remaining tray or breakfast things. Aware Mum was still glaring at her, she picked the tray and returned to the narrow kitchen.

Mum followed. How she got the cloud above her into the narrow room Beth didn't know. Beth braced herself.

After she put the tray on the worksurface next to the sink, she slid it away from the edge. It would just be her luck to knock it, sending everything crashing to the floor, breaking more crockery.

Mum, of course, was ahead of her. 'Be careful,' she snapped. 'You know how clumsy you can be.'

Only when you're around. Beth kept her mouth shut.

Mum stood in the kitchen doorway; there was no way she could be passed. Beth put her hands on her hips. It would only take the slightest lean, left and right, for her elbows to nudge the cabinets either side of the galley kitchen. There was nowhere near as much space as in the kitchen in Jake's flat, Beth thought, then hated herself for making such a comparison. Every time Mum and Dad had had to move because of her, Mum's kitchen had reduced in size.

'You've been nothing but trouble, Bethany,' Mum spat out the words. 'Ever since you were little, even before the… before Owen. Now look at what you've done.' She tightened her grip on the photo frame and shook it at Beth. 'Ryan's in trouble.' If nodding could be vicious, hers was. '*Your brother.*'

'You think I don't know that?'

'You want him to get hurt?' A creaking came from the frame. 'He's my son. I'm supposed to keep him safe.'

Once again Beth clamped her mouth shut. *Of course I don't want him to get hurt. After all he's done for me.* Beth knew Ryan had protected her, had fought off bullies, both in and out of school; he had put himself between her and those who meant her harm. True, he hadn't been there when Callum had attacked her, but it had been Ryan who had taken her to hospital. She owed him.

'I don't know why you're bothering with the cups, Bethany. We've got to go and get Ryan.'

'Yes.' *I know.* 'Have you phoned Dad yet?'

'This is all your fault. You *made* this happen. Oh, why couldn't you…'

Beth could feel her own anger accumulating. 'What?' the word came out like a bullet. 'Why couldn't I be more like Ryan? Is that what you're staying? Ryan. To you the sun shines out of his every orifice. You always preferred him to me. Even before... before Owen. Why?'

'You were always so difficult. He was the clever one. Never a problem. You though...'

'He was the favoured one.' Beth knew she had gone too far, a direct hit on an exposed nerve.

'Don't you *dare* tell me you weren't loved.' Mum was suddenly filling the kitchen, seeming to expand with rage; her face once again passing through burgundy and heading towards the colour of Jake's bruises. 'My children. I loved both of you. You... Both of you... I worked... I shed tears for both of you.'

'But never equally.' The words were out before Beth could stop them. She thought of the single bloody track down Jake's cheek, as if he'd been crying from one eye.

'*How dare you.* You ungrateful... After all I've done for you. After everything *you've* done to this family.'

Beth had no answer to that. She spun and looked out of the kitchen's small window, not daring herself to speak. She could feel the heat behind her, bursting from Mum. Could feel the disapproval, expanding and filling the kitchen like a gas, forcing out breathable air. All the time her own anger filled her veins, threatening to explode. She gripped the worksurface. It was becoming a choice between fainting or facing Mum and saying things she could never take back.

Then the doorbell rang.

Beth shut her eyes. Jake had returned.

CHAPTER 32

It wasn't until they were well on their way that Jake took the opportunity to ask the obvious question.

Mum was in the back of the car, leaving messages on Dad's voicemail with a voice becoming so increasingly clipped she was barely using words. Beth was in the passenger seat, giving directions, while trying to use the rear-view mirror to check on Mum. Beth wasn't surprised Dad's phone had gone to voicemail, and it was clear he wasn't going to pick up, especially when Mum had begun her message with an almost shouted, 'I know where you are and what you're doing.' Beth didn't know what Dad was playing at but not answering seemed sensible. He would know by now how much trouble he was in.

It was as he was changing up to fifth gear, once they'd joined the A27, that Jake extended a finger and touched Beth's side. She glanced at him, surprised, and he mouthed, 'What happened?'

Beth shook her head. The atmosphere between her and Mum when Jake had returned after getting the car would have been obvious. It must have felt like walking into a sudden hailstorm; even a normally oblivious man would have noticed. Jake had taken a step back and blinked, confusion clear on his face as he looked from Beth to her mother and back again, but he'd said nothing. Now, in the car, she couldn't tell him. Not only because she couldn't find the words to explain what had happened, but also because Mum was in the back seat; she may be concentrating on giving Dad a bollocking, but Beth knew from experience that Mum's ears could pick up a furtive comment from a mile away.

'Come off at the next junction,' Beth pointed left.

'No, Bethany,' came the raised voice from the back, mid tirade. 'The junction after.'

'Mum—'

'You don't want to lead him wrong, Bethany.' The subtext, Beth knew, being: 'You already have.'

Beth threw up her hands. 'What Mum says,' she sighed.

'We'll discuss this later,' Mum said into the phone, then disconnected her call. She leant forward and for some reason felt it necessary to raise her voice. 'It's quicker my way,' she stated.

Beth sat back, massaging her palm, and let her mother direct. It was easier than arguing. When she looked at her hand, she could see the red line caused by the impact of the photo frame was already fading, so she began prodding the top of her left leg, pressing the thick material of her knee-length shorts against her scarred skin, fighting the urge to expose her most recent scabs to her sharp fingernails. The thought of picking at them made her shift in her seat, eyes half closed.

The whole journey took about twenty minutes, and as they approached Southsea esplanade, Beth's felt her heart rate accelerate. It felt like sitting on a rollercoaster during its initial slow climb. And not just any rollercoaster, but the one she was avoiding looking at. In the distance, over the yacht-dotted Solent, she could see the Isle of Wight. The spire of Ryde church, on the hill behind the town, pointed to the sky like a rocket during countdown. She hadn't been back to the Island since she'd been escorted off by frighteningly large, loud and rough members of Hampshire Constabulary. She'd had no desire to return. Given the choice now, she'd make Jake spin the car right around and break every speed limit as they fled. Never seeing the sea again would not be a hardship. She sucked in deep breaths of the salt-tanged air, holding them, in an attempt to slow the pounding in her chest.

'Look, Bethany. The funfair. Do you remember when you didn't want to go on the rides? You spent the whole time in tears. You were ruining it for everyone until Ryan said he'd go on the rides with you. How he managed to fit in some of those baby rides I don't know.'

Ahead was a low building: the amusement arcade. Dark and empty. Across the top of its left-hand side, in a font that looked out of date by at least half a century, were the words *Clarence Pier*. Above the right-hand side ran *Golden Horseshoe*, as if the place were desperate to be mistaken for Vegas. Between the two sides was a burger bar, on the roof of which sat a yellow and blue building, like a small, low block of flats. Above this, a rotunda with a ring of windows offered views over three-sixty degrees. Beth always assumed it was part of the burger bar below. To her, it always looked as if a child had tried to force a round peg into a square block. To the right of the arcade, ominous and silhouetted against the sky, waiting expectantly, was the dreaded and terrifying rollercoaster. Unable to look away now, Beth saw the track was compact, low with no steep drops – nothing but a child's version. When she was little, it had seemed the biggest, scariest thing ever. At least until she had become the Island's most famous murderer. Nothing moved on the rollercoaster, not even the gulls perched on the rails. The funfair wouldn't wake until at least eleven o'clock.

As they approached a roundabout, Mum indicated the car park on their left even though Jake was already indicating. They had their choice of spaces.

Jake grinned as he got out the car. 'Shall we pay for parking or let Mikey get a ticket?'

'Tempting,' Beth said. 'But…' She dug into her old and shabby handbag. It normally lived scrunched up in her rucksack, so it was just large enough for her purse, phone and a few essentials. The leather was cracking in places and the seam on the strap was fraying.

'You know,' Jake's grin turned from playful to bewildered. 'You're very law-abiding... for a murderer.' He pulled his wallet from his pocket. 'I'll get this.' He strode off to the ticket machine to investigate.

Beth called after him. 'I'll get the hovercraft tickets then. Just over there.' She indicated the travel office, but then felt stupid. It was as unnecessary as Mum's final directions to the car park. The ticket office was obvious, both from the large Hovertravel signs and, to its left – behind a wall of Perspex splash guards – the hulking shape of a hovercraft. Beth glanced back at Mum, expecting her to comment on Beth's stupidity. Mum, however, was still clambering out of the back seat, muttering about the unnecessary height of the car and studiously not looking at the words gouged into its side.

Beth sighed, looked at her watch (nine-forty) and, without waiting for Mum to stop her, began jogging for the ticket office. Within a few paces she realised just how hot the day was becoming. She gave thanks she didn't have far to go: with just a road separating them, the car park could hardly have been closer to the ticket office. At the window, she asked for three one-day returns and, no, she didn't know what time they would be returning. 'But I hope we will,' she muttered as Mum walked up behind her. Mum said nothing and just stood, tapping her foot, so Beth pulled her credit card from her purse. She went to hand it over. And stopped. 'No,' she said, pulling it back and turning it face down as she did so. 'Not that one.' She replaced it in her purse and pulled out the card for her business account. It didn't carry her name. In her mind's eye she saw the woman at the till spotting who she was, pressing a hidden button, ringing alarm bells, and calling over other Hovertravel employees who would inform her she was banned from ever setting foot on the Island. The woman didn't look up, just keyed in three open returns. Beth winced at the cost, certain she wouldn't have the future work to pay for this. Mum still remained silent.

Jake joined them and they walked into what was optimistically called the departure lounge. It felt small, like a doctor's waiting room. To Beth, it was filled with tangible anticipation. Salt-encrusted windows offered a bleached view across the Solent to the Isle of Wight. Leaflets, magazines and piles of promotional material for the Island's attractions filled racks and were piled on the windowsill. When she'd last been here, she'd been an over-excited little girl, expecting holiday adventures. Now, it wasn't eagerness she felt, but fear of what she might find, especially if Ryan and Callum had already clashed. Would the police have been called? Or, oh God, an ambulance? Another stabbing? Would someone try to contact Mum and Dad about the confrontation? Were they trying now?

To take her mind off such thoughts, she looked at the other passengers: twenty or so including some wide-eyed restless youngsters, most of which were at the windows, gawping at the Solent, the rest standing at the glass door, waiting to be let out. Despite the occasional chiding, none of the children could keep still. Beth could understand it; she remembered how Ryan's excitement at the sight of a hovercraft had been infectious. She had feared there would be more tourists, that getting seats would be difficult. Maybe it was still too early in the day.

A rhythmic movement beside her caught her attention. Mum's fingers were plucking the shoulder strap of her handbag as if playing a musical instrument. One foot tapped the floor – toe and heel, toe and heel – and she licked her lips in a way that suggested they were dry. Beth hadn't seen her mother this nervous since she'd had to steel herself to deal with the police, court officials, social services and, of course, tabloid journalists.

The glass door opened, the first travellers had their tickets checked, and Mum spoke with what seemed forced jollity. 'So, how long have you two been seeing each other?' The words fell over each other, as if pulled into the silence between the three of them like air rushing in to fill a vacuum.

'Sorry?' said Jake.

'Mum!' snapped Beth.

Without thinking, the three of them stepped forward as the queue began moving.

'Just asking. When did you two meet? You didn't mention it, Bethany, on Saturday.'

Beth was aware Jake was looking at her, his eyebrows raised in expectation, as interested in her answer as Mum. Beth glanced to the side. 'Oh, look,' she said. 'How are non-English speakers supposed to cope with that? It looks like it should rhyme, but doesn't.' She pointed to a sign promoting a travel pass, combining a day's bus and hovercraft travel: a Hover Rover. She thought about the overseas authors whose papers she edited – well, used to edit. Their English was not perfect but was infinitely better than the only second language she had been taught at school, French. And it was because their English was not perfect, that she believed she – or someone like her – was vital in making their attempts at academic writing understandable and publishable. And yet, now, publishers thought such editing skills were no longer necessary. A sign of the times, everyone wants their academic papers to be published instantly, speed rather than accuracy, everything needs to be fast rather than *right*. She felt a sudden desire to talk to someone about it, an urge to express her fears over her future. As she waited, she realised it was the one worry she could share, and maybe it would even be a release from her burden. Then she saw her mum, eyes narrowed, still waiting for an answer.

Beth shook her head. Ha, the very idea that she should discuss her worries with her mother.

The three of them took another step closer to the door, and still Beth couldn't bring herself to speak.

It was Mum who spoke first. 'I apologise for my daughter.' She stared into Jake's face so her meaning was clear. 'Bethany does need someone to look after her.'

Jake shook his head. 'Frankly, Mrs Garway, I've only known Beth a few days, but I can say that, without doubt, she is very capable of looking after herself.'

If it wasn't for the fact that they were now at the door, Beth would have hugged him.

She showed the tickets to the official, and they exited onto a concrete ramp. It slanted down to their right, to the sea. The waves were closer than Beth expected; the tide was coming in.

Ahead of them sat the hovercraft. As a girl, Beth had always been in awe of its size, and was surprised to find it still felt huge – it filled almost her entire field of view – and also how small the passenger cabin appeared. The front of the craft, painted red, white and blue with a stylised Union flag. On the esplanade, excited faces were already pressed against the Perspex splash guards, waiting for the craft to take-off. For some kids, watching a hovercraft fly was not an everyday occurrence; even for the locals it seemed it never lost its novelty. Beth stopped, as did Jake, both of them taking in the cockpit raised above the bulbous white body, which itself was sitting on top of the black deflated skirt – Beth could smell the hot rubber. The two fans at the rear looked out of scale, as if they were from an even larger craft.

Beth heard Jake mutter. 'Wow.' It reminded her of Ryan.

Mum touched his arm. 'Not been on one before?'

He shook his head.

'This is my favourite,' she said. 'The Island Flyer.'

'Mum, how can you possibly have a favourite hovercraft? What possible difference can there be between them.' Immediately, Beth felt sorry for the other hovercraft in service, which, for whatever reason, in Mum's eyes didn't match up to this one.

She found herself on the receiving end of one of Mum's beloved looks: *are you really questioning me?* Mum returned her attention to Jake and a friendly smile appeared. 'If you ask Des, he'll lecture you all day on it. he'll tell you all about it. And I mean *all*. I can't tell you the number of times he's told us this…' she made finger quotes in the air, '…is the world's only commercial passenger hovercraft service. My advice? Don't ask.'

They climbed up the steps at the front. Beth had never been on an aeroplane, but from what she'd seen in movies, she felt this was similar, if wider. Pairs of seats ran along the sides, by the windows, while rows of three seats filled the central area. They found three spare in the middle section, near the back; Beth sat with Jake to her right and Mum to her left. Stuck to the back of the seat in front of her, was a sheet carrying details of what to do in an emergency.

After a brief safety announcement, the hovercraft made a great fuss of rising, if only a little, above the world, which then seemed to simply slide from under them. It was as if everything had become frictionless. Beth was thankful the noise precluded any conversation and, now she was aboard, she remembered how Ryan had got the two of them straining to hear or feel a difference as the craft passed from the concrete ramp onto water. As before, she was disappointed. Looking around, she saw the youngsters, especially the boys, thrilled and fascinated at the thought they were flying inches above the waves to an island. She understood their excitement, but couldn't share it. Instead, she felt dread about what she would find. It took a few minutes before she realised she wasn't the only one. Mum couldn't keep her legs still, her fingers tapped the handbag in her lap as if sending out SOS messages, and Jake chewed his bottom lip. Beth found herself scratching at the leg of her shorts, trying to get to the scars beneath, but not reveal them. She forced herself to stop, but it was hard. If it were anyone other than Ryan, she wouldn't be making this journey.

The three of them sat in silence, each absorbed with their own thoughts, fears and hopes, as they crossed the Solent.

CHAPTER 33

The tide was coming in fast, each wave reaching higher up the sandy beach than the last. When the tide was out, Beth remembered, Ryde beach was so flat it seemed to go on forever. There were times when the sea was no more than a thin slash of silver in the far distance. But when the tide changed, owing to the flat, shallow beach, it came in a such a speed the unprepared would just have to run. A hovercraft, therefore, was perfect in such a landscape: it could travel as far as it wanted up the shore whether the tide was in or out. The ferry, carrying foot passengers from Portsmouth, had to moor at the end of Ryde Pier Head, and the pier itself, to the younger Beth, appeared to stretch halfway to Portsmouth. It even had part of the Ryde–Shanklin train line on it, with stations at either end of the pier. Dad had once explained that the pier had to be long otherwise the ferry would beach itself if the tide was out. Now, looking at the pier, everything appeared to Beth smaller than she remembered. The wood was weathered and rotting, the piles shabby, and the train very obviously re-painted ancient carriages from London's underground network. Such underground trains don't die, she thought, like pensioners they just retire to the Isle of Wight.

It had taken just nine minutes for the hovercraft to cross the Solent, and Beth, Jake and Mum set foot on the Island as a train rattled passed, on its way to Ryde Esplanade and then Pier Head station. The sound transported Beth back to childhood visits to London – back when she had a normal life, before she became infamous. Before the murder.

'Blimey,' said Jake, wiping the perspiration that had appeared on his forehead. He winced, and Beth couldn't tell whether it was from the hot sun burning his fair skin, or his still-sensitive nose and the bruises under his eyes. 'It's got to be at least a couple of degrees hotter over here,' he said. 'Just in that distance.'

'Have you got a hat?' Beth already knew the answer. He hadn't brought one when he'd fled from his flat, and there hadn't been one in the car. 'Stay in the shade,' she said before he could answer.

'You two are alike in that way,' Mum said. 'Bethany always used to suffer in the sun. We could never sit out and enjoy it. We always had to find somewhere in the deepest shade. Do you remember that, Bethany?'

Beth didn't answer. She had other things on her mind. As she suspected, Dad wasn't waiting for them. Even if he'd managed to get the nine o'clock ferry, he'd have been pushed to get here by now. However...

'There,' she pointed. 'One of those must be ours.'

Two cars, with their taxi logos, were waiting near the footbridge, over which the quickest of the hovercraft passengers were already climbing. It took them over the railway line to Ryde bus and train stations, and to the town.

She strode towards the cars, speaking the name she had booked a taxi under: Jake's name.

The driver of the first car beckoned them, and they climbed in. Beth in the front. Jake crossed behind the vehicle to get behind the driver.

'Yaverland?' the driver looked at her as he started the engine.

'Yaverland,' she agreed. A chill blast from the vehicle's air-con should have felt refreshing, but it was nowhere near enough to cool her nerves.

They drove off, past the newest parts of the town – the ice rink, bowling alley, funfair – and out of Ryde.

Even with morning traffic, the journey took less than twenty minutes. As well as running on a different time scale – a lot of places didn't open until mid-morning – the Island also worked on a different geographic scale to the rest of the country. Places were just closer together. Yaverland was a village north of the town of Sandown yet still on Sandown Bay, only separated from its more popular neighbour by the Isle of Wight zoo.

Beth zoned out of Mum's constant chatter – tales of Ryan's and, where necessary, Beth's, youthful adventures on the Island. Beth was surprised the taxi could move, what with it containing the three of them and the elephant in the car that Mum was so studiously avoiding. A couple of times she came close to the reason Beth hadn't returned to the Island, before she veered off to another story about Ryan.

As they rounded a corner on the crest of another hill, Beth could see Yaverland and Sandown before them, all the way across the bay to Shanklin and the cliffs beyond. The sea appeared too blue, looking more like a tropical ocean that the English Channel.

Beth tensed and the driver misunderstood. 'Some view, huh?' he said.

'Not my favourite,' Beth muttered.

A hand tapped her shoulder, and she twisted to look back. Mum was leaning forward. 'Are you all right? If you don't want to do this, Bethany, you can get out now.'

'Mum!' Beth shot a glance at the driver. There was no recognition of her name or, as far as she could tell, association between her name and their destination. Even if he was a recent incomer to the Island, she'd made the national news for over a week – he was easily old enough to remember.

'Mum,' she said again, wanting to add, *don't use my name*, but unable to.

'Just saying,' said Mum, sitting back. 'If this is going to be hard for you, you can wait here.'

'Don't you want me? Is that it? Why don't you want—'

'I'm just trying to help.'

'Look,' Jake raised his voice. It had that edge to it that Beth had heard when he spoke to Callum. 'We're going to stick together. Yes?'

Beth nodded.

'If you say so,' Mum agreed, but in such a way it was clear she didn't know why Jake was making a fuss.

The trees obscuring the view to the left tapered out and, over a low hedge, she could see the parched grass on Culver Down, it sloped from its highest point behind them to the bay ahead. It was where Mum had found her after she'd killed (*no, murdered*) Owen. She had no memory, and no one would tell her, how she got from Aunt Mary's onto Culver Down, or how close to the cliff edge she came. Beth wondered now if in her fugue state she'd had a plan.

Would everyone's life have been better if I'd jumped?

She pressed her hand against her thigh, and tried to concentrate on what was ahead, what she could expect to find. Images filled her mind, of finding a shattered front door swinging open, of blood in the hallway, of finding a body slumped against the wall. Whether it was Ryan or Callum, her mind's eye flinched from revealing.

Her mouth felt as sandy as the beach ahead. It took her several attempts to clear her throat. 'Next right,' she managed to tell the driver. Mum didn't correct her.

Around them sat holiday bungalows. It had always been a joke between the two families that the Calbournes lived in the only house in Yaverland with an upstairs. It wasn't true, but wasn't far off.

'Then up here,' she indicated. 'And let us out anywhere.'

The driver turned as directed and, the moment she saw cars lining one side of the narrow road, Beth realised her mistake. She should have asked Paul what car Ryan was driving. At least then she'd know if one of them was his. She'd be prepared. A blast of anger at her stupidity rocked her and she clutched the seat.

The driver found the one clear spot where he could pull close to the kerb, and let them out. Instantly, the heat of the day hit her. It felt as though her skin was tanning the moment she stepped from the car; she wished she had sun cream, sunglasses and a hat. Paying the driver in cash, she told him to keep the change, and waited for him to leave before raising her eyes to look at Aunt Mary's house. The place that haunted her nightmares. An unremarkable detached house, with large bay windows and a garden now looking unloved. She never thought she'd see it again for real.

And frankly, she thought, she never wanted to. Squinting in the sharp, stabbing sunshine, she began walking towards it.

Jake fell into step beside her, Mum a pace behind. Beth looked at the downstairs, then upstairs, bay windows. Nothing moved. At least nothing she could see. She had a sense, though, that she was being watched. Her back itched, her neck burned in a way that wasn't due to the sun. Was a journalist going to report on the funeral? A hack already here, waiting? She halted and looked one way then the other along the street, then at the parked cars.

'What's up?' Jake followed her gaze.

As far she could see all the vehicles were empty, but that didn't mean someone hadn't ducked down, and then of course there were the blinding reflections. She put a hand up to shield her squinting eyes, but it didn't help against the dazzle. Anyone could be watching her.

'Hmm.' She shook her head, spun on her toes and led the way. For some reason Mum was hanging back, unwilling to take the lead; as Jake didn't know which house held Beth's nightmares, she had to be first to step on to the garden path. There was no gate. Brittle weeds thrust their way between the flagstones, and the small lawn to the side of the path had been neither cut nor watered. It was difficult to tell where the yellowing grass ended and the flowerbeds began.

'A shame,' she heard Mum say. 'Mary had such pride in her garden.'

Brown weeds and sharp tufts of grass smothered what, Beth assumed, were once the flowers. Wilted and withered, they clearly hadn't seen water since the heatwave began.

Contrary to her imaginings there were no windows broken and the front door was intact. Beth exhaled, relieved so far.

She hesitated, then pressed the doorbell. A muffled *ding dong* emanated from inside, and she stepped back, braced. Jake stood to her right. Where their shoulders touched it felt uncomfortably hot. Any other time, anyone else, she would have stepped away.

Footsteps approached, the door opened and Callum stood there, wearing the same off-white T-shirt and khaki cargo shorts as when she'd last seen him, and much the same angry expression. He also appeared to be gripping the same knife.

'Wha...' he said and, in the time it took him to take a step back and register who it was, he composed himself. He glanced at the knife in his hand, his expression no different than if he'd been checking his fingernails. 'Haven't seen Ryan, but I'm ready for him,' he growled.

A car door slammed and Beth glanced over her shoulder in time to see Mum open her mouth to speak.

Then things sped up.

Callum made a sound, a guttural animalistic noise that Beth couldn't believe could ever come from a human, and when she looked she saw his features were contorted, lips drawn back, his teeth so tightly clamped he was snarling, and from deep in his throat he made that terrible sound again, made it a fraction of a second before something shoved Mum so hard she fell against Beth, so hard it drove the air from Beth's lungs, and what felt like a hurricane followed through, hitting Beth and Jake simultaneously, knocking them aside so that Beth found herself staring at the cracked and discoloured paint on the doorframe, and she cried out, more in shock than pain, and she heard Jake do the same, their cries joining a scream of 'No!' from Ryan as he continued his charge through, into the house, flinging himself at Callum, who tried to raise the knife up, but too late, Ryan knocked it aside, out of his hand, so that it fell point first to the carpet, and then the two men crashed to the floor with Ryan on top, punching, hitting, pulling at Callum's flapping defensive arms in an attempt to get another shot at Callum's face, as arms and legs flailed, and fists flew, making the two men look like some single flapping, thrashing creature until Callum managed to twist himself enough so that he could start rolling the two of them onto their sides while groping for the knife and, centimetre by centimetre, he forced himself on top of Ryan, who, aware of what was happening, shouted, 'Run, Pudge, Run!'

But Beth didn't.

CHAPTER 34

Beth shouted so hard, so loud, it came out a scream. She didn't know what she yelled, she intended 'Stop fighting!', but she had the feeling it was as unintelligible as Callum's guttural exclamations. Whatever it was, it erupted from somewhere so deep and with such force it scraped her throat raw. She didn't think she'd ever screamed so loud.

She tried again, and to get attention she kicked out at the nearest leg, but whoever it belonged to didn't feel it. To them it was just another impact.

It was Jake who stepped forward. One of his hands wrapped itself in the neckline of Callum's T-shirt and – reminding Beth of a schoolteacher stopping a playground scrap – he yanked hard, pulling Callum up and free. There was a ripping sound, cotton being stretched beyond its limit, when Callum leant forward and plucked the knife from the beige carpet. Jake pulled Callum up and shoved him against the wall, forcing a croak from Callum's throat. Callum's free hand plucked his misshapen and ruined neckline from his throat. It exposed a livid pink line.

'You ripped my fucking shirt,' Callum snarled, kicking out at Jake. His foot barely connected, but it was a feint. As if performing a backhand stroke, he swung the knife, slashing through the air, leaving a thin ruler-straight red line across Jake's palm. Jake didn't notice; he stepped forward after the knife had passed, clumsily managed to catch Callum's wrist, and then twisted it hard until the knife fell. Callum swore and struggled, and Jake twisted harder and kicked the knife towards Beth. He shoved Callum back against the wall, palm against the other man's chest. It was only when he saw the blood on Callum's ruined T-shirt that, confused, he looked at his hand and realised he'd been cut.

Seeing Callum subdued, even if only momentarily, Ryan slid away across the carpet until his back was against the hall wall, his chest heaving.

Callum moved as if to get to the knife again.

'Just try it.' Jake was no longer in the pacifying mood.

'Stop this!' Beth yelled and felt it tear at her throat again. Much to her surprise, they all obeyed. Callum and Ryan's faces were so contorted with fury and fear and hate she barely recognised them. Jake, however, appeared to be waiting for an excuse to lash out, his anger finally surfacing. Even Callum seemed to sense this; he leant back, blood from his nose trickling to his lips. In the manner of someone leaving something precariously balanced, Jake removed his bloody palm from Callum's chest. He pulled a handkerchief from his pocket and wrapped it around his hand.

Ryan recovered first. 'Run, Pudge,' he took a wheezing breath. 'Don't listen to him. You know... Ow.'

In the narrow hall, Callum kicked out, managing to catch Ryan on his shin. Jake caught Callum's shoulders and threw him against the wall again.

Still in the doorway, Beth took a deep breath, feeling the sandpaper rawness in her throat and taking a sliver of pleasure in the discomfort. 'I. Said. Stop.' In one movement – one that was too reminiscent of her nightmares – she plucked the knife from the floor and banged the handle into the door frame. It left a dent in the wood, cracked the paint and sent a loud thud echoing along the hallway. She didn't care about the damaged woodwork.

Catching his breath, Callum leant against the wall, one hand behind him for support, the other pulling at the stretched neck of his T-shirt. Hatred burnt in his eyes.

That shirt's beyond repair, Beth thought, then wondered why such a thing had occurred to her.

She swallowed and tried not to wince. 'Now…'

'You know it was his fault?' Callum thrust a finger first at Ryan, then at Beth. '*You* might have murdered my brother, but it was *his* fault. I'm gonna—'

'Don't listen to him, Pudge, Mum. He's—'

'Oh, my.' Mum barrelled through as if Beth wasn't there. She knelt before Ryan, who was sitting on the floor, back against the wall, legs stretched out away from Callum. 'Ryan. Oh, my boy. Are you all right?'

Before Ryan could answer, Callum – his rage just about under control – spoke, his words snarled. 'My mum kept his diaries, you know. Owen's diaries. She didn't show them to the police. She was—'

'Don't believe—' cried Ryan.

Callum thrust a finger at Ryan. '*He* knows what's in them.'

Ryan shook his head. Not to deny anything, Beth thought, but in an attempt to stop listening.

Beth might have held the knife that sliced Jake's hand, but the daggers in the glances exchanged by Callum and Ryan were far, far sharper.

Callum's attention turned to Beth and Mum, accusing. 'You know what Owen wrote?'

Beth had a sudden urge to lean against the doorframe, let it take her weight and then sink to join Ryan on the floor. A wave of nausea passed through her. Sourness filled her mouth.

Must be aftershock, she tried to convince herself, *or adrenaline.*

'Get away from me!' Ryan tried to kick out at Mum, but the angle made it impossible. 'This is your fault.'

Mum remained crouching before him. 'Ryan, dear…'

'No.' Ryan looked up at Beth, his face a picture of desolation, and she was shocked to see tears fill his eyes and roll down his cheeks. She didn't think she'd ever seen him cry before. Never. The five years between them meant she'd never known him as a little boy. He'd always been her big, strong brother, who always came in and saved the day. Watching him cry like a child was terrifying, like seeing your home go up in flames. Breathing became difficult, as if all the air were being sucked from the hallway. She wanted to look away, but the hallway itself, even the faded floral wallpaper, held too many memories.

Ryan sniffed. 'You know what one of my earliest memories is?' He was looking at Beth, but she was sure his words were targeted at Mum. 'I remember, Pudge, the day you were first brought home. From the hospital. Clear, I remember it. Mum and Dad standing over the cot looking down at you, staring at you. But they weren't smiling or proud. And I remember, I remember Mum saying, "We've made a great mistake".'

Mum stood. Took a pace back and stared down at Ryan. 'You remember that?' Her tone and features emotionless. She could have been an automaton.

Ryan nodded. 'I felt so sorry for…, for Pudge, I promised myself I'd do everything I could to look after her. But then…' he looked down, as if watching his tears fall into his lap, '… one stupid, stupid remark. Trying to… Owen was a year and a bit older than me. When you're a teenager, a year's a big thing, it makes a huge difference.' He looked at Callum, then at Jake. 'You know. You remember what it's like. The raging bloody hormones, the urges, the absolute confusion about yourself, but total certainty about everything and everyone else, the overwhelming desire to

326

be understood but the crippling inability to express what you want to say, what you're going through, and the utter longing for acceptance by…' He sniffed, wiped his eyes and nose with the back of his hand, and started again. 'I wanted to be on Owen's good side, to be his friend. He could be… with that year, at that age, he just seemed so cool, so I… I… told him…' He looked up and down the hall, as if the words could be found hanging in mid-air, then his head dropped forward into his hands, and his words became muffled. 'I'm sorry. I'm sorry.'

Callum spoke, his voice stronger than Ryan's but not by much. Jake stepped closer, a warning. The scarlet stripe on the handkerchief expanding and deepening in colour. 'You told him,' Callum said, 'he'd be in with a chance with Beth. That she could be persuaded to let him—'

No!' Ryan looked up, his wet eyes red and swollen. 'No,' he repeated. The way he shook his head gave the impression it was too heavy for his neck. 'That's not what I said. You must believe me. I never said anything like that.'

'According to his diary you did. He believed Beth… well, that she'd eventually let him… The way he wrote about her—'

Beth spoke before she realised. 'I was nine! Nine, for God's sake.'

Callum looked from Ryan to Beth. She was shocked once again: in his eyes – *Callum's!* – there were also tears. She couldn't tell whether they were of sadness or rage.

'His diary. His fucking diary.' Callum shot Mum a sideways glance, and in that moment Beth glimpsed the ten-year-old who would have been mortified about swearing in front of his elders. Then the image was gone. Callum ploughed on. 'I wish… Owen had just turned sixteen, and desperate to… you know, lose his… what he wanted to do to Beth. And, and I just hope Mum never read what he fucking wrote.' He glanced at Mum again. 'It would have… Now, now I know what he was like. All those years after he was gone I had girls coming up to me, telling me what he had done to them, or tried to do. I never believed them. I got into fights with them, I… I… hurt some of them. What they said about Owen. Accused him of… Turns out they were right. All of them. He was…' He looked at Beth, rage competing with sorrow, and he slumped against the wall, just about managing to stop himself slipping down and joining Ryan on the floor.

Mum broke the silence, her voice just above a whisper, looking down at Ryan. 'Is that why you did it, then?'

He managed to nod, but it looked as if it took all his strength. 'I couldn't tell you, could I? It was my fault. All my fault. I realised what Owen was going to do… and ran after…' He looked up at Beth, eyes glistening, snot bubbling from his nose. 'It was me. Me. I killed Owen.'

Beth stared at him, not understanding. 'No,' she said, but without any force. Blurred images from her past became sharper. 'I remember now. Owen had a knife. I fought… He dropped it. I picked it up, lost control and stabbed him. Again and again.'

Ryan shook his head, and offered up a sad smile. 'Yeah. You did. By the time I got there you'd gone, and he was struggling in the paddling pool. I knew he'd blame me, tell everyone what I'd said about you. And what they'd think about me. I was scared, at what he'd done, and what *I'd* done. I picked up the knife. I was the one who held him down, under the water, until…' He shrugged, defeated. 'It was me.'

Beth stared at him, the only clear thought that, surely, Ryan was doing his best to save her again.

'I don't believe you.' She shook her head, trying to force more memories into focus; attempting to remember what she'd been commanded to forget.

'I wasn't out there quick enough,' Ryan sniffed. 'I…

Remember that vase that was broken that night? Owen did that.' He looked at Callum. 'But he blamed you for it.'

The way Callum nodded gave the impression all his muscles had calcified. 'Mum believed him,' he said. 'Mum *always* believed him. Never me.'

Through Ryan's tears there appeared the briefest smile. 'You got sent to bed early. Your Mum went up with you because you were complaining so much. It got both of you out of the way. I only realised what Owen intended when he followed Pudge out… When I realised he was gone, I ran out…' He forced his wet eyes back to Beth. 'But Beth, you'd already… you know. And then… when Mum came out… She saw what I'd done.'

'But… why…' Beth almost jumped at the jolts of memory that hit her, like images of a tightly edited film: Mum calling her name that evening; Mum finding her on Culver Down, Mum handing her the knife, blood still on the blade, Mum's white face thrust close to hers; Mum stressing, over and over: 'this is what you killed Owen with. It is, isn't it? Isn't it. It's what you did. You did it. You lost your temper and stabbed him. You did, didn't you'. She remembered grasping the black handle, staring at the slick blade, terrified.

Beth stared at her mother, the silence broken by a car pulling up outside and the sniffles from Ryan and Callum. Beth realised she felt empty, scooped out, floating in fact, rising untethered in the hallway. She looked into the new void within her, knowing she should be feeling blazing anger towards both Ryan and Mum, but there was nothing. Not even cold, cold ash. Glancing down, she found she was holding Callum's knife. She was tempted to try a small cut in her flesh, to see if she would deflate like a balloon and whether she would land in a world where everything made sense. And still she floated, now high above the hallway ceiling yet able to look down on the tableau to see how small everyone was, how silly Mum appeared, standing over a sprawled Ryan, while Callum looked on, trying to sort out his own feelings, and Jake stood guard, working out the best thing to do.

And then she crashed back into herself with such force she shook. 'Mum.' She had to fight to stop the words flooding out. 'You *knew*. You knew it wasn't me. All these years, and you knew it wasn't me.'

Mum reacted as though she was already bored of the argument. 'Of course I knew. I found them, Ryan and Owen. What was I going to do? Let Ryan go to prison? He had so much promise. *He* was the clever one. *He* was the one the world deserved. It was a simple choice. Ryan would go to prison, but you were too young. We could keep the family together. What else were we supposed to do?'

Mum, I was almost raped!

Beth looked to Jake and Callum. Both were slack-jawed. The stain on Jake's handkerchief was seeping through. Behind her, a car door shut.

'*You* did it?' Callum whispered, staring at Ryan. Jake moved in front of him, sluggish, uncertain.

Thoughts and images whirled and swirled and collided in Beth's head, and then they simply stopped spinning; with an almost audible click, they slotted themselves into place. Now she remembered Owen rushing up behind her, making her jump, then pressing himself against her, looming over her, the feel of his left hand on her, over her mouth, the confusion on his face when she'd struggled, when she'd knocked the knife from his hand, the way it had fallen, the blade embedding itself into the ground, the panic with which she had ducked and grabbed the protruding handle, and... She swallowed and found her throat was still sore and realised she was gasping as if she'd been submerged for too long and had only just surfaced.

Ryan was crying openly now, his sobs loud. 'You have no idea what you did to me.' Tears and spittle and snot flying as he shook his head at Mum. His hands were gripping the carpet, as if scared it would be pulled away. 'Do you know what it's like trying to live a life you don't deserve? While my little sister…' He broke up into wracking sobs. It took several loud sniffs before he had control again. No one else spoke. Beth didn't think they'd even breathed. 'University. Every job I had. I knew I didn't deserve it. I knew I should be in prison, *deserved* to be in prison. Punished. But I was free and someone else, my baby sister, was suffering instead. You know what knowing that does to someone?' With a huge sniff he leant back against the wall, banged his head against it. 'I'm sorry, Pudge. I couldn't… They made me. I know that sounds weak. But I didn't know what else to do. I should have been living your life, running all the time, scared, and you should have had mine and… I'm so sorry.' He looked at Mum, and Beth could see the hatred in his eyes. His mouth moved but he couldn't bring himself to say what he thought. He banged his head against the wall again.

Beth was trying to get her thoughts in order when Callum spoke, his own anger now dominant. 'Aw,' he said. '*You've* had a hard life? You've suffered have you? What about me? Owen may have been a… dick, but he was still my fucking brother. You think your life's been hard? What about me? I never knew my Dad; my brother was murdered; my Mum lost interest in me. And I *fucking did go to prison.* You know what they do to you there? And you? You! You just walked away and now feel a bit sorry for yourself? You…'

He flung himself forward, trying to get to Ryan, but Jake instinctively put his arms out; Callum bounced back, his face screwed with fury, and glaring. 'I'll break you in fucking half,' he said, thrusting his face inches from Jake's.

'*Stop that!*' Mum commanded. She stared at Callum. 'Your brother was obviously a monster. My Ryan did the world a favour. He deserves a medal.'

Oh, well done, Mum. Way to calm things down. Beth wanted to move from the doorway but was still unable to step into the house.

Ryan leant and stretched, put out his hand and touched Mum's ankle. 'No, Mum.' He looked up at Beth, and the desolation on his face shattered her heart. 'What are you gonna to, Pudge? Now you know. Are you gonna tell—'

'No, she's not.' Mum spun to Beth. 'Are you.'

'Mum…'

'She knows what'll happen. She wouldn't do that to her brother.'

Beth waited for the familiar anger to explode. But it never happened. Instead, it was as if the hallway had extended and opened up and Beth could see down it into the past, see everything that had happened over the last twelve years – the injuries others had suffered because of her, her own anxiety, fear, paranoia and pain. The sleepless nights, no friends, the continual relocations. Everything that should have happened to someone else. To Ryan. Could she pass that on to Ryan? Not Ryan, no. Not her big protective brother. Yet, if she didn't, she'd have to keep living the life she had. This was her chance for a normal life.

A hand touched her shoulder and she turned her head so fast it hurt her neck. Dad stood behind her. She had no idea how long he'd been standing there. He was looking at Mum.

'You told them then,' he said flatly.

Mum glared at him. 'Don't claim innocence. You were part of it as well. You agreed with everything.'

Dad nodded. 'For my sins.' He'd put on a black tie, black trousers, but not a jacket; he'd come dressed for a funeral. Beth stared at him and – in the same way as when she was editing and there was a sudden intuitive understanding of what the author intended, and in the same way the utter certainty had hit her that it was Mikey's car, not Jake's as she'd assumed – the last piece slotted smoothly into place.

'Oh, Dad,' she said before she could stop herself.

He glanced at her and, in that moment, knowledge passed between them.

Before he could speak, Mum went on the attack. 'What are you doing here, anyway, Desmond? Hmmm? Why are you dressed like that? You never told me you were going to Mary's funeral. You know I wouldn't have allowed it.' She took a pace towards him, then a step back as if she couldn't let herself get too far from Ryan. 'You lied to me. Look what's happened. Where were you? I had to deal with this and now everyone knows everything, and you were no help, as usual. Why didn't you tell me what you were planning? Look what I've had to deal with.' She turned, not to look at Ryan, but to scowl at Callum, before returning, her glare turned up to full power, to Dad. Beth squinted in its familiar intensity. 'Ryan could have been badly hurt. Our Ryan,' Mum continued. 'Yet where were you? What type of father are you?'

'Oh, for God's sake Belinda.'

'Don't you shout at me.'

'I've been giving it some thought this morning. Do you know what keeps us together? Do you know why I stay with you?'

'No.'

'Neither do I.' He paused, waiting for a comeback. When none came, he said, 'You want to know what type of father I am? Shall I say or will you, Beth? You know, don't you. You've guessed. Put it this way, Bel: from where I'm now standing, I can see my daughter and my two sons.'

CHAPTER 35

It was as if someone had switched off the volume. The void of silence was so deep it made Beth wonder whether the shock had sent her deaf.

Dad stood there, attempting to look relaxed, thumbs hooked into his trouser pockets, eyebrows raised, waiting for a reaction. He was stiff though, his body tensed – clearly acting.

After an age, when the only response was disbelieving stares from everyone, he shrugged, affecting disappointment. Beth became aware of the thumping of her heart, but it was impossible to tell if she was hearing it or feeling it.

It was Dad who created the thick quiet, and he was the one who gently broke it. 'So, I'm guessing, Callum,' he said with forced nonchalance, as one would if giving simple directions, but at gunpoint, 'your mum never told you. You see, after Ryan was born, Belinda, here,..' he pointed and Beth looked at her mum, '…wouldn't let me near her for, well, for years. That's why there's five years between Ryan and Beth. An eternity. So what was I supposed to do? A man's gotta…' he shrugged again. 'We all know that celibacy, long-term, well, for a man, that way leads to madness.' He gave Callum a gentle smile. 'And your mum was having trouble with her marriage, and she made it obvious to me she was more than willing; she wanted it and, like me, was desperate. Get it when you can, that's what I say.' He stared at

Mum. 'With you acting as you were, well, what was I supposed to do? And I don't know whether Mary told Gavin, or he worked out Callum wasn't his, but either way, he left and never came back. And good riddance. We're all better off.' He paused. Exhaled. Still no reaction, although now the stares were not quite so disbelieving. 'Don't know about you lot, but I feel better for having said that.'

'So,' Mum spoke each word with care, 'it's *my* fault?'

Dad answered with the sort of shrug only men can do, the one that says, 'If you say so'.

'Hang on,' Callum mumbled. 'My dad?'

Dad put his hand on Beth's shoulder. It felt kind and reassuring. 'Come on,' he said, walking past her. 'We all need to talk about this and work out what we're going to do next. All of us. Let's get a cup of tea.'

'Wait,' whispered Callum.

Mum's eyes were fixed on Dad, but Beth couldn't tell whether they were wide with shock, surprise, anger, or confirmation of long-held suspicions. What Beth did know was that this wasn't just the quiet before a slight storm, these were the last few moments before detonation. She clutched Callum's knife tighter. When Mum lost her temper, any second now, Beth wasn't about to give up this knife. That would be too dangerous. This family had stabbed too many people. Ruined too many lives.

She watched Dad give a smile reassuring smile to Callum as he squeezed past and stepped into Aunt Mary's house – the step Beth was still unable to take.

What on earth are you thinking, Dad? Have you turned suicidal?

She had a sudden memory of one family mealtime, with Dad making a passing throwaway comment that he didn't think the sausages weren't as tasty as the previous week's, and the resulting

335

explosion. Two plates were shattered and a fork ruined. Mum embedded it into the tabletop with such force the handle bent. They'd never had sausages again.

'It'll be all right, Bel.' The smile he offered Mum was sad, the sort used at a funeral. 'I just decided this morning, we've all been living with so many lies, and if you were going to tell the truth then so was I.' He stepped to Ryan and held out his hand. 'Come on, son.' Beth couldn't believe he'd turned his back on Mum. Static filled the air, as if there was an approaching electrical storm. Even Jake, Beth noticed, who had no experience of Mum's temper, could feel it. He braced himself.

Beth watched, stunned, as the black cloud that had bubbled up over Mum evaporated. And quickly. Her shadowed frown softening, her muscles relaxing, cheeks expanding, lines around her eyes deepening until… until she was smiling. A huge smile. The sort Beth had never seen anywhere near Mum before, except in their wedding day photographs.

'Oh,' Mum said, now grinning so hard Beth figured it must be hurting. Those muscles hadn't been stretched in decades.

Beth stared, dumbfounded.

How was it that families could always, *always*, surprise you? Even when you've grown up with them, still they can always manage to wrongfoot you.

'Oh, Mary,' Mum said, her hand moving to her mouth. She looked around the hall, speaking to no one and everyone, as if giving an acceptance speech. 'Mary said – she used to taunt me – that she knew something I didn't, that she had the biggest secret, and she would never tell me it. I used to say to her, "Mary," I said, "secrets always come out in the end", but she would never tell anyone, just used to act superior, teasing me, and now look, I was right. Secrets always do come out. Hah. Mary.'

'My dad?' Callum muttered. 'My mum? You—'

'No!' Ryan was now standing, still holding Dad's arm that had pulled him to his feet. He had turned pale, his skin suddenly loose. He looked terrified. 'Beth,' he pleaded, 'Now you know what I did... what are you going to do... will you tell?' He turned to Jake. 'Will you?' And Callum. '*Will you?*'

Jake looked at Beth. It was clear he knew he had no right to answer. Callum though, had now slumped against the wall, his legs shaking as if with cold.

Welcome to the family, thought Beth, unsympathetically.

Callum stared at Ryan, hatred and confusion swirling, like oil in water, in his gaze. He tried to step forward, but it was as if his legs wouldn't carry him and he slumped back against the wall. 'I can't get my head around... You're my brother?' His voice a croak.

Ryan's voice wasn't much louder. 'What're you going to do?'

'You killed Owen? All this time I thought it was your fucking sister, then I read Owen's diaries and knew you'd encouraged him, and now...,' he shook his head, his voice getting stronger. 'And now I know what Owen was fucking like and... I've been in prison for fuck's sake. I wouldn't wish that on anyone, even you. But, Christ, it's not up to me. You let your sister, *the whole fucking world*, believe it was her. She's had to live her life believing that. Your *sister*. Who would blame her if she now clears her fucking name?'

'She wouldn't do that to her dear brother,' Mum stated with utter certainty. She put her arm out, encouraging Ryan to follow Dad into the kitchen for that Great British cure-all, a cup of tea. She nodded at the blood-soaked handkerchief abound Jake's hand. 'And let's get you sorted out. See if you need any stitches. Although how we explain it...'

'What about me?' Callum shouted, looking at everyone in turn. 'What about fucking *me*? What do I do now?'

Mum looked at Callum, 'You,' she said, 'first of all, mind your language. Second, you have a funeral to go to. After that, then we'll all discuss this like…'

Family? thought Beth.

'… adults. Now, though, Des and I, well, he needs some things explained to him.'

She ushered Ryan and Callum, too bewildered to resist, towards the kitchen. They did as they were told, like children. Mum didn't look back.

Beth watched them go, still unable to take a single step into the godforsaken house. She blinked and found she was retracing her steps down the front path, out onto the pavement, which she followed, oblivious to everything around her, deafened by colliding thoughts, blinded by visions of the past and possible futures, battered by disbelief. Overwhelmed. She could be free. She could prove her innocence. She wouldn't have to keep on running. Could settle down. Fantasy images played out in her mind, of her sitting down and chatting with friends (imagine having *close* friends!), of sharing her life, of just being able to talk to people about how she was feeling, of boring day-to-day worries. She recalled how strange yet fulfilling it felt to help Jake in his kitchen. Could that be real life? *Normal* life? *Her* life? She just walked, one step after another, with one part of her mind knowing where she was going but not admitting it. If she did clear her name, she thought, what would that do to Ryan? And Mum and Dad? The case would be re-opened. Their lies exposed. *They deserve it*, one voice in her head shouted. Another voice, different yet exactly the same, tried to shout louder, *you can't do that to them!* Ryan, she realised, would be charged and imprisoned. His life totally ruined. *Good! Look at what he let happen to you!* She shook her head – *He was trying to protect you!* – as she followed a footpath onto Culver Down. Feeling the ground change under her feet, she looked down. Grass had taken the place of concrete and she was surprised to notice she was carrying a knife. Callum's knife. Not Owen's. Not the knife she had stabbed Owen with, not the knife Ryan had then used to finish the job while letting her take the blame. She shook her head again, No, that was unfair. It was Mum. She had made Ryan lie. He must have been in shock, just as she had been, unable to think straight. For Mum it would have been easy, easy to convince him that it was best if his sister took the fall. She was so young. Yet part of Beth, a part she despised, wondered just how hard it had been to persuade Ryan. Really? And just what was for the best now?

She looked down, the knife swinging into view with each pace as she marched up the slope. Here she was, striding out in public, up a steep grassy hill, carrying a six-inch blade. Did no one notice? No one care? Or was it that they didn't dare approach her, for everyone knew who she was. Except, of course, she wasn't. She wasn't who she'd believed she was. She wasn't a murderer. Not the Island's Killer Kid. Not the Maid of Murder, the Baby-faced Butcher. The weight of the knife in her hand felt good, reassuring. Not just to make meaningless dashes in her leg, but to finish things. Permanently. It would be the best thing for her family, she realised as the incline increased and she trudged further up the hill, all the time coming closer to the cliff edge. There was a fence: stretched wire bolted into wooden posts. In places the wood had rotted, and the bolts were loose. Easy to pull out. If she was gone, Ryan needn't worry anymore. Everyone else would believe justice had finally been done. And she'd be free from the bickering and barbs of Mum and Dad, a relationship which – thanks to Dad's revelation – was certain to be re-evaluated.

She squinted against the too-bright sun, looked up at a sky that felt too low, within reach but without a single cloud to break up the unending canopy. The air tasted thick and oppressive.

Lowering her gaze, fraction by fraction, she found the ruler-straight horizon, then the sea, which was several shades darker than the sky, and – far below – waves, relentless waves, throwing themselves against the base of the cliff on whose edge she stood. It wasn't even a chalk cliff, that was further to her left. Here, it was sandstone red, vertical in places, sloped in others, dotted with lonely bushes and clumps of grass. Noisy gulls swooped and dived. Lowering her gaze even further, she saw patches of yellowing grass trying to survive on the dry, cracked earth, then her shoes. It wouldn't even take a full pace forward. Not even half a one. No more than a shuffle. And then there would be peace and quiet and the world would be safe from her, and Ryan would be okay and she wouldn't have to listen to Mum and Dad bickering. And, of course, there would be no more worries about work or money, or lack of it, and about privacy from the press, or lack of that as well.

Looking up and to her left, she saw the Yarborough monument on the highest point on the downs, looking like a finger pointing the way to heaven. She looked the other way, feeling the heat of the sun on her neck; down and to her right was Sandown, its pier sticking out into the bay, and beyond that Shanklin, with the vertical white column that was its lift – she had more than once taken this from the town, down, down to the esplanade – and beyond that there were more cliffs, this time falling from Luccombe village. Fossils had been found in those cliffs, she recalled. In fact, evidence of dinosaurs had been discovered all around this area. Her gaze returned to Sandown, to the dinosaur museum, a white building designed in the shape of a pterodactyl. Dinosaurs. Animals, dead for millions of years, now extinct, and the world had carried on regardless, uncaring. The way it was.

All it would take was the shortest of steps forward and…

'Beth.'

She didn't turn, but she did nod. 'Yeah?' She kept her eyes fixed on the point where the sea met the sky.

'Time to come back now.'

She nodded again, and shut her eyes. The razor-sharp line of the horizon was still there, imprinted as an after-image. She felt herself sway, her eyes sprang open and she turned, with care, to face Jake.

He was alone. Concern was written over his features and the hand he held out was wrapped in fresh kitchen towel. It had a repeating blue pattern, and a red line that was expanding, staining it.

That's gonna sting later, she thought, followed by: *Even if you don't need stitches, you ought to go to hospital, to be on the safe side.* She blinked in surprise at her follow-up thought: *I'll come with you.*

'Beth, do want to give me the knife?'

She looked down, stared at the knife in her hand, and felt a smile curve her lips. She took a step closer to Jake, away from the edge. It was just a knife, she realised. It had a sharp blade, but so what? She had control, she could be trusted with it; she wasn't a danger to herself or others. The idea that there was some sort of power to be gained by making cuts in your own flesh suddenly seemed ludicrous. Still, Jake had asked. She held it up and passed it to him, handle first.

'Thanks.' He put both hands behind his back, as if he were posing for a wedding photograph. Beth could see the perspiration on his forehead and cheeks, his skin gleaming under the intensity of the sun. The swollen purple and brown bruises under his eyes shone.

She could feel her own skin beginning to burn.

Jake should be wearing a hat.

'Come on,' she said, taking another step towards him. 'Let's

341

find you some shade.' She held out her hand. And stopped. 'Oh, God.'

'What?'

'I'm sounding like my mother.'

CHAPTER 36

Beth watched as Jake toured the office, moving in a series of right-angles from desk to desk as if in some elaborate game, as he handed out invitations. People's reactions when they realised it was for an engagement party fascinated her.

Every recipient, male or female, without fail rose to their feet, broke into a big smile, and either shook his hand or hugged him and gave his back the American-style double pat. The two women in the office both gave him a quick kiss on his left cheek. Jake couldn't stop himself grinning.

Is this how normal people react?

'He looks proud,' Sue said, arriving beside Beth.

'He should be,' Beth nodded. 'He deserves it.' The white scar across his palm was the only sign of what had happened three months ago.

'Heard from Mikey?' Sue asked, as if making casual conversation.

'No. You?'

Sue shook her head. 'Anyone else and we'd have had the police in. He was warned over and over; we told him, if he's selling our code or ideas to competitors and gets caught, there'll be no mercy. None. No matter what. I can be a heartless bitch sometimes.' She smiled. 'Just ask my ex.'

Beth didn't want to follow this up but knew she had to. 'Has he made a decision?' She kept her voice low and her eyes on Jake.

'He's still considering options,' Sue whispered. 'But I think you'll be okay.'

Beth swallowed. 'Thanks, Sue,' she said, forcing herself to keep the irony out of her voice. 'For everything you've done.'

Sue waved her hand in a dismissive gesture. 'I'm glad it's all worked out, so far.'

Beth didn't feel particular relieved, and still didn't know whether or not she could trust Sue, and in particular Sue's ex. Beth had never had close friends before, and it hadn't occurred to her there could be people whose level of friendship was ambiguous. She was never sure how to act around Sue. It made her feel uncomfortable, and she wondered whether Sue knew that.

They were standing by the desk Beth normally used when she came into the Leamspa Games office. It was invariably unoccupied. For all she knew, it used to be Mikey's workstation. Two tall monitors stood on it, acting like a barrier from other desks. It was as if the company had saved money on partitions by supplying the biggest screens.

Mikey had been dismissed the day after Sue had confirmed his dealings. It hadn't taken much investigation on Sue's part – and it definitely hadn't been her intention, or so insisted – but after their night together, Mikey had boasted about his extra income. 'What an idiot,' Sue had said to Jake back in August, when he'd phoned her from the Isle of Wight. He and Beth had been standing outside St Mary's hospital in Newport, and it was the first opportunity they'd had to speak to Sue. Jake had explained the real story behind the Island's Killer Kid until Beth had snatched the phone from his bandaged hand and begged Sue not to tell her ex-husband the story. Sue had refused, sounding regretful, and explaining that, despite everything, she still felt some loyalty to him, especially now she had the combined guilt of not only spending the night with Mikey, but also the betrayal of firing him from the company. Besides, if what Jake and Beth said was true, then it was an even greater scoop now. That night, though – Sue told Beth later – she and her ex had discussed it, and he had decided to sit on the story for a while. He wanted to investigate whether, long term, there would be more money in writing it as a work of fiction.

In addition, when Sue had understood Beth's profession, she had got the company to offer occasional freelance work: copywriting, editing and proof-reading promotional material. Recently, Beth had graduated to helping write scripts and plots for some of Leamspa's more story-led games. Even Mr Lottan had had second thoughts about going public; the idea of the press pack lurking outside, ready to pounce, proved too frightening for him. Besides, he'd got a promise from Beth that she would do some more decorating.

Looking over at Beth and Sue after receiving his latest hug, Jake waved. If his grin gets any bigger, Beth thought, it'll be painful. She felt a pinprick of guilt: he'd suffered more than enough because of her.

He made his way to Beth and Sue, zigzagging between workspaces.

'Hi, er, Liz,' he said. Beth didn't think he could stop beaming, even if he wanted to.

'Congratulations, again,' she said. 'I'm positive you and Shreeya will be truly happy. And Dashee will have the best Dad in the world.'

'Thanks,' his grin immediately froze, proving Beth wrong about the happiness and turning his expression into something she recognised: worry wearing a happy-face mask.

Oh, no. What have I said? Can I take it back?

There was a tremor in Jake's voice. 'I'm not sure,' he said, shaking his head. 'I mean, me? Me, a role model? What do I know about bringing up a child?'

'What does anyone?' said Beth.

'They don't come with an instruction manual, you know,' said Sue. 'My two are teenagers now. They could pass for real humans. They don't seem to hate me too much. Well, no more than you'd expect, so I reckon I've done an okay job. And if I can do it, despite everything, then… You've just got to encourage the little one to think for himself, and teach him to be responsible. Beyond that? Out of your hands.' She threw up her own hands.

'But—'

'Just remember,' Beth kept her voice quiet, 'it's a parent's job to do what they think's best for their kids.' She paused for a moment, before adding: 'And it's the kid's job to forgive their parents for that.'

Jake nodded, but the manner in which he looked away, at those still at their desks, half-hidden behind their screens, clattering on their keyboards or staring into space, made Beth think he didn't completely understand. He would, though. Eventually.

'Speaking of which,' Jake said, turning back to her, 'how are your Mum and Dad?'

'Keep saying they're going to separate but, like, I've seen no sign of it myself. In fact, it's as if they've found something they'd been looking for, something new and big and important – and different – to argue about. It seems to have given extra life to their bickering. Sometimes I think they're actually enjoying it. Other times…?' she shrugged. 'Who knows?'

'Your brother? And…' Jake never mentioned Callum by name. Beth didn't know whether he chose not to, or was unable.

'Callum sold his Mum's house and has gone travelling on the proceeds. Said he needs to "find himself". Sound to me like he's trying to lose himself. Or at least his new family.' She attempted a smile. 'And who could blame him?'

The three of them stood in silence, watching the activity in the office, Beth aware one of his questions was still hanging.

Ryan – and Mum – had pleaded with her, begged her, not to go to the police, not tell the truth. It didn't make any difference. What they feared, she already knew: Ryan just would not be able to cope, either with prison or with the sort of life she'd been forced to lead. Besides, she'd lived with the paranoia, the secrecy, the fear for so long she was used to it. The more she thought about it, the more she supposed, if it all disappeared, she would miss it. It had become part of her existence. This was her life. She didn't know anything else.

Acknowledgements

While I have tried to keep *Crying From One Eye* geographically accurate, there are occasions where, for dramatic and narrative reasons, I have had to play fast and loose with locations. In particular, Regency Court is entirely a figment of my imagination.

My undying thanks go to Annette, my first reader, for her help, support, patience and for putting up with me. Thanks also to Larry – I just wish you could have been here to see this book – and Liz, Kenny, Milena and Morgan Waterhouse.

For their perceptive and invaluable feedback, as well as their support and encouragement, I am greatly indebted to the Milverton Writers (www.milvertonpress.com), especially Tanya Pengelly (www.tanyapengelly.com), Charissa Brain, Raef Boylan, Grace Carlini, Sophie Petrie, Brian Sigmon (https://briansigmon.com), Andrea Mbarushimana (www.andrea-mbarushimana.com), and of course the best mentor, Jon Mycroft (www.jonmycroft.com). My stories wouldn't be what they are without you guys. Thanks.

An anthology of stories from the Milverton Writers will also be published in 2025. Watch out for it.

Also requiring an honorary mention, is Mike Turner. This book simply wouldn't have happened without him. His feedback was invaluable, and he offered fantastic advice when it came to publishing. Check out *The Many Wolds Bazaar*, and his Amazon and Goodreads author page for more info.

For their support and love, Lee, Jean, Steve, Pauline, Georgie and Jen Joy need to be thanked.

Special thanks also to the late Dennis Jones (and his book *Links to the Past*) who gave me the opportunity to experiment with self-publishing.

I mustn't forget those from the Warwick University Writing Programme, especially Ian Samson, Will Eaves and A.L. Kennedy. Likewise, thanks to West Dean College and especially Greg Mosse who persuaded me to do an MA.

For their encouragement, even if they may not know it, Erin Kelly and C.L. Taylor deserve to be mentioned in dispatches.

Big, litre-sized thanks also go to Karl Anderson and Darren Jones for all the beers and the laughs.

Thanks also to Ian Mercer, especially as I seem to be the only writer whose stories he reads.

Of course, I couldn't forget Polo and his posse, who claim I'm still a work in progress. I'm doing my best, boys.

Mark Kermode and Simon Mayo have accompanied me over many years, decades even. And, of course, hello to Jason Issacs.

Mention must also go to Lynsey, Phil and Oliver Stockwell; Lynwen and Ian Wood; Gill and David Valenti; Phil and Bev Bennett; Nick Wright; David Rashleigh; Warren Tam; the Oscar Film Society.

The following have also been influential and given me inspiration. Their inclusion in this list, however, should not be taken to mean I have had any interaction with them. None of them bears any responsibility. In no particular order: William Goldman, Stephen King, Chris Brookmyre, Elizabeth Haynes, Alex Marwood, Steven Moffat, Val McDermid, Jeffrey Deaver,

Acknowledgements

Richard Matheson, Alistair MacLean, Desmond Bagley, Nicci and French, Shirley Jackson, Steven Millhauser, Steve Cavanagh, Abir Mukherjee, NJ Cooper, Alex North, James Mitchell and, naturally, Douglas Adams.

Finally, of course, thanks to Mum and Dad for encouraging me to read. I wish you could have seen this.

About the Author

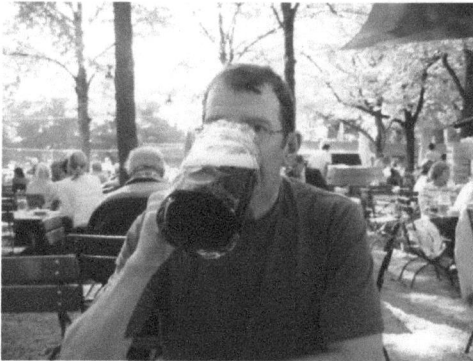

Pete Waterhouse began telling tales in childhood and hasn't stopped. What some dismissed as daydreaming definitely wasn't just him being lazy. A degree in physics convinced him that, while he found science fascinating, he'd make a really rubbish scientist. Making stuff up was just so much more fun than having to be, well, factual. Luckily, he stumbled into a job in academic publishing that allowed him to read about scientific progress, but without having to do all the hard work. He became editor of a number of academic journals and is now a freelance writer, copyeditor and proofreader.

He has always written short stories to entertain friends and family, but when one story ended up being the length of a novel, he decided it was time to take things seriously and enrolled in several courses, including at West Dean College and Warwick University, where he received an MA in Writing. That particular story, however, is now hidden at the bottom of a drawer and will never see the light of day.

He's still making stuff up.

You can find him on Instagram at petewaterhouse_writer

Also by Pete Waterhouse

UNINTENDED CONSEQUENCES

WS - #0093 - 040925 - C0 - 198/129/21 - PB - 9781806540235 - Matt Lamination